" **COME W**

"No," A

He came

felt his aura, stone cold, a fastening cold, grim and ravenous—an undecaying mockery of life.

Blindly willing unbelief, she backed away. He stood behind her.

She twisted away, and he was there.

She ran, but he was before her, ever at the turning, like a minotaur: dark marrow, in a maze of bone. She stood.

"You have called me," he said. Cold, insinuating, dry: he would have her, devouring herself as carrion, undying.

"Ariane," said his daemonic voice. "By your name, you are bidden. Eyes to ravens, soul to Annis: but the flesh is mine. . . ."

WORLDS OF IMAGINATION

MOONWISE

by
Greer Ilene Gilman

A ROC BOOK

ROC
Published by the Penguin Group
Penguin Books USA Inc., 375 Hudson Street,
New York, New York 10014, U.S.A.
Penguin Books Ltd, 27 Wrights Lane,
London W8 5TZ, England
Penguin Books Australia Ltd, Ringwood,
Victoria, Australia
Penguin Books Canada Ltd, 2801 John Street,
Markham, Ontario, Canada L3R 1B4
Penguin Books (N.Z.) Ltd, 182-190 Wairau Road,
Auckland 10, New Zealand

Penguin Books Ltd, Registered Offices:
Harmondsworth, Middlesex, England

First published by Roc, an imprint of New American Library,
a division of Penguin Books USA Inc.

First Printing, February, 1991
10 9 8 7 6 5 4 3 2 1

Roc is a trademark of New American Library, a division
of Penguin Books USA Inc.

Printed in the United States of America

For Delia, who undid the knots,
and for all who sang the skein:
the voices out of Cloud,
and Lucy

I

Silly Sisters

There was a green bough hanging on the door. The year was old, and turning lightward, into winter. Cold and waning, at the end of her long journey, Ariane looked back the way she'd come. Bare woods, bright wind that shook the rain from naked trees, a stony slant of field: the earth lay thinly here. The trees stood lightstruck, hill beyond blue glaze of hill. Then it darkened again, turned cloud and clods of earth, and crow-blotched trees: a drizzling thaw.

She turned back on the doorstep, and stamped her muddy feet. *While we poor wassail boys do trudge through the mire* sang mocking in her head (though her tape ran silent). *They* could beg, she thought ruefully: they brought things, garlands—Dear, oh dear, I've done it now. What if she isn't home? What if she is? Too late now. Should I turn my coat? Or break a twig of holly? Snare a wren? Would I know one?

Softly, she rapped at the door. No answer but the wind. *Cold by the door,* it sang. Louder. Again. A crow yelled. Round the side? Another door, a garland, muddy boots. She peered in at the window. It was dark in the front room, so she saw her face, a late pale moon, and trees with brass pulls and leafless tallboys and a chair of yew; but a fire burned: she saw it in the glass among the branches, burning in the air.

"Sylvie? Hye, Syl?" No one there. The rain came on, sudden, cold and sharp. A wind in the door blew it open. She went in.

Doleful and crumpled as a child, Ariane sloughed her

3

bundles, dumped her books and bags and suitcase, and wriggled out of her backpack. Her air of gravity and desolation was, she knew, rather spoiled by her wraggle-taggle trail of clutter. In the eluding mirrors by the door-way, in her dark coat, she looked a cross between Prince Hamlet and King Herla's rade, distraitly wandering through time. In comes I, little Johnny Jack, with my obsessions on my back. An owlish, cat-stumbling sort: but her own absurdity did not console her.

Dripping, she wandered toward the kitchen, ill at ease. She had no place here. Time, that had changed nothing in this house, had estranged her; yet she knew no other haven. She hung back at the doorway, at once fond and guilty and forlorn, coming back to what was never hers. She'd not been asked.

She'd written, there was nowhere else, she argued: Sylvie never answered letters, being Sylvie. It was like her to be gone when Ariane had come, ardently, apologetically self-heralded, after two years and a journey of three thousand miles, and a hobnailed scrunching taxi clear from town; like Sylvie to have left the doors unlatched, and the kettle withering on the fire, the windows flung open to the cold breath of winter and the rain. She held things lightly, being rooted; as Ariane clung and hoarded, blindly hurled. All the same, the dereliction struck her with a squall of misery.

Snatching the kettle, hissing and scorching daemoni-cally, from the stove, she backed into the drying rack, which collapsed into the ashes like a fainting stork, all legs, and plumed with tatty underwear. "Ouch!" she wailed, flinging down the fiendish kettle, and sucked her fingertips. But there on the hearth lay a note on torn paper, blown from the table: "Back. S." She laid it on the kitchen dresser, weighted with a cup. Could fill that with one of her gifts, she thought: a paper bag of stones, those veined and marbled sea-worn counterfeits, pebbles with chocolate inside. Sylvie'd like them. She began to feel quite happy, a cup unspilled, a new moon turned.

She forgot she'd wanted tea. The stones were some-where in her baggage, by the door. Slowly, musing, she began to walk, not back, but farther in. The house was the same as it had been in Nan's day, spare and unkempt as a wood. They held things light in Sylvie's family—does a wood hoard leaves?—yet they were drifted over, rooted in the sweet nourishing decay of loved ephemera, while the gaunt tallboys and gatelegs and settles stood unchanging. Nothing was ever lost, but became their earth. The air was bone chill, and smelled of woodsmoke and camphor, leafmould and must and lavender. In Ariane's memory, the rooms were not so small nor light; she saw them now as in a wordless dream, emblematic in their sober naturalism, only subtly aslant: a table moved, a book left open. The dissonances made an eery harmony of parallels, fifths and seconds.

She wandered into the low dark dining room, hung with black-a-vised ancestors: Herons and Farranders. She remembered on her first tongue-tied visit, Easter, back in college, Sylvie's showing them by nicknames, with teasing fond disdain: "Pooh, Geordie Whelps." He stared back, dotish, heavy-lidded, in a ram's-bottom wig. Nan, Sylvie's grandmother, that great gaunt dry brown heron-striding woman, had paused in her carving at the table head, with a collop of lamb on her fork, to remark with affable ferocity, "Poxed. That is not the Heron nose, which is aquiline." Stiff and shy, the ghostly Ariane of years ago still fumbled with her scarred unwieldy ranks of silver, knives and forks, her heart dunted with amaze.

She crossed the dark hallway. Here was the keeping-room, with its wide cracked boards and blood-of-nightingales scabrous rug, on which she and Sylvie and Cat and Thos, Nan's grandchildren, had played wild scrabbling flighty games of cards. She had once found an iron key between the floorboards, fitting nothing. On the tallboy was the Persian jar; above the mantelpiece, the flecked unsilvering myth-turning mirror, and the shells: great conches brown and smooth as horses' skulls, and wentletraps and a rose-branched murex. The moled and dappled ink-stained desk, inlaid with oak leaves, held a bowl of amber beads, a hairbrush, a half-eaten sandwich, and the nine of swords. From a roofbeam hung the nest of fretted ivory, sphere within sphere, like a model of the old earth-kernelled, angel-riddled cosmos. Ariane fingered the dusty books, brown and green and red: sermons and astronomy and natural histories of other worlds in this, with woodcut mandrakes, leviathans and falling stars; foxed pages of myth and ballads and stern unchildlike fairy tales, with crabbed footnotes and brightly crayoned-in initial letters.

Ghostly, fleeting, she saw Thos again, black-eyed and fallow-haired, wary and curious, with his Rackhamish long thievish fingers, peering from the cupboard in the chimneystack; she saw Cat, round as a wren, brown and birdclaw fastidious, breaking suddenly into a ranting midnight dance, with her bosom bounding from her nightgown. They lived elsewhere now, outside, and came and went.

Turning back, she touched the dusty workbox, horn and ivory. Long ago, yet still entangled, Ariane held out a skein of wool, far lighter now than any cobweb, for Nan's wraith, Norn-somber, with her gnarled and withered oakroot hands, her horn-buttoned Jacob cardigan, and her knot of dogwood hair: all were gone, were earth. The mirrored hall was empty where Nan strode, tall and witless in her hundreds, like an oak unleaving, stern and dry and rattled by the wind. She'd died of a lightning stroke within, and Sylvie'd gone on and kept house, and her hundred acres, and her kingdoms: all wood.

Ariane turned at the creak and sway of floorboards: wind, no stir of Sylvie's coming in. Again, she heard her, nowhere, singing as she laid the table with plates long broken, bread of air.

No one in the pantry: shelves of china, blue-and-white, or birds of paradise. Knives, pancheons.

At the foot of the steep back stairs, she paused. There was Sylvie's door, unlatched, and cracked a little on her badger-hole: a dark and bosky, slanting room, northeastward, not too far from earth, in the ell beneath the catslide roof. The box would be there that held the Nine worlds, hers and Sylvie's: leaves on leaves of memory, and a handful of bright stones. In thought, Ariane turned back the curved nailed lid; she read the fall of leaves, the stones. Unlethe, Cloud.

Not yet: only in unbodied dream is there no shame of trespass, as there is no fall in flying, no death but waking. Not at all, perhaps. It had been too long since they had walked there. The door was lost, thought Ariane; the cards were blind. In dreams, the longed-for object clouds and changes, fading; in the soul, it cankers, like a nail in living wood.

She lingered in the china closet, staring out the shivery window at the woods, at the garden veined and knotted with the roots of woods, and at the cloud-affronted light. Hill beyond blue whalebacked hill rose lightward, transparencies of stone, all etched with runic woods, enduring. She had known their green unison, their tongues of fire; so read time past in bare notation. Winter had distilled.

She remembered racing to the sunken lawn, spattered with the blood of ripe and unripe mulberries, to snatch the bounding, wind-berserking linen from the line, half a minute before a storm of hail.

She remembered a game of croquet, played by mothlight on their cant of crooked lawn, amid the gangling bygone lilacs, and the rose-thorns and the currants, in the Lyonesse of dusk. Their set was old, the heavy balls and mallets battered colorless, and the iron wickets grim as Newgate gallows. It was a fierce and freakish game; the air was flawed with wild giggles, pibrochs of ecstatic fury, threats and jeers and ranting taunting triumphs. Ariane was battle-drunk, amazed by her own rapacity. The others played elusively, erratically as moths: now belantered in the bushes; now undone by the backlash of a clacking, cleverstick riposte; now flying with uncanny grace through hoops that should have been unassailable as rainbows. Ariane stonewalled. Her floating, fluttering muslin skirt was caught and rent, entangled in the thorns of roses, where she skulked with cunning strategy; the others unpicked her from the brambles. Another stroke would take her within the edges of the woods, darkdrowned already, though the sky was still pale green and starless.

She remembered running in the pasture with them, in the November dusk; they were being people as yet unknown to her—ah, but she would never know them, they were elsewhere, sliding from themselves to other selves, three and many and one mind, teasing her with an uncomprehended joy. "Look! A falling star!" they cried. And she, her own cloud, had run after, never quite seeing what they saw, but ecstatic with the rumor of transcendence.

Now, standing by the lightstruck window, Ariane thought, O but I never heard her when she sang; it was like those falling stars, gone before I could say, how beautiful: beautiful in going.

In remembering Sylvie's voice, she heard it rise, travelling as if through years, like starlight from a long-cold, hanging stone. Clear and poising as a sword, it sang a descant, moving contrary and closing to an unheard music: as if she sang with her past self. Her voice fell like a leaf on silence, to touch the music rising from the dark: a dance before an empty mirror, strains of wintry shepherds and of bitter queens.

> Now open these windows, open, and let me in:
> The rain rains on my good clothing . . .

Ariane was silent, neither song nor shadow, but the glass in which they met—O now the I is crystal. She held still, but the dance eluded her, as light glances from a crystal, uncaught. She heard Sylvie laugh, somewhere beyond; and turned and clattered through the house, to where the voice had been.

No Sylvie. But the kitchen door stood open, and a great rook's nest of kindling lay inside. She turned back through the dining room. Sylvie? Eyes of Farranders, clouds of wig; a bitten pear on the sideboard; rain beating on the glass.

"Hey, Air?" called Sylvie, still elsewhere, still farther in. "That you?"

Back went Ariane through the narrow hallway, past the mirrors, and a draggled woollen scarf hung on the newel. In the keeping-room, the world-in-world of ivory dangled in the draught; a comb of tortoiseshell lay on the floor. Back she turned to the hallway and met Sylvie coming back the other way, brown and thin and quick, re-echoing in all the dim unsilvered mirrors.

"Hi," said Sylvie.

"Well, I'm here. Sorry if—"

"Got your letter. I left the door unlatched for you. Well, I can't find the key anyway."

There was an awkward silence. Ariane looked side-long, shyly, at her friend: at Sylvie's odd quicksilvery face, long-browed and beaky, brown as oak leaves, speckled like a wild bird's egg; at her old unwadding sheepskin jacket, dark with rain. A grove of Sylvies in the glass. Herself reflected, pale amid her tangled hair, bright and shaky, like the moon in a puddle.

Sylvie, unabashed, stared back at Ariane. The moon's cheeks turned suddenly pink, and crooked with an anxious mirth, a willed and wicked gravity. "What's this?" Ariane tweaked the wet bundle tucked under Sylvie's arm. "Lord Gregory's kid?"

Startled, Sylvie gawked, then laughed, wild and sudden as a storm of birds. "Oh, the *song*. Deea. *The baby's cold in my arms, love, Lord Gregory, let me in*," she sang, and held the swaddling out, a loaf of bread.

"Bewitched," said Ariane, graver still. "A changeling. If it yells when you toast it . . ."

"Deea. Changeling. It's wholewheat." Sylvie smudged back her lank hair, soberly. "Just ran over to Maire's—you know, up back of the hill, with the sheep—for some stuff I was out of. We got talking." Her black dog ran in, scrabbling wildly on the boards, rucking up the out-worn rugs, and toused at Sylvie's knees; then turned her eager muddy paws on Ariane, who backed nervously. She found dogs chaotic.

"Down!" Sylvie scratched between the dog's burry ears, absently, walking toward the kitchen. Ariane followed. "I like the coat," said Sylvie. "Like a high-wayman."

"The woman they couldn't hang," said Ariane; then wheeling, "Stand and deliver!" She snatched the loaf. "Ha! 'Tis Fitzgranary. The Scarlet Pumpernickel."

In the low dark kitchen, Sylvie turned out her pockets: loose tea in a plastic bag, soap, a jar of honey stuck with leafdust. "Pooh, I meant to get butter. Maire usually reminds me what I want, but she was a bit distracted, the goats got out. Oh, sit down, you've been travelling." She shook the kettle—bone dry—and filled it, and made up the fire, and propped up the clotheshorse, all the while drying her hair with a dishtowel. Then she put a dish of apples on to bake, and set to cutting bread for toast. She sang as she worked, as the rain fell, as if its falling were her plainsong. To and fro she went, lilting nonsense, and snatches of a ballad: cold by firelight, the wind and rain; and colder still, the grave.

Ariane sat drowsily. The rain railed at the windows; the kettle thumped and purred like a cat curled on a drumhead, by the whirring fire. There was a smell of woodsmoke and of apples baking, of damp wool as their coats dripped, of toast and wet leaves. There were books on the table, now as always, amid a clutter of inks and brushes, crumbs and nutshells: histories, a rough thick sketchbook lying open. Ariane leafed slowly through it.

It was crammed with oddments: notes and scraps in Sylvie's scrawl; old letters; leaves; then unexpectedly, a postcard from Ariane herself, from England. A white queen of walrus ivory, goosegog-eyed, and hand to cheek in toothached shrewd dismay. She turned it over—fox-red eighteenpenny stamp, a date two years before—and read the very small black text, as barbed and plaintive as a bird's tracks in snow: scratching for crumbs, she thought, appalled. ". . .What did you think of the poems? Did you get them? Comments & arguments humbly rec'd, also garlands of hemlock, raw nightingales' eggs & c. The last Arval bit you sent is wonderfully evil; though trust not in a witch's praise nor ravens' flattery . . ." Blushing, she turned it over. But Sylvie, flicking at the crumbs, caught sight of it and grinned. "Kept her. Thought she looked like your Miss What's-her-face."

"Morag? Dowdier. Much dowdier. And the umbrella— God, she was a redoubtable old rhinoceros, poor thing." The ash-witted antiquarian for whom Ariane had so long and so painstakingly collated folklore had died, in mid-fascicle, leaving no scheme nor sense of her entanglements, that her presence had made scholarship as the spider makes the web. Not being formally arachnid, Ariane was severed—snip—and so turned out, an unpapered alien.

"Should've left you her cottage."

"Nieces." Ariane sighed. "Not so much as a jump-rope rhyme." She stuck the card in the sketchbook and went on.

One page was all a maze of umber sketches—hands,

leaves, stones, strange leering faces—all in Sylvie's nervous line, no right way in: at its heart, a weird luminous
painting. Night: an endless branching passage, wood
carved with moongrey woods, woods turning hall, with
queer worm-eaten faces in the bark. A child walked, her
hand outstretched on nothing; far beyond, her clew of
cobweb glinted in the moonlight. O but I dream that
still, sometimes, thought Ariane: that I find the door.
"Are you doing the Curdie books?" she asked. "I like
how you've done the light, that wash. And those squin-
chy faces."

"Can't get Irene right yet. Too wispy." Sylvie had
made the tea loose in mugs and was now fishing out the
leaves—most of them—with a spoon. "I think there's
some milk." Ariane looked inquiringly at Nan's great
ebony and silver teapot, black but comely, cobwebbed
on the dresser. "Oh that," said Sylvie. "I forgot. I keep
the keys in it, and stuff. Guitar strings."

"Valentines," said Ariane. "Soldiers' buttons. Small
change in faery gold. The odd ring of power." The tea
was good and black, though dreggy. Ariane turned the
page. There, no bigger than a hazelnut, O there, green-
blue, unearthly, sailed the Ship, its mast a tree, great—
rooted, and its leaves far-drifting stars. It sailed in the
winter sky, a constellation in Cloud, of the Nine worlds:
one of theirs. Sylvie'd not forgotten.

Ariane looked up as if to speak, did not, went on. A
sketch of Maire herding goats. Two children in a labyrinth of stone. A dry leaf, red, like an odd mitten. Real:
it fluttered out. Blank pages. She would have turned
back; but baleful, fastidious, the cat came and crouched
on the book. Stone, said his gaze, I am stone. A crom-
lech. One of Maire's Long Meg's, she remembered:
Timour the Tartar. Been out fighting, she thought: one
ear was torn and stitched. Cloud-grey, unwinking, he
stared.

". . . *in search of Lord Gregory, may God I'll find him*
. . ." Fumbling blindly in a dark high cupboard, Sylvie
brought down a jar of jam, and blew the dust off it, then
rubbed it on her leg. "It *looks* like 'Bluebeard,'" she
said doubtfully, peering at the spidery label. She dug out
the moldy wax with a knife, which she licked. "Seems

all right. Blackberry. Kind of winy." Ariane cut her a hunk of bread and Sylvie stood munching it, slathered with the jam. "Not bad at all." There's Ariane gone full moon, she thought, looking shrewdly at her face: all crazy and bright, but she never stays. She sickles. Eats herself up. "So you're back?"

"S'pose so." Having journeyed to the bare green hills and stone circles of her long-imagined England, and arrived elsewhere—a flat in Hampstead, to be exact— she wasn't all that sure she'd *been*. Well, this time, she'd set out for Sylvie's woods, Nan's woods: her long-remembered Arden. She'd arrived, as always, somewhere else. (On a boardwalk in Bohemia?) It was always farther in. "It's strange, being back, it's so frail—all those wooden houses, like milkweed. And the trees." She looked at Sylvie, long and brown, a little sharper-boned; still Sylvie, like an oak that holds its leaves through winter. "So how've you been?"

"Oh, pretty quiet." Strange having Ariane here. Nan— well, she's earth. Still here. Air comes and goes. Watching and wanting. Not the moon, exactly—ghostly. Could take her on the long walk, back of Maire's. Could draw. "So you've stopped writing?"

"Damn, I'd forgotten," cried Ariane, and went rummaging through her pack, ransacking boxes, marbled papers, stones and skeins, entangled in unsilvering angels, and wiry stalks of heather; tapes of travellers, and dog-eared notebooks. She went to smooth a page, and a photograph fell out. "Not that," she said, turning it quickly over.

"Deea. You kept *that*?"

It was a black-and-white snapshot, taken point-blank and dazzled on Maire's lawn, on May morning, ten years back; and kept in notebook after notebook: Sylvie, slouching barefoot in the cold early spring, farouche and flighted, with her elsewhere gaze; Ariane, scowling in a cloud of hair—quattrocento severity—in a draggled flouncing skirt, and rose-wreathed broad straw hat. The silly sisters. The sisters Grimm.

"I do comb my hair now," said Sylvie. "D'you remember Thos in the brass earrings, he and Cat did us telling fortunes? Said I'd meet a dark stranger, and the goat butted in?"

"And I'd journey. Ah," said Ariane, unearthing a small bag tucked away in the obscurest corner of her pack. She shook it out. "There. See, it's really me, I didn't fall at Waterloo. Or Flodden. Take your pick." On her hand lay a silver ring, bent and blackened; she had found it writhen in an oak root. Its stone was elsewhere, was the star of the Nine worlds.

Sylvie laughed. "Oh, that," she said. "I remember," and she held it to her eye.

0

Hallows

He walked in the Cloudwood that they were to fell, had felled long since; though where he walked was autumn still, amid the flocks of leaves alighting on his face, his sleeve, his hair. He shook them from the folds of sleep. The nuts were brown and ripe; they clustered, thrang as stars. He filled his pockets as he walked. Awd coat were tattery as leaves, he thought; he'd weared it for as long as hallows, longer far as he could tell, being all athwart o years: no time at all. It blawed about him, tawny, same as wood. He thought as he'd taken coat frae off awd flaycraw in a field, and left sticks bare; though strange remembering green, since none were i't wood to keep, nor out on high fells, nobbut stones. Ravens were. He'd clapped and cried them frae't Law. Ate souls, did yon odd ravens. Picked eyes. But they's scant i't wood, he thought. Awd craws fare ill. And wandering, he pulled and plucked the hazelnuts, the brown and starry beechmast, ash-keys, acorns, letting fall as many as he took, so many hung and ripened, fell and leamed amid the leafdrift, far and farther still.

Birds sang, but flurried, shrill, it being fall of year. They waked; and through the branches of the trees, the wind spilled leaves of light and shadow, leaves of dust, like the souls of all the birds since Eve. Times, though he could not spell, he riddled at the wood, the tale the leaves told, falling: no end to their tale, no spring, however far he walked.

All afternoon he lay beside the water, and watched the leaves rising from the dark to touch their falling shadows from the air, bright, haily. Being still where leaf and its foretelling image met, he did not know if he rose or fell through time. For times he had risen from a sleep to find his clothes tattered to a heap of leaves; or having fallen like a swath of grass beneath the scything moon, as pale in its wandering as a homeward mower, he had waked in the cold fog on moorland hoar with frost: a stark and sunburnt, rainbleak scarecrow.

Straying to the high farms, he had found the hail and hurl of words were strange, though stones and dogs and the glances of uneasy pity were the same. And ale was, and fire. And bread. Times changed, as time did not. They who had slain children in the fields, sowing blood with corn, hung garlands; still the seeds grew tall and winter died. Come wakenight, they stoned the wren, poor Jenny Knap, and hanged it in a crown of green, with rimes; they fired thorn, kept lightfast and langnight, so the sun would turn. They danced the years and died. But in Cloudwood it was endless hallows. There no wren was slain, no seed was scattered; though he cried the ravens from the turning wood, no winter ever came to green. The gate was lost.

Times, having drunk clear water from the cup he held, he had dreamed the wood in spring, had slept beneath a drift of blackthorn, cold and starry with the green to come; and had waked in a foul dyke under snow, in a snarl of rusty wire, starving on Cloud Fell. Once, from the nuts he had gathered had sprung a hazel tree, and branched from his side, and borne and withered, in the space of a dream.

The cup turned all to shadows. Lying by the water now, he held it, wood and handworn. Fitted hand, he thought: his own and other's. Lad at given it were light-born. Last. Not see'd him sin, nor any face i' Cloud. No soul. Hawded cup fast for him, not breaking troth, not having else. He bent to fill it. See'd lad's face i't water now, he thought: aback of him, all gowd and shadowy i't leaves. He would have spoken. But lying there, adrift in leaves, he knew he slept, was waking. Even now, as he touched the water, before the leaf-wakened rings had vanished, it was dry; no hand met his. The wood unrooted.

The world was naked now. He lay on Soulsgrave Hag. Standing stiffly, he looked about him to the twelve winds, tasted frost. Far below, he saw the sheep driven to fold, keeled and curded like froth on the ale-brown moor. Lambswool. Eh, but he were mortal dry. He saw the maze of stone laid out across the common land, and learned its changes, walls and folds and gates; he saw the wire glinting like gossamers in a hedgerow. It was time to move on. Winter haled him. Stooping, he found a can of half-bright tin, clagged and rusting: poor stuff, but hawded water; it 'ud do to seethe in.

Coming over Cloudlaw in the miry dusk, he met with Awd Mally, grey and stumpish, looking out on her domain, the clouds of earth. He touched his slouching ragged hat to her, louting down a little, hesitant and stiff; and hailed her, softly, warily. Long time since he had spoken. Moved by an impulse between awe and fondness, he ran his fingers over her harsh face and breast, seeking the blind faint marks, like runes, beneath the lichen.

Tha'st tholed a few fell winters, awd lass, he thought; tha'st seen wood and waste. Cawd now: would tha like my awd haggard coat?

The stone was silent. She had never spoken to him; she was not always there. Some said she walked the moors, peering and prying into sheepfolds, owling after souls. But he thought that she alone stood unmoving, though all else turned: hills, clouds, and reeling stars.

He slept in a ruined sheepfold, back of Cloudlaw, and dreamed: he lay on the fell, stark cold and turning to a cloud of stone, stars icy at his cheek, unturning. He was blind. His mouth was stopped with earth, ribs hollowed round a heart of stone: but hands took root, thrawed sinews down and downward, warping. He were tree. Awd craw i't branches cawed and cried: *Bone, bone o branches, ah, and eyes o leaf, o leaf.* Leaves falled away til dust. Bones stood bare. But hands, they hawded fast, they warked i't earth. Hand scrat at summat sharp, not stone, but fire-warked: cawd iron, siller, gowd. Awd broken ring, he thought. Awd moon. Could never get it back i't sky, were darkfast. Cawd and dead. But the ring grew fast to him, turned O and handfast. Moon leamed under earth. O now he saw: the fell was cloud, and starry back of cloud, and deeper still. And all turned headlong, he was branching into dark and moon, turned lightfast with his roots in sun. Broke leaf. Bright swans above him, and his leaves arising in a crown of wings, and crying out: a thrang of birds. He woke to a fleeting sense of joy, winged with a glory and taloned with want.

Starved and starkened with the cold, he shuddered in his rags. Sheep were warmer to sleep among than stones; he had often shoved some baleful-eyed indignant ewe from her frowsty nest amid the bracken: it made for tallowy dreams, but snug. He rolled over. It was a heron-grey morning, in the backend of the year; cold and bright the springs of water ran, and wealed the moor with silver. Northward of the stones was rimy. There was hoarfrost on his coat, made it fine as any lord's; and in his hair, all starry when he tousled it.

He sat and reckoned. No bird nor hare had fallen to his stones, none were caught in his springes. They were wary as he, as he knew with rueful compassion (though some creature had filched his rind of bacon as he slept, and doubtless some furtive nests were eidered with his tawny hair). No bones to char, over a fire of thorn that spat and rang in the grease of innocence; no blood to mourn. He slapped among his leaves of rags. No oatmeal, begged at door; no salt; small hoard o nuts frae't

Cloudwood, though likely owl nuts, being awd as he. No roots, no eggs, and t'brambles all wizened, devil-spat-upon and scathed. No drink, wi'out yon becks ran ale. No breakfast. Eh well, then he could thole.

But the bield he had lain in was a tumbled shepherd's cot; he saw there was a hearthstone black with long-cold fires. Standing, he traced the maze of fallen stones, pale with moonfaced lichens: house-place, byre and fold. The rough grass was a garth, bewildered now; long time since there'd been worts to pull, or roots for digging from that stony earth, but he found windfall apples, withered, sweet. There was a windbent knot of thorn trees, rowan, hazelnut and sloe; their leaves fell light on water, on a wellspring running cold and bright away. Cloud ale. Crouching beside, he found a little shard of delft; he rubbed it with his thumb. A flint of sky. The leaves whorled slowly in the water, and spilled away down the stony hillside. He filled his cup and drank.

Looking up, he saw the gnarled bent trees, still bright, against the stony clouds of earth: Cloudlaw and Cald Knap, and t'Ravenscar, and all beyond and bleak. He'd been here afore in autumn, i't hallows o't year.

He waked. The wood was hallows, in the fall of leaf. He walked; and endless, pale and dark, they fell and fleeted, drifted down. He slept, and dreamed of falling, lying silent at the roots of Cloud; as tattered, leaves on leaves of wood, light leaves of shadow fell and covered him, their tale of years his dreaming. Even as he woke, the wood had faded and the hills stood bare: Cloudlaw and Cald Knap and the stonefaced Ravenscar. Looking out, he saw a dark smudge on the hillside, walls of stone: a stead. Could beg his bread and ale. *A soul, for hallows' sake.* All ragged, in his tawny coat and slouch of feathers, he went on. *A soul.*

He came upon a thorn hedge, bright with haws. No gate. A lalling from within, of birds. Wrens, dunnocks, thranging to the bitter sloes, and whirring, knapping at the haws. Among them all, he heard a low voice singing, like a mother to her bairn, a lass at her work. He'd not heard rimes afore, he thought: but tune were awd as Cloud. He bent to see.

Caught in the thorn-hedge, torn and unaware, he
gazed at the dark lass in the orchard, combing flax among
her goats. Leaves falling plashed her hair, her apron, red
as heart's blood, unbaneful. Leaves lay bright on the
sward about her. She was low and earthborn as a windbent tree, as wild and black as sloe. Thorn blaws fair,
he thought: pricks deep. Brown hands, she had, and wick
as birds. Small breast, and white as may. As red, and
sweeter than the haws. Her lap, as deep as hallows. And
her face, hid curving in a cloud of hair, as bright and
small as lady moon. Wandering, as the moon gives light,
she sang: of a hare; of a harp of bone; of a witch that
laid a spell upon her son's outlandish lady, plaiting witchknots in her hair.

The lass bent her dark head. With rough deft hands
she sleaved the flax, that caught on them, as strands of
her true and harsh and dusky voice caught and clung to
him. He pressed closer in the thorny hedge. Intent upon
her skeins, she never glanced at him; but at the clamor
of the birds in the laden branches, she turned away and
upward.

He was lovestruck, knowing all at once with his heart
and body her fierce roots, her branches, and her crown
of light, dazzling as the thorn that flowers leafless, by
the moon: her green enduring and her frailty. Sitha, how
she turns, bright as rising. His blood hung beating in his
tree of veins, it beat against the thorn. Lief, let me in.

No gate. Her thorny hallows was an O, another law.
No. Cloudwood was the O, was endless. She was closed
beyond him, in the turning world. Would dance, and
bear, and die. Caught in the prickle-holly bush, he gazed
at the last pale crescent of her face, in its tumbled cloud
of hair. Then she shook out her apron, and went in.

And she was dead. Her cote had fallen, stone from
stone. Her garth lay all unhedged, and wild and tangled;
though her songs had rooted in his heart, thriving spare
and windbent through the wintry years. Her spring still
filled and flowed away; the bright leaves fell on it. He
crouched beside. He had slept in her bower, in her hall,
but out of time, lying hard between the clouds and naked
Cloud. Cawd lap, he thought. He'd waked in hallows, in

the fall of leaf, another year, no year: the wood was endless, like a knot, an O, undying and ungreen. He'd not find heart on it, he thought, no featherbed nor lass nor love: no gate aback o Law. No dance. All others died; he waked alone. Gi'en ower when I taken cup, he thought ruefully: wood's what I is. Mazy. But I given lad my word. We's ae and other. He still held the cup, handworn, half full of clear brown water. He drank. Were sweet as keeping-apples, times. And bitter.

Stone had fallen now from stone; but on the ancient windbent trees hung flawed and fiery apples, haws and hazelnuts and sloes. He gathered what fruit he could, groping for windfalls in the rough tall grass, and clambering in the branches; but he left a teind to the trees, and another to the wren, and said his carol. He lingered all that afternoon in the pale fitful sunlight beside the beck, cracking between two stones his handful of nuts from the Cloudwood: some bitter, and most shrivelled, owlnuts full of dark and must; and now one sliding from its silken husk, leaming, like a lass from her smock, sweet and brown.

Sylvie's brown hand, with the black silver ring on it, laid down the Hallows Tree, turned over the next card: the Sword. It depicted, in a rough hand-colored woodcut like a ballad sheet, a traveller, clad all in brown and flaunting rags, and brave in cap and feathers, striding with drawn sword against a green dark wood; ranting, long and lithe by owl-light, beneath the sickle moon.

"It's darker than I remembered," she said, and laid it on the quilt with the others, all anyhow. She turned the next: a child of stone. Naked, greenish-grey with lichen, with a cracked cup in its hands, it stood within a ruined maze, bewildered in a wintry garden, leafless, blind with thorns.

"A journey," said Ariane, touching the Sword. It lay between them. "Rebirth. And the Cup's mourning, or retreat: a labyrinth. If we were playing." There's Sylvie's card, she thought, there's mine: the blind maze turning inward and the journeying, the dark and light of one moon.

"But we're not," said Sylvie. "It's not a real fall." She turned up another card. "There's the old Hare gone head over heels. Well, he's rightways for you. Backwards fortunes." A weird fall anyway, she thought: one of those back-and-forth endless ones, the same knots over. Cat's cradle. There's the last of them. The cards lay scattered on the quilt.

She and Ariane sat cross-legged on Sylvie's whale-backed bed. The quilt was mothworn, fumed in camphor and woodsmoke, drifted over in leaves on ancient leaves of sleep, in falls long past of ghostly cards; they huddled on its somber folds. Its quarrels were of sad, rich colors: seal-dark, sloe-dark, the heartsblood red of ballads. Sylvie traced its fells and fallows, brooding on its wintry uplands, herself shadowing her hand's journey. She poked at a threadbare faded patch, fir once, now willow-green. "Falling to pieces," she said.

"It's the same as ever," said Ariane. The Sylvie-ness. It has to be.

Sylvie's room was dark and slanting, scarcely higher than her fourpost bed. She'd brought in boughs from the woods: green, bitter firs, black pines, their wintry harshness wild and strange against the withered-rose-brown garlands of the paper, foxed with age. Dry needles sifted down among sloughed clothing and leaves of books, the windspill and welter of a sibyl's cave. The air was chill and musty, secretive. Wind whirred in the wavery glass; the husk of house creaked and shifted. Briefly now, the sun was dazzling; they'd lit the candle

all the same. Unseen, tremorous, its dry lizardstongue of
fire dwelt upon the air.

The chronicles were here, in stacks of tattered notebooks, in tin trunks and dusty cardboard files, the years
unbound and spilling over. They were written in two
hands, crabbed descant and a hurling scrawl, antiphonal.
They two had pulled out all the leaves of years, remembering, returning, as the light had turned, the candle
wasted on the sill. The box lay open, with its curved lid
and its hasp of iron. It had no key. On the floor lay
Sylvie's curling maps, held flat with books; a stray leaf
from an herbal, seed and calyx, in scrabbly ballpoint; a
grieving face amid calculus notes; her tales of Alder, and
her codices of Lune, prosaic historiographies of mythic
kings.

Ariane's small heavy hoard, the worlds-in-little that
she carried on her back, lay cradled in her lap, unpacked,
not fallen far. She held them one by one, the dog-eared
and exquisitely close-written little books: her lapidary of
angels; her runes, nine alphabets of trees and stars, illuminate; her list of names, mythologies and spells; her
witches' breviary.

In Ariane's poems, the leaves spelled prophecies in
falling, the blood of the warring gods rained down as
crystal. In Sylvie's commonplace, there was a gravity of
pain, naked, unenskied; and reckless joy. She wrote of
betrayal, madness, and the deaths of kings; of thrones,
dominations, falls from virtue and from power; of the
will toward evil, and of love.

"It's weird," said Sylvie, "writing without the cards.
Stuff happens."

The cards were Ariane's. They were a sort of tarot,
whose outlandish figures were the constellations of the
Nine, their sun, and moon in all its phases. Ariane had
taken for her starry images the songs and ballads of this
earth, as if what Sylvie sang were true elsewhere, not
tales but law: the tongue-worn relics of an otherworldly
mythos. In her cards, Child Rowland's tower was the
dark of moon, unchance and turning; and Burd Ellen
played at ball amid a sort of Pleiades, her errant star
eluding sight. Not a fall, though bright as leaves, the
images lay scattered on the bed: the Sword, the Ship,

the Harp of Bone; the Gallows and the Wren; the Witch, whose knotted hair was galaxy; the Virgin, or the Sibyl, scattering leaves of prophecy; the Nine of Trees, called Hallows; and the Tower and the Hare, and all. With these, Ariane forespelled the patterned changing fortunes of the Nine, ascendencies; and Sylvie told their ends.

Sylvie gathered up the cards, and packed and shuffled them. It was tough to get beyond, she thought: chancy, intricate. A fugue, a leap of faith: like shooting rapids in the dark. Like being dreamed. I'm out of practice. Riffling the cards wickedly, she turned to Ariane. Her face was teasing, daring. "Want to? Keepsies."

O but I could never follow you, thought Ariane, I never saw; I burned you like a candle in my dark. "It's been—oh, I don't know, perhaps there's nothing there."

"We could look," said Sylvie. Kneeling up, she burrowed through the windspill papers, clearing space for the game. Ariane had made it to defend the naked act of imagining, as guisers hedge their sacrifice in the weaving of a knot of swords, in fool's play and in dance: absurd and formal and fantastic. Sylvie'd taken to the game. The worlds were marbles, moved in patterns on the squares of quilt, until one last, the odd one out, was left: was earth and heaven for a turn. Then starry to that world, its zodiac, the fall of cards laid out would cast its fortunes. Scenes, persons, fates: a tale was spelled, obscurely, in their constellations. Sylvie would unriddle, seeing narrative in what had fallen: what befell.

Sylvie hauled the box onto the bed, and crouched over it, looking for the shabby velvet bag that held the worlds; her dark hair fell about her face. Distracted, she unearthed a cache of stones, licking them to bring out their essential clarities: the birchwood, the leaf-eye, the swans. She found owlnuts and fircones, and an old childish drawing of hers, a flight of crowned and mantled cats, Thrones and Powers of a discarded world. Winged and numinous, they searched the air. "Pooh," she said. Her voice was shaken at the edge of laughter, like a sail lying too close to the wind's eye, confronting ritual.

But sheering from the bright impending moment, Ariane said, "Wait."

Sylvie, unknotting the strings of the bag, glanced up.

"Pen's dry," said Ariane; and kneeling up to find the ink, she looked about at leaves, and thought: the wood's where Sylvie is; she scatters Cloud. And still I fret, I hoard. Now, as then. She touched a withered drawing. She was ill at ease in her inheritance, the dark and turning hallways of the tower, and the wood: afraid of losing herself in it, afraid of trespass and of loss. Coming late and anxiously into her kingdom, she had then hung back, a stranger, longing and unsure. Not bright, her realm, but stony dark: it was the moon had borrowed it, had left it cold as cloud. And there she stood. It was Sylvie, holding light her great dominion, who had met her at the door, walking out to feel the wind and rain.

It was Ariane's first year of college, at the turning of November: the leaves hung fire, whispering; the wind blew cold. Coming along the woods path from the library, she heard a wild clear snatch of ranting music—*"with me fine cap and feathers, likewise me rattlin drum"*—and there came a straggly dark dishevelled girl, striding along barefoot on the brown leaves and gravel. Throwing down her books helter-skelter by the path, the girl flung herself headlong in the sopping grass. All the loose-leaf papers flew away, unheeded on the wind: sibyl's leaves.

"Deea! There goes Alder."

Ariane, solicitous, respectful of the slightest scrap of prose, went stamping and snatching and scrabbling after them, through prickly bushes, through and through the puddles, and the smoke of bonfires, burning leaves.

"Gotcha!" said Sylvie. She rolled over and sat up, holding a dwarfish wrinkled baleful toad.

"They're all I could catch," said Ariane. The blurred and crumpled scattered leaves were stories, and notes for stories, and dark outlandish drawings, in among assignments, scribbles, and labnotes on the eye and fugal counterpoint.

"Just some stuff," said Sylvie, cramming it away, all anyhow. "Hey thanks." She'd pocketed the toad. Bright and sober, she looked at Ariane. "Do you think writing about, like, other worlds creates them? Or are they *there*?"

"Infinities," said Ariane. "Not counting odd ones."

By that winter's end, abruptly, shyly, Sylvie had let her in; and for five or six years they had created as a dyarchy, ruling Sylvie's old childhood kingdoms, Thorn and Alder, and discovering Unlethe and the others. Ariane had walked with Sylvie's stride, through Sylvie's branching woods; as Sylvie, with another's eyes, had seen another, lapidary world. They had been as close and contrary to each other as the dark and light of one moon.

But as Sylvie's chronicles had branched from rooted wood, and borne and scattered leaves, lightly on the wind; as Sylvie had walked farther, lost and found herself amid her green and ancient wood, Ariane had spiralled inward, spellbound by her own intensity of patterning, Gorgon to herself. Awkward and unconfident, she had found the bright jewel in her head, so had repudiated whatever dies, and so had lost what dances. Her lapidary love had grown, slow, crystalline, and not quite poetry: a handful of hail-seed. Her world and Sylvie's had diverged, the eye of stone from the quick and changing creature. Now the ring, the O rejoined them, and began it all again.

Well, it's my turn, Sylvie thought, Air's shying. She held out the pack of cards. "Longways?"

"What? Oh sorry, yes. Go on, astonish me. Strip tarot." Capping her pen, Ariane watched as Sylvie laid them out, nine of the thirty-three. A fall. "Like a hall-way. With doors."

"Doors, I like that." Sylvie turned one up, warily. "What's behind here? Rrahrrr. Slam."

"No exit," said Ariane. "No thread." Her face quirked. "It's tarot cards all the way down."

"Hush," said Sylvie, turned graver, eyeing the cards. "Gallows, oh good. And the Swans."

"Winter," said Ariane. "Snow. A birth, a voyage, transformation."

"Rats, it's always winter. The Scarecrow, reversed."

"Famine. A wasted sacrifice. A barren field. Innocence betrayed."

"Eyes picked out," said Sylvie, fiendishly. "Piece of cake."

Ariane grimaced back and went on. "The Tower. The Light Horseman."

"Looks like he gets crunched. The Witch reversed—that's a tough one; it wants to be another story. Un-unbinding?"

"Either way," said Ariane. "Done and undone. Riddles, knots. The end's not so grim: Wren. Hare. Ship. That's it."

Sylvie wore the stoneless ring, turned blindly inward on her hand. She held out the shabby velvet bag. Turn and turn they drew from it a child's glass marbles, the seed of worlds, their darkness voeled or veined with whorling nebulae, cracked and starred with genesis of light: Cloud, Unlethe, Perran Uthnoe; Alder, Idho, Thorn; Far Lune, Anthelion, and Ravenser Odd.

Nine worlds of crystal, whose star was Sylvie's ring, and Ariane the dark binary, now occulting, now revealing fire. In silence, they set the cosmos in its order, and cast the blind and labyrinthine fortunes of its kings. They two were numinous, yet in exile, wanderers returning through abysmal dark to their kingdoms, which were unchanging, being stones of crystal; and yet in Cloud, the drops of blood upon the snow could not be unspilt, nor the dark ship of Unlethe sail against the wind. "The gods are haggard," they said in Thorn, "they come from darkness and return." The dance went on in silence; they caught and shifted the worlds in their endless patterns on the quilt. Now one, now the other held the eye of crystal. It was done. A marble, green as wintry dusk, lay on the quilt alone.

"Cloud," said Sylvie. She touched the first card, hesitant: the Swans. "Cloud. Winter."

"Swans," said Ariane. "They're rising, so it's winter turning. So it's white, it's all and nothing, birth, rebirth. It's travelling. Unbound. Like out of sanctuary, prison. Out of hallows."

"Hush, there's someone. Riding hard. And like a mantle blowing. Moors. And a tower. The gate's iron." Sylvie's voice was sliding, strange. "Cloud. Winter, and the year not turned, the old year dying. In the ninth year of Arval's reign, from his keep at Varth. . ."

Ariane caught herself and hunched over her notebook, scribbling minutely and desperately in her Chinese-slippered hand. The tale was evil. The end was holy, casting shadow before it. Sylvie crouched behind her tangled hair, speaking in that throaty, sibyl's voice; her body swayed. She was the burning glass. She was quicksilver that consumes what it touches, drawing in the dark to make it silver. Ariane had said once, tell me how your dreams end, don't wake up. Sylvie had walked far into nightmare, willing sleep as she might drown herself with stones. Barefoot, threadless, in the labyrinthine dark, she had brought Ariane a garland of its galls and fungus, the cold sweat of its medusa-branching trees.

Now as Sylvie spoke, the horseman, unhorsed, unmantled, was beheaded; his lady, great with child, stood by; snow fell. Ariane still saw the constellations and the ambiguities, the patterns of the cards; and Sylvie walked the onward road.

A crossroads. Dusk. A stranger? Faltering, her hand laid down the Gallows, hovered on the Witch. "His mother, standing . . . No."

Softly, Ariane put in, "She could. The Witch is either way; she's out of hallows."

". . . and his mother, standing by the hallows cross . . .unhh."

As the candle leapt up, avid, to a sudden darkness, Sylvie paused. The sun had turned long since; the wax was all but gone. ". . . and she . . . I've lost it. No. Gone." Sylvie's face by candlelight was shadowy, autumnal; one long dark slanting brow was scarred. She pinched the wick with her long fingers, as if she were plucking a leaf. Darkness.

"The Witch . . ." said Ariane. "Go on."

Sylvie switched on the light. "Later, okay?"

"But it's there, the turning back."

Bending, Sylvie pleached the quilt. "It doesn't fit."

"But it's the card."

"It's not how—They wanted somewhere else. Things happen."

Ariane capped and uncapped the pen. "Not if . . ." she began.

"Babel," said Sylvie, raking the cards together.

Ariane took down her gawky hair and put it up, biting on a bristle of her tortoiseshell hairpins, like the tusks of a truculent boar. She dropped a pin, and retrieving it, let trail the fringes of her crow-dark shawl. There was a ratscrabble under the bed, and the slutswool-grey cat streaked out.

"Ffft, Tamburlaine!" Sylvie rose in a hail of marbles. She caught him and swaddled him, willy-nilly, in the afghan; and finding Nan's Great-Nan's embroidery scissors, she began to take his stitches out from his torn ear, gingerly, while he writhed in an ecstasy of fury, clawing at the quilt, rending the forests of Unlethe.

In the bright thin morning after, they walked out to Sylvie's woods, bearing cans that clouded on the air, that spilled a froth and fume of water through the muted fields, beyond the wire-strung stone wall. They walked among the naked trees, with their coffee cans full of slopping hot detergent, and their putty knives, scraping away at the spittle-white larvae of gypsy moths. Dinah plunged and weltered in the brushwood, checking out a rumor of squirrels. Ariane trailed dreamily behind; she juggled and clambered, and snagged her blue scarf.

Unsnarling it, she saw that Sylvie had gone further on, light as any leaf, unvexed, into her element. Though she wore heavy boots, her stride still had the heron-stalking nicety of bare feet. She bore her tools to hand, her blade and lethal brew.

Ariane trudged after, cumbered with her knife and tin, like emblems, these her sword, her fuming cup: hieratic, as if posing for a tarot card; or else as Fool, in some Brueghel proverb. The Knight of Moths. The Mazer Wood. Her trees blurred with fantasy. She could not, with staring, turn them elsewhere, to Sylvie's world; could not, for wanting something other, see them now. Only moving, she bore herself away, with the illusion of imagining, as if running from the earthly forest made it Cloud.

"Jay!" called Sylvie. "See him?"

Ariane looked up. Thin bluewashed sky, bare trees.

Sylvie stooped, prying up a rusty can. "Yuck."

"Some old grail," said Ariane.

'Blecch," said Sylvie, uncrumpling a sodden wodge of newsprint. " 'Teen Mom In Rock Star Shock: He made me his love-slave.' Deea. Arval strikes again."

"A maid betray'd," said Ariane. "Let me see."

" 'Kidnapped by space aliens!' Geez Louise."

"Same as Tam Lin," said Ariane. "You know. Hold me fast and fear me not, I'm the father of your blob."

Sylvie laughed, and stuck the trash in her pocket. "What a dump. You missed some, over there."

They moved on, scraping, through the threadbare woods.

"It's these oaks I'm worried about," said Sylvie, from a stand of huge and shabby trees. "They're all infested." Touching an old scar where a branch had fallen, she turned to Ariane. "D'you remember? Where you found the ring?" Ariane nodded, though she remembered somewhere green. The ring had grown fast to the gnarled root it encircled, inlaid as on a knuckly hand; its stone, perhaps, lay buried in a hundred years of leaves. "Nan used to come here," said Sylvie. She scraped furiously, an avenging dryad, tearing ropes of grapevine from the bark.

Ariane gazed about; she thought she remembered now, through a green mist of vanished spring, the slant of hill, the rocks: all skeletal. Does green have shape? Or does the shadow of a dream have bones? But now

the trees stood wintry, bare. Scant leaves still clung; they
rattled, dry as mummy. Downward from their great
gnarled roots, the brook ran sinewy among the stones: a
flock of them, grey wethers, goats. The walls had fallen
here; the folds were forest.

Sylvie sang as she worked: hoarse breathless snatches,
wintry songs. She had a cold coming, and her voice had lost
its middle notes, had dropped to a raven's croak, shrilled to
a wren's reed, a bat's cry. It whispered, ghostly. Yet a few
fierce notes rose clear and poignant, unimpassioned as a
bird's. Here Ariane's enmythed remembrance and her
imagining of Sylvie touched—now—as leaf to leaf's shadow
on the water. "*. . . a mantle of the burning gold did keep
him from the wind . . .*" Sylvie set down her can on a
flattish rock, and flourished her blunt knife wickedly,
across her throat. "And then—kkkkkhhhh."

"Tea," said Ariane demurely. "Tea and honey. For
that throat." She grinned. "Or rum. I like the moth-
drowning shanties." She stirred the glutted water, pen-
sive. "Could you do Lord Gregory? You never sang it
through, not the end."

Stooping, Sylvie spun a pebble at the brook. It curved
and leapt; then struck a rock and sank, on two notes like
a stonechat's: clack and clonk. With her hands thrust in
her pockets, standing, odd and brown among the trees,
she sang. "*I am a king's daughter . . .*" Her voice in the
wintry air was fogbound, plangent; but as the story took
her, as she sang, it rose through cloud to a high clarity,
green and pure as nightfall and the shepherd's star:

> I have built a bonny boat
> All covered with pearl,
> And at every needletuck in it
> There hangs a silver bell.
>
> But I'll take down that mast of gold,
> And set up a mast of tree,
> For it does not suit a forsaken maid
> To sail so royally.

Unmoving, knife and tin forgotten, Ariane held fast.
How thin the world is, she thought; and felt the welling

up of hills of sea among dry branches and the stones. The woods were drowned in insubstantial leaves, green as water; they trembled with elusively incrystalled light. Light caught a branch, a tree still leaved with shards of bronze, and they were flaws of spirit, fiery tongues. A brightness—O the Ship, indwelling in the wood, unsought. Cloud's stars lay hidden at its roots, earthfasting what was air and other. Its shadow was of fire, and its leaves of light: the tatters of a fall, foretelling, spelling silently all chances of the Nine in one, in now. The stars held all in gravity: held still the leaves, unfallen prophecies; held fast the Ship, unsailing.

Now, she thought, I have fixed this sight eternally, have caught my soul in chains of stars. Pausing, phrasing this, Ariane let slip the moment, losing what she held; then seized. But it had clouded. When she came to where the star had fallen, it was jelly: cold, timorous, diffuse.

Now and elsewhere in Nan's wood, and by the grey northern waves, Sylvie sang: ". . . *so I'll leave now these windows, and likewise this hall, for it's deep in the sea I will find my downfall.*" She croaked the last note dismally and giggled. "Silly wench," she said. "Well, poor thing, she did get stuck with the baby—but she just gave up, like that." She thwacked her icy glove against a tree, and her can sloshed over. "Drowned," she said darkly, coughing. "Let's go in, it's getting cold."

After lunch, they sat on Sylvie's bed, and listened to her tapes, and drew. Or rather, Sylvie worked; Ariane crouched staring at her paper (blank and virginal, neutral pH, that the uncreated image might not fade); not drawing Sylvie as the brown girl, as she'd meant, but laying out her pencils in uneven spectra, colors of the music. Caught aslant in Sylvie's mirror, her face was bright, unfilled: a late and crescent moon, reversed, unwaning in the glass. Her eyes, in its thin curve, and cloud of hair, were innocent, grey-blue as dusk. Beyond her, deeper in the speckled glass, Sylvie bent to her shading, all intent as candleflame. Her dark hair brushed the page. Her face was oddly faceted, but caught by light, possessed: now darkly lucid, now dazzling blank, beyond Ariane's slow dogged skill of hand to capture. Tentatively, she set down a shaky umber line—a jutting nose—erased it, stared.

If only Sylvie wouldn't *move.* she thought. Glancing woefully aside, she saw her own pale mirrored image, smudgy with longing. *I see the moon, and the moon sees me.* She ducked, abashed. She thought of herself as gaze, and would forget that she was earth-turned, had mass and face and gravity. Beside her, Sylvie tapped her pencil.

"Can I see?"

"Not yet," said Sylvie, hunched with the drawing on her knees. Ilorin and her dead love's mother. An unquiet bed, a sleeper waked, a figure at her bedhead, witch or revenant; but she was turning something else—a stone? A crossroads. Dusk and snow, a stone like a grey-cloaked woman, silent. Or a witch? Sylvie turned it sideways. Wind, moorland? Or a moonlit bed? Goes either way, she thought: like what Air sees. Like dreams. But stories? Could you tell them either way? I wonder. Stories go one way, they go on. There's choices made, there's turnings. Gone is gone. Or now and somewhere else, like ghosts.

"Had this weird dream," she said. "There was this necklace, like a moonstone. Nan had kept it for me—in the dream, I'd seen her wear it, oh, for years—she had it in the tallboy, only all the drawers were very small and square, like an apothecary's; and she couldn't find it, they were full of leafdust: it was years and years. Like tea. She gave me some."

"Like tea," said Ariane. "A cup of oolong syne. What happened then?"

"I woke up." Sylvie started drawing, light and sure. "I thought, well, it's *there,* Nan has it, somewhere in the house. I'd lose it. And I thought, that's what you meant: it's hallows. It's what stays. The rest goes on."

The tape had run silent. Ariane put on another, wordless music. She combed her hair out with her fingers; braided it; set straight the swaling candle on the windowsill, and made little pallid moons of wax, pinching out noses and ears, and trailing hair, like a comet's Arianemoons. Her sketchbook slid from her lap.

The cards lay scattered all about her. Sylvie had been

playing with them, had left them as they fell. Ariane felt a pang of jealousy for her creation, so lightly held, profoundly known, yet occult to her own desire; she longed for Sylvie's careless grace of insight. She had never seen the lands beyond. She smoothed out a bent card and began to gather them; then paused, looked sidelong. Sylvie worked on, unheeding. Ariane half turned aside. Warily she shuffled and covertly laid out a handful of the images in a wavery huddling sort: not longways, but a knot of nine. What then? Knotting and unknotting the unravelled fringes of her shawl, she fell into a blurry revery.

Here was the Witch, a mirrored figure, dark, undark of moon, chiasmic; there, aslant of it and sinister, the Wren turned tail. Unlight, unturning. Blood. And there, the Swans, reversed: black frost and barren labor, the weaving of nettleshirts in silence to unspell; earthbinding. The Cup was inmost. Being stone, the child was blind; the water of the fountain wept for it, slow tears, unsalt. The cup it held was cracked: the moon lay drowned in it, unseen, as deep as heaven in the shallow leafy water.

Now, she said, I am that O, that eye within the maze, the moon's garden walled in thorn: my clew is light. Now I will journey outward, will undo the knot of thorn. Will see.

Beyond her lay the wood, Sylvie's element, undreaming. A wind in her boughs stirred Sylvie's darkness, shook the rain from her bright leaves; it shivered starlight in her living water. Even in her stillness she was poised, like the moon new-bent in heaven, like a sword. Ariane had only to find the door into the wood—Witch or Wren or Tower—and walk through it as Sylvie did, becoming wood and journeying and moon, at once the traveller and the tale.

She could not. She was darkfast, vexed and riddled at every turn: a captive in the black-thumbed, ink-blotched garden, in the papery henge of cards. Staring, she unfocused; the woodcut image slewed and blurred. She saw only the configured cards in a knot of mirrors, oppositions, ambiguities, turning ever inward to the maze, the cup, the moon: which was illusion, a mirror at the heart.

No other where. She stared harder, till it broke in tears, dissolved: the water's tenure of the moon.

No door, no dance, no clew. Uncrystal.

Ariane wrenched up her hair, stabbed in the pins. She gathered up the cards, aligning them, neat as orphans, two by two. Eleven, twelve, thirteen. She sifted through drawings, shook out folds of quilt, leaves of notebooks. Twenty-eight, twenty-nine. "Sylvie?"

"Huh?" She was hunched up, shading to the music, her fingers livid with blacklead. "Oops." Sharpening her pencil all over her lap, she squinted. "Something weird about that face: the light falls two ways at once."

"Sorry, could I just look under you? I can't find some cards."

Sylvie knelt up in a flurry of woodflakes, clutching her sketchbook and sneezing. "Bless you," said Ariane, as Sylvie fumbled for a hanky, smutching her nose with the blacklead. Ariane worried the pillows, ransacked some pajamas and the crocheted afghan (shaking out an apple core); spied out the nightstand drawer, half-open, spilling socks; hung head downward to peer under the bed, where an odd library book and a hairbrush lurked forlornly: turning up three scant cards at length. Two by the candlestick, amid a wrack of crumpled tissues, and one in Sylvie's shoe. Giddy and furious, with her hair come down again and draggled in the dust, she righted herself. "I can't find the Sword."

"Oh well," said Sylvie, straying back to her drawing, "It's in here someplace." She glanced vaguely round the room. "It'll turn up."

That night, Sylvie's cold spilled over. Tea and lemon drove it back, skulking to her larynx, where it sulked. Ariane looked anxiously at her, shivering in a seedy cardigan over threadbare striped pajamas; at her damp brow and red nose. "I should go; you're not up to this."

"Pooh," said Sylvie, in a fierce whisper. "Two days. Tempestuous but brief. And where'd you go anyway?"

"Ravenser Odd," said Ariane, unclouding. "It's the Styx. Could I get you some tea, or an aspirin, or anything?"

"Oh, that's kind of you. Tea. No honey—it makes me

sniffle. I think there's some brandy in the sideboard."
Feverish, she twanged at her guitar strings, droning a few
mournful intervals. ". . . *a little while after*—damn—*a letter was wrote* . . ."

Ariane leaned on her elbow, in drowsy sympathy.
"God, you sound authentic. Like a wax cylinder of Caedmon's nurse. Go to bed."

When Ariane came in with the tea, Sylvie was
crouched splayed on her bed, amid splinters of glass,
hunting brilliant nervous droplets of mercury over the
sheets with a spoon. The atomies jigged in mockery,
assailing her shifting knees, elusive and importunate as
fairies. They beaded like breath on the fibers of the blanket. They spangled and fled. "Alien marbles," she said,
chivvying. "I smashed the thermometer."

"What about the glass?"

"Oh, never mind that. I could *breathe* this stuff. My
hair could fall out." She was beaming. "Aren't they
neat? All the little bojangles, all over. Blobs. Whoops!
Gotcha."

"You'd go mad," said Ariane. "Like the Hatter. Over
there, by the pillow, a whole invading galaxy. The Huns
of Elfland wildly rolling."

Sylvie chased two, one, seven bits, over the fuzzy
sheet. They were tarnished now, saturnine. "I hate dirty
mercury." Grimly she tipped the last droplet into a phial.
She held it up. Then heedless, deliberate, ecstatic, she
decanted the bright shivering creature on her hand.

The wind had changed, turned northward. Sylvie's cold was waning, as she'd prophesied. She tinkered with a lantern on the broad bare kitchen table, trying out stumps of candles. "Pooh," she said. "None of these fits." It was all the same to her if they brought a flashlight to the woods; it was Ariane, self-consciously, who clung to the icons of ritual, to candlelight and salt and garlands. They were going to Nan's woods to wake the moon with carolling, wassail the trees: a Cloudish ritual, said Ariane, the last of winter solstice. It was dark of moon. The sun had turned a twelve-night since; the moon was turning: not the year's great doorway, but its wicket-gate. Behind lay hallows, and beyond, the cold uncertain way, and rising light.

"Snowing again," said Sylvie. "Crazy." Kneeling up on the bow-backed Windsor chair, she fumbled in her jacket pockets and fingered among a handful of gritty coughdrops and fircones and frayed guitar strings. "Ah." She secured the candle with a twist of breadbag wire. After she had lit the wick, she hung over it, wrenching up little screws of paper napkin, and flaring them. Here and gone, she thought. Hey, where'd it go?

Ariane watched her. The brief firelight glanced from Sylvie's scar-browed gaze, that slash of constant lightning. She burned with an elusive intensity of focus, now and nowhere, like a star caught in dangling crystal, fleeting and inconsequent in semblance, though it gravely shone elsewhere. Sylvie blew the last wisp of ash from

35

between her fingers: ashes of dandelion, midnight
o'clock.

Ariane went back to rummaging through the lower
cupboards, saucepans hurtling down with a din like the
Wreck of the *Deutschland* on a reef of Rastafarian steel-
drums. She found a dwarfish black iron skillet, spidery
with neglect, and a swart and rusted stovelid: they would
make a fine clangor, struck with wooden spoons. Wap!
And the boggarts would flee. "Hey, Sylvie, don't you
wash this stuff before you put it away?"

"I think Nan used to. Why?"

Ariane scoured them a bit with a wad of newspaper,
and stuffed them in her empty backpack, turned out to
make them room. She wore her ruffianly greatcoat,
caped and cuffed and quite staggeringly heavy, of mole-
ish dusky wool, with rather fewer silver buttons than
designed. It hung to her heels. With the wooden spoon
she brandished, striding and swirling, it gave rather a
Dulle Griet air of absurd panache, of rag-and-bone fan-
tastical swagger: *so boldly did I fight, me boys, although
I'm but a wench.*

"Missing anything?" said Sylvie.

"Marbles. No, other pocket. Here's a spoon for the
Badger—"

Ariane grimaced at the glass and swept the candle-
ends from the table, cramming her pockets. They were
made to hold any number of pinchbeck watches, fat as
turnips, and witches' tinderboxes, amid packs of greasy
tarot; they bulged with her turned-out oddments, crazy
and endeared: her notebooks, her pens, marbled papers,
tapes, talismans and skeins of silk. They were her beads
and budget, her familiar loving imp, Pyewackett. She
couldn't help it: living rootless and only waveringly present as she did, she needed touchstones of her existence.
I clink, therefore I am.

Sylvie unwadded dampish paper from her boots, toss-
ing one crumpled clot for the cat to wanton. Another
fell short of the fire; Dinah sniffed at it. "All right, all
right, we're just going," said Sylvie, swallowing her
tea. Stone cold. Throat's better, anyway—touch wood.
I can sing.

Ariane wriggled into the straps of her bag, oddly hunchbacked beneath her greatcoat's cape, and peered into the coldly Stygian depths of the refrigerator. You poured cider on apple trees, for the charm. What libation would you pour out on forests, root beer? An academic question: technical liquids comprised milk, ketchup, and expired eggnog. She slapped together a tunafish sandwich, dry, on greening bread. Toward the middle of the loaf seemed all right. "Want one?"

"There's some cheese somewhere," said Sylvie helpfully. "From Thanksgiving," she added, cramming on her knitted cap. "It's Maire's. I was saving it for company."

Ariane prodded the tinfoil, peeled it back. "Cheese turned self," she pronounced solemnly.

"O dear."

"It's gone all Arvally, 'veined with an evil magnificence,' " she said, wickedly quoting Sylvie's notebook at fifteen.

"I like kings that way," said Sylvie. "Black-hearted, not clabbery like Arveth." She paused, winding her brown-and-grey plaid scarf round and round her hand. "All marbly. There's a point . . . It's a kind of symbiosis, like lichen: evil and nobility living on each other's decay. There's a balance." Dinah snuffled fondly at the cat, who, with a shrug of withering disdain, leapt up on Sylvie's shoulder.

"And then they get all moldy-souled and decadent," said Ariane. "Evil cheeses. Anarchic."

"Ow," said Sylvie absently, patiently unburring the cat from her collarbone. "No. Chaos is narrowing. There's no complexity, no choices. It's like not waking up from nightmares: they're the wild country, but if there's nothing beyond, there's no further in." She poked the cheese gingerly. "Eeugh. That's arrogant." And ingenuously: "I hate cheese."

"That's high treason." Ariane primmed her mouth, demurely sly. "He's probably been in there debauching the creamcheese. Nice innocent country lass. Caught her at the bedmaking."

Sylvie laughed. Hunched up in her chair, scarfed and mittened, in her stocking feet, she sang. ". . . *but she said that she'd led such a contrary life, she said that she'd*

never be a young shepherd's wife." And miming:
"Thrum. Thrum. Thrum. Guitar in gloves. *Here's my
sheepcrook and my black dog, I give 'em to you*—oh,
buzz off, Dinah."

Ariane spluttered crumbs of sandwich. "We could wassail Maire's goats. Mairzygoats. With the cheese—*O
lilywhite billy*. Or we could go around and hang little
Walkmen in the branches. Cold metallic nightingales.
Techno-carols. Whirr. Sprong. With endless loops of
tape, like Tibetan prayer-wheels."

Sylvie laughed, tumbling about on the floor, and tugging her other boot away from Dinah. "Walkthings.
Deea." She sat up, breathless. "Hey, the lantern's
burned out."

Ariane rekindled it, with a new stump of candle from
her pocket, warding it for a moment with the hollow of
herself, until the quarrels of light were still. Then she
latched the glazed iron door.

"All right, come on," said Sylvie.

By candlelight and the dark of moon, out into the owl-
soft and ragged snow, they went, banging the storm door
behind them. There was a thump and flurry as the black
dog ran past them, bound on her own night errand. The
uncurtained light fanned from the windows. It was barely
dark, and at the turning of the year; the starved and
wintry landscape lay under snow, like a beggar dying in
a kingly gown. Dark and silence and the soft oblivion of
snow, the pure and primal earth: as if with her wavering
candle, Ariane began the world.

"Deea! It's slippery!" cried Sylvie, clutching Ariane's
sleeve; and down they went, hurly-burly, flapping like
scarecrows, and staggered up again blind with elation.
The candle danced dementedly; yet strangely, stubbornly, did not go out. Stumbling like Brueghel beggars,
snatching at coat-tails and embracing thorns, they slithered down the snowy hill to the bourne of the rising
wood, farther than in spring.

> For to seek mad Tom o 'Bedlam,
> Ten thousand years I'd travel:
> Mad Maudlin goes on dirty toes,
> For to save her shoes from gravel.

Still I sing, bonny boys, bonny mad boys,
Bedlam boys are bonny . . .

Sylvie chanted breathlessly, taboring her hand; and
crouched, as the scything, dispassionate regard of a passing car swept by them. Ariane fell over her, and sprawled
in the snow. The earth was stony, poor pastureland,
beneath the swathe of swan-white mantle. Cold and
sharp, there was snow down her collar, and up her
sleeves. Lantern? She'd dropped it. There, everywhere,
its werelight mopping and mowing. "Hey!"

"Hush. What's that little stumpy person?" said Sylvie.

"What?"

"You missed it, behind the rock." A sly, delighted
whisper: Sylvie was teasing, thrilling with a joyful mischief. She crouched, hag-browed, and ice-daggled with
the drifting snow, breath-bearded like a Lapland witch,
amid the horns of a fallen branch. "Look," she said
gravely. "There's a hare, see? He's running. That's
where the stone wasn't."

Ariane tumbled up, shaking out her greatcoat and
beating her mittens. Swan fell from her softly, a feather-
cloak, as if she were the elderborn of air: another fall
and she would fly. *And the lovely owl my marrow,* sang
Tom o' Bedlam. She shook the snow off like a botched
transformation, flailing and flapping crazily in a whirlwind of plumes. "Ogham," she said, stomping. "Ogham.
Ogham. Ogham." The knot of stones stood huddled.
"Folk rocks. They do Celto-boogie. Sacred doo-wop. Da
doo rune rune."

"New wave?"

"Hah! *The punk I scorn, and the roaring boys'
bravado.*"

A wild storm of giggles, but the wind's eye was eery.
Ariane bent close and whispered. "They're hiding in the
trees."

She felt the dazzle of Sylvie's spirit beat against her
glazy soul, like the impress of the wings of winter, feathers of the frost—ah, let me in—as if Sylvie were her
daemon. And as well, and unavowed, there was the
enchantment of a briefly hovering seisin: Sylvie sang for

her alone, a wild bird to her hand. *O that is the blood of my grey hawk: she would not fly for me.*

The center's relative, thought Sylvie, peering through the falling snow: things curve round it, like the night where there's a candle burning. The lines of pattern change. Or like the game when Ariane plays. She's the rock. Then there's away and toward, there's farther in.

The candle still burned, canted over in a drift of snow, like the moon in a cave of cloud; it curved and crazed the brittling ice. As Ariane set the lantern upright on a stone, the candle swayed; between frost and fire, the glass cracked. Flawing wildly and furling, the fire dwindled to a sullen squint. She undid the latch and steadied it, nursing back the little leaf of flame, with fingers turning wax. *Hold fast, and fear me not.* In the wood, the ice fell, ringing sweetly as bridles.

They had come to the drystone wall, almost drifted over, a weal of snow. Beyond lay thickets of bayberries prickling the snow, and the small wood, crabtrees and alders, witch hazel, and buckthorn with its tawny leaf; beyond again, the river and the firs in their mourning plumes of wind, and a great candor of snow, flawed with trees. The whiteness clung, leaving a frail rim of black to each branch and bole: a wood of lunar negatives, ensilvered as the moon had waned, all bitten to the rind with dark. The stone-throated fall of water was muted with black ice.

Dark of moon. A turning of the dance ago, and it was glory, it was new, thought Ariane. But now the starry dance hung still and fierce; the hopeful grass lay under wood, like a hare beneath the falcon's foot. The dark had whelmed the islands of high summer, clouds of stars. Would they rise to Sylvie's singing, bright as Phoebus with untrodden dew?

A hundred years ago, thought Sylvie, this was fields. Still here, it's all still going on, the fields of summer, and the leaves of years. The moon's possibilities: it's time and patterning. What turns. But the earth's like running on in counterpoint. Nan's woods and Air's, and all the falls. What turns, turns round again. The same and never. Dark of moon. Midsummer eve. She envisioned the sweet drifts of silvery grass, dusk beneath a paler sky; she saw, elusive in the air, the hunting swallows and the fireflies, black and burning celadon, flying in scissoring, enweaving dissonances, contrary and resolved. The moon rose, in the branches of a green and ancient thorn.

Further on, she thought, it goes on.

Sylvie clambered between the wall and the wire. She took the candle from Ariane and went on, low and bright and wavering, a shepherd's star. The ice on the river held. Ariane followed warily, cumbered with her pack, ensorcelled. Did they walk on clouds of air? Hold fast, she thought. The star holds fast.

Over the stony water Sylvie, glimmering, paced and turned about. "Here," she said. They had come, by another way, to Nan's grove. The trees were obliterate with snow; the paths among the stones were blind. Their lantern trembled on the air, a burr of light, a hallowfire, rayed against the stony dark. ". . . see now," she said. She ran over a broken spectrum of notes, and began to sing. "*All under the leaves, and the leaves of life. . .*"

Her voice, harsh-edged, held in a wild pure clarity, like the green dusk through a hedge of black wet branches, a lovely desolation. Clouded, yet it gathered to a grace; as in the bleak and leafless hedgerow, the mist hangs trembling from the thorn. Her graces were sharp-winged and sliding as the swallow's flight: reverberent, her music skeined the air, wove night and candlelight on hands of branches, bent and black and starry.

Ariane would not sing, but echoed unaware, like the shaken metal of a bell. With their pots and wooden spoons, they raised an iron clangor, forging a wintry cage for the sun upon the cold grim anvil of the dark, trampling wildly and gravely round and round in the snow shaken from the branches, and deeper into the wood.

Drunk with holiness, with dark and snow and the carol of the trees, from within the frail sanctuary of light, Ariane said, "Wassail the moon."

"There isn't any. Here. It isn't here." Sylvie was shadowy, still as a candle of ice.

"You bring it back with carolling, to blow and bear the silver apples. Or hunt it through the wood, with a cage of branches, and knots of black ribbons, of night and the snow: please to see the king."

It was clearing; Ariane saw a star, and another, and a knot, and then Orion, shivering in his rags of cloud, cold and heartless as a tinker. A soft clump of falling snow put out the candle. And there was a moon among the branches, rising in its crescent like a crown of horn, like a delicate elusive ship whose mast was tree; and the branches were another wood.

She took Sylvie's sleeve; the body beneath it trembled like quicksilver. Then Ariane held nothing. Terribly, vertiginously, her knowing overturned: chance became design, the constellations of another world.

"Wait," said Ariane, as Sylvie walked away. "Oh, don't." It was dark, it all had turned. She knelt, fumbling desperately with cold wet shaken hands. The candle would not light.

Bright and heedless, Sylvie ran. Her random moving had a pattern, a willful necessity. She sprang, shying and swerving amid the trees of her ghostly wood, now bright, now shadowy as they and horned with shadow; leaping as a child does being the horse, the prey and huntsman all at once, as if she followed something swift and wary: a hare or a hedgerow bird. The moon. She cried out once, clear and shrill, and cold as Orion's sword. But she herself was the sword, the lightning, whose substance is all spirit, act and being fused inseparably in one fleeting stroke of will: ah, but in what hand?

Ariane scrambled up and ran after, helter-skelter, clagged with ice and cumbered hopelessly with doubt. Now one, and now the other wood held sway, so that she shrank at shadows, stumbling on air, and crashed headlong into wraiths of trees as harsh and sinewy as wyrms. Malicious twigs snatched at her face and hair; ice pelted her, and owls assailed her, falling silent into snow. Vexed and desperate, she lagged, while Sylvie ran on unamazed as moonlight. Araine caught and wrenched her foot and fell.

Looking up, she thought that Sylvie wore a mantle of the light, flying out like burning silver on the wind; that Sylvie hung moveless, as the cloak flared out, and the wood fleeted, like cloud before the moon; that as fire graves the eye with its shadow, so this brightness was the impress and afterimage of the dark. And then it seemed, achingly, as if she and Sylvie were two things, as if the moon and its dark were sundering, the bow in its curved brightness bent and the bleak cold asperity of stone. Two things: the journeying and the cold and ruined tower. And then there was nothing there at all.

II

Darkfast

Dark, back of Law. Unhallows. A stone and a thorn tree whispered together, leaning close in cold embrace.

Time, said thorn to standing stone.

Not time, said stone to thorn.

Back of clouds, the moon rode, cold and ancient, and unfast: light rounding in the lap of shadow, dark gnawing at the wasting light, childing and devouring.

Dead and graved, said dark of moon.

It turns, said moon. Turns O.

O's naught, said dark of moon.

As the dark of moon was stone, the moon was flowering in light; and round them stood the starless hills, the naked clouds of earth. They two were sisters. One lay in the other's arms: the old moon dying, and the new reborn, each child of her devourer and mother to her death, each childless and unborn, undying.

Far and beyond them, round them on the naked fells, a ring of fires blazed and leaped. The dancers, earthborn witches, flared from shadow, with their fiery, their storm-dark hair unbound, their mantles flying out, caught fast with thorns of iron, stained with blood. They fleeted, and were past. They called on darkness, craving light of it, light bound. They danced unhallows, and the winter's death.

They wake, said thorn to stone.

The sisters met, as always, now and nowhere, at the lightspring and the fall of years, at hallows and unhallows eve: they met as tree and stone, unlightfast, fast in earth. They bent and whispered, as they had before the years were danced, before the lightborn children came. No time was then, but in their turning. They had waked alone. They two in elder days had borne the sun and moon, borne stars that fell and drifted, fleeting like the leaves of years; of falling, they had spelled the earth and sky.

No more. The stars were lightfast now, unturned, and turning in the endless dance. The children of the lightfall danced the ring. Winter and the fall of leaves, and green and summerlong, the sisters never met in earth; but dwelt in moonwise, cronying, entwined: though dark and O kept still their secrets.

They were one. Light eaten by its inward fury, crown rising from its root in darkness. They were moon and dark of moon, bound each in the other, changing yet unchanged: the journey and the tower, A and O. Their turning spelled all things by sort of stars, by lightfast and the fall of leaves: fates told long since, and still foretelling, falling true.

Two sisters and one being, turn and turn. One dance. They were the raven and the owl her marrow, nightfall and the lightspring, earth as grave, as lap. They met at hallows and unhallows eve; they danced. Turn all, and one was two again. One waking from her halfyear's spell as stone, as thorn, would walk the earth; the other in her turn would wake and watch, bound thornfast, leafless through the dark of year, or lightlong as a standing stone.

Stone waked at hallows, striding, calling down the snow. She rode the wind and hunted; she did rage. Desiring nothing, she devoured light, leaves and all. Dead of winter, dark of moon, she danced unlightfast at the sun's new grave, ranting air to ice. She danced; yet could not still the springs of light. It rose, beyond her hand. Time and time again, it turned: the wren died for the wintersake, and rose; the lightborn dancing waked the sun. And still, and still, she rimed the earth to stony sleep. She bound night fast in stars.

But her other winterlong kept thornfast, rooted deep in stars; within her bounds of tree, hedged round, she watched by the dying year: spelled leaves on fall of leaves, waked sun in her great lap. She lapped it in a cloth of snow, she lulled it on her knee. Moon rose and journeyed, owling after souls; yet where she was indwelt, was hallows, small and endless, and the eye of Cloud. Come thorneve, at the green unhallows, when the blackthorn and the white had flowered, and the hallows O was turning dance, dropped hands to let moon through, then dark of moon in turn was bound. She cast away her staff at hallows' roots, and turned to stone.

Reel turns, said stars in branches.

Riddles, knots, said standing stone.

Who'll cut the thread?

Nor dark nor light.

The other comes, said stars. She sails.

Deep's endless, said the dark.

Unfast and fast, said fall of leaves. Bears light.

Not time, said stone to thorn.

Time is. They wake.

Wind in the budding branches, white as stars. Wind raged about the witchstone, cold and still. Storm rose, a storm of ravens' wings, unseen but flaring out in fire, in the wakefires burning, leaping in a ring of writhen gold from hill to waking hill, unmoonwise, and unclosed. A brooch of fire. Ah, it pinned night fast on Law, it held it darkfast. The stars whirled away; they left the branches of the sky swept bare. The witches whirled away in ash. Cold and fiercer still the wind. It danced unhallows and the endless night. It danced the sun and moon to stone. It danced unlightfast of the stars, and it turned nothing. Nothing there.

Yet there on Cloudlaw, time before all times, the Ship had come, made landfall, lightfast. It had sailed out of winternight beyond the dark; its mast was a branching tree, great-rooted, and its leaves far-drifting stars. The Ship sailed on; the lightborn kindred it had brought still walked the hills of Cloud: unearthly, yet the guardians of wood and wild, the children of the endless dance.

There on Law at dead of winter, dark of moon, the children had kept wakesun, dancing nightlong with the turning stars. They danced as stones, took on earth's burden lightly as a cloak. They turned the wintry night to branching, and the stars to leaves; they wove a garland of the dark and light to bear the winter sun. It waked. Earth bore, as it had graved, the sun and moon; its crown was rooted in its dark: but turning in their winter carol, the children bade the earthborn, moon and sun, to rise; they called them to the dance. They wove them, with them, in the starry hey. Unfast in earth, yet they kept troth: the knot, the lightfast of the earth and sky.

Now, here, at hallows' end, the thorn stood leafless, with the old moon tangled in her hair. At dawning, she would dance her sister's wake. Time before time, in their circle old as earth, the dark of moon had turned, turned stone; as the moon had flowered from the thorn. It was her time. For half a year, outdwelling, she would walk the fells, wake summer, while her other stood on Cloud-law: cold unhallowed stone.

Has turned, said wind in thorn. I blow. I bear.

And I did hunt.

And will in turn, turn stone. Time is. I call you.

No.

The wind was still. The ring of fires died to ash. The stone at the crossroads seemed to shrink: not stone, but a dark-clad woman.

No, the witch said. Time is not.

Will you not dance?

I walk. Keep hallows, and your cage of thorn: I go by Law.

And I by light. Will you not turn?

Have bound whatever turns and dies, forever, else-where. I am I. Unbound and shadowless. Do you not see my crown?

Beyond them in the paling dusk, there stood a broken ring of stones, small as children, still as death: the dance, caught stonefast as they turned, the longest night. The witch had thralled, unsouled them. She had struck their bodies into stone. The ring had stood from dark of moon to dark, unturning since.

Not all. Some breaking from the dance had fled; but dark still hunted them, took souls to crown her void, struck stones of light. Beyond hallows lay no wood, no fastness: Law, and ravens' fury, and her hunt. She walked.

When the ring was closed, no dance would be, nor turn of year. No leaf nor moon, no starry carol nor the quick brave sun, but cold unchanging death. The stones lay scattered like a witch's hoard on a gravemound, on the bones of earth: her body once, denied. Her crown was death.

Crown? Aye, or crow's shackle, said moon to dark, said owl to raven witch. All's one to thee, and naught; and yet unclosed. Stoneblind: thy shadow's still behind, and done's undone.

The witch said nothing. Rising from her ungraved body, she was air and darkness, shadowless; was naked immortality, sheer crystal: but her hair streamed out in storm. The blood of lightborn was its jewelling, was clotted in its fury; blood fell, sharp as hail, to earth. A child lay broken on the stony Law. She'd done with it, undone. Crying out, her ravens thronged to tear its eyes. Their greed unstarred the night. But silent, cold, she bore its soul away.

She rose, unflawed and starless, crowned with souls; but the moon's hook caught in her, not light but void. She'd torn it from her, bound it darkfast and unhallowed, graved it; yet it scarred: a talon's wound, slashed over and over in her endless planes of night. She was gone.

May eve. The moon hunted, hunchbacked, cold and ancient, in a great sharp brough of ice. Would snow by morning, biting leaves. She owled after souls, to bear them to her rimy tower: not of stone, but nine-walled, gateless. Soft, inexorable, she stooped and slashed: all fiercely shining but her sweep of dark, her iron edge.

Dusk, back of Cloudlaw, now and nowhere. A black frost and a bitter, windless, starry on the thorn. A henge of stones, no taller than a ring of children in a game, but cold, cold as death, and pale as bone, unturned. Unsouled. Not all. Not endless yet. Leaves fallen, pale and bleak, beside a blind vain stone. They'd caught in rime, in fall on fall of prophecy, or fates long told and past. The Sword, said leaves. The Wren. The Ship.

Ariane woke to the sound of icy rain. The clock said ten to three, implacable; the light of afternoon was raw. Sylvie? I was crazy, I thought you—No one there. A shadow on the wall, a wind.

She had not slept until long after light. Waking and waking, she had seen the trees starkened with the rigor of the dawn; had heard the wind go softly on the stairs to bed. The candle—O but that was dream, Sylvie's going with a rushlight through the house: for it was wood, was ruined tower. Nan drew shrouds of snow across the mirrors, laid a stony child to sleep in quilts of leaves: all dreams turned inward to the maze.

Rising, sick and dazed, Ariane stood on her bare feet. The boards were chill and dusty. She had not undressed, or unbraided her hair; it hung in frazzled sallies. She went to the uncurtained window and looked out, and saw the snow was waning, all but gone on the hillsides. Ice bent down the trees. Sleet railed against the roof. Small change. She thought, Sylvie didn't wake me. She's asleep, she came in with her candle, late; and saw her burning, flaring out in silver fire on the wind. Ah no.

Ghostly, hesitant, she walked downstairs, and slowly through the silent house, not calling out. Hall and kitchen, keeping-room and shed, even Nan's dark mirrored room: no Sylvie. (The moon rising in the wood, the stone—) I am waking, she said; I am cold. Her face was shadowed in the mirrors of the hall. Nothing had been moved, yet all was changed. The house seemed mute, unsouled, and she not life but trespass. She moved

unwilled, as if she had no self at all, but were merely the
still voice that walks in dreams, that says: that tree is
Sylvie; now the stones will move; the ship will sail. *Wake
here*, it said, *the other walks*.

At last she stood at Sylvie's door. She could not speak.
She knocked, too softly to be heard; then sharply. No
answer. The latch clinked as she went in. The room was
empty. Sylvie's clothes lay sloughed among the fircones,
tissues, notebooks. There was dust on the branches of
yew. She saw her breath. A wind could scatter worlds,
leaves of paper, light and all. All wind. No Cloud, no
Alder, nor Unlethe. There were never any worlds.

But waking, she remembered running, stumbling in the
dark and calling. *Wait*. No Sylvie there. And then, no
woods: she'd come to empty fields. Below her, lay a
waste of snow, unbroken, and a rock beside a stunted
tree. As she stood, the tree shook, silent, bare of snow.
An owl flew. It was morning.

Suddenly, Ariane stripped the bed of its quilt and blankets, so that it lay bare, bleak and snowbound: nowhere,
Sylvie's kingdom. Stiff and bright, a something fluttered
from the shaken folds of quilt: the Sword. Cold with
knowing, lightstruck, stone, she saw it fall.

Crouching on the bare cold boards, she hugged and
huddled the awkward bundle of bedclothes, fiercely to
herself. She was crying, but no tears came: she wept dry-
eyed, howling and gnashing, like a witch. O Sylvie, I
have nowhere left. The owl—She bit her wrist to turn
the thought. Unwilled, her night came back. She had
dreamed of finding a gutted, undying owl in the clothes-
dryer. Mangled, bone and feather, it hung clawed to the
steel mesh, tumbling and rending, and staining the linen
with dark blood. With baleful eyes it stared at her, daunting and compelling; in its ribs lay an uncorrupted jewel,
a soul, for which she longed, and dared not take.

She stood. She folded up the quilt, quite even, with
its brightness inward. Then she pressed her face to the
cold glass of the window, and thought: the rain is uncre-
ating Sylvie. Snow translated her, the spell's dissolved;
as if a dryad's tree were burnt to ash. Damn the rain.
And damn the turning moon. She went by dark of moon:
that door is shut between the worlds. I cannot hold her

light unbound. How then? Call down the frost to seize her into stone? Turn back the year? Or catch her falling star? I'll bite the moon to dark. I'll rime her. Rime her. And the wood—

She turned in fury on the room, the leaves, to scatter them; and stilled herself, stood trembling, aghast. No, thought Ariane. Not woods, not Sylvie's—*Rime*? What am I talking about? Unhinged. Here's Sylvie—Nowhere? That's impossible. I saw—But gone. No sword. No supper even. And she hates to leave here, all her—Hell, I've got to find her. How? Tell Maire? That Sylvie's, what—? Not dead. Not here. I lost her in a game of cards. I can't. Stay here? And wait for her, wait until she's back and tells me what she's seen? And wait until they come and ask where's Sylvie? No. Keep house for her, this house? (*Keep hallows*, said the voice.) Shut up. Nan's woods, and Sylvie's, all the—What I wanted, all the ghosts, the childhood, but I didn't mean like this. Not empty, not alone. Not mine. O God, I've messed it up already.

Rueful, careful with remorse, she crouched and picked up the Sword where it lay. The brown girl ran on, long and light and ranting, by the new-bent moon. A journey. There and back again. As clear as that, she thought, shaken with a crazy clarity. No dread. A queer cold lightness. No worst, she thought, it's happened. The knot's cut. Well, I'll go look for her. *Beyond the wide world's end, me thinks it is no journey.*

Ariane hauled up the rattled window, to a gust of cold sharp rain. The candle on the sill blew over in the haily wind. She set it upright. Not by dark of moon, but candlelight. And back again. She left the window open, so that Sylvie might come in.

The kitchen fire was out. The cat skulked in the ashes, wailing like the soul of famine. Ariane pulled on her boots, still damp and stiff; flung on her ashy coat; put out the leavings of the tunafish. She thrust the Sword deep in her pocket with her useless precious hoard, her runes and candle-ends, the ring. She was going to Nan's woods, to the turning place. The wood was deepest there, and there the light had been, was still, if she could cross. There the ring was found, and Sylvie lost; there the other and unearthly moon had risen. Would the tower still be there, the dark of moon? The door? And what beyond? Another wood, a labyrinth? She had no clew. A journey. She would try the door.

The rain had stopped. It hung as heavy mist, pale, brumal. Sleet pocked the lying snow, as scarred and shadowy as the moon's face: the sea of storms, the sea of darkness. It was starved away to ice in patches, glazing over haggard grass; hung rattling, bony on the branches' marrow. Somewhere, everywhere, dull and dreadful, was a roaring, a rumor of the querns of giants, grinding bones. Ariane began to pick her way downhill, where she and Sylvie had slid and ranted, down toward the stonewall and the lantern wood beyond.

Going warily on ice, she'd not looked up. Now shaken by the drum and tumult, she caught hold of a branch and stared, filled out the astounding clamor with the vision: a rout of water ramping wildly from its stonebed, towering with ice. She clambered onto the wall and clung. Whirling and shattering on the rockfall, daemonic in its hurling frenzy, the torrent broke, like the blasting of a hill of adamant. Thronging, thunder-black, it roared and tumbled, ravening with floes.

Where wood had been was winter islands. Stones and trees stood rootless in the flood, estranged. She looked across the water at the fretted landscape; where Sylvie had set the lantern was drowned.

Unheeding, she slid and scrambled down onto a spur of rocky ground. She took another step. The raving water tore at her booted leg. Another step would hurl her down. She cried out aloud, seized by a fierce dry fury of longing; and she cursed the water and the wind.

She turned and ran upstream, blindly, like a routed drummer dazed with horsemen, skirting the apocalypse. She had to get beyond, she thought, not thinking of the world behind, but running, running from desire. Beyond was Sylvie, and the candle. And beyond was journeying, away, away from time. A leap from now to nowhere.

Skirring on the glazy rocks, snatching wildly at trees, baffled at the rusting snarls of wire, splashed with mud, she pelted on. The river left no earth to her; she was driven back onto the wall, from stone to stone, then slithering on icy leaves, up beside a waterfall, scrambling, deeper into slanting woods, further back in winter.

The stillness caught at her, there, amid the hoarded death of leaves, and the quick trembling of rain. The wood was sheer ice. She stopped, breathless, and sleeved her face; walked on a few steps, and looked.

She was lost. The trees hung down like witches' hair, in knots, in rime. The water here was black, backed with an eerily abstracted flittering and writhing of spume. Across a narrow strait from where she stood was an island, a stone no larger than a saint's ship, and masted with a dead unrooted branch. It was island but for a great clot of icy thorn and leaves that baffled the water. The knot was black and intricate; where the river tongued it, it was bound in ice. Seeking the way onward, through, away, the water had for a thwarted moment stilled, and turned to stone. Stillness bred on deadlocked stillness, stone on stone. She marvelled how it spelled itself, raging into silence, like a witch tranced in her own mirror. The desire was Gorgon to itself. And still, and avid still, the water spelled itself to sleep.

How beautiful, thought Ariane, how terrible: the Witch's bones. A light struck then; it caught the glass-wood out of time, all clarity: a rime forever spelled. The ice-bent branches rang and glinted. And the stone and mast of tree shone silver. O the Ship, she thought: time rode at anchor for her, now, but only now. The ship would sail. Hold fast, and it would carry her. She'd not be left again.

Crouching and trembling on the bank, Ariane hesitated, her glance flickering from rock to raging water. Coil after coil of collected nerve languished unleapt. Come on, body, she thought, nothing to it, cat's leap: up, horse and hattock!

No. She found herself sprawled in midair, which was absolutely impossible; and fell like a cancelled angel on the rock, winded, stunned and clawing.

Christ, that was a crazy thing to do. Her will was still wavering on the bank. Her heart lurched. She was strad-dled, sliding off; benumbed, she found a kneehold, and grabbed the branch and hauled herself up. Her braids had tumbled down, her coatskirt was soaked. The ring fell chiming on the rock. O hell. She caught it, put it on.

And nothing changed. No journey. There she sat, time's fool.

The ship's caught fast, she thought: I'm spellbound. Riddles, knots. What turns, unturning? Dark of moon? The moon itself? If Sylvie could unravel, see how time translates—ah, but Sylvie's nowhere, she's the travelling, the light. Unbound. She journeys lighter of herself. But I am darkfast. I hung back, I held on: so I am left the knot, the fastness for my own.

Angrily bereft, she stared at the knot of ice: herself, a cold and thwarted puzzle. Apology and need and bitter envy lay dark within, the marrow of the witch's bones. Crack the glass, she thought: undo the labyrinth of thorn. Let go.

She crouched gingerly, awkward on the tilted rock, and tugged on the obstruction. It was fast. She knelt, wedging her knee in a crevice, and peered through the crystal to its perplexed and rotting heart. If I leave it, it will thaw. No spell in that. Then smash it, smash it and the ship will sail. She hammered at it with a stone, and saw how the ice clouded at the first infraction, starred and shattering in flaws of brightness. She laid bare and broke the marrow of dark wood.

Break free, she thought, break all the spells. Jackstraws, jackdaw's nest of sticks and bones: all vanity, all glass. Her passion was a sort of folly, to set with Tom who sieved the wind and seethed in eggshells: for what she would undo, she did. For all she thought of travelling light, she held the faster to the dark, her rage.

I'll not be left behind, she cried. I'll not be bound. I'll not possess what I must keep, nor give nor take what I desire. I'll sail, I'll sail away.

Let fall, she cried, and flung away a handful of black leaves. Unpatterning: the Sword, the Wren, the Harp of Bone, all hurled asunder on the flood. The Witch. *It turns*, said no one. *Either way*, the other said. But casting leaves away, she would not hear, cried *Babel!* to herself. No spells. I'll sail away as Sylvie ran, as light.

But ritual denied is riming still; and rime run backward, rite. The Witch is mirrored in the Witch. Unfast and fast, by moon and dark of moon: the law of Cloud holds still. Two witches turn: one walks, one wakes, and waking, spells the traveller on.

I wake, said Ariane within. "Break free," she cried aloud, and never heard their voices, dark and moon.

Dark's fast, said one. *She ravels light.*

The other: *Done's undone.*

And Ariane, undoing knots, undid the crazy snarl of light, of dark, that bound her will; combed out her daemons, long as wind. *I fly*.

Can I get there by candlelight? sang Ariane within. I'll sail upon a millstone. Sweep clouds beyond the moon— Hey, Sally Lune, thy broom! And hey! for Tom Rynosseros. But I will find bonny Maud, merry mad Maud, and seek what e'er betides her. She felt the old wild joyful terror of nightfall games, of Babylon and hideand-seek: rhymes darkening to conjuration.

Out: I'll weave no rhymes, nor garlands of the thorn; I'll weave no nettleshirts for swans; earthbind no airy spirit, catch no fleeting star in frost. I'll frame no cage of bones for soul. Break crowbones, ravenglass. Unspell the leaves and scatter them; wind, whirl the stars away as straw. I'll undo, and I'll undo. I'll leave no lyke for raven's fee: the fury of the dark will not devour—

Ah, but then, what then? A dark thought struck her still; the stone was moveless in her hand. What use? The river never would run back. Her bitter joy ran dry. She thought: I've let her go.

And so she had: but which? Unloosing knots, Ariane had not worked at catching up with Sylvie, now, but at her going on. The dark ship sails before the wind, and gone is gone: for time combs all one way, for all its vexed and tangled knots, toward death. Yet moon after dark of moon is ever newly born. It turns. *I walk*, said Sylvie, long and light; and Ariane as dark of moon, unbound and turning after, said, *I wake*. Undone and done.

The witchknot broke and lurched. Like a band of steel, the water poured and breached, relentless. Her stone was island, still was fastness; but the light was elsewhere, fleeting on. The sails of her spirit hung slack. She would have a cold landfall of it.

   * * *

Ariane lay sleeping, wrapped in Sylvie's quilt. The
sheet was strewn with cards: the Tower and the Bones,
the Ship reversed. The moon had set. The ice slid, shattered on the earth; the earth was strewn with broken
twigs. Her body's sleep was heavy, falling downward
from her bones like rotting snow. She lay like a sodden
branch between oblivions, dark water and dark air,
caught in a glaze of dreams. They were too thin to bear
the weight of her desiring; they broke beneath her like
crazy brittle ice, entangling her in cold weeds and current
time, while Sylvie's spirit was upheld, light and heedless,
running on.

The Witch lay on her pillow, at her cheek. A mirrored
image, of a woman like a leafless thorn; but rooted in
another crown, another witch, as in a glass; the old and
new moons tangled in their hair. *Unfast and fast*, said
one. *Unbound*, the other said: *I walk*.

Her body slept. Elsewhere, the scything and the
ghostly falling flowers of the snow ran on before her,
light and dry; the black unbodied grasses bent. The trees
strove against the wind like dancers iron-bound, their
fury ravelled into branches. High in the embittered air,
the owlmoon hunted, following unwearied through the
clouds. She felt the shadow of its taloned cold. Yet all
was illusory, and might crack and send her tumbling
through dull clouds of sleep; or warp into a dream of
endless rooms, the mazes of the ruined garden. She bent
on, laboring to dream. The wind effaced her footprints.

Then the moon had changed, sharp and shrunken.
Down a long and thinly wooded hill, through tumbled
rocks and thorns, she walked. As the hillside rose and
broke in scarry cliffs, she bent to it, and made her way
on willed and abstract feet, and knees and hands, up the
high bare broken scarp, and over the rigg. Thorns tore
at her; she did not bleed. The water of the ghylls ran
silent, dry.

She came to a dark bare slanting field, stony but for
crouching thorns, and eight or nine low gravemounds: a
dark unholy place, a place of bones and coins. Before
her stood a wall of stones. Beyond lay moorland and
wolfish fells: a rougher darkness, set with solitary, pale,
unwalking stones. The moon had set. No Sylvie: she was

far beyond. *That way lies back of Law*, said the dream.
Ariane clambered over.

The light was real. She saw the stone of chaos cracked,
and the archaic light laid bare within, arrayed against the
dark. She saw unbeing starred with genesis. Dazzled, she
raised a hand before her eyes. A child was crouched
beside a great stone, harboring a candle. She had waited
there a thousand years; the wind of her coming had not
yet stilled. About her there were trees, where nothing
was; and nothingness was not.

That child is numen of the wood, its soul, said Ariane's
still voice, her dream: the face, the hands, are seeming.
They are what I understand, the cloud of my unknowing.
She is lightborn.

Shining through its cloak of leaves, glanced fleetingly
by wind, her body was unearthly, cold and clear: the
starry blue-turned-green of dusk, encrystalled to the eye,
yet nowhere, inessential. Wood was the light she cast,
her cloud: it haloed her. A world warped about her candle, flawed and tremulous with leaves, the leaves of life,
and bright with fallen rain. An O, a hallows green as
spring, and out of time.

Ariane came toward it, a half step. The water from
those leaves she could not spill; the weaving of that flame
she could not stir, with breath or hand: that light was
crystalline, and she the wavering shadow, fleeting and
consumed. Yet to the child's slight breath it swaled, beating on the air in tongues of unknown language, and was
not sundered from its wick. Stone and sky and leaves,
the candle and the lightborn child were—O green and
starry, they were one, and all else nothing.

O, thought Ariane, unsouled with longing. O the
light—

Blindly she came forward, and her hand met darkness,
a reluctance frail yet absolute as death: the candle's burr,
the unwalled citadel of light. It seemed no greater than
her hand, and infinite. Not air, nor stone, but the untena-
ble, the other; and herself the dark.

The child rose and came to her, and she was in the
wood.

Within was darker clarity, enigma: a remote and formal frailty. She might have touched the child's face, if child it were: grave and shadowy, its light reversed, occulted. She had taken on a dwindled seeming, out of myth, or as a mirror of Ariane's unsight: a green and seely spirit, child-small, yet ancient out of mind; elusive and as frail as rushlight, cold as stars. Her face was new-moon thin, green-pale as moon on blackthorn. Her eyes were purely iris, of the green cold grey of afterstorm. A stone hanging at the child's throat twisted slightly on its chain, now lightstruck, now darkly lucid, flawed. Her sky seemed indwelt in it, in stone as in her eyes, the soul and essence of her being.

All else was shadowy. Her hair was dark as cloud, as huge and shadowy as woods where birds wake, silent; and her clothing was obscure, sky-black, and quilted faintly with stars. Before the candleflame, her curving hand was leaf-red, veined with knowledge. Then as the child set the candle on the rock, its flame grew still as frost, as small as a wren's tongue. Yet they were within.

"How have you come?" she said.

"I have walked," said Ariane, the words of the ritual assuming her voice.

"I walk still."

Bright and momentary came a vision of the child walking like a star by morning, calling forth the wood in stony places with her thought and tongue and hand, waking and enduring winter, lest the earth forget the way of the dance, and the leaves their voices. The wood was all her body, root of her rib, and bone of her branches, nerve and sinew of her dance. She told the falling of the leaves, the flowering as stars: her name was endless.

Ariane gazed. Yet even in her awe she caught a dazzle, an infraction of the light: not dance, but crazy, swift and jagged as the swallow's hunt. A glance of moon. A sword.

"Is Sylvie here?" She knew as she spoke that these were not the words she had to say, but asked, "Can I follow her? Is this the way?"

The soulstone twisted. "Not by candlelight; she is not lightfast, but the Sword."

Cloud's stars. The Sword's turned up, but strangely, as another's fall, another fortune's bright ascendant.

They had never played this game. "Is she—will she come back? The cards—"

The child spoke gravely as a sibyl, taking up the dance, the web of words, from Ariane's unravelment. "It was told long since, yet still is telling, lightfast and by fall of leaves: all souls are stone, unturning, that should dance, but one and one's the other. Winter's crown's not light. The ring's not yet undone that is the Sword's undoing."

Riddles, knots. *Unfast and fast*, she had to say, but said, "But it was both of us, we made the game. Why can't I follow her?"

The dream was changing, the ritual confused. The wood no longer seemed a little haloed world, enisled in darkness; but took within itself the dark and all unhallows: boundless, shadowy, alluring. Now Ariane could see the nightblack stony river, beyond which Sylvie had gone, too far in her bright heedlessness; having set herself to pluck a garland of pale flowers on the farther side, or come to the dark tower, among thorns. Not as traveller but as the tale, Sylvie went, called out of earth and now to be the sibyl's falling star, the lightning, light unfast: the Sword.

Go after her, thought Ariane; and felt the nightworld shiver. It would crack. The wood was in the stone of light; beyond lay nothing, waking. In the rents of dream, she lay profoundly still beside a dying fire, and the ashes sang like birds of crystal. *Where? Nowhere.* But the moon cried, *Now.* Her desire was perplexity, raging into walls of thorn. Not being the Sword, how could she journey? She was the dark of moon, the Tower; or the Witch, ambiguous, undark and dark, and clagged with silicate desires, knots, entanglements. She was the Cup: stoneblind, she held her mirror to the moon, held nothing as it fled away. Yet she stared beyond the burr of light, into shadow, into wood.

The child said, "That is not your way."

"What are you?"

"What I do I am."

She rose, unclouding, green and nowhere. There were leaves in her, and eyes; the birds would wake. Ah no, thought Ariane, afraid that she would snuff the candle, annihilating even Sylvie's loss. O stay, she cried, unvoiced: I wanted—Leaves, the new moon in a cloud of dusk her curving face, the candle burning. Eyes. The wood was in the light, and Sylvie in the wood; the light was fleeting. It was leaving her. Earth, water, air had turned her back. By fire then. Not journeying but light was hers: then she would have it, apprehend the very marrow of the crystal.

She stretched her hand, and felt no candle where it stood. I am asleep, she thought despairingly: I'll wake and cry with loss and longing, desolate. Oh, I've held nothing, not the light, not Sylvie—Yet she curved her hands, as if around a moth, blindly feeling darkness and smaller greater darknesses within, unheavens; and she found the light between her hands.

She cried out: for her soul became the wick, her scathed nerves twisted into fire. The lightning spoke through her, shrill as a harpy. The leaves were burning on the branches, unconsumed; the sibyl's leaves were burning on the wind. The ash was snow. Her brazen talons scythed within the child's ribs, grating on the bone; she laid it open. Owl-stiff, her hair was clotted with its formal blood. She caught its soul, a stone made of light.

Yet its face and body hung clear of her, beating upward, winged and transcendent. Unclouding of its mortal semblance, it was crystal, dark yet fiery as if new-blown, its eyes unearthly and serene, its heart sky-black, recollecting myriads of knots of stars; and then in the bitter cold of revelation, the image cracked. It fell in dry and shattered motes of light. Ariane stood desolate and barefoot in the leaves in Sylvie's room, with a curved handful of withered snow.

Waking in her bed, she rose. She pressed her two hands to the cold glass of the window. They burned. No blood on them. Fumbling, she took Sylvie's quilt from the welter on the bed, and walked downstairs, trailing sleep like a broken wing. The night tasted of bronze. Her head ached. In the kitchen, she set the kettle on the ring with a dull clang. The lamplight was bleak, unendurable. She thrust her bare feet into boots, and threw on her old coat. Then she caught up the quilt and a flashlight, and went out the back door.

It was very dark. There was no snow, but in the shadows, and the trees stood like faggots of used-up lightning. The earth was splintery with thaw. She could not endure her light; she switched it off and walked by the fall of the land, on the stony common land of dark, stumbling in the icy grass. The child was not where she expected, in the lantern wood beyond, but closer, lying in a little hollow in a field. Its face was hidden, but one hand lay outstretched, leaf-red and torn. All about its body in the dying snow were flurried scars, as if impressed by an agony of wings.

It was a girl, when she turned her over. She lay light and stark as a dead bird, all ribs, one hand clenched at her breastbone. The breath raled at her new lungs. Ariane wrapped her in the quilt. Though wasted as the old moon in her arms, the child was an awkward burden, and there were wire fences: several times in that slow journey, Ariane had to lay her down in the icy mud, and twice she fell. As they came at last to the house, the rising light struck blank and silvery through its windows.

She laid her burden on the kitchen settle, and knelt, blindly tracing its brow and eyelids, its tangled hair, grieving at the unearthly tattered hand, veined fanwise like a leaf. The child stirred, crying out long and noiselessly, writhing like a dry branch consuming.

Ariane sprang up, and ran to the hearth, trampling sand and water over the smoldering logs. She was stained with the ashes of the wood; her hands were wan. She wiped them. Then she wrapped the child again, and lit the oven. She swathed the one torn hand in gauze; the other, clenched, would not uncurl.

Then she sat on the ground beside, and watched. The wren's song piped in her head. Blankly, she turned out her pockets: the Sword, the candle-ends, the ring. She turned it over and over in her hand. Cold and endless. Cold. What have I done? Undone. No witch—There are no witches, no Cloud. Nothing but a pack of cards. This is crazy, Sylvie going in a silver fire, and the wood, the child falling in light—

But there she lay. Not spirit: bone and blood and hair. A body. Ah, but not of earth: unearthly, strange. Of Cloud? But she and Sylvie made that up. And they had never thought of such a child; had called no beings *light-born*. And yet she'd dreamed of them: they danced on green hills, out of time. She'd read such things in tales. She'd not believed in them, no otherworld; yet obsessively she had made boxes for them: her book of runes, her spells and labyrinths, her crystals. She'd sent Sylvie after, into dark beyond to fetch her daemons. O she'd wanted them, the lightborn.

So others had, she thought, defiant. Witches. They had raised stone circles in their awe—O here be light—to spell such dancers' starry carols, hold them earthfast. They had left groves unfelled in twofold holiness: green leaves but fleeting, earthfast; leaves of light. Had any ever caught a god? They had—ah, but they had crowned and slain their weeping children for the sake of winter's death. Blood for the lightsake, for the sun's returning. And in turn for the child's fall had Sylvie—?

No. She went as the other came, as light, unbound. Then I—Ariane winced, not turning where the child lay bound, naked, in a cage of bone. Could I have caught her, called her spirit down? But how, from where? I am no witch. I meant no evil. O God, it all went wrong. She came uncalled, as messenger, as light. She told me, what? Riddles, knots. The Sword's undoing. Was she Sylvie's moon that she ran after? If I'd run after then, and not undone, not done; if I had seen—

Not by candlelight.

There was no refuge, for she knew this thing was of her calling, neither straw nor wren nor sacrifice, no scarecrow image of the winter's death: no image, but the child itself, naked and newborn. After a long while, she was aware that the eyes had opened, and were iris, blank and lightstruck, as if they stared into an abyss of light.

Waking, the child was fierce and frail and haggard. She wandered, wrapped in Nan's grey dressing gown. She moved intently as a dancer, though no grace was left: unbalanced, one hand still at her breastbone, clenched. She said nothing and heard nothing, heedless of the trailing gown, but walked and walked in her mazes. Nothing sprang from her passing. Bewildered by a wall or glass, she would transmute her patterning; or waver, caught between mirror and mirror of the hallway. There was no center to her labyrinth, no death, no light. It hung like a web, unseen, and bowed beneath a weight of rain. It broke.

Her eyes would not correspond with the light. She was not blind; they darkened to her own unearthly sun. She stood at length in the little attic room, whose walls, angled like rough crystal, broke the quarrelled light in wraiths, in dancing, and she gazed at these hieroglyphs of light like one seeking her exiled language in some archaic tongue.

Ariane had followed, close as the dark of her moon, unwilling gaze. She watched, fearful that the child would run away, turn fiercely on herself, her body, mad or willful in despair. But now her mind slid furtively away, away from silence, trees. She could not hold this bitter glory of birth any more in focus.

Damn her, I was dreaming, she thought. There was no candle. I should have blown it out. She turned toward the child, a moving caught between caress and violence, and ending in angry reverence: she barely touched the hollow of her throat.

The eyes regarded her. "I see what I am," said the child, and falling on the ground she raged in silence, clawing at her face and body. The stone fell from her unclenched hand and rolled across the floor. It was a cloudy marble.

It was nightfall. Ariane set down the lamp. The child lay
shawled in Sylvie's dark old tattered quilt. She lay in the
little attic room, that was high and bare and looked out
on trees. She was turned from the lamp, a candle in a
sphere of glass, gazing at its light-shadow on the wall.
Her hands spoke with it, silently; their shadow was leaf-
red. Drowsily, she spelled with them, whispering a little
wan and wraithlike autumn into being. A breath would
sever it, the lamplight frail as the down of hawkweed,
the leaves touched with frost and trembling. The image
of her dandled stone hung like a distillation from gossamer. She wore it knotted on a strand of silk.

She had not spoken again after she had stormed, but
had drunk snow from the shade of yews, and suffered
herself to be bathed. Kneeling up in the shallow tub, she
had watched the dance and dazzle of the element; her
skin was pale, enwoven in the watery light, as the underleaves of sallows. Now with her eyes half-closed, her face
was childlike, though bleak with weariness and scathed
by her own hand. The image faltered; her hands fell,
folding like leaves in a spring drawn backward. Her face
was hidden.

As Ariane bent softly to snuff the wick, the child
started awake, crying out in a strange unsyllabled voice.
Her eyes were black with fear, unirised. She hurled herself at fire, struck glass.

Ariane's throat made no sound as the lamp shattered
on the floor and the child plunged after. She clawed at

67

the bedclothes, groping for the sundered flame. No candle: it was out.

Ariane caught hold of her, wound and weltering, blind mothworm, in the long pale nightgown, in the glass. "Are you crazy?" No one in the eyes. She stared at her, the stranger in her arms. *No child, there is no child*, it said. She felt like shaking her; instead, brushed back the tumbled hair. Touching the long eyelids and the brow, she saw what the child foresaw, as if their eyes were one: a waste of darkness, like a sea of ash, unislanded, yet thronged with cruel and scarry rocks, against which her spirit broke in salt. Death, thought Ariane, afraid. She's dying. I will die. Not now, not yet. The small sharp face was stony. Heavy-eyed, it crumpled—Oh. She's tired to death. She doesn't know. "It's sleep. You have to sleep," she said.

Whirling round, away, the child flung up her arms, crying out a word to whirr among her branches, as her soul leapt up in leaves of spirit. All mortal shape was gone. Windbent, illusory, a tree branched in the air, an O of trees, enisling her; and then her sanctuary withered and was gone. She was not alder, not the witches' tree of hallows and of transformations. The blood broke afresh from her hands. Flecked with the dark drops, she crouched amid her crowblack avid hair; her face was bitter white and starry, small and myriad: was flowering on thorn, was frost. But a frenzy in the gnarling branches shook the ice, consumed the tree: not sloe.

Ariane, thralled and cowering amid the shards of glass, cried out to her: but her voice was quelled like a flake of fire in the wind, the storm of prophecy. The child spoke the Sibyl's alphabet, dispersedly, unspelt and scattered on the wind: the eldest runes, whose names are trees. She spelled her name, which was endless, against unnaming dark.

Gathering herself to a greenness, wind-wakened, she sprang, and was shattered against stony sleep: not ash.

She was low and writhen. Her tawny leaves were birds; they rose, unleaving, plaintive, and were mute. They beat their wings in vain, withering on the wind: not thorn.

Nor yew, though the air trembled with green darkness, drowned and netted about her sinewy and hollow ribs.

Nor sallow, whose underleaves of silver-grey flickered in her palms.

Nor birch, which branches at the road's beginning; nor rowan, bright as blood, the witchbane; nor the wise and lowborn hazel.

Nor grey-cloaked beech, whose name is book; nor apple, whose root is Arthur's sleep; nor the tree of winds nor winter's door, not oak nor holly, nor any rune took root. All were illusion.

The images shrivelled in the scathing air. The child's mortality deformed them. It made gorgons of their transcendent leaves, harpies of their branches, warping with unearthliness the human shape, so that she seemed a child racked within a tree, or horribly, a grovelling thing, unrooted, taloned or arachnid, on its belly scaled with bark. Yet she spoke with her body the holy book of trees, alpha and omega, beth and idho, leaves of prophecy of light. Wild and despairing, she danced out her revelations, drubbing her unrooted feet against the void undrifted boards, until the body failed her, and she lay broken on the floor.

Ariane crouched beside her. Shaggy and hulking, she felt herself as dark, overshadowing the slight child. She had seen the storm of trees; had felt the fleeting wood as runes; read nothing. Babel. Yet the spell was there; the ghosts of leaves still dazzled in the air. All vain. The child was flesh, not mad but mage; the wood was gone. The dark was greater than her spell. What dark? thought Ariane, and felt her looming self. Her shadow. "It is not death. It is an image, sleep."

"No. I have walked in death. Roots are. Unmaking." The drenched nightgown clung to her ribs, paling as her breath was drawn, then grey, pale and grey; her face was haggard. "I will forget."

Ah no, thought Ariane. What if the child forgot the wood, the being light? Another fall? She had seen her walk twofold, in the woods of Cloud, in holy woods of air, at once the green and the burning tree. Undone, and then undone, thought Ariane: her desire had felled the sacred grove, immured its daemon in a falling castle, in

chains of nerves; but Lethe would unsoul. And yet—She
bent to raise the mortal child, the child the god consumed; and bending, touched her stone by chance. She
saw. The light, O the light was stone. Still there.
Unskied, her soul caught fast in stone, as her spirit was
in bone and hair, she might still coalesce, transcend. Go
back. If she could find the way. In the forgetfulness of
sleep, the god would die, dissevered utterly: not light,
but tallow and a clouding stone.

Let her wake then. Ariane flung back her head, and
wrung and raked the tangled hair before her eyes. I'll
wake with her, she thought. Go back, somehow: a journeying through stony dark to her green rebirth as numen,
backward to the springs of light.

But how? She saw the child lying wracked on the
floor, unwilling her bones. How far could she walk,
in that frail body, to seek a country not of earth?
Already Ariane's head whined like shaken metal with
exhaustion, and her bones ran lead. She saw herself
like a bearward on a desolate moor, tormenting and
pinching the thing in the cage of bone, to keep awake
its needleseye of immortality, how long? The child
would die with waking.

Let her die? Ah no. But if she did, would the soul—?
Ariane turned, and stared at the uncurtained window. It
was dark beyond the room. She saw—what if she saw?—
the phoenix soul beat down the walls of bone and tallow,
laying bare transcendent light: not death, but genesis.
She saw the stone uncrystal.

No. It was wrong, it was horribly wrong, unnatural, to
let the child die in an alien body: no wood unleaving, no
starry cloak to fall away, sunward like dissolving snow,
but gristle, membrane. Let her sleep. Let go.

Sylvie. O but Sylvie's there, she's in the wood. Would
Sylvie die within that sleep, O God, would she be lost,
annulled? Go out like a candle? The child's wood was
all her being now. A green thought. Annihilation. Out.
Ariane pressed her heavy eyelids. She could not imagine
Sylvie's face; she had never seen her purely, never seen,
had made a scarecrow Sylvie out of rags, a mockery.
There was nothing left.

She twisted in a paroxysm, turned against the child, as

if in dying she'd become fell Death; and stayed. The
child had not flinched, not seen. Ariane hunched up,
huddling the quilt into her lap. She saw the obsidian
eyes, incurious with pain; the hollow of the throat where
the pulse beat, bird-quick; the ribs, exposed by the torn,
redundant gown. The child was shivering, intently silent.
All her will was bent on waking; she was stronger than
the body, she would die.

That is not your way, thought Ariane. Let Sylvie go,
you've let her go. The child is here and now. Amid the
shimmering whingeing in her head, she heard Sylvie's
voice: no sense, but an elusive northern lights of laughter: ". . . deea! Poor thing . . ."

With utter certainty, she knew that she could not
endure the child's dying. They had to sleep. "Come. I
won't leave you. I'll go with you." She stripped her of
the gown, and clothed her like any naked child. The
sark was woven of mortality; it burned her hands like
nettleflax. It scathed.

The child tore off the gown, and lay naked on the
floor, unmoving.

Ariane wrapped her in the quilt; when she flung it off,
she wrapped the child again, and again, and held her
still, as cold and silent as a stone. She waked the lullayed
child, she rocked the corse asleep. For all her willed gen-
tleness, each movement felt like a betrayal: she shrouded
her in lullaby, hung cold circlets on her brow and wrist,
and called them dream; barrowed her in blankets, earth
on earth, heaped fells of stone of darkness on her head.
She held her fast, though in her vision it was a naked
child she thrust beneath the stones, into the darkness
where no roots are.

But the child was her dark as well, no telling which
now waked, now bore the other: this unbounding of their
eyes a last defense—ah, see what you have done,
undone—or utter frailty, unwarding. Her grave was Ariane, and Ariane her lap, as the branch is mirrored in its
roots. She was the leaflorn stolen girl brought sunward,
out of night and under earth. Their common earth. Yet
she was lightborn, though made stone, made bone, was
light; and Ariane her dark of moon: the childing, the
devouring dark that eats, that bears the moon's new edge

beyond its waning. Unmoving, cold, the child held back the dark. As she grew stiller, her terrible innocence grew purer, the simplicity of a stolen child who will not sleep in fairyland.

Ariane herself longed for sleep: an inverse lightning crazed her brittle sight. Stubborn with despair, she stroked the salt-rough, wolfish hair: a dry caress, unsteady. Against the images in her mind of stone, against their common waste of dark, she wove wraiths of consolation—ah, but there are forests in the dream, beyond—murmuring in broken phrases of sleep, of sailing to the islands on the rim of morning, of stars in the water in the air; but she made no fleeting ship. She had no voice to raise a world from nothingness. The sea was dry, inimical. It rose, and did not break: great fells of dark, and flecks of paler stones. The woods grew dim.

Towards dawn, the islands of the quilt arose from darkness, muted and elusive shades. Ariane bent over the haggard child. Her breath raled, drawn harshly from the owlknot of bones. Her hair started up, harsh and ravenbleak, channeled with salt sweat. Her nose beaked abruptly from her face; her lips were cracked, and brownish-mulberry. Her eyes had clouded, glazing over the dark breaking of iris, whence the soul had fled. Ariane rose softly, and laid her on the bed, beneath the quilt. She stirred, like grass unburdened of the snow, and closing Ariane's hand in hers, she slept.

> I'll take down that mast of gold,
> And set up a mast of tree . . .

Sylvie?

The star rose; the dark ship sailed, light-laden, in a galaxy of foam. Not withdrawing from that blind and mortal touch, Ariane damped her sobbing with her streaked hand, and rawly wept, for the light unmade, and the journey begun.

The door of the keeping-room stood open. Nan held out a skein of wool. "Come in," she said, "and wind this off." Ariane took up the skein, and watched the ball grow, round and grey. The sun lay slanting on the workbox lid, inlaid: the tree of horn, the moon of ivory. The basket by her chair was full of leaves, some pieced in patchwork, red and brown, some pinned. The needle in a fold of it shone silver. "Well," said Nan, "you'd better take her back."

Back and forth went the yarn, and round and rounder grew the ball, as grey as cloud in Nan's brown knotted hands. Ariane said nothing, watching and remembering the way. It wound, unwound from her. Then she held nothing; it was all to do, all done.

The ball was done. "That's yours," said Nan. "I'll keep it by me." And she rose and put it in the tallboy with her skeins. She looked at Ariane, a measuring glance. "Don't sleep much now," she said. "It's in my hands."

"Here's your scissors," said Ariane. They were lying on the patchwork. Deeper in the pile of leaves, she saw, were other pieces, stars of Sylvie's old grey trousers, patches of the child's blue starry coat, and neatly cut, a quarrel of her own mole-colored greatcoat, with a silver button dangling still; and deeper still, green leaves and leaves of bluer green, as clear as sky. "What's that going to be?" she said.

"A sail," said Nan.

* * *

Sleep cast Ariane softly onto light. A wave had borne the ship from her, withdrawing: dry and fathomless, the sea of dark. She clasped a fragment of the dream, an image fading in the cloudbright air. She woke. It was heronlight, a grey and recollected morning. The child lay sleeping. Her upturned hand lay on the pillow; her face was hidden in a cloud of dusky hair. Softly, stiffly, Ariane stretched. Her ribs creaked, curving round a holiness. The child's sleeping wove a bower of unearthly peace, of utter frailty: a little hall of rushlight held against the dark. Between grief and remembered grief, the dark of waking, it said only, here, I am here.

She stooped, and quietly gathered up the shards of lantern glass like fallen petals, curved like calyces of frost. Withering, she thought. Some edges of the glass were brown. She held them carefully on her palm. On the wide boards were dull red stains, overlaid, like skeletons of leaves. She walked down through the shadowed rooms, holding herself like a new moon, like a candle, bright and frail; though the wind of reality had fallen strangely still. In the dark front hallway, she saw her light shivered from awakened mirrors, as if from a dusk of raining leaves.

Beyond the door were naked branches in the mist, and cloud beyond clouds of hill, pale greenish white with frost. She walked across the sunken lawn, gnarled with roots, and the bewildered stony garden. Her bare feet scarred the rimy grass. Kneeling on the black earth, she buried the glass at the wood's edge, among the roots of a thorn. She watched the blood bead slowly on her hand, a slow dark jewel. Then she went in.

She bathed in cold water; combed and coiled her hair; made tea in that holy light. Tea and limeflower honey, oatcakes with wild plum jelly. (Whose? Nan's? The writing was blurred, but the wax had held.)

The child slept still when she returned. (Here, said the candle, I am here.) Ariane stood and gazed at the high white room, as if she had never seen it: a child's, slant-roofed and low-eaved, with the chimney shouldering in. A pure and complex shape, she thought, like hands folded overhead. There was a

white chest, carved with ivy; a shelf, with a blue jug
and a branch, a wooden angel with a sword; a few of
Sylvie's books, and her quilt on the bed. Ariane sat
by the low window; she leafed through a book, and
saw nothing for the inessential light. Her book seemed
more bright than language, overlaid with fleeting, falling images of runic light, leaf-enwoven, a breviary of
dreams. She could not have told a word of it. Now,
only now, her waking shadowed the child's sleep, two
and one, one thing: as the stone and the bent of
brightness are the moon, as the dark tower and the
green and endless wood are one, the tale, and the
journey is the coming into light.

The child stirred, murmuring; she turned, and fell
again to sleep, as still as the leaf falls on the water. Ariane got up, and stood beside the bed. She brooded on
the child's face, no longer wolfish with death. Yet its
clarity seemed deathstreaked, flawed and clouded from
within. Asleep, she is the stone, thought Ariane: still
green, still elsewhere. Light and cloud. O but she is beautiful, beyond imagining, and strange. The light is in the
stone, and she will wake.

She went back to her corner, by the window in the
eaves. The blue tattered book she had not seen, now
saw, was fairy tales by George MacDonald: the book
that Sylvie had been painting, that Ariane had read in
childhood, so young that it had seemed not fantasy, but
foretelling not yet understood; its remembered images
were like a dream foreshadowing a lost reality. Years
later, coming into strange rooms in her soul, unswept but
tapestried, she would think: but I have been here before.
Now she read the tales again, for they alone did not deny
the wood. Their darkness was hers, at the roots of light.
Their towers were forests, endless rooms of wood, bewildering the solitary traveller. There were lamps beneath
the earth, in halls of stone. Her thread was lightfast,
tenuous, unseen. She wandered deep; yet all labyrinths
led back to the child sleeping. At her cheek was cold
glass, and the bare branches and the mist beyond; her
way turned inward still.

Halfway through a tale, she looked to see the child
awake: there, like a star rising from the water, paling

into conscious day. Her eyes were dark with sleep. One hand touched the air, questioning.

Ariane knelt beside the child; her hand mirrored hers, did not touch. "Don't be afraid."

"I am. Where?"

"In a house. You've been asleep."

"Water."

Ariane held an earthen bowl of tea to her dry lips. She seemed bewildered at the greenness on her tongue, tasting the fragrant bitterness of leaves, of death distilled: the water at the roots, unearthed. As if, thought Ariane, I had waked blind, seeing light only with my hands. "What are you called? Do you have a name?"

"No. I have forgotten." Unnamed, thought Ariane. Unrooted.

Leafblind, the child's hand lighted on her stone. Here, I am here. But curving round, the fingers touched the hollow of the throat, and startled: she had felt her pulse. The soul dangled, cold unearthly dusk, yet clouded: deep beyond deep in that eluding clarity, a star hung falling. "It is closed," she said. "It is stone, and I am not. Not inward."

"I saw it, it was light. And leaves. The wood was there."

The child was quiet. She let go the stone, uncurled the hand. She saw it. Ariane set down the cup, and gazed at her. The child was seeing earth. She touched her face, the long eyelids and the scarry brow, as one might touch the fossil of a leaf. Each hand traced the other, with mothwing delicacy. She tugged a little at the nightgown, as though it were some tough and curious nerveless tissue: a caul, perhaps, or webs of membrane. She tongued the buttons, clicking and comparing them against the teeth and thumbnail. She sleaved out a strand of hair with breath. She traced the quilt as Sylvie had, green and greenwood and wood, faded patch on patch. Wafting the sheet above her head, she lay in cloud, in moonpale underlight. She twisted about, and ran her fingers round and round the spirals of the wooden bed-rail, like branches with the ivy stripped away. She knelt for a long moment, turned toward the light; she stared at the clouded hills, beyond the glass, and at the fall of rain. "I saw her in the sleep."

Sylvie? Or the child that was? "Will you go look for her?"

The child slid to the floor, and waded, as if through deep leaves or dark water, weltering in time. She could not find her way at first, having no sense of common light or cornered space, but groped in the leafless air. Touching briefly, turning, glancing, she joined angles, curves, translucencies. She made of light and space and moving an aethereal geometry, a pattern like the instar of a crystal, but stoneless, pure entelechy; like an abstract constellation, like a web: a complex rose. It broke.

"Other stars," said the child. "Beyond—" and she touched her stone. "Beyond what I spell. Out of dancing." She looked about the room again, another way. She traced the ivy on the chest, touched the blue-white rounded jar, a formal heaven. She stroked the poppy-head angel: a rough, endearing figure with its wings as shaggy as fircones. The child tousled it; then crouched and turned the pages of the book. Black and white. "What . . . the curving, thin? Treegarths. Runestaves."

"It's a book. A patterning. What I know to spell."

The child traced the rim of the cup, moonround, and drank a little tea. A flaw of pain seized her, scarring her eyes.

"What is it?"

"Brooch. Caught here." Her hand touched the hollow of her throat. It was bare.

Ariane stared, uncertain.

"Abyss," said the child dolefully, touching her ribs.

What abyss? Her death? Her world, unsouled and starless void? She stared bewildered at the child. Riddles. Eyes. What brooch? Sharp bones—O heavens, she's *starved*. And her throat's sore. Talking. "Wait," said Ariane. Light with simplicity, she ran.

Half an hour later, she came slowly, steeply, up the bent stairs, heavy-laden. She nudged the door with her shoulder. The child stood at the window of the high room, staring out at the rain, unearthly still. Ariane came

in, and set down her tray. The child turned to her.
"You're cold," said Ariane. The still voice within her
said, *colder, by and by.* "I've brought you some things,"
she said.

Rummaging, she had found a robe of soft thick wool,
of deep and muted mingled shades, cloud and earth, like
an autumn dusk before a storm. *Though worlds of wan-
wood leafmeal lie . . .* Unconscious of her gaze, the child
stroked, pleated the rich stuff; rucking her dejected
nightgown up about her ribs, she stared down at her
body. Ariane pulled the gown off over her bent head,
and the awkward crook of elbows, like espalier gone
wrong. The child eyed the offcast pallid thing. "Thaw,"
she said disdainfully. Ariane robed her in the nightfall
wood.

Wrapped in it, as in a covert, the child sat on the bed,
and drank her tea, sucking the leaves from her fingers.
Ariane gave her a brown pear, which she took, and held
as if it were a small wild bird. Ah, but Ariane had
dreamed her so. Though in the sleep she had not known
her, a grave numinous figure, a spirit or an angel
cloaked, unsummoned, who had walked beside her
among green hills bare as waves. Her wings had been an
inward brightness. She had poured forth wine from a
brown pear, the gift of a beggar, before the dark envious
witch who had sought to bind her.

Now the child hesitantly bit the pear, and studied the
half-circle of scars. She ate it, seeds and all. She cracked
and sucked a raw egg from her palm. Her cheek was
smeared with sun, absurdly. Day, thought Ariane: her
summer aspect, that whose fires had beseeched? She
drank the cup of milk as though it were bitter, yet
holy. "They poured it on the earth," she said. "The
stone drank it." And fiercely, "They stain us with
their blood."

A silence. Ariane fumbled in her pocket. She found a
skein of silk, and made a cat's cradle; the child watched.
Drawing it from Ariane's fingers, she threaded it with
crystal drops, and swiftly, intently wove. She held a
handsbreadth of darkness and a web of stars. Trembling
with light, the labyrinth of heaven danced between her
palms: the constellations of Unlethe, of Cloud: the Ship,

the Sword, the Wren. Her face held a gravity of delight.
As suddenly, she eclipsed the sky, and cast it down with
a delicate little clatter, a string of stones, a string. "It
breaks," she said. "There is no dance, the ring's
undone."

The silence streamed away like water from a broken
pool, like fire, unbeing and becoming. As she sat, the
child ran her fingers through her tangled hair. A knot.
She sleaved it out. Another, in a ratsnest, and she
worked and pulled, as if unweaving, weaving dark; but
baffled, tugging at the knots.

Ariane knelt down beside the child, and combed the
nightdark heavy hair, cloudsoft, and mingling with the
silence, with the air. It was not black, but dusk, a darkness full of leaves and owls, elusive shades of trees; she
saw the glimmer of a moon just set, or rising. She untied
the witchknots, one by one. She knew she must not cut
them. The combing put a stillness on her, a trance of
moving; swayed, unknowing what she did, undid, she
ravelled out the skein of cloud, unstarry, dark and light.

The child sat quiet, dandling her soulstone on its
thread. The stone was blue turned green, serenely dusk;
though clouded now, as if with storm, or with the smoke
of burning leaves, a freakish umber. Its scarring was a
frost within. Her eyes, as she looked through it, were
like the dark of moon, all iris. She let it fall. Flickering,
her hands moved, as if they wove a half-forgotten rhyme,
of stars long set beyond her sleep, of woods unfelled: a
shadowy and haunting innocence. She was telling over
her hornbook of leaves.

Ariane walked deeper in the wood, a cloud-green
dusk. No moon. The light was a thorn in flower, was a
thorn in bloodred leaf. She spelled the tale the leaves
told, falling, and by light of stars. "The root of the thorn
in stony earth found a jewel, a brooch of golden and of
silver birds: it clasped a cloak of earth. Heavy was that
mantle, bright that beast-jewel: cold the hollow crown of
bone, unwrought, that bore them light. The tree took
root in him, his bones were branch; the fall of leaves
bled for him, the thorn drew sword, the garland fell as
snow. Of his heartsblood sprang the haws the bird ate,

the little dusky-cloaked wren, whose cry was this: O my child, my branch, *a chraobh, craobh.*"

Crieve, crieve, echoed the bird's cry, shadowy and plaintive on the thorn: ah, crieve, *craobh*, O my branch.

Ariane laid by the comb—there, lighter now; looked up. The day had gone. So brief. And then the sun struck fiery through the glass, a fallow tide; the bed was adrift in leaves of light, fallgold and fleeting, though the child above was dark: a lopped and leafless thorn tree, rooted deep in brightness. Dusk.

Ariane lit the candle in a white bowl filled with water; as she set it down, the rushlight swayed and trembled, water-haloed, like a mirrored star. The slanting dusk was swayed, was eaves of autumn branches, tawny with afterlight. She bent and touched the child's brow, gently. "Sleep well, Craobh."

Damn her, needing pomegranates, thought Ariane despairing: where am I to get them up here? In the dull red anxious dream she hunted one, formless and flittering from shelf to shelf of withered fruit and rusted knives and forks, wrapped up in stained and scrumpled leaves of notebooks; she paid a hundred times with witched silver for a twisted empty bag. The child would die without a taste of it. The fruit she held at last was shrivelled: it split, spilling from its rind a rain of seed, bloodred and hard as crystal, hailing and hissing on the dusty floor. Down on her knees she groped, grovelling in dim corners, anxiously gathering the elusive precious ruined grains. A need, at once obdurate and shadowy, compelled her. She was seized with an absurd frenzy of rage, stamping and ranting in a dwarfish fury, Herodian lullabies, until the seeds danced and rattled on the floor. She bit the pocked and rufous rind to shreds, and spit; with her naked sword, not sword but beak and claws, she stabbed and slashed the featherbed, until its obscure outlandish countries hung in tatters, until absurd and baleful as a tumbled owl, she choked with the whirling of the dry untransforming snow.

Waking, she stared into the angry dark. The nightlight had gone out. A vein in her eyelid throbbed and twitched. She felt Craobh's sleep beside her, naked and insistent as a newborn cry; she wanted only to get away. She thought she put aside the blankets, with hands as heavy and unselved as wool; but each time she rose in will, her body lay, still and swaddled, until she sank again, dark into its moveless dark.

When she woke again, it was not quite morning, rainy. She got up. The stump of candle stood in its sootsmutched glass; there were splinters of wax in the water. The child slept, face down and hard. Ariane took up her book. But Irene's lamp had no holiness, bleared and withering; her thread snarled and clung. Ariane felt oppressed with the weight of attics and of stone, bruised with the trampling of rain. It was hard to read, so dim, and bitter chill. She stared at the sleeping child.

Until she wakes, she thought, I have what I desired: a fallen star in chains. A necklace of another's soul. They always give what they are asked. And Craobh will wake, and change, and need, and die. O what am I to do with her? I can't see, I'm tired. Wake.

Lying down in her twisted sheets, she read by half-light. "—you must take off your ring, and put it under the pillow of your bed. Then you must lay your forefinger, the same that wore the ring, upon the thread, and follow the thread wherever it leads you." She drowsed again, uneasily, unknowing that she slept. She thought the child left the ring, not the ring, not stoneless, but with an eye of fire, beneath a rock, and walked out into a nightfall wood, her robe and not her robe, a stormy autumn, full of brief, eluding gossamers. Ariane woke at a small sound. The child was standing at the door.

"Craobh?"

The child said nothing. Scrabbling, touching iron, she cried out, as if it were deadly cold. She lifted the latch with both hands and a great intensity of will, as though it were ninefold spelled against her. Ariane rose and slipped after her, fearing she might fall, or come to willful harm in her errancy; afraid to break the spell.

Beside the landing, the great unbranching bole of the chimney climbed. The world was skyless, overcast with slates. Hard rain, thought Ariane, and wondered that they were not wet. The boards were high, but as no hillside is, unrooted in the earth and hollow. Step by step, the child went downward. As she walked, the house grew shadowy; her will denied it, turned it to a cloud of stone. Ariane saw darkly through the stairs a stony ghyll; she heard the drumming of the rain on slates, yet saw a storm of wind, a soundless fury, back of Law. It's turning Cloud, thought Ariane. Craobh's walking there. She's found the way.

Coming down into the hall, Craobh stood: on either hand, unsilvering confronting mirrors, face beyond cold face of silence. She chose the darker way. Above the wide bare moorland of her journey flew no birds; no trees stood earthfast, and the water ran far and swift below the rock. They walked among great scattered stones, and scant and windbent thorns. At their feet was bloodred lichen. The door beyond stood open, low and dark.

Ariane saw the fire, ghostly on the hearth, but elsewhere leaping bright and furious, wood raging into air. It burned on the wintry fell at dusk: a witches' hallowfire. She drew nearer to the child. Craobh stood. Then in one swift and complex movement, she came to the bonfire. Her dance was lovely and inexorable as scything, herself the grass; the cold blade gathered in its bent her last and standing brightness and the crouched terror at her roots. She said nothing, but heard with her body the annunciation of the fire. Bright and terrible, in a storm of tongues, it spoke its compacted memories of leaf, its prophecy: in the unbeing of the wood, the changeless light.

Craobh laughed, sudden as a falling star, whose death is brightness. "Not all, not all. Her crown is broken. One will dance." Turning, she fleetingly, fiercely, clung to Ariane, and hid her face from the angel of the fire. Before the other's arms could understand, enfold, she broke away, unchilding, turning wild and strange, toward exaltation and the leaping dance.

"No," said Ariane. "Not by fire. Craobh, it burns." She held fast to the child. The hill vanished. There were ashes on the hearth, long cold. Her voice shook. "There are other doors, there must be."

Craobh was still. She held the soulstone at her throat. She was disjoined: the I of stone that saw, desired; and the child that fire burned, the dancer broken from the dance. "No woods. I am the last."

Ariane was mute. The child's touch troubled her with somber joy. I am her dark; she turned to me. Not strange, for so the moon's reborn, and after winter, leaves. I am her roots, she thought, and Craobh my branches, the leaves that drink the light and drift on the wind, far-seeing: my wings, my presence, and my eyes. She is far and now; and I am earthbound, darkfast, blind and obstinate. I am her memory and her winter sleep, her sinews and sustaining. I hold fast. I mole.

"Craobh," she said. "Your wood—is it still anywhere? Is Cloud? Would it be there, if you came back to it?"

The stone hung turning on its cord. "Cloud's where it is."

"Can we get there by walking?" Or shall we sail in the wicker basket, or sleep, or summon the owls of the moon to bear us away? She remembered being very small, being carried off on a dark wild day alone in the back seat of a black blunt car, round and leathern as a lizard's egg. She was sitting in a wicker basket full of clothes; it creaked and the rain plashed and streaked and ran together on the window, and she was there.

"Travelling," said Craobh at last. "Travelling is there."

Like the Sword, thought Ariane: like Sylvie's card. No falling star unless it falls. No worlds. "Sylvie left things, stones. We could try." In the corner by the door, she found a blackthorn stick that Nan had used, shoulder-high on Craobh, a staff. "Here." Not by dark of moon. Not fire. Air? "Is there a way?"

"Door's the way it's found. Dark is one." Craobh stood with both hands on the staff, unrooted here, unleaved; the air was thorny with intent. Then slowly, unmoonwise, she turned round through nine of the twelve winds. The cat, slouching mouseward, caught wind of her, went hunchbacked, horrid, black-eyed, as if Craobh were walking lightning; spat and fled.

"Catechumen," said Ariane. "Bless you."

Coming softly on the clotheshorse, crouched beneath the crookback stairs, all sticks and rags, Craobh bowed and gravely hailed it: how far, lief mother? Back o't wind. How fare? By light and law. What turns? A silence. They went on.

They came to Sylvie's door. Ariane undid the iron latch for her, and followed Craobh in. They stood at the bedside, the fourposter that was stripped to the bare essence of a grove. Craobh touched the sheet. No leaves. Black wood, and bleak with frost. She laid her staff aslant the bed's four staves, a rune. Walking about the room, tentative, aware, she touched the boughs of withered fir; dimmed the glazy mirror with her breath, and drew patterns in the unclouding.

Ariane, in her corner, thought that Craobh was laboring to translate herself through a language not her own, an alien gramarye. She sought an alphabet of things to hand, having lost the speech of transcendence, which is being. For all her frailty, she was tough, perhaps in vain. She seemed enduring as crystal, which utterly dissolved in cloud and turbulence, will star, instar itself again in blind immortality of pattern.

Craobh found Sylvie's box, and knelt to unriddle it. Bridling, Ariane held back. Let me, she wanted to say, you don't know what it's for; and thought, did we? Craobh sifted through its spill of papers, scattering them like sibyl's leaves about the dusty floor. She brailled the blind impress of vehement typescript, researched the coil of notebooks with her tongue, held watermarks to the light. She stared for a long time at the drawing of the winged cats. Ariane saw with a small resentful grief that her touch had defaced it, leaving streaks of ash and blood. The child looked up at her: on her palm lay a fircone, dark and incurling and morosely barbed. "You," she said. Groping in the corners of the box, she brought out the hoard of stones and owlnuts; she scried the marbles, enigmatically.

"O!" said Ariane, lightstruck, crown to earth. She found, held out the stoneless ring. "O look, is this your dance, your other stars?"

The child turned it over in her hand. Cold and endless. Her face was shadowy. "Time was—O that was lightfast, as the dance was shadow. It turned."

"Then will it—turn?"

"No. It is." A silence. "Lightself, though no dance is. I am not. I can break things. Bind them. Bite." And colder, clenching it, she cried, "Ring's for a raven's fee, foretelling: nothing comes of naught." There was a fierce witchlook to her face and tumbled hair, as bitterwhite as rime, and black as thorn.

Ariane shrank back, dismayed. But swift as she had flared, the child clouded, pale and dwindling, duskier. Her hand lay open now. She touched the frail bent ring. "Light still, unturned and turning light. Elsewhere. Not seeming, stone, as I am now. Unfast and fast."

"But it's Cloud's," said Ariane, imploring. "Isn't it?"

The child held out the ring. "Take it," she said. "The one or the other's." Bending her head, Craobh took the soulstone as it hung against her naked ribs, and slipped it off. Her hands were full, chaliced close to her. The soles of her bare feet were black. She rose unspilled, and standing by the bed, she laid her stones and touchstones out in patterns on the desolation.

Long after, Craobh half knelt, falling back on her heels, on the high bed within the wintry stand of trees, amid the figures of her occult game, like a priest-astronomer amid a henge of stars. She was silent. She had labored on intently, wholly possessed, through the morning and beyond.

Ariane had watched and waited, crouched and paced: a stranger at an interminable and holy rite, uncertain of epiphany. Rejected. Snubbed. She'd *tried*. She had offered all her store of talismans, and Craobh had shrugged; they were, it seemed, unwanted, as the ring was transcendently aloof.

Doggedly, unhopefully, Ariane shuffled through the cards a hundredth time: they held no magic. She stared resentfully at Craobh, who was going where Sylvie had gone, beyond the dark of moon. They were all leaving her behind. She longed to unspell the child, unriddle in a dazzling insight what was vexed; conjure Sylvie; juggle stars. She longed to run away through the woods, to dance to rough-edged ranting music. She would've liked to stomp in a few puddles. But afraid of missing the revelation, she hovered, useless, anxious, torn, until the relentless involutions of the spell drove her to a frenzy of kitchen-straightening—mere anarchy, and nothing left to eat, the child would starve, the cat was lost, damn them both, poor things—then back to her unread book, unreadable; and at last to the attic room for Sylvie's quilt: where in the light the image of the child distilled, with brief and piercing clarity, a vein of crystal in the blood.

Furious, mute, she came storming down to the bed, and clawed the air at Craobh's shoulder. "I didn't ask you to come. I didn't make you. You're the god."

Craobh started. The maze of stones and marbles tumbled in a heap against her leg. She turned a thornblack boltwhite glare on Ariane, who faced her stonily. What have I done? Undone. She felt the shards of crystal in her blood, flintsharp; but said scornfully, "Go on."

"That is not my way, by dark of earth," the witch-child said. "Thy fell's thine own." And soft and harsh, she said, "Unriddle: art thou flayed of stone? Skinboat, and thy mast's of bone, the river's of thy blood. Will sail—"

Craobh hid her face. The rising spell broke off. Ariane, outfacing darkness, felt it slide, dissolve; felt cold. Craobh gathered up the stones and laid them out again, as if she would deny the fury of the dark in her, the ravensblood. "It won't come out. It won't ever come out," she said. But the hands went on, trembling with a fury that seemed to appall her, as if the body were a pack of hounds that pulled her down.

With a sudden slash of her arm, she hurled the stones.

They struck the mirror, cracked, cracked through within. Brief stars. They rained and rattled on the floor.

Stonestruck.

Nothing fell, no end. Craobh's hand went slowly, blindly out. Gone? She found her soul, tangled by its cord round her sleeve.

Ariane pushed back her hair. "O God, what a mess." She gathered up the scattered marbles, all dishevelled wandering stars, and put them in their bag, and tied the string. She pulled the covers straight, unfolded Sylvie's quilt. "Look, Craobh," she said. "Look, it's earth. You've got to start somewhere."

A negating stillness in the body.

She laid out the quilt as invocation, against the bleak geometries of Craobh's winter, conjuring by its mortal beauty her own belief, as one lights candles to recall the sun. There were other quilts, she remembered; Sylvie had shown her, years ago: "But mine was Nan's." What stays, thought Ariane; and saw Nan's cloudy skein, and saw her basket full of leaves. I see. I dreamed them, but they're true. They're all here in the house, somewhere. All here, and somewhere else. The leaves and all the clews, and—Oh, in Sylvie's dream, the moonstone. What she followed and she left behind. "Craobh, look, what if the old things in the house are Cloudish? Ways to Cloud, like where it touches earth. It's like a rainbow's nowhere, but it has two ends. We have to start from where we are." Caught up with her lightblown intuition, wind-possessed, she tugged the lowest drawer. It stuck; she coaxed it with a pencil in the keyhole.

Another quilt lay folded, star on star. In a poignant hail of camphor, she shook out its quarrels: slate-blue as storm, and brown as winter earth, waled and furrowed. It was pricked with threads of sharpest palest green, and patched and crazed with crowdark tatters. She thought of a shivering scarecrow child: the wind, the wooden clapper, and his cry as the birds took up into the air.

Another quilt lay beneath, harsh and delicate as winter. There were fans of cloud, pale as Thule or louring, and quains of broken stone, of bronze-veined greyish-black, all splashed with drops of crimson; it was bound with Lapland witches' knots, that rein the wind.

Craobh had clambered from the bed. She stood at Ariane's back, silent and curious as the moon, that has seen
all and is reborn unknowing.

I must not turn round, thought Ariane, and shook out
another quilt. This was wild moorish fells and hags, a
country of stone and heath and stunted thorn: browns
and purples, with one sly reynard-colored patch. Another,
an autumnal wood of oak and beech. And crumpled as
new leaves, the last, green on green in an acuity of
stitches: spring and moonrise.

The room was a little world of them, bright and
rounded on itself, an O: the end and morning of creation.
Ariane thought, how beautiful, how strange. If Sylvie
had slept beneath one of these, would she have gone into
another tale, a farther journey? Would Craobh have
been another sort of spirit? Have I done this right? she
thought. Did each quilt lie on the marches of another,
realm beyond realm? Or overlaying them, could she
move in a web of journeys all at once, through earth
and air and water, fire and transcendence? Counterpane,
contrapuntal. She began to layer, to see what quainings
coincided.

She was caught up short by scent. Beneath the acerbic
mothbane, the moorland quilt smelled faintly, elusively,
of earth and leaves. Had Sylvie lain out on it some summer's night, beneath the counterpane of stars? There was
so much, so much, she could never know. She held it on
her lap. *Why should I sit and cry, pulling bracken, pulling
bracken?*

The dry unrimy snow of camphor fell. The child picked
up one of the mothballs, as from a cold and addled
clutch, the swans flown, the nest ravaged; her face had
a bitter, scrumpled look, yet curious. Soulegg?

Ariane took it from her. "No, O my love, O no, it's
dead. It never was alive."

So here we are. Ariane sat among the drifted quilts.
They were earth, but not the way, she thought: their
tales were long since told, pieced and plotted in their
making, dark and bright. Handfast. They were like the
ring, unturning; though the bent black starry ring was
high, and they indwelling powers, earthfasts of the fields
and woods, each bound to one dear ancient place. They

were what they were. Nan's earth, Cloud's stars. They
stayed.

What journeys? Moon. And dark of moon. Leaves
falling—

"Sword," said Craobh.

Ariane looked up at her. She'd wrapped herself in the
ballad quilt; it hung from her shoulders, flawed and
splendid, the unregarded tattered earth. Her hand was
silver, like an oak-leaf veined with frost.

Sylvie's mercury. Tucked away, in one of her flashes
of impulsive wariness. "Oh, Craobh," she said, but
laughing. Thos had found some as a baby and had drunk
it up. A charmed life, Nan said: the eldritch stuff had
merely plunged straight through him, jigging mockingly
as faery silver, irredeemably fickle, in his unpinned dia-
per. A goblin market. He had crowed, unharmed. Ah,
but he and Sylvie were alike in that, invulnerable as air.

Craobh clapped her hands and scattered silver. It fell
like seed on the scarecrow quilt, or bright as rain. "Like
that. Unfast."

"And fast." The clew's tied to a ring, the ring's left
in a bed. *Of the kingdom, the key.* That's here: Nan's
cradlesongs, her starry lap. Her keep. And will be here,
still hallows, dark and bright, so long as we are travelling.
We know by the moon. It turns, it spun the thread that
leads through all these crazy toys, wherever Sylvie—

"Craobh, look. *By light and law.*" She held a kaleido-
scope to Craobh's eye; the child's face, still grave, grew
bright. She took the glass and turned. It had nine changing ends of crazy glass; though Sylvie had best loved it
naked, its tumbling crystals turning chaos to geometry,
and what-have-you to infolding stars of light.

"Riddlebox," said Craobh. "There."

So Ariane turned to the tallboy, pulling out the little
drawers. Laocoon of kite-strings, kneesocks. Cards. Marbles, as yet unnamed, their swirling clouds or chains of
light held moveless in eternity. Craobh shook her head.
A bird's skull in a ring box, on carnal velvet; stones and
waterglass. Ariane wound up a pair of stubby clockwork
sneakers that toddled, dementedly steadfast, to their
doom. "No. Wood," said Craobh, still searching.

There were draggled feathers, birds' eggs, milkweed.

There were lead tokens from vanished games: a flatiron, a ladle. There were little boxes that held clots of mold, or nothing. Flowers? Berries? Craobh leafed through foxed and withered tiny books, sere as oak-leaves: *The Garland, or, The Child's Reward; Toads and Diamonds*. Ariane switched on a spray of fine colorless filaments, that had made a fountain of light; but the batteries were corrupt. "Poof," she said. "The Fairy Wandsworth. Sorry, ducks, pumpkins is off." Rose quartz, with a wraith in it. Jacks. Scales of mica and of butterflies. Garnets dark as jam. A wormy nut.

In a lower drawer, they found plain cardboard boxes, spilling wooden jigsaw puzzles. "Woodspells," said Craobh. Spells? Ariane remembered scenes of woolly innocence: the tabbied sleep of cottages amid their gardens; children bringing May; huntsmen on horses brown as gingernuts; sheepfolds and hayfields, with lads and lasses in their garlands of straw.

Yet within the painted images were hidden shapes of wood, much loved: trees, stars, and crescent moons; a pair of spectacles amid the thatch; a teapot daubed with cloud; a child in the standing grass; a scythe; a ship caught in flowering thorn; a goose of reynard-colored sky; a cup in a hazel-copse; a sprawling hare, haunched with nightfall; a swan tumbled in a countrywoman's apron; a hunchback with a bundle of wood, whose nose Thos had broken. He'd filched other pieces for his games. Ariane remembered the oilcloth, owl-shaped scar among the sheep. When the puzzles were done, they were tenacious, hooked and barbed and burred, as delicately intricate as thistleseed: you could pick them up and shake them before they tumbled into atomies.

Craobh turned these over and over, as if they were a text in some archaic tongue, the linear A of woods: not for their babbling prose, but analytically, for their grammar. Unravelled, it might weave for her.

So Ariane went on alone, still winding Sylvie's clew. At the very back of the lowest drawer, beneath the quilts, she found a little rattling hoard of tapes. She put one on her player, and heard Sylvie's voice, as green and pure as wintry dusk, but caged in a tawdry blare of brass: a freak recording, for somehow in the labyrinth of air and wire, a daemon impulse had pervaded. Witched. Yet fleeting as the moon through rack, she heard a clarity: ". . . *turn wood* . . ."

A spell. For swift as darkness closed on it, she saw Craobh's face, mooncurved, and turning into leaves.

With her thumb, Ariane pressed rewind, and heard the whirr of the tape reeling backward as she walked past Craobh lying mute amid her solemn toys: rewind; and stop; and play. Too far: she broke in upon the aeolian tumble and confusion of sounds; then abruptly as the rock's arising from the sea to which the wild swans fell, unwinged at dusk, the song began. It was Sylvie's song, she thought, though unknown to her until this evening; so that strangely it had no memory of Sylvie in it, was anonymous as a bird's cry. It was brief, three verses, sung to a bare modal melody; its lyric haunted and eluded her. She had the shape of it, odd clarities of sense, but fading in and out of storm. It ended in a catch of breath, a sheared-off giggle; and then the melancholy roar of tape.

Again. The sea, the rock, the fall through cloud. ". . . *turn wood* . . ." she thought it said. She'd seen Craobh's soul in that, seen Cloud. But that was all at first, when caught, baffled, she had thumbed through the ruined palimpsest of tape, hearing islands in unmeaning tumult: a grand daemonic St. Walpurgis station, beneath the iron and the veniced glass of northern lights; a stridor and a gibbering—*light leaves*—of spectral geese, of daws—*and catch*—a cry of gabbleratchets; witches' sabbats, hurling backward on the whirlwind—*turn*—and raving; tumbrils of apocalypse, and the rancor of the horns. *Turn crows?*

Again, for the moment when the darkness spoke, the wood arose.

Again. Were the thorn trees a dance, the dancers stone? ". . .*catch hands and turn* . . ." And then the breaking into brief lament, yet timeless, ritual: so that it hovered at the break of light, of joy.

And if not Sylvie's, whose?

Craobh, wrapped in her autumnal robe, had poured out all the puzzles on the floor of Sylvie's room, pell-mell, and wood-side up. She lay or knelt, intent upon some deep design, a labyrinth or rune, as if she would

spell eternity with the flakes of wood. Some shapes were
thick inlaid or scattered on the floor, strung only as the
stars are, in the constellating mind. Some were heaped
in cairns, some laid on edge, ring within ring, in frail
henges. Some dangled from a string: the hunchback, the
hare and the moon, turned horn downward. She moved
among her tesserae as if her hand were shadow to her
mind, crying out softly only when her forgotten sleeve
brought down a volute of the brittle architecture,
whorled and spiralled as a shell.

Again. Ariane sat crosslegged, writing out the scattered words, minutely, with thornblack impassioned clarity, as if there were no alphabet, as if each letter were
the thing itself, O creation. But they made no wood,
without the voice. Again.

Craobh laid down another piece, withdrew her hand,
considered.

It was dark. The light that had dazzled on a straw hat,
hanging with its faded wreath of flowers, had shifted,
paled and died. There was frost on the panes, a scrawl
of rime, coarse-burred and cross-grained, combed and
tangled, like the lines of an engraving magnified until all
imagery of sense was lost, and only the intent and tremor
of the graving hand was left. It might have been the
shading of a traveller's face, encountering the dark
knight on the road; or the horrid bristling of a witch's
woodcut imp; or the plume and rachis of an angel's wing,
wind-ruffled in its piercing flight.

Again. It wuthered back. As she listened, she walked
in spirals, up and round the stairs, to the window of the
attic room and down again past Craobh in her other
maze. All paths were blind. The journey had an end, an
eye of wood: she'd seen. Would see. She walked and
walked the maze, now brooding, and now flurried,
launching vision like a riddled kite. ". . . *light leaves
. . .*" And skirring on a rug, she fell and scraped her
knee; the black box flew from her hand, the wires tore
away and dangled. She swore, but it lay unshattered
when she picked it up, buzzing away to itself like a looking-glass insect. ". . . *fall, would fall . . .*"

Again. She boiled the kettle dry as bone; drank cold
stagnant tea, with the spoon still in it; ate broodily: burnt

corners of apple from the pan in the sink, crusts and ends. She walked, back-thumbing and forwarding, pulsing on a word or the waning of a note, obsessively, until as pure ear she heard nothing: quavers, phonemes.

Again. No coordinates.

Again, and in the middle of a note, it blurred and faded, weltering—ah hell, the batteries—as if it sank, like Atlantis, but in a sea of mercury.

". . . *turn stone* . . ." it slowly said.

Ariane took off the headset. In the dazed silence, she heard the storm, the dark wind blowing that bent the trees with weight of dark, that heaped drift on curving drift of night. No rain, no stars nor cloud, but the rush of wind. Wrapped in her small metallic tumult, she had not heard the sky. She was standing in the attic room.

And then for a moment out of time, she was air and elsewhere, of that unruly storm of spirits, sinews of the wind, that rose whirling on the wild unhaily hurly air, their plumes commingled in sublimity of dark: fell with ecstasy, lordly in the dance. Far below, she saw the lamp in Sylvie's room, a burr of light aloft, a star: small as a child's marble, small and far as Cloud: a seraph's eye. *Turns O*, said wind in heaven.

Ariane was by the window again, within the glass, before her heart had beaten, or her lungs drawn breath. The light glinted from the plumes of frost, the silent impress of the wings. She let the curtain fall.

She walked down through the still house that curved about her, sweet and silkworn as a nutshell. It was after four. The light was on in Sylvie's room. Craobh still knelt there, caught in ring within ring of wood, rose-branching, spined and delicate. Her wood took up the bare unpolished boards, like wintry thorns bewildering a ploughland. She was hedged within. She could not move without tumbling all, so worked inward and inward on her whorled and windling spell.

Ariane sat on the heap of quilts with her arms about her knees. She stared at Craobh, seeing clearly now the odd sharp curve of nose, the inset of the eyelids, long and shadowy, the hollow of the throat: how strangely beautiful and not, unearthly; how unchildlike, flawed. But the flaw was essential—O she dared not, could not unravel how—the dissonance like a mode in music, haunting. A torn sleeve was turned back; a blown hair clung to the cheek. The gritty soles were clenched with intensity of travail; one hand hovered, one upheld her cheek and chin, corbel-wise: crabbed, but unfolding, fanning out in moments of release. She flickered like a candle and resolved, pale and straight. Here, said the rushlight, I am here. The wind blew, and she was not quenched. Oh, thought Ariane, but I am happy.

After a time, she was aware of a stray puzzle piece, almost at her feet. It lay beneath the quilts, half-hidden by the box: a branch with a few long oval leaves and a crescent moon entwined. *Turns O.* The vision in the song, she thought: it all comes round. Moon. Dark of moon. A rune, a mast of tree. She picked it up, and turned it over. On the face were painted grey-white, close-mackerelled clouds—No, sheep: for there was the shepherd's crook, slashed brokenly aslant the shapes of leaves, there and not. The moon's bow was the shepherd's nose.

She turned to Craobh, enisled in her wood of spells. O look, she thought, look up: the moon. The child was elsewhere, gazing cloudily beyond her wood. Ariane held up the spray of moonwood by its stem, as in a quattrocento painting: branch. The child looked up, said nothing; but her face unshadowed. Cloud turned star.

Ariane knelt up, leaned out across the web and galaxy of wood; as bright and silent Craobh leaned out toward her, each mirror to the other's bent. They met as angels, hand to hand. No leaf was stirred. One gave, her other took the moon and branch. Craobh laid it down upon a dark small pool of floor, unerringly, as if to touch its rising shadow from the water, bright, annunciate: for in that glass, no drifting star, no leaf, can fall awry.

She sat back trembling on her heels, and drew a breath. Her sleeves slipped down her lowered arms. Her face was milky bright. "There," she said. "O she had gone such a long way in. Will you come?" She looked with the sweetest gravity, and then grimaced a little, out of weariness and the falling-off of a long-sustained solemnity; she rubbed her heavy eyes, a little swayed. Her sleeve brushed the wood. All the unregarded pieces fell, in a dry delicate whirr and clatter of unbinding, spiralling rose-leaf outward from her, naked at the heart. She sat and toyed idly with a handful, letting it fall through her fingers as drowsily as sand and rosy shells. "I'm sleepy," she said.

Ariane looked at the bleared and recollected face, bone-thin, and trembling with light and sleep. She stroked back the tousled hair. "Me too."

She went out into the kitchen, and scraped up some cocoa from the bottom of the tin, bending a thin old silver spoon. There was powdered milk. She stirred it up on the fire, and poured it into mugs, sipping as they overbrimmed, and slightly burning her tongue. They were good mugs, a little crazed, but handpainted: Titania and her green rade, horsed upon swift-running hares; and the babes in the wood, dying rosily beneath their coverlet of birds. She took them up with great sleep-drunk gravity of balance, sipping as she walked and they slanted. Now and then she paused to rub each instep on the other heel. Her bare feet had left a trail of the flakes of wood, like scattered leaves: they clung. It was morning, heron-blue, not very light. but cloudier, pouring and pouring milk into the clear and bitter night. No outwalled dark, no hearthlight: all the air was one dim and misty cloud.

Walking into Sylvie's room with her drowsily unspilling mugs, and the eggshell puzzles crazy underfoot, she saw Craobh lying asleep on the quilts, with her gown rucked up about her, and one arm outstretched on air; so she set down the mugs, and crouching to cover up the child, she toppled and fell asleep beside her.

Ariane woke looking upward into light, light mirrored from new-fallen snow. She thought Craobh had unmade the world. Still with sleep, her self was lightface, silence where the dream and waking met: Sylvie rising from the dark to touch the shadow of her starry fall, as leaf to ragged leaf; the snow fallen, that the light could rise. Ariane sat up, shawled in blankets, and looked out. The morning sky was dark, a greenish-gray like clouded jade. The hills lay uncreated, pierced with the fire-rose of waking trees. Snow fell on snow. Craobh slept. *Now*, said a still voice.

Barefoot, shivering, Ariane got up. Crouched and burrowing with blind cold hands through leaves on fallen leaves of wood, dark earthy quilt on quilt, she found the small hard root of things, gnarled as iris root: the bag of Sylvie's worlds. She held it fast. The box was lying on the naked bed, within its formal grove. She left it there; as soon, she would walk from the house, and close it, leave it lying in the winter fields, among bare trees. Beyond lay uncreated hills of cloud. She would carry genesis with her, the seeds of light. So imagining, she lay, and slept again.

In her dream, it was snowing. Craobh came out of the dry reeds, far taller than her head, and plumed with morning. In the lull of snow, they alone had voices, faint and harsh, whispering together. Craobh's staff was dark among them: grey-gold and ravenblack against the snow. She carried in her grey woollen palm an eggshell, small as a wren's, unbroken, clouded green and pure as her own iris. *The winteregg,* said Ariane's still voice. It held, within a whirl of plumes, the unborn winter sun.

Later, by the kitchen fire, Ariane knelt before the child, tying on a pair of duck boots, wadded with old stockings. Between them, they had dressed Craobh in odds and ends of Sylvie's clothes: a shirt long as a shepherd's smock, grey and brown; a pair of old grey woollen tights, cross-gartered like a berserker's. Then came two sweaters with the sleeves turned back to the elbow, far upland green and a deep stormcloud blue, one over the other. Over all she wore her robe. She had found a four-winded Lapland hat, of hawthorn-scarlet wool, enwoven with runic creatures in white and black. She had kept Nan's blackthorn, as a staff for her travelling. They were walking to Illyria, to Maire's farm, for bread and goat's milk and honey.

Ariane sat back on her heels, oddly light-hearted and unpossessed. She had no idea how they were going, whether in or out of time, in dreams, in symbol, or on foot; they might be back by dark or never: there was no packing for such a journey. In the end, she had taken her notebooks and the ring and Sylvie's stones, a cup and dry socks, the tape, her pen; she wished she had some chocolate. And tea. She had bundled the maelstrom back into the drawers and cupboards, helter-skelter; had banked the fires and washed the saucepan. Cat? Gone hunting. And the dog off hunting Sylvie's moon. Long gone. There was nothing to feed them anyway, and scant enough for breakfast: a handful of oatmeal and a withered apple. She would scatter the oatmeal to the birds.

She stood and swung her backpack on, under her great-coat's cape, giving herself an absurdly sinister hunch. She grinned. *The next that comes in is Awd Nan Furbelow; she's as ragg'd as a sheep and as black as a crow*—What then? Oh, eggs and beer. *And I hope you prove kind*— I hope the goats aren't out.

Craobh stood for a moment in the doorway, stunned with light. She raised her hands, and the snow flocked to her, feathering, until she seemed half swan; then suddenly she leapt away unwinged, as light as a hare over the snow. Ariane pelted after, headlong as she'd slid with Sylvie, wildly floundering. Craobh's fleeting shadow fell and rose, in a long-drawn descending curve, an unbroken thread between them. They came to the river.

Here, after the eiderish drifts, all was delicate: the snow thin and watermarked, a glaze on skyblack ice, the web of branches. Craobh? The child turned, a hand at her throat. She dazzled. Lightstruck, Ariane saw fledged sun, her eggshell dream fulfilled. Illusion faded. Craobh held her clouded stone, cold green and heavy, vain of any seed of wings. Ah, but stone's no realer than light, thought Ariane. They're metaphors for soul, a way of seeing. But the body—

Far below, she heard the jingling and scraping of the plow, riding in triumph like Tamburlaine, above the salt-thawed vanquished snow. There was the scent of wood-smoke on the wind. "Craobh, there'll be people. You don't have to come."

"Longways now," said Craobh.

They clambered over the far wall, going the back way up Orion Hill, and through the fields. Illyria, caught spare and sailing into light, was a saltbox, slanted house among tall trees and a hodge-podge of sheds. Maire came out of the patched grey barn with a pail in each hand, balanced to the sway of milk, haloed in the silvery reek streaming out from the door.

"Well, town plow's been," she said. "Come get warm." She was fine-grained and workworn, as silvered, tough and spare as an ash-handled rake; though canted back with child, bulging roundly as a ladle. Her jacket was unzipped from the bottom.

Through the narrow crack of doorway, Ariane saw musty golden air, short straw, the rout of goat kids leaping and clashing in a wild mockery of a morris, as if to shawn and crumhorn. A border side, she thought: black-faced, shaggy and anarchic. A huddle of highnosed sheep to one side, perhaps in the Cotswold tradition, discussed the performance in discreet Sharps and flats; and Sylvie's black dog wove in and out like the Fool. Cuckolds All Awry.

Maire bit her gloves on, and pulled the door to

and barred it. Ariane took up the snow-sunken pails, and followed her, past a coarse crotchet of wire fences, edging the unmade garden, past the mother of all woodpiles. Sylvie's dog lolloped after. They went in at the back door of the farmhouse, stamping on the withered linoleum.

"Scat! Dido!" The cat on the table paused, printing its ginger paw disdainfully in the swathe of dough; then leapt in a swift arpeggio from table to shelf to draining-board, among the seedlings in milk cartons, and away. Ariane, unwhirling her snowy scarf, sang under her breath: *Ha! bonny lass, are ye baking?* The snow was melting on her eyebrows. Her feet weren't there. "D'you like oatcakes?" said Maire.

Ariane nodded. Through the door, she looked in on the low-beamed keeping-room, serenely chaotic. Skeins of wool and bunched herbs hung from the timbers, wraiths of dried flowers from the rough high summer. By a chair stood a wicker basket full of half-sewn patch-work, like Sylvie's quilt, but other worlds. A loom crouched on the floorboards, framed like a wave-worn leviathan, warped with bone-pale linen like baleen. Beneath, among its stranded bones, with a hoard of spin-dles and egg cartons, lay a very small child in overalls, peering out at her.

In the pure dispassionate windowlight, a child of nine or so, as tall as Craobh, stood fiddling. She had pale tawny deadleaf hair in plaits, and wore a flowery muslin skirt and legwarmers. She bowed her fiddle stiffly, with a stalking grace, her ungainly stride becom-ing music, as a heron rises into air. At a sprawled note, she broke off, and stepped backward, with her hands at her sides and her chin dropped, grimacing; then came into the measure again, as if into a turning rope. She played, with such dancing gravity, "The Gift To Be Simple."

Maire was taking their boots and gloves. Ariane turned back to Craobh, and saw no child but a wintry spirit, lightborn and unearthly cold. She glanced at Maire with sudden dread. Would she not see the otherworld, the witch, in leaflike hands and eyes? Cry out at Craobh's unearthliness? But Maire, serene as ever, peeled off the sodden scarf, looked rueful at the spangled hair, the raw, embittered hands. She stroked Craobh's hair with absent tenderness, and the stars were water in her hand. They fell with impartial sweetness on the trampled floor and seedling herbs, set out in cartons with the faces of lost children; on the sacks of onions, battered toys, and a green narcissus in a bowl of stones.

"I'll hang your stuff by the stove," said Maire.

"Sylvie isn't . . ."

"Guess not," said Maire. "Just shove Rolag off the couch, will you?" she called; but the grey cat was stalking away. Ariane cleared away a stack of books and socks, and sat down on the jaded couch, as bony and accommodating as a carthorse. The sheepdog, Dhurry, twitched and grunted at her feet. Craobh wandered around the room, flinching when she passed the fire, though it crouched low and slumbrous as Jerome's lion, mumbling old logs. She seemed unaware of the children; she moved in a windless place veined with music, bright and inconclusive as gossamer. She turned from web to viol, as though she would reconcile two grammars, the brief bright tongues of mortals. Fleetingly, fiercely, she danced, though to unheard music, whirling in wild dishevelment; and was still, as though a flaw of wind had died. At her back, the fall-haired fiddler turned the page.

Maire came in with a trayful of good earthenware, handthrown and subtly slipped. "Molly, love, put that fiddle down, come talk."

"No, please, it's lovely," said Ariane.

Molly frowned, rose-cheeked and severe with pleasure; twisting the tuning pegs, she tweaked and plucked the strings: they jangled faintly. She launched, with shy and watery fervor, into "Easter Thursday."

"Well, it is," said Maire. She patted her belly. "Dances to it; likes contras."

"Do you receive in Dolby?" said Ariane.

Maire poured out the tea, and took up her patch-work, sighing. "This one is for me, if I ever finish it."

"What's it called?"

"Don't know. I made it up. Drowsy Maggy."

Ariane watched the brown hands, the bright needle. Quarrels of dark air, of starry night. "Are the ones at the Farranders' . . .?"

"Some. And my aunt's, and her gran's, and on back." She bit her thread. "On that side. Not the Hughses. They don't—well, Aunt Kate, she's Aunt Caro's friend, she borrowed my good scissors once. Turned out she'd lost an earring in her typewriter. Tried unscrewing the whole thing. Screwed the scissors," she said ruefully.

Ariane sipped her tea, politely, oddly puckered: lapsang souchong, with the new goat's milk. It tasted of black fens, full of bones and chalices. But the oatcakes with the honey were still warm, and there was toast and applebutter.

Craobh bent and crept under the loom. The small child wriggled out and ran to Maire, flinging up his heels, shyly burrowing his head into her knees. She caressed him. "Hey, Tavy. Mind the pins, love." Craobh lay head on arm, gazing up through the warp-strings at the hanging flowers, out at earth. Around her, the loom seemed as spare and as nobly sprawling as the Plough and Stars. She set the spindles twirling, one by one, on the wide-boarded sky. He came back, spilling the dance with his feet. "I'm a rhinoceros, if I want to."

"I'm a tree, if I want to."

Molly crunched up her bite of toast. She glanced at Craobh, quick-eyed and wondering, and gave her some. "What happened to your hands?"

"Happened?" echoed Tavy.

"I don't know," said Craobh. She turned and watched Maire piecing. Clack! went the cranesbill scissors; and the needle, the one-eyed bird of silver, bright and furtive as a kingfisher, went darting and minnowing away. Craobh's face was curious, regretful, almost wistful. She opened and shut the scissors, with both hands, and fingered a silvered-bronze pin in Maire's workbox, a shawl-brooch wound with odds and ends of silk, and rattling with lacemaker's baubles and beads.

Maire knotted her thread. "Oh, that, I found it under the floorboards. Want it?" Craobh nodded.

Tavy plucked at her clothes. "You dance," he said. "No more," said Craobh. "It's not my turn."

They stayed late; through the window, Ariane saw cloud combed with fire, before they rose: a kist of winter's carded wool. Above, the sky was pure and clear, the goatstar tremulous. There was a new moon bent in heaven. Ariane wished on it; then frowned, bewildered: wasn't the dark of moon last week, when Sylvie—?

Maire put down her scissors. "Time you were going. You've got a ways." In the kitchen, she packed a lot of knobbly bundles: oatcakes and crumbly cheese, smoked fish, dried fruit, a honeycomb, a square of chocolate. She'd found a pair of Molly's castoff boots for Craobh, and old grey trousers, and a jack-knife. "Sylvie left it here; she'll want it sometime." At the door, Maire gave them a lantern, looked out at windless dark. "You'd better go round by the hill," she said.

They walked up the pasture in silence. Craobh held the light. Ariane trudged after, stumbling dreaming in the drifted snow. She thought of the leaving fire, of the quilt in Maire's brown hands, the fields of nightfall and of cloud: their tale of Drowsy Maggy still untold, still telling. *So it snowed, one starry night* . . . Wake up, she thought; looked up, and saw the tale around her, dark and bright. Nan's earth. Near and far, elusive as the moon, as unentangled, Craobh led her over a stone wall, and through and under the woven, whipping branches of Nan's woods. It was rocky underfoot. Clagged and cumbered with the snow, she lagged, unwarily, and snagged at every step, bemused with light. She'd lost sight of the moon.

They had crossed the water, and they walked upon unearthly hills of cloud. The star went on before her, dancing in Craobh's hand. Her soul upheld them, not stone but cloud, and fallen cloud, and fells of cold sheer night. Around them stood faint stars, alone, or in great broken rings, pale henges, cairns. They danced on the abyss of Law, unfallen; and the clew was light.

But Ariane's envisioning was shadowy, insubstantial as spring snow. It was mined with a rising world beneath, the whaleback of shouldering time. The stars were fading into water; cloud was thawing into time. She heard the light brooks running on, unspelled from sleep.

For a moment, the light faltered, and the world was wire fence and scrubby trees; then it flared, and they walked on the dark bare hillside, stony but for crouching thorns, amid pale standing stones. Beyond lay huge unbroken dark, of sky or moorland. *Back of Law*, the witch-voice said. The edges of her vision warped and shifted, slashed; the touch of things, their voids and contours, seemed disjointed from the image. She looked for the turning moon. The sky had cracked. They walked into a blackness shaped like a rough-cut spray of wood: a black unmoon entangled in a void of leaves.

They came to the great stone. Ariane touched it, before she saw. It was dark and rough, enisled in shadow. It was real. A stillness came on her, remembering the spirit that had waited here, light within her wood of light, her iris of green leaves. The child set the lantern on the stone. She turned to Ariane. "The ring's lightfast: it stays."

Ariane found it. As the cold still voice within her bade, she knelt and scratched a shallow hole amid the roots of thorn and icy stones: there in dark, that is light's grave, time's lap, she covered up the endless turning stars.

Craobh clambered on the rock beside the waning candle, and knelt. Baring her neck, she slipped from her cord and star. She drew the bronze pin from her cap and pierced her throat; she watched the falling of the slow dark jewel of blood. It lay like garnet on the rock; and there she set, green as wintry dusk and cold, immortal, the stone that was her soul.

III

Cloudwise

Lightbreak. Endless wood, a fall of bloodred leaves: unhallows. They were elsewhere. For a flaw of time, it was not Craobh that lay upon the rock, but a darkness winged and ancient, bound in her frail ring of soul that seemed to wane, devoured, as the slight moon embraces her own death within her holy bent. And then, O but slowly, the mooncurved brightness overcame: no light unearthly form, but as a child, as body and green soul, dissevered still, still Craobh. The child was wounded in the quick hollow of her throat. Her blood veined the rock.

Cold and timorous, her heart hare-quick, Ariane crouched cowering amid the thorns, holding the child's red cap in her two hands. She stared at the thorn-isled rock, the inmost in a maze of stones and ice, and at the leaves falling in the wood around, slow and ardent as Craobh's own blood. "This is your wood," she said.

Craobh lifted her face and rose trembling, coming rounded again like the moon in water that was shaken: pale and passionless and still. She slid from the rock. She had not let fall her staff; now she leaned on it. The trees became her silence, dying leaf on leaf beyond her spell, as if her soul unbound them.

"It is what I am," she said at last. She took up her stone. Still other. Bowing her dark head, she slipped through the knotted cord. Her soul turned blindly at her throat. "It is late," she said. "None dance. Perhaps none walk: the way is changed."

There was no way but wood, no wood that ever grew

on earth. Endlessly it branched and fell, as if to music, strangely graced: a bent and modal tune. A Lydian wood. It was the wood the child had danced, but wordless now, unspelled. The trees were nameless, neither ash nor oak, nor any of the book of runes, but falling and undying leafwood, A and O. No sense of lyric nor of prophecy endured, caught up in branching music. What it spelled was silence, an endless knot of death. Boles and boughs were greeny-black, like a bloom on infinity. They quenched and daunted light. The leaves still were falling, slow as shadowed birds whose death foreruns them, bronze or sullen red. No bird cried out, caught in the dreamless air, nor any creature scurried on the earth. No sun, thought Ariane. She saw no sun. She turned. "O Craobh, we can't stay here, Craobh, Craobh, I'm cold."

The child lifted her face, pale and fierce, exultant. "They ride."

They? Ariane stood shivering. Blood on the rock. She vaguely thought to hide Craobh's stone, her long fierce harrowed wounds, like owl-scratches—from what eyes? She could not bear to look at them herself.

Craobh turned and spoke, unseeing Ariane. "Light bides. The owl's way, not the raven's, and by nightfall: thorn is hallows."

They crossed water. Cloud was labyrinth. Yet Craobh, for all its turning maze, went hawkwise for some haven, far and perilous. *Light bides,* thought Ariane: it was the wood that turned. She knew no quartering, no west nor east, only away from the great stone, the doorway: farther in. And then no star but Craobh. She hastened after. But something, sharp as briar, plucked at her, importunate: unease, distrust. She lingered and looked back, then flurried desperately; she ran and halted, turned. As in a dream, each way not taken was unmade. Had she turned quick enough, she thought, she would have seen no wood, but naked crags of stone, though it mocked eternity with its great-rooted and far-drifting ancient trees.

She thought that the wood was not wholly Craobh, but gravely altered or possessed, turned even against its soul. It seemed bent toward a fell unchanging immortality, the ending of creation. The very air seemed crystal, scant

and sharp to breathe. With fearful clarity, she studied a
fallen leaf, as it brushed her sleeve; it seemed a mimicry,
a leaf of inlaid stone, even to the curl and ragged edges
of decay, that mocked with cold eternal blind minuteness
the frailty of death. It had an eery beauty, as when a
stick walks and preys, or a lichened stone discloses wings,
is flaked with moths; but this was stillness mocking life.
The leaf had eyes.

She lifted her face and saw that she had strayed.
Craobh walked in the slanting forest, wide and far below,
amid the dusk and drift of autumn. But the leaves hung
still, the air was stony. Craobh, she said, not aloud,
afraid. The child paused.

The stillness broke. A fury hunted them, cried death.
She felt its naked malice, yet could see no earthly thing:
a storm of silent wings, a crouching whirlwind, dark.
They ride.

The child ran blindly, in a great dry tumult; she sprang
and stumbled, hunted headlong through the rocks. Wildly,
Ariane ran after, nowhere, whipping back a madness that
assailed, possessed her blood, a frenzied terror of aban-
donment, calling out in the wounded air. The fury of the
silence stooped at her, the wings, it tore, it tore, O make
it stop—

In a sudden rage, Ariane wheeled and cried out to the
wood, "You let go!" Storming the leaves' whirlwind, the
thunderface of silence, flapping wildly in her coat, she
hurled what came to hand: Sylvie's knife.

Stillness. The torn track of leaves, ending there.

Gone.

She felt a moment of triumphant terror and release,
amazed. *Babylon is fallen.*

Craobh—No, wait, the knife.

Anxiously, she darted back and grubbed and scuffled
through the leaves where she thought the knife had
fallen. All her fleeting glory fretted away, lost in rake
and ransack and scrabbling haste. She was stupidly
bereft. She envisioned it so clearly: a horn knife, with a
jangling keyring, and a blade and a broken half. It was
Sylvie's; it had routed dark. But the knife was gone forever, and she dared not stay.

She found Craobh just beyond a stony stream, sprawled

shuddering, her hair and face splashed red with fallen leaves. Her eyes were blind and bright. Ariane knelt beside her. Touching the child's face with trembling fingers, she saw the rade of huntsmen she had blindly routed: ravencloaked, or pale as dying suns, their bodies bitter white as frost, flint-clear, and flecked with dark immortal blood that rained like crystal on the earth. They carried knives of bronze or stone; their harness was of writhen metal, gold and grey-black, veined with crimson, of the lightborn blood inlaid: night-fiery, like a turmoil of windwyrms. They were crowned with iron, wrought as thorns; and pale as its flower sprang the foam from goat-rough horses, cruelly spurred. She saw the stone-fire struck from brazen hooves. And she saw the ravens, iron-beaked and taloned, but with moonwhite naked breasts, and witches' hair, like cloud, like fire flaring out. Silently, the horns cried havoc. *Darkborn*, said her cold still voice: their prey is souls.

"Craobh?"

The child was still. "Not for them, her crown. Not stone," she said at last. "You cloud."

With shaken hands, Craobh fumbled for her stone, and drew it forth. Of her will, she gave the stone to Ariane, folding her hands about the soul, so that bone and blood were calyces of light. Ariane caught breath. Receiving, she was spirit, light bent outward into wood and branches; her thought was leaf. She sprang from roots of nebulae, was branched, and flowered into stars, falling, fleeting, and too bright for pain. Her hand closed on the stone.

For a long time, she sat, holding the child on her lap, stroking the tangled hair. It was dusk, and the leaves were covering her, as if she had died in a ballad.

They lay huddled among roots. Craobh slept; Ariane lay wakeful, strangely unafraid. The child's frail trust, her need, still troubled her with joy, a wintry exaltation. The soulstone had annealed in her a rune of unturned turning stars. She felt it still, as blinding light still blackly dances, swiftlike, in the crazy eye. Dark, undark and bright: her taking of the candle, Craobh's turning with her soul, until she could not tell whose moving was embrace, whose shadow. They were one.

Falling into sleep, she felt the touch of other sleepers, ribs and knees of rock against her body. Sleepers? Staring into dark, she saw a knot of stones, a broken ring, bound darkfast, naked to her apprehension. They were lightborn, and she saw. Like one who has tasted birds' blood, and must willy-nilly understand their grieving tongues, she was changed. She saw with the eyes of Craobh's unearthly kindred, eyes of tree. The witch had torn the heart from her, and given back a heart of stone, cold stone. She stood among the others, still as death, undying and unsouled: a ring of stones, none taller than a child, that crowned the naked hill.

But that was a dream. Craobh had cried out in her sleep, and waked her. Or she herself had cried: Ariane could not tell. She lay in darkness. The sky cleared in lakes of cloud. The stars were strange; or else she had forgotten what webs her constellating mind should draw, forgotten names. No. The thread was broken, and the Sword had scattered in the dark.

That too was dream. Waking, taut with fear, she lay and stared at the dark, beside the child's slight wavering breath. She recalled the high white room, and saw Craobh's hands, enskeined with heaven, fling down the cradled stars. No stars, she thought. There were no stars to know the world by, none by which to travel. Seeking light, she held the child's cold occult soul. It gave her dark of soul no light, no more than any stone.

At the break of light, Ariane woke. Craobh's hand was on her hand. The child was gazing at her. Waking stark with chill, beyond all known consoling dawns, she thought, What now? The child's afraid, she cowers like a candle in the wind. Yet nothing stirred. She had Craobh's stone, she'd know if—wouldn't she?

Ariane sat up. She touched the child's face. "Craobh?"

No answer. Craobh was elsewhere, in her dark of moon.

"Craobh, the owl's way, do you remember? Or back to the stone?" O Craobh, it's your wood, your wood.

Craobh's voice was rush-frail, plaintive as a bird's rehearsing ancient grief. "You were in the sleep. I couldn't find you."

Slowly, Ariane held out the stone. It dangled in the
air between them. "Craobh?" The child looked elsewhere, at a cobweb hung with dew. She plucked it, held
it to her throat, unseeing that the drops of water fell.

"Mine's clouds of stars."

Mad, thought Ariane. O God. And no way back.

Darkness and a cold despair. They could walk, or they
could lie together in a hollow, until the hunt, or want,
or stealthy winter took them and they woke no more: a
vain death that would be. No birds would cover them
with leaves. None here but ravens.

So the travellers went on, amid unending trees, beyond
the moon and north of nowhere, in an endless knot, as
far as Ariane could tell. She chose no way. Chance
caught them up and wove.

Craobh walked like one bewildered; Ariane, as in the
labyrinth of another's soul, as in a waking dream. She
had forgotten why they came. She dreamed of walking
in a ruined tower; ghostly to herself, she brushed with
cold reluctance through the veils of withered arras, dry
and still, to reave the naked cold undying jewel at its
heart. Between unwilling trespass and desire, complicit,
she was caught and cobwebbed. But the tower was a
wood, the wood became her thought, unleaving: wary of
her furtive rootless self, desiring leaf-fall, darkfastness
and unending sleep. Still her body trudged on, a shadow
with a child as shadow, unhopeful and astray.

But straying through a grove, she shook the cold bright
mail of water from the leaves. As it fell on her, she
roused. *By light and law.* She thought of Sylvie striding,
hoarse and quick and reckless, with her sword: here, in
this unearthly autumn world, but in its spring, far and
green beyond imagining.

Sylvie?

Cold bright scattering: hold fast. Now, before she fled.

Ariane flung herself into the thorns, wild and heedless
as the one she sought, badgerly intent, holding fast until
she woke and saw: it was not Sylvie she held, but a little
scrubby tree. It was like a red oak, with curled dishevelled stubborn leaves, sharp and brown and thin; it
splayed and straggled. In a wood of archetypes, it was
beyond all praises odd. But now the grove was birch and

rowan, ash and tangled thorn. She saw red berries, silver bark. She stared, and rejoiced in waking; gave rueful thanks to the sting and sopping, blessed the thorn: she had jumped into a bramblebush, and scratched in both her eyes. She had Sylvie again, not now but here. She broke a spray from the oak, by its leave: for remembrance, for panache, defying spellblind sleep. She stuck it in her hat.

Now she thought the wood seemed shabbier, imperfect, as if the mode had changed; the branches grew awry, the leaves were brown. She felt no present horror of the hunt. They seemed thin and archaic, plaintively eery as a horn-dance by daylight: a frail dub and piping on the wind, a ghostly clash of horns. Perhaps, clouded in her fog of flesh, the stone was veiled from them. For now, they had withdrawn. Touch wood.

Craobh eyed the twig. "The others' wings were black."

Ariane trudged on. She sang tunelessly beneath her breath, ballad after ballad, tenaciously remembered, in her flat and errant voice, reed-thin. She sang of wintry lovers and of jealous kings. The slow leaves fell and bled for them, the shadows of her earth. She sang to waken Sylvie's echo, rising out of dark to touch her falling descant from the air, as leaf to leaf upon the mirrored silence.

But death and gramarye go ill with wandering; they are for fire and sleet and handwork, hearth and loom, and scrubbing pots. For walking in a strange wood with a ghostly child, they are cold comfort indeed. Ariane's throng of shadows seemed a clammy gang, corpse-candles all: drowned, betrayed or hanged. The wood daunted her, and the glass was empty. She fell silent. Then setting her cockade of oak-leaves, shakily defiant, she began again, with her fine cap and feathers and her drum, rattling the dry wood.

Craobh whirred and lingered from branch to briar, adrift, inconsequent. As they went, she gathered haws and beechnuts, acorns, sloes and mushrooms. Craobh ate these, heedless as a bird; but Ariane would not. The sloe she bit at scoured her tongue. She ate sparingly of their hoard, the oatcakes, cheese and honey from Illyria.

Afterward, she sat and turned out her bag and pockets,

to see what she had got. Exaltation is no mood to pack in, she thought ruefully. A comb would have been nice; also a toothbrush and some ink. And soap, and iodine, and blankets—ah, but bless Maire for the chocolate. What else? String, for birdsnares? And a kettle. Oh, and matches, though she would not have dared to break a dead branch of this wood. Also tea.

Craobh eyed her, drawn fleetingly to the jumbled brightness. She touched an unsilvering pilgrim's badge, threaded on a strand of crimson silk. Ariane sifted through the jackdaw heap. She caught herself singing again—*"What care I for my goosefeather bed, with the sheet turned down so bravely, O?"*—and broke off laughing, between absurdity and dole. Oh, she did care, very much: and for breakfast after. She found her runebook, and pressed Sylvie's twig between the pages, for safe-keeping.

The afternoon was windless, grey, unshadowed. It grew wintry on the farther hills, all wreathed in mist. It clung to the trees in glittering salt, and plumed the becks with crane-grey desolation. The leaves were rimy. Far and white, the shafting sun paled cloud with wraithlike glory. Ariane would turn and stare, at no one, at a sword of rime, a shadow. *Let me in.* The cloud was caught with light, was cloak for some vague fleeting shape; but dulled with cold and wandering, dream-slow, she was eluded.

Then it came. She heard, not wind, the dry thrash of a creature among the leaves of the underwood. The hunt. She sprang round, wild with terror, warding Craobh. The roar of leaves came onward. Slow, and stranger than the hunt. It was a sere quick tumult like a flock of birds, whirring in the wraiths of summer trees; a dim dry clacking, like the far-off clash of horns; and prickling in her small hairs, frail as gossamer, a thread of dreamlike eery piping, now and nowhere.

Ariane stooped. No stone to hand. No knife. Stick? None lying, and she dared not break the wood. She touched the soulstone at her throat. It put no vision in her mind, good or ill. Blind in the uncanny mist, she turned and turned; she could not stand against the other, seeing none. Beside her, Craobh was still, twisting her dead staff.

What it was came wraithlike, bent, unhallowed, moving warily amid the roke: a shadow crowned with horn.

Ariane stood earthstruck, stark with fear.

It was a man, slight, neither old nor young, but faded, tawny as a winter leaf. He carried a bundle of thorn on his back; that was the crown. He wore all faded brown, in leaves on leaves of tatters, pieced and patched, hedgelinen and a beggar's-opera greatcoat: half woodwose and half tinker. His face was sharp and somber, cornered as a nut and creased; furze-browed and beak-nosed, with hazel eyes.

Astonished, he stared at Craobh. His gaze was rapt, fierce and homely as a rushlight, that brought both comfort and a throng of shadows. It flickered at Ariane, amused, wondering, commiserate; then back at Craobh in puzzled awe. He slung down his load of thorn. Rubbing his nose a little shyly, consideringly, he half knelt and laid down his knife, hilt foremost at their feet; he did it awkwardly, a fumbling touch upon a pipe or strings unplayed for many years, a long-forgotten grace.

"Come, tha'lt be starved wi cawd, lass. I'll not hurt thee," he said to Ariane; and as she stood amazed, "There's ravens sall, an tha stays for them." He glanced at Craobh. "She'll walk no farther."

He gathered up the child, scant and stiff as his bundle of thorn, black and white as if she flowered in his arms. Ariane followed, cumbered with the sticks of firing, with his knife stuck in their twine. Craobh's head lay on his shoulder, and her arm trailed drowsily beneath his broad-brimmed battered slouching felt, and his jauncing draggled feather.

In the green sky a haloed moon was rising, hunchbacked and transfigured, in a maze of cloud; they stumbled in the weaving dusk. It was yet owl-light, more puzzling than the simple dark. Beyond a dyke and a ring of tumbled stones grew trees in a bewildered knot, low and writhen, on a round green knowe. He shouldered his way through, and Ariane clambered after, coming to a rough green castle, drunk with the lees of light. At his back, the storm broke in a tree of branching light, and another, and a third: a grove of birches, winter-bare, in utter and aloof tranquillity; but then the sky was shat-

tered with the thunder. The leaves stormed before the
sudden wind, thronging thick as witches in the wild and
haily, hurly-burly air.

Swift and nimble as a hare, he ducked into the hillside.
He laid Craobh on the earthen floor, and crouching,
teased and coaxed a fire from the thorn, adjuring it in
soft exasperation. Then he brought in a cupful of hail;
and dazed with weariness, Ariane could think only, how
strange, how marvelous, to drink the stones of heaven,
windfalls of the lightning. And again she felt the cold
immortal hailstone at her throat. For a while she sat
stunned, like one taken from the sea, out of a storm of
marvels.

"Meal somewheres," he said, rootling in his coat; and
held out a dusty palmful, mixed with twigs. Then she
bestirred, burrowing in her pack for goatcheese and dried
apples, and muddled up some rather lumpy oatcakes on
the hearth.

The stranger tucked Craobh up in his wraprascal coat:
knobbly with sloes and nuts and oddments, ruinous, it
reeked of leafmould. He had taken off his slouch hat;
his fall-brown hair was tumbled. He warmed something
from a leather bottle in a crooked stoup that looked
oddly like an old tin can. He made Craobh drink, and
Ariane, and took his turn. The small ale swayed through
her veins like a tree of molten bronze. He curved his
cold fingers and his palms to his wooden cup, and bent
his face into the fume of ale. By firelight, he looked grim
as Dante; then it caught the rings of frail gold in his ears,
that wove light on the air.

At length, Craobh sat with her knees drawn up, the
greatcoat cast aside like moorland by the climbing moon,
her face crescent in a cloud of hair. The hillside was a
hall of stone. Behind her in the wall was carved the ruin
of a face and wing, so like her seal on the dying snow,
that night she had lain naked in the field, that it seemed
illusion, the afterimage of transcendence. Yet it was
Craobh who was consumed in stillness, and the stone
that broke the firelight in leaves of gold, of shadow. With
her chin on her hands, she stared. The traveller was still
as she, as silent, amid his flickering, fantastic shadows,
like a rooted tree alive with birds.

The stranger never spoke, but looked at Craobh as if at a new-risen star, a marvel long-foretold, unlooked-for, hanging in still clarity above a cloud-shouldering hill; yet a companionable wonder, the first star of winter, with its calendar of frost and fire: as if she bade the shepherd in. He bent, as if to touch her scarring throat; drew back. He fed the scant fire, twig by twig.

Ariane gave him the last of the goatcheese, and an ashy shard of oatcake, juggling it with chary fingers. "Where is this place?"

"I't Cloudwood. Now and then; or not." He caught her glance at the stone image of the child. "They's flitted now; they'll not come wake us wi their stir."

"Who?"

He turned the cup in his hands, staring drowsily into the fire, so that even the will o' th' wisp dance of his earrings was still. His voice was a little mazed, with ale or sleepiness or awe, dark and soft beneath the raving wind. "Ah. Yon lass is another such—tha knaws, light-born—as bairn at given me t'cup. I thowt he were t'last."

"Here?" Soft and wary, as if she held a glow-worm in her hands.

"I't Wood, as they were to fell, back end of a year. By t'water I were, all my lone, ligging i't leaves and laiking, cracking nuts. 'Will tha drink?' says no one. Lad. He were no taller nor a bairn, all fallow, hair and hood and all, as wan's a winter leaf i't leaves. And then t'sun leamed thruff and thruff him, bright as t'burr round a candle. A, thowt I, wha's aloft? being flawtered wi't light; and allt water runned away thruff me hands, 'How dosta like Cloud ale?' says he. He's hawden his cup to me, and I did drink on it. I see'd him—he were light. Sithen, I's not waked. I's ever i' this hallows wood, and all athwart 'o years. All beside is shadows; they die." The cup was empty. He looked at her. "Wood's what I is."

He bent toward Craobh, and all his throng of shadows swaled and scuttered, goblin-beaked and backed, and etenish. He mowed at her, to make her laugh, as if all fears were lanthorn mummery, hearthtales innocent of harm. She smiled back in sudden plain delight. Then rue-fully, bemused, he said, "But tha's nobbut bone and blood, poor lass, tha's light and not: a scranny piece enough, but no waft. Tha'rt wick as I. Why hasta not fleeted wi thy folk?" He glanced shrewdly at Ariane, in her swashing greatcoat, and turned back to Craobh. "How does tha come by yon rantipole?"

Ariane, huddled in the dark, began, "I . . ."

He shrugged, and delving in his pockets, sat idly toying with a handful of his oddments, cracking nuts. He cast about for a stone, groping in the ruined wall where a root had thrust it down; and started, sucked his palm. He dug. Unearthing something small, he bent toward firelight.

"Eh, well, I's blessed," he said softly. In his hand was a bent and blackened stoneless ring, too dull to catch the light.

Sylvie's? thought Ariane.

He tried it on his thumb. Too big. He looked all dazzled innocence at Craobh, and held it out. "Would tha like a fairing, lass? I's gauds o my own." His earrings winked and glimmered, lightstruck, bright as moths.

Craobh looked full beyond him, dreamily. She took the ring, and looked through it, through her cloud of tangled hair, serenely grubby. She laid it on her palm. Her air was grave and lordly, as of one for whom black cherries are rings of dragonsblood, and withered leaves are gold. "You keep my wood for me, shepherd; I must sleep." And then she slept, lying on the taloned root, as at a griffin's feet.

Ariane covered her with her own greatcoat. Then she came and poked a twig into the fire. It blazed up thinly, blue and alien. Its few leaves curled and clawed with fire. Nearest to the heart is loath to speak: it clots. "Did you . . . have you seen others in the wood? A brown girl?"

But nodding by the hearth, he turned the dark ring round and round, and did not hear. Soft and sudden as a rushlight going out, he slept.

Ariane meant to wake, and see if the woods faded and the moon stood still; but the fire burned drowsily, the dark had walls. Waking in the night, she heard the wind, a weird angelic gabble of voices, as if the wild stars hunted, clamorous as swans—O the song, Sylvie's wood arising out of storm, she thought—and dreaming that she rose to look for Sylvie, that she found her fiddling at a

tinker's wedding to an owl, while she herself must play
the moon as drum, she slept again.

The morning light was green with frost. The hearth
was cold, and the harsh stones feathered with grey ash.
The others were awake and away: not far, she heard
their voices. But the piping had ceased. How they'd
woven in the hey, the owl in her moony scarf, the tinker
in his leaves of rags—Hey, wake up. Ariane lay, sleep-
heavy, rounded inward on her dream; strangely heavy,
for as well as hers, the tinker's coat was over her. It
stank of musty leaves. Dismayed, recoiling from the gen-
tleness that preyed on unwary sleep, and through and
through pervaded with its foxearthy fume, like a tisane
of a thousand autumns, she shirked it off. O dear. He
meant it kindly, she supposed, repenting of her sullen
dignity. His coat's all he's got. Rags. Patchwork. Ah.
She lugged it gingerly into her lap. Look, yet another
country, cloudish wood. Oak and beech and hazelwood,
and—hullo, an ecosystem. Creatures. O dear. Arrgh. She
flung it down.

She went out into the light, into a green hall, roofless
under heaven, cloud and stone. Craobh sat beneath a
low, gnarled thorn, amid the ruins of the broch. They
who had dwelt within had graved her image in its stones,
thought Ariane, remembering the lightborn child, the
wood ensouled, a turning of the moon ago; yet they had
fled, their keep had fallen, ages past. And still the child
endured, still green and ancient. She was playing with
cobnuts from the tinker's pockets.

He sat on a green bank, beside a tumbled wall, turning
Sylvie's ring round his thumb; he rolled a nut at the child.

Odd and odd made two, and Ariane one other,
strange, outlandish.

Rather stiffly, she said, "It's late. Sorry."

"Hallows yet," he said. He had cut himself a staff, she
saw, and was thwittling it, turning and rubbing. Now he
took it up and set to work. As he worked, he muttered
softly to himself. "Hmm. Hah." His face was wried with
concentration, an absurd severity of enjoyment. He straked
his knife against the stones, trying its edge, and let it fall.

Thrumming very softly with his fingers on the wood,

he spoke, half sang, a skein of nonsense, fa and lilly ba. The tune grew haltingly, as he remembered; it became a haunting ancient rhyme. "*. . . by lang and light til Babylon . . .*" It was the tongueworn remnants of a song, still older, rubbed until only knots and knarls of rhyme were left. "*. . . wi Tom alone, and Cutty Joan . . .*" It was ancient and as battered as his mazer cup, carried through the years beyond its making. So many a fine thing is sprung from earth, is shaped and worn away by hand or tongue, with loving use descending from above the salt to cot, to kitchen and to cradle, from hall to hedge, and last, all unconsidered, to the tinker's budget. "*. . . but Jenny Knap's th' eldest born, and cowers i' th' moon . . .*"

Bending to his work, he grimaced with his beaky face, pleasurably, as if the music grew within him, song and singer, wood and artisan at once, shaping his green thought to the long slow twisting of the phrase, as a craftsman curves the living tree for timber.

> We's hunted her thrae Babylon,
> By moon and dark o moon;
> Gi's siller for to light her wake;
> She's bare a hally crown.

He caught breath between two notes, and smiled, wry and wide-eyed, dazzled as the wind on water. The child laughed in her green innocence, fanned to brightness as she sat, amid the maze of fallen stones, amid the narrow crimson leaves that fell, and splashed her hair with illusory, unbaneful blood.

Beyond the green castle, all ways again were wood. What now? thought Ariane. She'd packed; the tinker was flapping about in his coat, fooling with things. Old home week, she thought. I hope they're all very happy together. Now he and the child seemed to be playing follow-my-leader, jumping on the rocks. Ariane turned away and hunched brooding, staring out at trees. Sylvie's anywhere in this. No asking Craobh what she was after: she's lost herself, forgotten wood and all. So it's up to me. O dear. She looked sidelong at the mazy tinker. And him?

"Are you coming?"

"Wood's where I is. Nowt else."

Turning to the twelve winds' quarters, the tinker spied the air. Crows? Ariane saw nothing: cold grey cloud; and below and endlessly beyond, the mottled mothwing drab and white of hoarfrost on unleaving trees. Craobh copied leaf-fall, whirling dizzily in her dance. All at once and askew, the tinker set out, scrabbling and staggering down the steep rimy hill, with Craobh at his coat-tail, slipping after.

Ariane lingered, wanting a word, a glint of wings, a rainbow—revelation. No sign was given. Warily, she touched the soulstone, and saw nothing: edgeways into lightning. Dazed, she let it fall. She stood alone. They're gone, she thought, panicking: I've cracked the wood and they've slipped through. They're leaving me behind. No, there: Craobh's red cap. For all the tinker's scuffling, he eluded sight, a fading rumor, leaf-brown amid the tattered vagrant leaves. She scrambled after.

They walked on in the slanting wood, seemingly astray. Ariane fretted: she wasn't quite sure how one quested, but surely one did it more intently? *The owl's way, not the raven's*, Craobh had said. Hadn't mentioned cuckoos. *Thorn is hallows*. Fine, the wood's all thorns.

As the hoarfrost faded, it became a mild, slithery, bemusedly cobwebby day, shabby and spattering, with freaks of sun. Now and then came a flaw of rain, rattling on the withered leaves like a vexation of squirrels, and always on the travellers, pelting them with dwarfish malice, while the sun shone faintly in the grove aside, the glade beyond. The water spangled and then damped their hair and clothes; they went slipshod with the leaves. Plastic bags, thought Ariane suddenly, dolefully imagining her notebooks mouldering in the damp.

I'm lost, she thought. They're strangers. Odd one out again. And I was just beginning to sort it out. Am I Craobh now, what she was? I have her stone. For that matter, she thought, eyeing the tinker doubtfully, he has Sylvie's ring. Cloud's stars. On his left thumb, falling off. (Under scrutiny, he sneezed.) Two's one, moon and dark: their changes are a dance. Three's strange. The dark and the light, and—O heavens yes, his thornbush (she grinned)—hey, the man in the moon.

Wet as a bird, stooping and sidling with abstracted ease through the thickets, the tinker sang, lilting softly to himself, with the fall of rain as drone: scattered woodnotes, and snatches of country tunes. Now he moved swiftly, with the sudden terse and freakish shifts of a skipped stone or a started hare; then ending back of nowhere, he would saunter along amid the trees, trailing his hand down their branches and rough bark, rattling the nuts in his pockets. Slouching towards Babylon. Or Bedlam. In and out, Craobh whirred and lingered, making forays after nuts, and flirting out at leaves, as if they flicked and fled her in a game. Caught you last. She'd got the tinker's feathered hat.

The leaves fell endlessly. They thronged with him. Walking, dodging after, Ariane became possessed by a delphic urgency. Surely he'd not come upon the ring by chance. It bound them. Surely they were meant to act. She caught up with him, flurried, almost crashing; then

hung back a step, breathless, shy. "The ring, the one
you found: it's at the root of things," she said, pink with
prophecy. Do sibyls blush? He ducked beneath a dripping bough. She ducked after, entangled, aspersed. "It's
a spell, I think; it holds light fast."

"Aye then, an tha will, it does," he said, nodding
sagely at her shoe.

"I left it in another wood, not Cloud: another earth."

Bewildered, he rubbed his nose. "Is't riddles asking?
I knaws another, and's dark."

"It's stars," she said desperately. "They're in two
worlds."

He turned and grimaced at a squirrel. "Like thy
cheek." This time, shyly recalling a sort of manners, he
addressed her elbow. "Wha's not?"

She began to feel a little giddy, as if she were playing
cat's cradle with cobwebs in the wind. Craobh was odd,
he was odd, she was turning strange herself. Half-
quarked. Some Cloudish charm on them. Unconcerned,
he shied a nut at the squirrel. It swore. The ring turned
loose, unheeded, on his thumb.

"Oh, be careful!" she cried, pleading, furious. "You'll
lose it."

"I's never yet. Not stars. Clouds or no."

I give up. Why *is* a raven like a writing-desk?

Crossing a beck, he hopped from stone to stone, light
and clumsy, never quite overset. The water jostled like
geese to market. Sploshing in the shoals, he halted laughing: the child had set his feathered hat sailing bravely
down the beck. It foundered, overfraught. "Hey up, yon
duck's rigged ower. Were hatched frae cuddy's egg." He
snagged it, and wrung it out, and they went on.

Ariane stravaged after, keeping Craobh in sight. All
at once, the tinker wheeled round sharply. "Wo! tha
munnot break wickwood," he said, canting his head at
her. She'd snapped a twig; still held it, stupidly. She
dropped it like a coal. His face was grim. "Breaks
hallows."

"Oh," she said, anxious, "Oh, will it call—?"

But already he had drifted elsewhere. "Odd garland
tha'd weave wi hagtrees. Would tha dance at craws' wedding?" he said, and flitted on.

She gazed at him covertly: would he take the stone from her, lightly as a jackdaw would, for its dangled glitter? Would he wander off and leave them, bewildered and bereft, to starve? Or was he fey, leading them nowhere but the dark of moon, to be devoured soul and bones by the hunt? Ah, but Sylvie'd gone nowhere. Could be that his nowhere was the same as hers, where leery reason could not follow. Moon and dark of moon.

Then ruefully she thought: he took us in. What harm in that? Poor sarkless scatterling, he's mad as Craobh, and near as scrawny. Did he beg his bread and ale? But where? And what of cold? How many winters had he endured unhoused, alone? What of Bedlam? O God, and the dark wild hunt, the ravens—wouldn't they be hunting him all down the years and through the wood for that cup of his? She shivered, imagining their storm of blind avarice breaking on him. What chance had bemused mortality, a staff and ragged coat, a cup and knife, against that fury? A leaf in a storm of fire.

No, she thought, looking up at his light gait: he's light as Sylvie. Birds of a cap and feather. He would drift through it all, world and wood, like a moth in a melee. The nameless child with the cup had chosen well for its guardian, Cloud's shepherd: the tinker was unassailable as light in water, out of dark's element. Who'd storm a rainbow? Lay siege to elsewhere? But Craobh had had no choice at all, giving up her soul willy-nilly to the next unstony hand. As good hide it in a paper bag.

Ariane stumbled on a root. They had come a fair way, she realized, for all their straying, and without stumbling over the brink of some unfathomed scar, nor blundering into sloughs. The trees were vexeder, cross-grained and wind-frazzled: their leaves seemed red with stooping, like crones over cauldrons. The shape of hills was strange. The green castle, that unearthly knoll, had long since vanished. "How far—?" she began.

The others were gone. Witched away? Ariane stopped cold, cast about for them. I wish they'd *say*—Not far, thank heaven. Craobh was sitting on the ground, making patterns with her hoard of nuts, scratching mazes with a stick. Her face was grimy and recollected. "Here's Babylon," she said. "His other's drowned."

The wanderer lay beside a little spring, inlaid with leaves, and falling leaves that changed the pattern, waking cloisons of bright water. Through the brown clear stillness rose a whorling thread of silver, flaw and origin and fate. Pale and dark, the leaves of shadow rose, and touched their falling shadows from the air, bright, haily. He was gazing in the water, talking softly, rarely, to himself, his other self; his hand was poised above its mirrored palm. His cup was beside him, nearly empty.

Curious, a little awed, Ariane stared at it by daylight: a burl of some whorl-grained wood, silvery-dark with age, though flawed with fiery autumn where most worn; not quite true round, like half a nutshell with a stumpy foot. A band of silver bound it at the stem, all tarnished. It was badly scratched, or graven; but she could not read the runes, if runes they were, and she dared not pick it up.

He touched the water, and sat up, not seeing her, with his chin sunk in his folded arms, hugging his knees. His face was drawn with weariness and unbelief. The leaves turned slowly on the water.

All beside is shadows, thought Ariane, remembering. He's wood. He's borne another's soul, long years: what soul is left to him? What earth? And if he's Cloud, the child who gave the cup—Had he gone mad like Craobh? Turned stone? She searched the stranger's face, saw bleak enduring, and a crazy innocence. Did bearing light do that? She felt the soulstone, heavy at her throat. Not all herself. Not yet.

She took the spray of Sylvie's brown dishevelled leaves from its hoarding-place, with anxious care: already their stifled curl had begun to crack. "What sort of tree is this?"

He took it, and studied it, fingering the dry sharp edges of the leaves. His touch was gentle. "Hawds leaves langest i' winter; last green i' spring, and bonniest. Thy brown girl, is't then? Nay, I've not see'd her."

So he'd not been asleep then, last night when she'd asked. "Oh," said Ariane sadly. "Thank you." She put away the twig. Craobh still was scratching in the earth, an armslength and a world away. Closer than Nan's woods. Ariane sighed. "Is there anyone else here? Or just trees?"

"None o thy gossips. Stones. Awd Malykorne." He spoke the name with a curious mingling of awe and teasing fondness. "Tha'd not gan call on her for a crack and ale, not while it rained craws."

"Why, what's she?"

"Witch, like. She were here afore t'wood." Crouched beside her, he mowed wickedly, hunched and claw-handed, miming malevolence; but creased with an owlish mirth. "Ista flayed o witches?"

Ariane grinned back, suddenly tickled. "I don't know. Does she eat paper?" (At the back of her memory, Sylvie's sly, delighted voice said, "Hush. What's that little stumpy person?")

"Gnarls it up for her breakfast. Fat ballads and bacon." Then all at once he looked quite sober. He spoke low. "What's aloft? T'awd ones—tha knaws—has rade out, and in hallows, after yon lass. She's nowt for them. They's not ta'en all, wood's here: but all unfast, all flittery-like, and stone's rising. I see'd i't water. Leaves falled on nowt."

Not mad, she thought, looking at his shrewd fantastic face: not mad, but cloudwise, innocent. He knows the wood: its huntsmen, and its dark of moon, its stones; he knows the lightborn. But these things are, they do not will the good or evil that they do. He's innocent of malice, and of greed, betrayal. I could be a witch. He trusts me as he did the child, as light. A given. Ariane twisted her sleeve button. It was hard to talk of dreams and visions with a stranger. Yet he would not think her mad. "I dreamed they were all stones, the—children. Standing on a fellside, in a—No. Not all, the ring was broken. It was dark. The wood was drowned in stone, like great waves."

"Stane's all what's under us."

As skull beneath the skin, she thought: but who could endure to see bones blearing through the face?

"And dark's aback o't moon."

Craobh plucked at his coat; she held a handful of sloes and haws. He brushed the leaves from her hair. "Nay, lass, keep thy cattyjugs: good burnt bannocks for thy dinner."

They walked on, from cloud into shabby light, and rain and cloud again: and still all ways were wood.

"Where are we going?" said Ariane at last.

"Find awd witch. She's moonwise, is awd Malykorne. Uncanny, like. Happen she'd knaw what's aloft, an she'd say." He barely nodded at Craobh. "Unspells. And spells. Tha'd best be wary o thy tongue wi her, think on: there's rumors of her porridge." This was not encouraging. Seeing Ariane dismayed, he hedged. "Hedgehogs'll say owt. They's arfish. She's nowt to do wi folk, no more as owls wi acorns. Nuts i' May," he added ingenuously.

Ariane thought that lacking mice, an owl could develop a taste for acorns. "Where does she live?"

"Aback o beyont." He frowned consideringly. "I thowt as we'd best walk athwart and away. She'll be where she isn't: if she wants to be found. We'll knaw by t'moon."

"Ah," said Ariane. "O dear, I'm sorry. What is your name?"

He rubbed his nose, in bemusement. "Hmm. Ha. Forgetten what. Happen it fell i't water." As if in his beclouded innocence, he thought one day to find it at the bottom of his cup.

"Ariane," she said shyly, "I'm Ariane, and she's Craobh."

"That's not her name: tha calls her."

"No. Yes. Oh well, what do they call you?"

He laughed, as if amused at a sudden memory, creased and dazzled. "I's heard mams calling out til bairns, 'Come thy ways, ba, come out frae't wood, Awd Nuttycrack'll get thee.' Langneb, I's heard, and Mazy Will. Awd Flaycraw."

"What?"

"Flaycraw. Same as i't corn: tatterwag. There's craws i't wood, right enough. Craws wi horns." Suddenly, he went rushing, flapping away, crying out and cawing, clappering to flight imagined crows. "Cark! Cark!" Craobh clapped her hands, flitting after.

Foolery, thought Ariane, laughing: O but something

else beside, some crazy holiness, half-understood, or slighted for her own, the stranger's sake. The crows, she remembered with a cold exultant thrill, were real. Could he flight so fell a brood with mummery? It seemed he had. The cup was borne by him; the wood was standing. They were walking in his sleep. Was that stranger than her calling Craobh? Than Sylvie's falling as a star in Cloud? Ariane looked up. The tinker's slight quick figure fleeted crazily away, borne up by a compelling brightness, whirled and whelmed like a leaf in a beck. His draught of Cloud ale, his wandering, had made him—no, not unearthly, but of earth as leaves its spirits are, sylvan and astray. He fetched up by a great oak, and called back, breathless, to Ariane, "Come by, come by, it's cluddering for storm."

She ran, caught up and cloaked by the wind, the dark tatters of the air: astride of winter. He was crouched beneath the thickest of the rattled leaves, with the child happed up in the skirts of his greatcoat. He looked up at the scudding tumult in the heavens, the greylagged gabbling of wind and rack. "Sitha, Arianty," he said. "Mallygeese." The sky had turned black as brambles; now it poured and pelted flinty rain at them, with spiteful elfshot accuracy. Craobh caught his hand, warily as if it were a shy wild creature, twisting round the tawdry ring. "They san't have that, not at swords, lass: need that gin we meet wi witches."

Half waking in the night, Ariane thought that Sylvie wound and wound the skein of autumn from her hands. Cloudwarp, said the dream: and moonwise, turn and turn about, they span the whorled and knotted stuff. But three were there, not two: dark Ariane, who dreamed; and Sylvie, with her bright cheek turned away; and last, another who was Malykorne, dark-clad and hunchbacked, ancient, cold and bright, whose hair was night-black wind, was birds. She held the snappish owl-beaked shears; they gnashed at air. The weaving drew them in, all three: it quirked at, tangled in their loose dark hair; caught up light ravellings of souls, and wound and winched them in its skein, gnarled up with twigs and leaves. As vexed, as giddy as she was, Ariane could not tell which gnashed the shears, which whorled or knit the starry skein. Turning, three were turned to one, their wise and clumsy dance a single clew. Light and cloud and dark reeled inward in a mingled thread, inwoven and withdrawn. Cold and brighter grew the witch as Sylvie waned, as Ariane spun round, spun out her self as light and dark: the crazy tangled reel was filled. The great moon slashed the thread.

Waking, as she thought, the fells she saw were not of earth, but cloud, fraying upward into swift blue air. She saw the moon, round-cheeked and sharp-nosed, owling after stars, in her mantle of the flying cloud; she breathed the bitter and the earthy air, fragrant with the death of leaves. The root she lay on was real enough. Against her cheek, Craobh's breath had blown a wavering island of damp; the tinker sighed and shifted in his tattered heap. The fire sank. Starkened as she was, she slept again.

After a cramped night, they had a cold breakfast, to sharpen appetites and tempers. They were none of them quite dry. They'd had good stones to lie on, though none seemed right for soup; and if water came in babbling plenty, the birds it seemed were witched: at least none had fallen for the tinker's snares. The fire wouldn't light. They coaxed and swore at it, while the sky turned from reynard-clouded morning into mist. Shepherd's warning. "T'goose ont fox's back," the tinker said. "Fat pickings for some." Scanted of game, they ate charred oatcakes from the night before; Craobh's pignuts; dry granola from Illyria; morsels of rusty acorns and withered musty crabs from the tinker's pockets, all tasting oddly of wild garlic, fircones and wet sheep. "What's hedgehog like?" said Ariane.

"Off elsewhere," said the tinker. He shook his aleskin. It was dry.

Before the unripe moon had set, green as a hazelnut, they walked on. The tinker had marked from what airt of heaven Mally's cloudgeese had flown, and had set out contrary. Yet turn as they would, it was all her domain, clouds and earth: all athwart. Now the slanting wood grew scarry, and they clambered down a tumbled ghyll beside a fretted and a stony water. It fell and ravelled, fell again. A vein of colder air fell with it. They rested briefly in an aldercarr, narrow as a needle's eye, and desolate. Among unburnished reeds, Ariane saw a heron. Stalking, priestly, he strode and clacked, and the light broke, plumed and dazzled, on the reeds. "Sitha," said the tinker. "Cloudlaw." For a moment in the wintry light, beyond the misty wood, they saw the fells, brown and bleak, rough-pelted as some slouching beast. "It's ower cawd for laiking," he said. "Let's on."

The wood here was low and crabbed. Pale threads of gossamer caught light and clung, ineluctably, elusively, across eyelids and cheeks and lips. Ariane spat them out, irritably. The leaves were dry and scurrying, the branches full of furtive wings. Vexed with spiderwebs, she stumbled into a thicket, enwoven with dead thorn, snarled like an old hairbrush full of sluttish combings; backing and swearing, she saw that it had been patched by some hand, clumsily staked and eddered. It was a hedge.

"Aha," said the tinker. "Sharp lass. If yon's not awd Malykorne's earth, it's summat worse."

"How do we get in?" said Ariane, doubtfully.

"If she wants us til."

Round they went, and round, blundering in the ditch of miry water at the roots, but found no gate. The tinker spoke to the thorns, mildly, with respect, adjuring them to unclose and let them through; he tried a rhyme or two, uncertainly, to no avail. He called out: but silence snapped his voice up on the wing, with impartial malice, as a nightjar hawks a moth. Ariane peered and prowled about the crazy thicket, but saw nothing: elders and nightshade; or lairing eyes. Craobh played in the ditch. Mazed and baffled, he glanced wryly at a spider on her web. "Run til thy mistress: tell her put kettle on."

At last where the hedge seemed thinnest, he set to, and bashed and daunted with his staff; but for every branch he trod under, a hundred importuned. Ariane tried unravelling; then caught in a perplexity of spiteful thorns, and lashed to fury, she tried to shove her way through, all anyhow, harled and snarled and harrowed, thralled and thrashed. Ouch, said cold reflection. Scarlet-cheeked and scattering hairpins, she had to retreat. Ramshackle as it was, the hedge would not let them through.

"Craws!" She looked at the tinker, who had hacked his way out again, and was nursing a bloody hand. He swore softly. ". . . cock rat it . . . tha bloody awd atter-cap, tha . . . Hecate-imp . . ." There was a thorn driven under his thumbnail, and a spider swung its malign geom-etries from his hatbrim. Twigs burred and bristled in his tatters: jack-in-the-wanleaf, a deciduous woodwose. Threads of his ragged clothing fluttered from the brake. Stooping, he retrieved a hairpin. "It mowt take root," he said dolefully. He glanced at Craobh, who was putting cobwebs in her pockets, as if to hoard their bright and scattering dew. "Yon lass mowt fly ower, straight intil owl's nest, whiles we stand mazed."

"What about your knife?"

"As lief gan mowing hell wi a moonbeam. And I dare not. Hay's hagged, right enough." He sleeved his nose reflectively, grimacing, with his mouth drawn down at eight-twenty, and his eyes palely and moonishly shut. Then he spun about, like a cat after a butterfly, intently distracted, fingering the air.

"Ah!" he said. "Hmm. No. Bugger," crouching and rising and twirling. "Arainwebs," he explained, harping the air like a March hare by moonlight. "Getten it." He traced a long erratic curve with his hand, the scrawl of a sun-blind astronomer. The thread of cobweb glinted, fitful in the air before him. Craobh, with her clew of tatty cobweb round her wrist, went and clung to his coat-tail, shadowing; and bemused, Ariane was caught up, and followed in the hey.

The gossamer led them a labyrinthine dance. Now skimming, now soaring, through furze and quagmire and among the stones, and through and through the trees, it fled: harping on the hedgerow, fleeting mockingly above the beck in great calligraphic flourishes, and rolling joy-ously in the slough as a dog in carrion. Three times round the hedge it ran widdershins, and thrice, and thrice again's the charm: wiry and witched and serpentine. He leapt and crept after it, weltering and winding, and Craobh and Ariane kite's-tailed him. At last he writhed into the hedge, thrashing about the mothy hovering of one hand.

"Now fort keyhole," he said, breathless.

And though she saw no shard in the hedge, Ariane followed, covering her face. The thorn let her through, though it plucked malevolently in passing, tweaking and tugging at her hair. Yet it seemed to her that Craobh wafted through, unvexed as moonlight through a grove, as a dream through tangled sleep.

They tumbled through the wicket-gate. Within the paling was a stony garth, leaf-choked and pallid, lank and rank with froward weeds. Some neglected gangling worts still grew, frost-blighted: skirrets, runch and mandragora, wormwood and sallowed onions. A rake clawed upward, ravenstark, beside a stony spring; a gawky rag of linen flapped from a bush. There was a furtive reek of burning.

The witch's hovel was a shrug of stone, owl-shouldered, with a steep and louring brow of hoary thatch. No windows did they see, but a low door, like a tooth; nor any living thing, save a disconsolate, pebble-eyed goose. It hissed them from the midden.

Ariane giggled in her sleeve, still giddy with the dance; a toyish fear was prickling in her thumbs. "Weregeese."

"Hush," said the tinker, stalking. Warily, warding Craobh with his staff, he advanced.

Rancor, said the goose, disdainfully, and turned its back.

Triumphant and shivering, with a wicked brilliance in his cheeks, the tinker turned about. He looked shy and bright, borne up by a formality beyond himself, like a child rattling a soul-box or bearing a garlanded wren, knowing that one who put him to flight would reap eternal winter. Softly, hoarsely, he chanted his rime:

> We knaw by th' moon
> That we are not too soon,
> And we knaw by t' sky
> That we are not too high.
> We knaw by t' stars
> That we are not too far,
> And we knaw by t' ground
> That we are within sound.

Still the garth was uncanny, thought Ariane: her dream of witches lingered. The door stayed fast. *Perhaps we shall call and see who do live here.* They stood all of a row like mummers, in the cloudy raw of winter, in the goose-green slather of the yard. They were all absurdly draggled. Gravely, he arranged Craobh before him, like a child of branches, settling her bright cap, and leaving the twigs of holly in her hair. He stood for a moment, wavering; then drawing breath, he took up his staff, to rap the door and raise the witch.

Peering shyly, shrewdly, round the low door was a brown-kirtled woman. She was stumpy as a little owl, huffed out with wariness, as if all her gravity were feathers, preening and blinking in the solemn light; ageless as earth, though the locks draggling from under her red cap and twisted kerchief were brown as winter fields. Her face was moonish, pale and round, yet with a witch's nutcracker profile, a sharp strong imperious nose and chin. Unexpectedly, she wore great iron-rimmed spectacles. She swept them a triumphant glittering glance.

"Nowt's brewed," said Malykorne, and made to shut the door.

Leaning on his staff, the tinker drew Craobh forward, pale as a morning candle, her unearthliness unseen in colder light. "We's not come a-begging, but to ask at rede, or hallows."

"Ah," said the witch, peering sidelong at the child, covering her quirked mouth cannily, with the back of her hand. Her face bobbed once, twice. "Well, tha can't be ower careful." She beckoned with her wooden spoon, and turned abruptly, calling, "Come in; but don't let t'wind out."

In the unwindowed earthy dusk was fire. Dark-dazzled, stooping after, Ariane saw nothing else; then slowly, ranks of earthen jugs, unglazed, some perhaps with faces, squat in crannies and on beams. Hard by them skulked the witch's pale and scrawny cheeses, pocked as moons; in the shadows, bones and eggshells, flax and horns and muted feathers; taloned candlesticks, thrawn roots; and withered apples heaped in cairns. A hedgehog curled asleep, or dead.

Amid the cratch of timbers dangled bunches of hoary weeds, and withies, and a scythe and crook. From iron nails hung the witch's pattens, her stork-shanked clumsy shears, a lanthorn and a mended sieve, beside a wisp of uncolored silk, so ruinous and fine that Ariane took it first for a cobweb. But the web was knotted, and so oddly moon-bleached, desolate; the other webs hung shawled and swagged as thick as slutswool, brooded over by a pale-eyed loom of spiders. There were dead leaves heaped and drifted in the corners, and a furtive ratscrabbling beneath; there were kists of clotted wool, and great withy hampers spilling grey goose down. The witch's iron pot crouched sullenly among the coals; it reeked and muttered. Her wolf-toothed carding combs lay by the hearth, ensnarled with rolags of stormcloud. The tinker sneezed. Bless us all, thought Ariane.

The witch laid aside her spectacles, moon-glazed and owlish, on a dusty shelf. She probably keeps them for answering the door in, thought Ariane: they'd last her. "Hawd tongue," said Malykorne to owl-eyes. "Watch pot."

She bustled, sidelong and lofty as a goose, rubbing wooden bowls clean with her elbow, scouring up spoons in her petticoat, ladling out dollops of something from the cauldron. Pease-porridge, Ariane supposed, or worse. She eyed it qualmishly: a slumped discouraged khaki mess, shimmering with slugs of muttonfat. There was no bowl left for the witch. She sucked a splodge of porridge from her knuckles, thoughtfully; and as she scurried about to draw them ale, went plucking and pinching morsels of burnt oatcake, crumbs and crusts and parings. She swept the hearth in patterns that her draggling skirts effaced; and stared at the travellers as they ate.

Craobh was delicately dislodging a small spider, like a stoneless pronged setting, from her lumps of porridge. Ariane fiddled gingerly with hers. She had expected the taste of sodden smoke, but not of pepper; nor the strings. What on earth was in it?

"Nettles," said the tinker wryly. Crouched next to her, he munched gallantly, morosely, his thin cheeks swelled, his earrings jogging like a jade's brasses. His spoon was much too broad. Wiping his mouth with the back of his hand, he took a long shuddering draught of ale. "Oh. Ah. Ha. That's good!" he cried, amazement spluttering his composed courtesy. Tripped up by delight, he danced on air, unable to speak for astonished laughter. "Hmm. Ah. Come on, give it ower." He drew his face together, knotting his furzy brows impressively, in a ferocious grimace of sobriety; but his face crazed with laughter, dazzled like water in the wind.

The witch blushed with a small sweet crooked pleasure, frouncing her apron, and pleaching up a draggled curl. Her mouth twitched. "Aye, that were a bonny few autumns." He nodded, still speechless, and sipped regretfully, lingering with sweet rue over the sop he had left him in the mug. "Best go canny, lad; tha'st drunk five hundred year already." She gazed at his recollected face, innocent as a silver spoon. Hers was serenely impassive, moon-blank. She thumped her wooden ladle on the cauldron. "Thy plate's empty."

Resigned as any donkey to the nettles, he set down his mug. The ladle dunked, impended. But meekly handing up his dish, he turned aside, glanced ruefully at Craobh. The child had not stirred or spoken; she sat like a poppyhead, spoon in the air. "Why, tha's had nowt." He bent, all concern and mischief; somehow, in his distracted care, mislaying his own spoon, eluding Mally's. "Asta burned thy mouth wi thy good poddish? Sall I keel them for thee, lass?" he said; and blew. Her hair stirred slightly on her cheek. Craobh was still.

Full gravely now, he smoothed her hair, and turned to Malykorne. "You see what yon lass is, nowther earth nor air. Could you unspell her? Or rede how it mowt be done?"

"Nowt for nowt," said the witch. He rose, and began

searching and slapping among his rags, ferreting in his pockets, offering what he had unruefully. She took from him and turned back his knife, and a tattered broadsheet, a silver penny and a shard of delft, acorns and oddments of string, his feathered hat, a flint and steel, five horn buttons from his sleeves, a rowel like a little wintry star, a cold hunk of bacon and an oatstraw pipe, peering and fingering, as she would buy a hare to jug.

"These," he said, regretful, and she touched the rings of gold in his ears, rather wistfully; but shook her head.

"No," she said, and "No," to each, tousling and mousing at him all unmoved, until at last she came to his old thin wooden cup. "Ah, I'd not mind hawding *that*," she said. "That's been filled once or twice."

"Cup's hawden for another," he said softly; but Ariane heard the dry tremor in his voice. Standing pale and somber on the rushes, slight, but resolute for all his tatters and his ale, he drew a breath, and shut his eyes. "Tak owt else afore."

Malykorne looked shrewdly up at him, from under her red cap, not too far from the earth. Her wooden spoon was tucked in her belt. "Not said I'd tak cup. Happen tha gans t'heavier for't." She glanced ravens at him. "There's others wanting, as tha knaws."

"Ta'en's not gi'en away. Owt else."

She stood like a chess queen of walrus-ivory, sallow and stumpy, absurdly powerful. Swift and sidelong, as if by whim, she caught his hand with the ring on it. A tarnished, trifling thing: she turned it round. "Doubt that's ower big for thee; tha'lt lowse it, lad."

He stared unhappily, betrayed by his own forgetfulness, and bound by his word: caught between the old trust and the new. It was Craobh who spoke.

"Not for the other's crown: her O," she said, with the barest crescent of her old grave numinous air; then more childlike, beseechingly: "You said: for witches. The one or the other." He looked long at her, and searchingly; then he laid the ring on Mally's palm. Without a word, she tucked it in her pouch.

Watching, Ariane felt a cold trickle of awe: the witch had Sylvie's ring. She could have had the cup; had left it for another pawn, but at her whim. What if she should

demand the soulstone? What if I refused? Would she
snatch it? Juggle it away? Her hand curled round it (O
still there); withdrew, fearing by her stealth to make it
coveted. The witch turned to her, fumbling for her
glasses. She perched them on her nose; and baleful and
dwarfish, drawn up in high-shouldered, quilly haughti-
ness, she cast a long appraising upward glance. Ariane
felt a ticklish horror, between laughter and dismay, as
one who feels the prickling of small talons; for behind
the absurd poppet portentousness there lay the shadow
of a drowsy malignity. She thought of her own soul
devoured and its shards spat out, in an owl-knot of fell
and bone. The stone slid on its knotted cord, cold against
her skin. "That is not thy own to give," said the witch
severely.

Slowly, reluctantly, Ariane turned out her pockets and
backpack, and the witch studied each talisman with
shrewd solemnity, twanging the hairpins and taking the
watch's pulse, fluttering the pages of the notebooks, all
awry: ah no, thought Ariane, no; but herself was laid
aside, belittled, spared. The witch poured out Sylvie's
stones and marbles on her hard wise palm, licking them
to bring out their virtues, holding each to her eye. "She's
a rare light wench; best keep these for her," she said.
At last she chose the last oatcake from Illyria, and bit
it, gravely as any child, and held it up to see each change:
from moon into waning moons, and into air and
darkness.

Ariane stared, near crying with bewilderment, or
laughing with astonished anxious joy: so little. Was the
witch mad? or maggoty? or darkly cunning? (Hungry,
said the tinker's face, and small wonder.) Was the ring
a trifle, or the cake bewitched?

Sucking the last morsel from her thumbtip, Mally
stared. "Eh! I's forgotten." She knelt abruptly and burrowed into chests and coffers, rose and rummaged elbow-
deep in jars, worrying the cobwebs and whirling up a dry
tempest of leaves and dust, and finding whatever it was
at last in the teapot, where she should have looked first.
Solemn and askew, huffed with stooping, but scarcely
grimier, she gave Ariane a blown eggshell. It lay, unex-

pectedly light, frail and freckled, on her palm. "For as it's needed, sitha."

Last, she turned to Craobh, and touched her hair with sharp strong fingers, tweaking and tugging out a snarl. From some fold of the child's clothes, she plucked a yellow leaf, and puzzled over it in the faded light, turning over its frail text of veins, her lips moving as she read; then taking it to the door, she gave it to the wind.

Ariane looked out over the witch's shoulder at her stony garth, and beyond. She stared. From within the thorny O, the eyot of the witch's hedge, she saw by day and waking what her eye of stone had dreamed: no wood, but a wraith of wood, a dwindling shadow on the fells. The way they'd come had vanished. Where was here? And which was Cloud? The wood had shrunk and shrivelled, waning: no more now than a copse like a clot of shadow, and a few tenacious spurs of thicket, clawed and clinging to the fellsides where the narrow waters ran; then huge moorland, and immortal barren rock. The garth lay all below the light, hedged in by scanty trees, and overshadowed by the fells beyond, the clouds of naked stone.

The wind had turned; there was winter in the air. The water on the stones was mute and dark, and feathery with ice: rimefast, its cold voice silent, that had spelled itself to sleep. And yet her spring still rose. The waking leaves sithed and rattled. "Come in, if tha's coming," said Malykorne to wind.

Turning back into the cold sallow dusk of the room, she no longer regarded the travellers. Unseeing them, she took their voices, took their wills, as if they had become no more, no less than the familiars of her hovel, blunt with dust and web, whose watchful silence wove her dusk: the wizened apples and the leaves, the combs of fretted iron; the travellers, no less of clay, nor warier, than the unglazed earthen jugs, obscurely mowing. All were still, all wakeful beings, earth and artefact alike, their bodies objects of uncertain use, obscurer age and provenance. Crouching, she dipped a rushlight in the fire, to make it flare. A gout of tallow burned her finger, and she swore. She set the rushlight cowering on a ledge.

It ribbed the room with shadows, curs of starved and slinking light. She stood, sucking her scathed hand.

Then stooping to the earthen floor, she swept up a handful of dead leaves. She shuffled them with both hands, very cautiously and clumsily. Some fell to dust. Having rubbed the board with her sleeve, she set them out on it, amid the candle-grease and puddled ale. She laid them out in a sort of clumsy fall, a pattern, never-ended: for the leaves, wind-warped and sidling, shifted. Some blew away, all unregarded. Others by chance, caught in cracks, or sodden or more sheltered, lay; or else by grave design. It was a simple naked pattern, sprawling as a constellation. It could have been a ship, or a ladle, or a swan; and then it changed.

Ariane stared at it, and made no sense; she felt no awe. She was tired. Cramped and cold and sadly scratched, snuffed up with wonders, she could no longer focus; though she longed desperately to long for visions, had a thousand times imagined such a moment overlooked and irretrievable, unseen in the foreseeing.

Now, she thought, I must be here and now, within the O, the witch's eye of Cloud. But where is Sylvie? Where is nowhere? Look. The fall is hallows, and a maze. The wood's beyond. What door? The one I see. O but the leaves are blank: no Wren, no Tower. And I am no witch, to owl by waning moon, or wind the clew of dark and tangled light, to find the way. Doors and only doors, and all of wood, of leaves. And yet unlike. Though all the leaves were wan, all shrivelled, some were fire-flawed and embered still, or veined or sullen red; others sere and holy, hale and brown. Oak and alder, hazel, ash and thorn. They were reaped from many woods and centuries, she thought, fleetingly to make one pack; as light, travelling from stones long cold, bright suns or fiercely dying, sundered by abysmal dark, is gathered in one knot of stars: Orion, or the Harp of Bone.

Malykorne leaned shrewdly on her elbows, biting her tongue and clutching her ears, so that her cap stood up in owl-tufts, and her thorny hair came straggling down. She put her head on one side, sly and solemn, peering crosswise and prying over her handful of leaves. Her long eyes, warped as trout in their wintry meres of glass, leapt

and wavered; her brows quirked, fierce and lithe as
otters. "Ah," she muttered, and looked severely at the
tinker, grim and sleepy on his bench; as though she
would wap his noll with her spoon.

"Tha sall wake wood frae thy sleep," she said, stone-
faced. "Be cloud i' thy cups: thy burden's light leaves
ont water."

She turned crossly to Ariane. "What's wick i't shadows? Swale-and-die. What's sharper nor thorn? Sword i't
leaves. See tha don't cut thysen."

Then swayed by an inward storm, eyes shut and ears
held, as if hailstruck, she crouched and turned away
toward Craobh. Her hands unfolded, fanning out. Her
voice was harsh, triumphant. "Stoneblind: sall have as
tha's craven, witch, craws ower crown."

The hands fell. She snuffed the candle, plucking the
flame like a dead leaf, thriftily, and rose. The pack of
leaves, forgotten, lay muddled in ale, or drifted scrabbly
over fire and fleet, and foundered in the porridge; one
alighted on the hearth, and was gone, in a small frazzle
of lightning. "I mun just see to't moon," she said; and
slipping on her pattens, she went out, clangorous on the
glazy mud.

The travellers were left in darkness. "Ah," said the
tinker pensively, rubbing his nose and shivering. He
sidled closer to the fire, tumbling rushes with his trailing
coat; Craobh burrowed in the drift of rags, as if the coat
were nightwood, and the cot of cloud. He drowsed and
nodded by the chary coals. Ariane writhed in stifled fret-
fulness. By the reek and glower of the witch's fire, she
could not see her book: she needed it. She had to write
the prophecies before they faded from her, unbodied and
immense; to bind before she could begin to see, to knot
the wind in runes. She needed the reassurance of the act,
the touch on callus, and the soft, configured scratching.
Would the witch bring back the light?

At last, groping warily, she crept to the low door and
peered out. The dark was gathering; the cold was eager
out of doors. The witch's hedge of stunted thorn served
only to whet the wind. She spied Malykorne coming from
the dusk-drowned wood, in her pale apron and her leaf-
red cap, solemn and officious: pit pat paddle pat! The

moon was setting, thin as the tinker's earring, in a swathe of cloud. The air was green with frost. Mally crouched and rifled a tuft of grass, tucked something in her pouch. Then standing awkwardly on tiptoe, she snecked the wicket-gate behind her. With her iron heel, she broke the cat-ice of the spring, milkywhite as blindness, glazing, and she knelt and filled her sieve. Huffing to her feet, in a cloud of breath, she carried it, brimfull of darkness, to her thorn, and drenched its roots with air; again, and yet again, she fetched nothing in her riddle. The dark was heavy; it staggered her. She took up her rake, arachnid, far too long for her. Within the paling of her garth, she raked the leaves thrice round, in patterns that the wind consumed. They rose, and flocked to her, unleaving as a storm of birds that cried out in her language, whirled and whelmed, and withering to leaves: her crown of wings, her messengers, her eyes.

Ariane, behind the door, stared unmoving in an ecstasy of cold, and exalted fear. Her soul hung shivering on her skin, distilled like breath on rough wool. No one else had seen. The witch on the rimy grass called down the wind, ensouled the leaves; she quelled the birds to flaws of tattered darkness: an image sharp as in a little stone of crystal, and Ariane's alone. Unwittingly, she held the soulstone at her throat. She had caught a falling star; she longed now to possess the wind, for mastery, and the wild delight of knowing dance. Caught between her fierce desire and a cold passivity of spirit, she hung for a long moment on the sill; then sharply and quietly she closed the door, and stooping plucked the huddled tinker by the sleeve. "Now!" she whispered. "She won't see us. Run."

He looked up, startled by the fierce unreason in her voice; in the dark she could see the mothy pallor of his nose and cheek. "What, ista fey? There's snaw ont wind. We'd not last midnight, not bairn."

"But she's thralled us, she'll keep us . . ."

"Frae't wind's teeth, and worser: not starved in a ditch fort ravens. I's walked nights i' winter." He touched her shoulder. "Think on: tha'd nobbut be craws' baggin, and cawd fare at that. Fire here; no wolves: nowt nobbut wind and witch comes thruff yon awd hedge, in or out."

"Oh . . ." She was biting her hands, in fret and helpless fury.

He took them from her face, uncrumpling them patiently. "Hush, lass. What if? We's not nettles."

They heard the scrape and clink of iron on the stones. The latch rasped, and Malykorne came in, with cold-clouded spectacles, and draggled to the knee. Her overskirts were rucked and tucked and twisted in a great untidy bunch about her hips, and still more petticoats hung down, leaf on gnawed and tattered leaf, patch on patch like a cabbage, dun and grey and brown. The great bunch of keys she wore dangling (but why? they had seen no locks) clinked like ice-candles on a bough. She knocked the clods of earth from her feet.

"Cawd night to walk abroad in," she said, heeling off her pattens; and she twisted up her flagging headrail, her elbows jutting and jerking. Leaves fell, dry and thronging, scattering as she moved.

Ariane saw them falling from the air: so light, so ruinous. Yet seeing, she remembered nothing, only that she'd seen, forgotten—ah, but what? A throng of light, her longing. O she must have dreamed, once, of a storm and cry of leaves. She saw them darkly now, as isles in Lethe, dim as from the farther shore of sleep. No. Not a dream, but something seen and hidden; not sleep, but a spell. The witch had brought in darkness in a cloud, like breath about her: a cold unknowing clung like mist.

Turned back against the witch's lethe-tide, beclouded, Ariane stared fiercely inward. She can't have the leaves. They're mine. Unleaving birds. But waking, unendued with the ambiguous clarity of sleep, she could not envision what they flocked to: a gnarled and dusky tree, a standing stone? All gone but leaves and longing, and an owl's shadow of cold fear. She had wanted, what? to storm them, snatch, as she had caught Craobh's lightborn body, to her grief.

Yet she had not. She had not run, wild and headlong, scatter-souled, into the circle of the witch's garth, not joined the fell alluring dance. It would have faded as she—No. Oh no, it would have fanged her. And she'd almost—Only now it came to her, how nearly she'd been had. Fool's-mated. She had passed, and had not known what trial by wanlight she had played. Somehow, blindly, she had won.

Shaken and uncompassed, Ariane felt a queer elation. Poor awd attercap, she thought, poor Mally: thowt I'd look canny on thy shelf, didsta? Well, tha'st not getten me, I's slipped thy web. Yon moths, yon innocents (she glanced pitying at him and Craobh, back at their endless game of cobnuts): not see'd what I has see'd. Won't nowther laik wi thee. Don't want thy clarty soul. So there. She fleered at Mally's back. The witch's soul, she thought, would be an old clay marble, knapped and cracked and crazy, with an owl's beak: it wouldn't even roll.

The witch turned, baleful, in her louring skirts, cloud-grim and glaring haughtily: what's this? A leaf flirted out from her petticoats, and wry and skittish, flittered almost to the ground; then rose, and fleeted round her head.

Craobh laughed, as sudden in delight, as light-borne, as a rainbow on the scar of storm. "O the pretty howlet!" she cried, her hands curving round air. Giddy, she whirled lightly round with the leaf, and turned again, as in a dance. *"But Jenny Knap's the eldest born, and cowers in the moon."* She plucked the leaf from Mally's hair.

"Tha sall have it for thy sake, my soul, and a cage o bone forby," said Malykorne. "When's time."

"When it's time, it shall be," said Craobh; and lifting her hand, she blew the leaf away.

Ariane saw, poignantly, their oneness, witch and child: the low and dark and earthborn flowering in light, as from the ash and grease of a candle springs its burr of fire, unbodied and invulnerable, yet naked to the wind. Then with a pang she thought: but I have thralled the child. I have bound her to time. Cered in mortality, she would dwindle, mute, translating tallow briefly into flare and reek, devoured and devouring. The stone hung cold at Ariane's throat.

The witch stared at Craobh, absurdly solemn, truculent and wistful as a rhinoceros who scries a unicorn in the mirror; Craobh gazed back quite innocently, as if at her face bleared in a tin ladle, when she knew no other glass. Without her pattens, Malykorne was barely taller than the child, but twice as broad, huffish and glary as a tumbled owl, as round and brown and stumpy as an earthen crock, the very pattern of her baleful jugs. Mally twitched the child's jacket. "Hey up, lass, tha's buttoned crooked. Dragged thruff hedge?"

Craobh looked up at her seraphically. A spider dangled from the witch's cap, swung lightly to her spectacles.

"Huh," said Mally. She took up her broom, and swept indignantly at the leaf. "Mucky trollops."

Ariane bit her lip. She felt ticklishly close to laughter, at her peril; like one compelled to sneeze, unveiling the dust of ancient kings. Were these the hips that haunched a thousand aprons? And above—O fearful symmetry, she thought. What the ladle? What dread grasp? O dear.

Lifting her fiery cheeks, she caught the tinker's eye. He was pinch-faced with propriety, crimped, like an apple tart about to burst. Hey, she thought, with startled pleasure: hey, he's with me. The odd ones out. Unlightborn, light in mortal wise. Still clad in crazy tatters of his wits, though shaken, he was fleetingly endeared to her: in all this otherworld, most earthly, unestranged. Witches aren't ticklish. Wickedly, she bent behind her hand and whispered. "Sitha: Mallybesoms."

He crazed with laughter, shaking silently; he would've cracked up at any daft thing. And with it, he played out a swift furious voluptuous mime, sweeping round behind the witch's bristling back. Mally turned on them, redoubtable, her spectacles flashing malefically. But reckless with a wild delight, half fear, like falling, he swept on and crowed out loud. "Mallybesoms. Ah. Howlyboggles." Ariane gave a muffled sneezing squawk and hid her face, shaken with a guilty glee. "Mallyjugs," she blurted. She stuffed her sleeve in her mouth, helplessly, and wailed, "Oh damn, now I've done it." Wonder if spiders have any small talk?

Mally eyed the tinker, broom on hip. "Drowned thy wits?" she asked, imperturbably.

"Lang since," he said.

"Aye, but none deep enough." (*Rancor*, said the goose, and turned its back.) She glanced quizzically at Ariane. "Why's tha cowering i't dark? Flayed o shadows?"

She brought the rush-candle, its light swayed and spilling from her hands. From that first she lit two or three candles more, and stuck them precariously in crannies, whence they snivelled tallow down the walls. They gave a feebly skittish light. One, more drunken than the rest, scorched a skein of mouldered onions. They stank. Mally wiped her moon-blank rimy glasses on one of her petticoats, perched them on again askew, and unrucked her skirts, wherreting them with the whirr and flap of sparrows in the dust. She scraped and prodded at the porridge, consideringly, and then slopped in a jug of cold water, and after it the tatters of a maggoty cabbage, sallowed as her petticoats, and a herring on a string, for a whet. The fish shone coldly, condescendingly, as from the heavens: fox-fired.

Not again, thought Ariane, dismayed, as Mally rummaged in the crockery for bowls and spoons, in a rout of spiders and a storm of ash: it's always six o'clock now. And never tea-time.

"Could yer fancy a sward o bacon?" said the tinker, dandling it alluringly by Mally's nose. "We's to spare."

She regarded it with her head on one side, cross and lovesick. "That depends."

"Alas," he said ruefully, "it's nobbut rusty thirsty scranny stuff to give, and salt as a beggar's curse." Stone-faced, she set the ladle by; and taking the cup from his hand, stumped off to fill it from her cask. Behind the witch's back, he grinned at Ariane, and whispered, "Small tithe, an we's scaped yon seething: not spoon lang enough to sup *that*."

She nodded, wry-faced. "It's the resurrected cod."

"Aye, and see'd yon cabbish? Ranting wi mawks. Forby odd spider, fiddling fort dance."

Mally's new maggot, for as many as will. The Mawktown Strutters' Ball. "What if we just politely said no?"

"She'd have our bones for bait."

Mally had drawn three mugs of ale, and filled the tinker's unforfeit cup for him. Returning, she caught Ariane gazing resentfully at the pale and inviolate cheeses up above. "They's gey green as yet. When there's nowt up aloft, nobbut air, they's done."

Ariane remembered the rind of moon setting beyond the witch's hedge, and thought: but it was nearly full last night. O heavens. Hey, a Cheshire moon. She looked doubtfully at Mally in her dingy petticoats, and grinned with sly delight. Moon turned self, she thought: like the slattern's cheese in the folk song. Whatever does she milk? Not owls.

The tinker dipped his beak into the ale, demurely. Then he straked his worn knife on his sleeve, and divvied out the bacon fairly, a speck for each. Two for Mally. Having found a not too battered turnip for Craobh, and wiped it with his coat-tail, spit and rub, he pared away the mouldy bits. The bacon was cold and unctuous, but cleanly enough, gritty but not rancid; the ale was bitter and charnelly to Ariane's tongue, and to Craobh's by her wry face, though the tinker liked it well. Mally saw that his cup was never quite empty; he drank, uncomplainingly: the tide wavered between them. Ariane scraped some dispirited stray and squidgy raisins out of the seams of her backpack. The hoard was quickly gone, flapdragoned. She was saving the square of chocolate for ragnarok.

After their scant supper, the tinker sat bemused, murmuring to himself and plaiting rushes, all askew, but solemnly as if he bound his soul in rimes and baubles. ". . . *Tom alone and Cutty Joan, but Jenny—*Craws!" The frail thing broke. He set it down with others, whorled and clumsy cages, thwart or crumpled, in a crooked row; took up a snatch of garland, and began again. *". . . but Jenny Knap's th' eldest born . . ."* Now and then, he'd twitch absently, and crack a flea. Mally filled his cup.

Ariane raked out her cottered hair with her fingers, unbraiding it, bitterly mourning that forgotten comb. She was longing for a cup of tea. By stealth, when Mally's back was turned, she found a scrap of paper from her book. Her pen was dry (overlooked, she thought wryly, like the gossip's cow); so she wrote the witch's prophecies with a stump of pencil. They looked spidery by rushlight. Flittery, as if they'd change. She hoped the tinker would remember, but she doubted it. He'd lost his name.

The child was bent upon another game of her devising, played with stones and sloes and hazelnuts against a shadow. They were moved in complex knots and mazes, turning to a broken music, silent, unresolved, and crossing darkly in a sky of mind; or else at random, scattering. She'd made herself a ring of cobweb for her thumb; a knot of bright and cloudy dew still clung to it, like stars in a braid of shadow.

Ariane drew back into the shadow of a cruck, a great balk of tree between her and Malykorne. There were roots in the earthen floor, like bones beneath the fell of rushes, very ill to sit on. Gingerly, she brought out the cold frail windegg from her pocket. It was green as wintry dusk, and flawed and clouded with a freakish umbered grey: speckled like Sylvie's face. Quite vain: as light as breath. No crack in it. No clew. She wrapped it very gently, round and round in her mitten, and hid it deep. She sat and watched the others' games, the owl-witch at her work.

Malykorne crouched wide-lapped on her low stool, and drew up her withy basket of carding: sluts and snarls of fleece, woolgathered on the moor, so clagged with muck and clotted up with thorns and furze and wiry tufts of heather. She raked away doggedly, and from the shearing of her combs came clouds, long and grey as marestails. They loured in her apron. As she carded, she sang. She had a rackett's ninebent astonishing voice, deep and harsh, with a curious damped resonance. Her woodnotes leapt unbroken into a queer frail piping, fiercely inno- cent, soulless as a wren's charm. There was no pity in that voice; its plaints were emblematic as a bird's. The tinker echoed her, attuned, unconscious as a shaken bell.

Abrupt and ancient and unkempt, her songs were snatches, plucked from passing mortals, caught like clots of fleece amid her willful apprehending thorns. Some were grotesque, some stark—a death in a severed line— and some haunting: clarty-black or cloudy wisps, or stained or rudded as with blood. Others were corrupt and riddling, all crux and no wool. Tu-whooing and lal- ling, stone-throated, she sang: "*. . . and every nail on his true love's hand, it were like to an iron rake . . .*" And then: "*. . . a mantle of the burning gowd did keep him frae th' wind . . .*" And taking up another clot of wool, she sang, "*. . . catch hands and turn, turn stone . . .*"

Ariane tumbled upright, crying, "Where did you get that?"

"I't cup," she said, and laid down a cloud.

Ariane sat down. She had nearly snatched the witch and shaken her for Sylvie's song: as well ransack the wind. She drew back against the wall, half-hidden by the massive cruck, with her arms about her knees. One of Craobh's hazelnuts had rolled away. The tinker gazed about, vaguely distracted, blinking and blowing out his cheeks. Mally took up her work, another song.

Half-consciously, the tinker had echoed her, in word-less notes and graces, chiming soft and seldom as the after-rain from leaves: now still, now closing in one fall and drone of music, water into water. Now as she sang, he came in; their voices rose in near parallel, a crossing harmony like the bents of an old barn, gaunt and noble, a granary of shadows. The witch broke off, and he flapped on for a phrase or so, naked as a startled bird, a martin in the eaves. Then he tumbled into silence like a hare down its hole. He laughed confusedly. "Eh, not bosky, is I?"

"Tha'rt wood." She filled his cup. "I don't knaw how it ends," she said. "Tha does." She stared, implacable as Caedmon's angel, hovering fastidiously above the Abbess of Whitby's mucky byre.

He bent his head, coughing and clearing his throat and sternly grimacing, harking to his hands like seashells; then he sang. His voice rose, ungainly as a heron, into grace. The cup of ale was at his hand; the wind was in the eaves, and the wood around them, rising to his note. He sang on, alone, and he himself became the green and bitter loves, the leaves, the deaths and journeyings. He was the harp of bone, the wren, the gallows and the sword, the ship whose mast was tree; he was the fool, the maiden, and the king, the witch and the unborn child, the hawk, the slayer and the slain. By his candle, where he walked was turned to wood, from darkness; there he made his endless way, amid its thorns and hungers, and the passing sweetness of its spring, unbowered but for light. Sylvie's song was woven in its branches, with the cry of ravens and of Mally's geese. It was a changeless world, beyond time; and yet within, the drops of blood upon the snow were not unspilled, and the dark ship did not sail against the wind; and yet again, the wheel came up bright with water from the dark, fatal and eternally reborn. The light is changeless, though the candle burns. Craobh sat up in darkness, listening; and Ariane unmoving heard, beneath the sun and the unwaning moon, long time and timeless, as the fire sank.

Huddled in the leaves and ashes on the earthen floor, adrift, she dreamed and started, drowsed and woke. His voice had fallen, lower than the wind, Novembered, dying intently as a candle. Rarely now, a note would rise, dark and momentary as a homeward bird against the last green clarity of evening; while all below lay dusky wood, whose roots drank deep of silence: one endless branching ballad and one journey, the shadow of his wavering rushlight. He drew breath. His hair was tousled. His eyes were shut, but his hands moved still, tranced and unaware, curving to one ear, falling, tallying, gnomic: ah, but see.

The witch eyed him as she would a lantern with a farthing dip in snuff: can I get there by candlelight? But where? All ways were dark; belantered and amazed, he lapsed into stumbling forgetfulness and babble, hush ba and lilly ba, fa and lillylow. Flickering fantastically, barely unquenched above his pool of ale, he guttered, swaled and sank, slumped among the ashes. Mally bent and tweaked his hair, as if to pinch the wick.

Wary, Ariane set herself to watch, solicitous for the child, asleep now at her side, and pitying the tinker's cold unrestful lethe. She pressed Mally's wooden ale-cup to her scorched cheek, then to her cold brow, and felt its grain, scrubbed harsh as a cat's tongue, exhaling a pungent and a musty breath. Her thousand scratches tingled like a walking-map of hell. She was sitting on a ravenshoard of leaves and bones and plundered hair; and surely, that was a brooch? A string of birds' claws swung beside her from the beam. Her head on her knees felt cavernous and unswept, its crow-haunted rafters creaking, sooty with unvented sleep. She nodded, twitched awake, tweaked back by riddling phantoms. The windegg lay in her pocket. A sly gift, she thought, impassive, precious, frail: bestowed with tutelary malice. "Tha can seethe water in't," the witch had said.

Malykorne still sat at her carding, crouched and

cloaked in shadow, like an old thorn tree hung with moon-bleached linen that affrights the belated traveller. Her lap was heaped with cloud. Ariane heard the rasp and rustle of her combs, tearing like blunt scythes, wolfishly. She heard the tinker's muttering as he lay, scrawny as a hare's old jacket, fitfully asleep. Craobh made no sound at all. The rushlight flared, and dying, caught a wary gleam: the veiled lustre of a Persian jar, rubbed bright where a passing skirt had brushed it; a sword; a web; a mirror; eyes.

The witch rose, uncumbering of her cloud, walking unperplexed through her cluttered hovel as the moon through a hedgerow. Her shears hung at her side, bright and cruel. She gathered up Craobh in her apron.

Ariane felt a sudden horror of cold and lightness at her back, as if she had grown a wing. Its feathers hackled; but her flesh was stone. She thought of witch-tales, of children seethed for a single bone, that placed beneath the witch's tongue would let her walk unseen; of blood caught in a cup of stone; of subtler cruelties of transformation.

Craobh's soul. But she'd've taken it, if she—No. Waited till we slept. Cry out? Cold iron. Where's the tinker's knife? I trusted her. Could I—Would Mally bleed? Or was she semblance, earth and wind, a walking root? Or—But that was dream, the witch as cold bright baleful moon. She was so small. So absurdly cross. In her own way she'd fed and housed them. Touch the stone? Beyond you. Light. She'd snatch it. Grab the scissors? See tha don't cut thysen, said owl. Her bread and salt. Oh, this is stupid. I'm scared. Ariane stiffened with an unsprung vehemence, caught up in chains of absurdity and compunction, afraid to make a scene. O why didn't he wake up?

Lightly as a dead wren, the witch bore the sleeping child, and prying open a cupboard door, she popped her in.

"No!" cried Ariane. "Ah, don't."

But the owl's pantry was a bed, high and narrow, with a patchwork counterpane, heathish grey and brown. The witch covered the child, tucking her up as if she were bread rising. Nettled with weariness, Ariane staggered up, to wrap herself in a coat and dignity, and topple on the straw; but the witch caught her up in her sibylline arms, plumy and inexorable, and laid her in the bed.

The sheets were coarse and clean as wind; the feather-bed as harsh and huge as air, crazing under her like cat-ice as she sank. It smelled of wormwood, and of leaves of alder, there, beneath the gnarled and bitten trees of the wild garden; her sleep was landscape, earth and sky. Within the O of cold green air hung linen stiffening with frost, wind-bellied, bound, ecstatic. They were souls in flight, straining and tugging at the pegs of green cleft hazel. A labyrinth of lines turned inward, pale within pale of dancers; dusk and thorny trees among them, woodcut black against the ghostly, moving sheets. The grass was botched with unripe apples, winter-blighted; hoar with rimed and blackened weeds. Dead leaves caught fast in crazy ice. Beyond, the fells were long and still; the pale moon set. It was dusk beneath the wintry star, amid the cold clean lines where Mally walked, slowly, with her creaky wicker basket, folding the sheets of light.

Naked and soulless, for her own shift danced among the linen, Ariane walked to the hedge. It was leafless, hung with frost. She could not find the gate. Far beyond on a green bank, Craobh slept, and from her side sprang a tree of thorn; her dreams were cold white flowers, knots of stars. Beyond again lay her wood, like a green wave going out. And at the wood's edge, but within, stood Sylvie, odd and brown amid the waking trees. She was turning away from her, turning back into wood. Ariane beat against the thorns. The branches were hawed with her bright blood, though she felt nothing. If only she had a sword, to hew . . .

Something in the hovel fell and clinked. Ariane started, turned and sank. The wrinkled firelight touched her eyelids, ah, hush; while at her back lay the moveless sea of hills, the tranquil storm. Beyond the draughty door of the wood, by ember-light, she saw the witch take the cup from the tinker's hand, and haul him up in her strong arms, as she would bind a sheaf of barley. He half woke, blinking at her in brief wonder, like a child at the moon, the unearthly and familiar nurse of sleep; and even as she touched his brow, he slumped against her. "Come up, lad."

She tumbled him in, drowsy as a heap of leaves, and he sank to sleep; so that all east of Ariane, there lay a wood of oak and beech and hazel, slumbering in an autumn like a keeping-pear, sweet and sound; and far below, the wanderer in his wood ran on, on to the green scarth at the world's end, cloud beyond cloud, the spring of time. And Ariane, waking for a moment, saw that the witch's hovel was not of time: that she herself had not lost Sylvie, had found and would not find her, nor had they ever met. She slept; and perhaps the witch herself clambered in, a cold serenity, but soft as wings: cloud or featherbed or fall of snow; the last that Ariane knew was, O the swans.

IV

The Moon's
Old Riddle

Looks like snow, thought Sylvie, craning into dusk
through edgeless woods at something far and pale, too
low for the elusive moon. Hey, but when had it stopped
being the moon she was after? Air? Sylvie turned. Hey,
where'd she go? No candle. Out? No snow. That's weird,
oh hell, that's scary. She looked up. No stars. She'd
never been this far before. If this were Cloud—Don't
freak, she told herself. You can't go back. Like dreaming: you just do it, you go on. And if it's somewhere
else? A fall, but crazier? There's still Nan's woods, back
there. That stays. And then there's choices here, there's
farther in. A story. See what turns up. She hunched her
shoulders, peering at the gloom. The whiteness, tatters,
flapped and whirred. Not dogwoods, anyway. Too wintry. Swans?

Stalking nearer, wary, curious, she saw a fierce little
stumpy woman, brown as mandrake, snatch an owl from
the air, and shake and fold it catty-corner, wing to wing.
But the owl was a ragged smock.

Sylvie clapped hands, as the leaves did: Hey, again!
Do that again! She craned closer in the thicket. All round
her, the thorns and hazels of the underwood were hung
with rags, wind-rattled, pale as cloud; and the moonfaced
redcapped woman stooped and stumped about her busi-
ness, snatching and subduing them, filling up her wicker
basket. How it creaked! The wind was getting up. The
rags bated wildly on the thorns in a bird's-wing rush and
clatter loud as fire; the air pelted down with twigs, nuts,
hailstones, thronging hurly-burly with the leaves, all

155

edged and unbodied malice. One, sharp as holly, drew a scrawl of blood from Sylvie's cheek.

Bruised and exhilarated, she wheeled about, slashing at the wind; and sidelong through the leaves, she saw the witch's thornblack scornful gaze, her dwarfish dusky figure hulked against the tattered glory of the light. Sylvie laughed out loud for joy: I see the moon.

The witch turned, calling out a word, and straight at Sylvie's eyes, moonpale with scything talons, stooped an owl. Sylvie caught it in her outflung arms. It was an apron. Stark with frost, windribbed, witchmoved, it had an owlish feel to it: quilly and malign.

Ha, got you! You'd tear me if you could, she thought, bundling it up; and she tossed it in the basket. Now what?

Behind you. Thorn is hallows!

Windblown herself and woven, tangled in the crazy game of tag, Sylvie darted out, and in and out, among the leaves and thorns, touched last! and chasing after scraps of scattering moonlight, owlets: all the little witches in the garden. Fox and geese. Odd bits of clothing, fine and coarse, and quick with wind: a cap with strings, a romping petticoat, a baby's shirt, a rag-tag shred of patchwork faded grey and brown. A child.

Hey, where'd it go?

To Babylon. Catch hands and turn, turn stone. With Tom alone, and Cutty Joan—

It's gone. Moon and wind.

Sylvie caught a shirt from the branches, hiding, and a rantipole smock, and all rags and tatters from the thorns. They were crabbed with darns, and dancing; wrenched and wrung and cockled; nettle-stitched with frost, or patched with leaves on patches; shrewd and innocent, and stuck with twigs, bristling with teased-out threads: all folding, cold and clean as moonlight, dovelike, doucely in her hands. Rags of linen. Not hers anyway, thought Sylvie, glancing at the witch's gnawed and sallowed petticoats: nothing like her shape.

Hedge-backward through the branches, bent and witchful, stalked the earthbrown woman, tweaking and twitching down her washing, with her apron full of pegs. Sylvie watched her, delighted. She liked her sharpnosed face: cross, aloof, assertive, imperturbable and wary; she liked her dumpy draggled figure, wind-mollocked and disdaining wind, though once when it rumped her petticoats about her ears, she turned and gave nothing a baleful stare, as if it were a sticky child. Her cap was snatched askew. She was all over leaves, and looked like an abandoned rookery.

One huge sheet was left, swagged and shaken on a thorn tree. Sylvie took two corners of the shroud of wind, coming with light measured steps to meet the witch who held the others. So they met: hand to gnarled brown hand, as dancers touch, stately to a cold weird music, breathless; then withdrawing. The sheet danced in an ecstatic fury, caught between their cornered gravity. Once, and halved; again, and quartered; and in ritual, she relinquished, and the witch folded away the light. The basket was full.

Sylvie hefted it, heavy as a thundercloud, by its worn and splintery handles. "Where's this go?"

"Tha's here," said the witch, loftily.

Sylvie sat down in the basket. Out of breath, she considered her scratches; what she saw might be illusion, but the thorns were real enough. And there was nowhere else, no sleep, no bed. It's like a falling star, she thought, the travelling's the light, and waking—Dark. How strange. Her hair whipped her face. She sneezed, and wrinkling for another sneeze, she fumbled in her pockets: guitar strings, cough drops—huh? Oh, crumbs of fir-cones—and a soggy mitten. No tissues. She grinned at the thought of the witch's clean handkerchiefs: deea, peck my nose off. Blackbirds. Wiping her nose on her sleeve, she remembered being little, hiding under a clothesbasket. It had made a woven night that creaked and murmured, pricked with stars. A tortoise-world. Here I am, going on.

The witch eyed her, sly, amused.

Sylvie stared back, but askew of her, abstracted: not working at the witch for now, but at her wood, by her light. The witch turned and got on with it. Back and forth, in and out, she bustled, twitching nothing from the twigs, winding nothing in a tidy ball. "What's here?" said Sylvie.

"What tha seest. Cloud."

A riddle: what is now and nowhere? Here. And where's here, anyway? Not Cloud. Well, not our Cloud, not mine and Air's. Not in the cards, but elsewhere, somewhere that I dreamed? Itself. But whose else could it be? And who's this witch here, counting clothespins, winding cobwebs round her thumb? Not ours. Messier than ours. Air'd like the cap, though. And the way she talks, sort of rustic: Clewed. Sylvie turned. A clump of scarecrow thorns; a muddied spring; a rake choked with fallen leaves. (A rake? In the woods?) Not quite a cross-roads, but a scrawl of indeterminate paths. Already she'd forgotten the way she'd come.

No way at all, but years. The witch was strange to her, but she knew this owly wood. Nan had told it. It was a wilder and more ancient forest than the green thin woods of her childhood. Its paths were older, ghostlier; its roots were dark. A ballad wood. It came with red squirrels and whitethorns; wolves, hedgehogs, sloes and witches; goose girls and swineherds and swans turned men. The birds would speak. If you tasted their blood, you would understand their grieving voices; and the leaves would tell their old dry endless tale in falling, and the paths would turn toward farther meetings, darker falls, and none by chance: the wood was all the tales that were. Though some were hidden in the trees. No clouds: they'd folded them away. No sun. No moon, but she would find it: it was in the wood, was part of it. A piece. By not staring, she would find them all: the witch's spectacles, the moon and stars, the sword, the naked skyblack children.

Twisting her hair, Sylvie looked at her bootlace, at the leaves by her feet. In the hollow of an oakroot, all tumbled together, lay an old thin faded nutshell, and a fir-cone (but the wood's deciduous, she thought) beside a hailstone like a ghostly marble. It was cold, and dusty with the mould of leaves, ephemeral; but burred within, scarred and skeletal with light. She held it to her eye.

The witch in the ice was bent and bleared within her furl of cold red cap, owlnosed, both grotesque and strangely shining. Sylvie laughed with wonder; then the stone was dark, and bright. Caught and swift and strange

within the eye of dreams, the visions altered. She scried
them, intent. But the ice was slurring in her fingers,
dwindling; suddenly uneasy, she set it down, fingering
the blind sweet nut for solace, the alien and prickly
fircone.

"Asta see'd owt?"

"A man in a brownish sort of long coat, asleep—or
dead"—she touched wood—"under a tree. White things
on a hill, stones, I think: they were sort of blobby. Moving. Dark like now, but watchful, and no woods: only a
stunted sort of thorny tree, but like a cold little person
too, or frightened, with her head on her knees, and
clouds of hair, crouched over a roundish little moony
thing. Mourning, or greedy, or afraid. She—it shone out,
the clouds were too thin to hide it. There was a kind
of—not aura—seizing, like a black corona, like an iron
ring, all round the periphery." She twiddled her hair,
frowning. "That's all. And your glasses. On that stump."

The witch settled them on her nose, and beckoned.
Sylvie tumbled up—what next?—and the witch set the
great creaking basket on her hip. No owl ever made so
great a rushy uproar through the leaves. Sylvie stumbled
after in the dusk. They walked a little way, eight or nine
steps through the dark wood; then crouching, the witch
tucked her burden in a bush like any other, and rose and
turned and with the flat of her hand, on tiptoe, pushed
nothing to behind them. It fell quiet. The wind was shut
behind the door. "I mun shut souls i't cupboard," she
said, "or birds'll fret at them."

They were standing in the wood, roofless to the sky,
unwalled; and yet within a fastness, hedged intangibly as
the burr of a candle is. With her eyes closed, she'd know
her hand was in the fire: so blindly, absolutely, Sylvie
knew they'd come into the witch's hovel. They were here.
The hallows stood, unseen and unassailable, unwindowed,
but with ways beyond and in. Beyond, she knew, stood
naked hills: wind and stones. Within, a furtive flickering
fire burned on a low rough hearth of stones; from behind
the door, she had not seen it.

The witch crouched by the spring, and taking a wooden
cup from her skirts, she filled it. Rising, she handed it

to Sylvie: black clear water, black and furry leaves, but flecked with pallor, twirling and decaying.

"Thank you," Sylvie said (and thought: me and Cat playing witches, this is flying drink, the time we drank the yew); but curious, polite to witches, irresistibly dared, she drank.

It was strong as death, as roots that crack the stone. Earthfast, she was light and still, and saw the stars reel round her through the rags of cloud: ship ladle swan harp of bone gallows wren witch tower hare light horseman scarecrow ship . . .

"Deea, what's in this stuff?"

"Ale," said the witch. "Come by t'fire."

Sylvie followed on her long light legs. The winter she had scarlet fever, the rain beat on the glass; the branches scraped. Nan's zoetrope whirled on the dark crazy quilt: hurled high in the wicker basket, the toy witch swept the cobweb clouds. The winking moon wore spectacles. Flying before the wind, Sylvie heard the gabbled fugue of geese. Woodwings. She ran down the bare mountain with the spider-cat behind her, fast, still fast, unmoving, while her grandmother's lamp fled from her down the sky. Two, one, seven tarnished moons. She jumped. The swan was Polly's apron blowing, was the White Queen's shawl caught on a thorny-bush that moved and snuffled: Mrs. Tiggy-Winkle whined thrice and once. The charm's wound up. The wind. Asleep. As we went round and round. Slow. Sick. The darkness cleared before the wind: the stars blazed out again. Shivering and swaying, she had forgotten which side of winter she was on, fall or spring: a leafless time.

They sat. The witch scrunched and wriggled down her huge hips, with a furious rustling, beside the fierce glowering fire. Her skirts were barbed with innumerable little wicked burs. She stared imperiously over her hulking knees. Sylvie slithered down. The leaves were dryish, crimped and rustling, but insidiously slick beneath. The cold barren field. Above its stillness, the sky was full of scudding rack and scurry.

"Yon's a night's wark ower," said the witch, gazing up at the clouds. She set a cracked charred vessel on the fire to brew: the ale and a handful of fallen crabs, stems, sticks and all. They withered, seething, brown as bat-wings, wrinkled, wry and leathern; abob, then bursting, frothing clouds of pulp and black malicious seeds. A powdering of dry leaves floated.

They shared the cup, turn and turn, sitting close as two gossips, but in witchful silence. Owls of a feather, drinking down the moon. Weird sisters. The drink imposed a clarity; it fulfilled and it took away.

Sylvie saw herself and not herself, black like a woodcut shepherd bent against a wind of relentless feathers, with her stick and bag, going up a moorland white with frost. She saw walls of dry stone, a knot of standing stones against the sky. She saw the hooked geometries of rimy heath. Ravens were after her, the iron ring was closing. The winter sun hung fire. She saw a cup of crazed and milky moonwhite porcelain, saw children sleeping in the wood, beneath light birds, dry leaves; leaves falling through the bitter tea, an anxious, exalted face: Ariane's. The ship was sailing, though its mast was a great-rooted tree, its leaves far-drifting stars. She was a sword in someone's hand. She heard a ring of enweaving musics, endless, small and clear and ancient, pure as gravity and light; yet creating all in beautiful complexity, like a carol of the cold rejoicing stars. She heard a darker voice than hers, rising from the earth to meet, to cross her falling voice; she heard the intervals, though not what they sang.

How long had she been singing? Her throat was hoarse and dry, it hurt. The candle's nearly out, she thought. What card? But Ariane was silent. Cramped, unknowing, Sylvie shifted her forgotten weight, and put her palm down on a terrible sharpness. O the Ravens. They take eyes, she thought; and woke. No Ariane, no moorland. Blood. She winced, clutching her pierced hand, grimac-ing. The fall was broken glass, half-buried in the earth. The quilt was leaves. Ravens? There were never any— No. That was playing, this is Cloud. She watched the slow dark jewels of blood, black by moonlight, in a slid-ing chain.

"What ravens?" Her cheeks burned. "Can I have some just water?"

The witch peered haughtily at her, arching her hand over the mouth of the cup, as if warding it from sly malicious thievery, from sipping beaks. Her lip twitched. Solemnly, reluctantly, she gave the cup to Sylvie. It held water, cold and muddy. Sylvie gulped it, and wiped her dry cracked wetted mouth with the back of her good hand. The other she wrapped in her scarf.

"Ravens is t'other one's: her eyes," said the witch. "They's not leaves, but ashes. Stoneblind hersen: sees nobbut what she craves, nowt as dies. Souls." Her hair had tumbled down in elf-locks, dark and stiff, about her face and shoulders, from beneath her dark red cap; her frost-blank glasses caught the firelight. She rubbed them in her petticoat. "Doubt she'll not regard thee, tha bleeds still; t'cup's not made thee light as yet, nor wood." She glanced at the scarf. "Would slay thee unregarding allt same, fort ravens' fee: has servants mun be fed. And thy soul's not all unglinty. Sitha: tha munnot ask nowt of her, or nowt s'll tha have; nor look in her seeming-glass, nor turn frae her dance."

There was a splinter of glass still in Sylvie's hand. She found it with her tongue and bit at it. "Do I walk there?"

"Back o't wind? Aye, and beyont. By candlelight: I's sent awd Tom-wi't-lantern on afore."

"Oh rats, I thought I'd get to fly. Ouch. Got it." She spat away the grain of glass. "And then what, when I meet the other one, the raven witch? Will I know her?"

The owl witch was not so absurdly huffed and rumpled as Sylvie first had thought. She had a fierce small gravity, but absolute, indrawing: she compelled. A root slumped on the fire, set flakes of ashes whirling, eyed with red, then eyeless, thronged like crows. "Annis? Tha'lt see whatever sark she wears. She is my marrow. Knots wind, stills water, gnarls stone. She'll not come i't wood, for that I's not swept. What's leaves to her? Cannot spell them. Keeps her hunt aloft, and her hall below. Riddles i't dark. Gnaws moon to't rind as wick as ever I can turn t'light."

Sylvie stirred the fire. "But that's balance, moon and dark of moon: it's a sort of dance. Like death. Things have shadows."

"Aye, but shadow casts no moon."

"So is she, is Annis, annihilating you?"

"Eeh no, not I: I were not made, I's no soul. Nor she:

we is and not, nowt else. We's eldest and alone. But
after us came lightborn. Cloud bairns. They's lightfast
and unfast i't earth, unturned and turning all: they dance
what is. Annis cannot thole them, for that they's souls
and sight, and work creation in her dark; cannot thole a
candle burning, for that it warps and swales and dwines,
for all she craves its light. Tholes nowt unfast: nor dance,
nor turn o't moon, nor owt as springs. Thinks she: why
journey, sint end is dark? Why make, sin t'soul is
marred, becoming such carrion as earth?"

"But the going on's the end, I thought. The dance is."

"Nowt's endless." The witch looked sidelong at her,
shrewdly. "Dance drops hands, light turns, owt's elsewhere and gone; but O's all endless and for ae: so Annis
thinks. Not asked thee. Has set her hunt on lightborn,
to bring them til her hand. They's stones for her ring,
s'll not dance, being nowt; and souls for her crown.
Thraws eyes to't ravens, dark her jackal eats owt else.
T'bairns has all but one and t'other one been ta'en:
stone-fast. Wood fades, waters fail, stars slur away.
Come ring is closed, all's endless, all s'll end but Annis
and I and dark."

"What . . ."

"Tha's my sword. Tha'rt to unbind their souls, unblinding Annis: will knaw knot when it's cut." The fire
fleered in her crooked spectacles. She bent forward and
tweaked Sylvie's sleeve. "I's given word to't wind o thy
coming. I has a gowk wi an egg s'd daze Annis, and an
awd flaycraw s'd daunt ravens. T'hunt's thy riddle."

"Right. Now?"

"I't morning. Thoo's asleep."

Sylvie laughed and pinched herself. "Am I? Are you
dreaming me? What if I wake up? But why do you need
me? You're pretty fearsome."

"Cannot come where I's not, cannot wound where I
is; she and I is ae thing." Her eyes said, come: the dark,
the real and unloving eyes. Cold white and ancient,
hunched within the devouring crescent of her self, her
sister dark, drawing on with her nightwind hair to dark
adventure, she stared at Sylvie from the eaves of the
shadowed wood. Elsewhere. Not a leaf had stirred.

Staggering up on her unsteady legs, elated, terrified,

Sylvie put her hands out to ascertain, and where the witch had seemed to be, touched nothing, wind and birds: a flurry of unbodied wings, a storm of talons, beaks, that rent and rent and drew no blood. Owl dreams. The nightwind hair was furies. Round she wheeled, and saw the knowing moon behind her, deeper in the wood, and ran and roughly hugged the wind. No moon. She turned again dizzily, March-mad, and saw the witch, crouched unmoving by the fire with her ale. All else had turned.

"Deea! What a headful of curlers." Sylvie giggled, drunk with rough games, flumping down beside her. The witch laughed, a dark deep bottly hoo-hooing, like a woodwind with the spit knocked out, jigging and enjoying, innocent of malice. Leaning crazily, conspiratorially, against each other, they crowed.

The witch recovered first, pursing up her dignity. "Eeh, my souls," she said. "Reyk me yon cup, lass." She turned on Sylvie her huge solemn face, and the ritually proffered cup. Though her cheeks were primmed and a wicked pink, she spoke gravely.

"Wassail."

"Wassail," said Sylvie, with mirroring mock solemnity.

"Wha's ale? Moon's." The witch hiccoughed.

Sylvie rather spoilt it, blurting into her beer. *Wassail the moon.* Hey, I saw your light. Come down and let us in.

Scrabbling down into the leaves for warmth, Sylvie found a cold sharp heavy thing: a rusted knife, horn and iron. Like her old one. It lay on her palm. She put it in her pocket. *Buttoning up me trousers*, she thought, yawning, smiling: then I'll go. I'll go quiet. *Cap and feathers.* Ah, this draught had made her drowsy. Dirty toes, she thought (curling them), Tom o' Bedlam, horse of air. Dark tower. The sky was all cloud; her bones sank to sleep. Walk there by candlelight. The wood was autumned with the fire. Drowsy, all adrift, she thought: Oh, I wanted to ask her what we were singing, when I heard the music in the dream. She raised her face.

But she could not speak. The cup, giving dreams, had taken voice and all, all that wakes. Her star was falling, she was lightfast. So she fell.

At some door or turning, she would need to answer with those riddling verses: they would be some clew or charm. The witch gave nothing but was needful, though darkly, in dreams, in runes, in mirrors. Nothing for the asking. All cloudy. All in knots. Nodding, Sylvie evoked her dream, remembering the music (had she heard it?) not as voices, but as wind in reeds, or birds. Her own voice and the other's. One clear and wandering, the other darker, spellbound, like a shadow tree in water: fall of leaf turned rising, roots of branching. A rhyme. But which voice fell, and which was rising, who was shadow? Who dreamed? Barely, she recalled a counterpoint, a crossing harmony, that lingered though the notes had gone; as rimefrost, breathed on and no rime at all, still ghostly keeps its crystalline instarriness.

Her hands were stone; she leaned against the witch's harsh quilly shoulder, snuggling in until only the cold crescent of her cheek was naked to the windy dark. With a comb of horn, the witch unbound and combed their mingled hair together, long, long and nightfall, Sylvie falling from the air in stars of soul. Eyes perseids. She curled asleep in Mally's lap.

Turning over after an unremembered iron dream, Sylvie woke. The dark was paling. Far below herself, she was lying on a huge bare hill, a cloud of earth, at the crossroads of no trodden ways, beside a hoary standing stone. Snow lay thinly in the folds of her cloak, a harsh and clumsy web of wool, gnarled threads of northwind grey; her cheek was on a grey skin bag, and in her hand a staff.

Ariane woke in sallow darkness. She had a minotaur headache, lurking and louring in her labyrinth of skull, sullenly insistent. It roared for bone porridge. Shaggy ill-made creatures, caveblind, blood-sacrifices, twitched and snuffled in their dreams of light. She lay awhile bewildered in the stifling dark: no wood, no sky. Earthweight on her. Gnarled roots, entangling—were they bodies? Am I dead? What she remembered of a moving whiteness, of souls, faded from her like snow in black water, elusive as a dream, but whose loss was sharper grief. Herself was the foul ditch, a soul's grave of spirit.

Her hand found a gall, a strangeness: the swaddled windegg, like a changeling at her breast, impassive, frail and false. Then panicking, she groped until she touched Craobh's soul, slewed round her side and cold still as hail, for all its lying with her. It had bruised her collarbone. Holding it, she felt a desolation and a lightness, like bereavement, a clarity of night. Malykorne had risen, had been sleep itself.

Mally's bed. They lay in the witch's cupboard, in a jackstraw heap of limbs. Some, thought Ariane, were hers. Waked now, she felt the bony weight of bodies, and the hulk and harshness of coarse woollens: rasp and rustle, itch and cloying and close air. Breathing. It was not to be endured. She fumbled anxiously for the door; there had to be a door somewhere. Her groping hand encountered, closed upon, a small rather gritty foot, cold and delicate; then touched, recoiling, skin and bone and filthy hair, yet soft beneath as foxfell. Oh. Oh dear. At last, scrabbling at the sallow crack of light, her fingers grazed the wooden sneck, only just within her reach, and stiff to work. The door creaked open a reluctant inch.

Chill draught and ashen light. Her eyes moved on clumsy cords and hooks; she wore a fox's mask of fever. Bed. Daylight. Frowst. Only three bodies, after all. Asleep. Craobh lay inward by the wall, turned as the witch had dealt her out: the Child, reversed. Oblivion. Unbirth. Retreat. She huddled to herself in shadow. All dusk, but a mooncurved cheek, a hand curled upward, mute and empty as a shell.

Between Ariane and the door, the tinker sprawled and shuddered, gawky, kneed and elbowed like a load of kindling. His face looked unsouled: a burnt-out turnip lantern, hollowed, grimy and collapsed, all nose and ears, and spiky tousled hair. He stank of ale and sweat and ashes. She couldn't move without waking him; and she needed desperately to get up. She lay fiercely still, with a burning-glass glare at his sodden slumber; so he woke, twitching and flailing feebly, like a half-drowned moth. "Not yet," he muttered.

"You'll wake the child!" Ariane whispered savagely, and rearing up blowzily onto her knees, taking the covers with her, she thrust open the cupboard door. (Alice with one foot up the chimney, she thought absurdly: poor Bill.) She loomed over him, wild-haired and blue with cold, frieze-mantled, like some ancient Celtic goddess of war. He shut his eyes.

"I think I's dying," he said hoarsely.

"Excuse me, I've got to get out," said Ariane-as-Badhbh, and clambered over him. The hovel was iron-cold, and her flesh shrank; but the frost put a formality on her, a stalking dignity, glazing over her queasy mortality with a chaste aloofness. As withered leaves before my chariot, she thought, and wrapped her coat about her, with a grandeur hobbled by the witch's crockery from swirl to abject huddle.

There was no sign of Malykorne; she was everywhere: a watchful silence, disquieting. Ariane poked about forlornly in the ashy dusk, unwindowed. She was wary: any leaf could be the witch, a web dishevelled could spell unchance. The fire was out, and reeking ash, the floor unswept. The hamper full of clouds was gone. In the cauldron, slops of nettlish porridge were congealed. She looked hastily away. A spider skated on a pool of ale, amid unscoured pots. What might have been a kist of meal, guiltily pried open, was full of feathers, eggshells, iron keys. The witch's spectacles mocked her from a shelf, and all the rude jugs fleered. No breakfast.

But there, thank heaven, was her bag, bulging and forlornly downy, like an errant Cupid. She shook it and cradled it, she slapped and brushed it off, rough in her fond anxiety. The tinker's hat, with its draggled feather, hung amid the mawky cheeses, and his heaped greatcoat lay in the dankest corner with the toadstools, perambulated by an anxious spider (no doubt muttering, *No more twist*, to itself). Ariane had a wicked impulse to try the witch's spectacles (O what does the moon see? Cloud?); but turned away. She saw a comb on the table, gat-toothed and alluring; but she dared not borrow: would likely elf her locks. Beside it stood the tinker's cup. A leaf lay in the bottom with the dregs of ale, in which her mirrored face looked awful: collied, fierce and wavering.

She laughed at this appalling vision, remembering the witch's narrow bed, seeing herself reared up, blue and horrid, over him, like a ballad run backward: lady-into-hag. No doubt with teeth like tethering-stakes, the better to craunch on blood and bones; and nails like iron rakes.

In her stocking feet, she padded shrewdly to the door, and raised the latch. No one forbade her; but she shivered, caught between disquiet and the fierce malicious furtive glee of playing witch. She let in a beak of light. Affronted, she blinked, behind her out-turned hand; yet after all, it was a sad grey morning, if morning it was.

The wood had come back. Crow-dark, it thronged the hills, it broke the stone with taloned roots: alighted, yet immutable, and old as earth. No leaves: had winter fallen as they slept? Had Cloud another door? The wood was shrouded in a roke of mist, ensnarled like the thorns in Mally's night-combed cloud. Within the hedge lay an O of rimy garth, moonwhite as if it mirrored sky. The rake lay clawed upward, stark as a dead crow. A hare's track

had torn stigmata in the frost, but crossways; there was
neither sign nor scar of Mally's passing. So then she
lurked within doors; had flown away; was not of earth;
or else was translated with the wood.

No leaves, thought Ariane: she's made it winter. And
Sylvie's wood was fall. I must have got up on the wrong
side of bed. Hell, they're all wrong. But even as she
looked, the earth came blackened through the dying
frost. The wind had shifted toward rain.

Ariane raked through her dank and sleep-snarled hair.
She could have crunched it up by handfuls, like dead
leaves. She felt a snuffling cloying scratchiness at the
back of her nose, that each breath grated raw as nutmeg.
She was getting a cold, she *never* got colds, and she had
no handkerchief: another thing she'd forgotten.

Turning furiously, she saw the tinker huddled up in
bed, hugging his elbows, his face wan and greenly under-
painted, like an old Sienese martyr. "There's a teapot,
damn it, there must be tea," she said.

"Don't tha drink it," he said forlornly. He had no
voice left. He sat with a sort of slewed dignity—penny
for the guy!—lolling stiffly in its pushchair, pitiful and
sinister. Gingerly, he groped for the floor. For all his
slightness, he stood like an old dancing bear, shambling
from foot to foot, mumbling old ends of nightmares like
a bone; but his head he bore like her windegg. "Ough.
Great fool I is. Daft sin I were born." He shook the
Persian jar: no water. He pressed it, like a cool and
formal heaven, to his cheek. "Where . . . ?"

"Gone, I think." So shivering and commiserable a figure made Ariane awkward, ignobly sharp, evasive. Poor
bare forked creature: and the use of forks was not among
her graces. Brittle with embarrassment, she turned a cold
eye and a scarlet cheek on the rushes. On the roofbeams.
Elsewhere.

Bemused, unvoiced, he whispered. "Dreamed . . . Eh,
did tha see her, did tha see t'moon? Could 'a witched us
sleeping, spelled owt on us: leaves, owls, arains."

"Turned yourself into a jug. And filled it." She could
not bear to talk of dreams, nor of that cold intangible
serenity, night-Malykorne: that was hers. Souls were
hers. Bodies, being earthly, could be made absurd: were

lighter game. And teasing broke no crazy ice, skirring lightly above murky compassion, abysmal trust. "Hey, maybe that's where they all come from, all her crockery ware," she said, envisioning the jugs a rout of chance-come tinkers—wap—unspelled and blinking in the rafters. "See, they're all a sort of bonny mad boys, a rag-tag gypsy lot came knocking at the witch's door, wassailing her, by ones and twos; they're faas and Toms o' Bedlam, lured in with ale, and drunken into lumps of clay. Circe-jugs."

Sadly, he rumpled his hair over his cold ears, and crouched unsteadily over the ashes. Stone-dead. Grovelling among the coals, she thought. He looked a wretched parcel of rags. "Ont ran-tan, were I? And wi a rare awd rantin wench forby: eh, no wonder I's getten a headwark. What's I done?"

"You sang." She looked at him, all smudged and slouching misery, and thought: he sang and there was wood.

O but she'd been crazy, blind, not seeing: he was one of them, like Craobh, like Mally. They were Cloudwise, they were wholly other. Numens. So he was, though unlightborn, bearing light of theirs: earthrooted and unfast in time. Immortal. The cup had made him Cloud. Would bearing of Craobh's soul turn hers to stone? Or slowly, light? No, look, he's bone and rags, bemused, no god—or lose her in itself, as he was lost?—and crazy sodden drunk on ale. On light. Another sort of odd: unnuminous, at once more earthy and unearthly light than she. Tom alone and no one. Mally's rushdip. He dwindled, bearing light; he drank and he was drunken up. He sang, and he was wood, unleaving, dying winter out of time. An endless fall.

Remembering at last, Ariane filled with rue, as a bowl of water brims with light, for the trembling candle, borne so far, and so desolately, so intently into shadow, and there dying; while the wood he had created stood fast, branching black and naked to the rain. The light had been his song. Seeking to recall the shape of that creating music, she heard none; but saw his dazzled grimace, saw the burr of the moving candle, far and farther away, through leaves that were its shadows. It was gone.

She tried to hold it back. Ah, wait.

No use. She tried to work it out, to puzzle at it: not toying light, nor sleight of hand, but law. Cosmology. The wood had been behind the door as they slept, unbounded as the earth, boxed in with cupboard, cot and hedge, closed in by inimical bare hills. Now the child slept on in the narrow cupboard, beneath bare rumpled fells of patchwork, and the wood lay all around them. It was smaller, being outward: for there was a beyond and a deeper in to it, like Sylvie's nightmares. The wood, thought Ariane in awed perplexity, was nested in a Chinese-box of Mally's cupboards, the further in the huger, by some metaphysical geometry. It was the way they had come, and would be their journey. Yet the wood was the tinker, branch and soul. The witch had devoured him to give it being.

Ariane half bent, abruptly moved to touch his brow; her hand jerked out impulsively. She started scratching her wrist instead, inexplicably come out in a bracelet of furious red bumps. "We ought to go. Before it's dark. Can you walk?"

"When's time."

She was reluctant now. The door stood open, the witch was gone, not a gossamer clung and kept them. But now that she thought of ravens, of the nightwood, it seemed the hut was fading: no hearth, but naked roots and stones, a midnight ring, that had caught what the wind had blown it, and as lightly would unleaf. By common light, it came unwitched, unsorting into elements: dry leaves, cracked clay, a rusty iron pot. The embers cold, it would be nowhere, moorland and a muddy spring. Yet she clung. Mally's hall was draughty as Stonehenge, as cold and uncanny, but it was all the sanctuary they had.

She scratched her shoulder-blade, her ankle. Damn! There was an archipelago of spots all down her legs. Measles? Some witch-plague? Owl pox. Another of Mally's nicely judged malicious gifts: but was it fatal?

The child stirred. Ariane went to see.

"Hush. Let bairn sleep," he said, "I think that's what awd Mally given her, same as like thine egg."

"And what for you?"

"My fill o dreams," he said somberly. Rising, he took

his cup from the board. He stared into it, grimly; then he tipped out the dregs. "We owt not slink away like beggars."

Ariane envisioned herself leaving a note for Mally, a dead-leaf bread-and-butter. "What, should we do the washing up? I wouldn't dare. Not for pancakes. God knows what she'd do if we meddled with her crocks. Set it hailing owls upwards. Scatter the sun and stars like jacks."

"S'd like to meddle wi her cellar," he said darkly. "They say as owl-nog's good for a headwark."

"She comes back and finds you, she'll gnaw your kneecaps."

He crumpled silently, his familiar dazzled mirth gone puckered, like an old balloon. "Mallyjugs," he said sepulchrally. "Nowt's brewed, were it? Nowt's strong stuff."

"Nowt stronger." Hey, got him to laugh. Poor old guy, he did look awful, pinched and tallowy, as if he really were a rushdip. Grease turned self, she thought, and coughed back a giggle. "Ah well, nowt's what it seems. You've got to watch that stuff—what were it? The Ravenser Odd ought owt? The extra-sec bec. The *vrai* crow."

But his brief bleared wincing smile had dulled. "Peace. Were ill thowt, and hallows on us." He shivered. "Cawd in here."

Ariane looked doubtfully at the scant heap of green kindling. "Could make the fire up."

"Hush." Startled, he looked sharper-nosed. "Wood's wick, it'd cry out to't witch. Yon's all her foxwood, awfish stuff: thorn, ash, owlers. Let be."

"How can you tell with the leaves off?"

He stared glumly into the ashes. "Soft now."

"And where'd they go, the leaves? It's awfully late out there. Must be quarter-past December."

"Peace, hawd thy clack. Tha's like a cat i' pattens, back and forth. Gan spin, an tha's wakerife, but let be."

But Ariane could not. She maundered on, shrill with a nervous gaiety, a strain of nonsense. "No leaves to hide in; we'll have to travel incognito. As Craobhtree and Goblin." He met this sally with distractedly polite bewilderment. "Soap," she said, "which you wouldn't know about." No answer. Something rustled. "Oh. Is that her?"

"Sleet. Soft now: cannot leave while't lass wakes. Cawd wind and worse nor wind to thole, beyont hallows: tha'lt wish tha wert crouchin i't ashes. There's wolves abroad, and ravens, and t'Awd One's jackal hunts." He made horns with his hand, quick and fearful.

Wolves? "But . . ."

"Run by thy lone til't hunt, if it likes thee, but I's getten lass to keep, and I's flayed and weary and mortal sick." He shut his eyes. "Spell i' thy book."

I won't go play, she thought, I'm not a child. And Craobh's in *my* keeping, she gave me her stone. Not him. And I've kept it from the witch, and the others, the hunt. (Jackal?) Not drunk myself stupid. Not lost my name. Or the ring. I won't—

O heavens, the prophecies! *Spell i' thy book.* "Oh, I get it," Ariane called out. "It's riddles." Fool. Her part was laid out for her, and she'd left it all undone. How could they go, without knowing their way? As the wood had been his labor, so the way must be hers. Night and light journeys. The maze, and the clew of words. Riming and unravelling. Gan spin, he'd said. And she'd dreamed the whorl of fates, the starry skein.

But was it Mally's arainweb, the sly moon's snare? They had given what the witch had asked, in faith, as forfeit; what she gave in turn, her spell, however tangled or elusive, must lead somewhere. The trial lay in seeing, and in holding fast, through all malicious or alluring changes, to the thread. She must not be bedazzled with the gramarye of words, light weaving glamour. The ring's the anchoring, she thought: the endknot. Lightfast. Leave that in Mally's lap and go by feel. Hold fast to the spell. And—Christ, where'd I put it?

Hunched over the bag on her lap, Ariane searched frantically for the scrap of paper. Not in her notebook. Not in her bag at all. She truffled wildly through her pockets. There. In the odd mitten, in the thumb, folded furtively away. Uncertain of the text, she'd not set it down in her canon. It looked all wrong in pencil:

smudgy, tentative. Spidery. How on earth was it spelled and pointed? It made no sense.

"Thy burden's light leaves," not heavy; or was it light, like moonlight, comma, leaves? And then it might not be burden in that sense at all, but refrain. Another song? Light, leaves, on the water. And a-down. Tom's a-cold. And "wake wood frae thy sleep," did the witch mean he'd wake crazy? As a tree? A moonstruck oak? Or would the trees sleep, until he called them? Damn. "Wake wood. Wake *wood*. What does that mean?"

"Thowt as tha knawed t'grammar."

"But you talk this way." She was rattling the paper under his nose. He looked wan and blank, and withdrew, like a worm into a nutshell. She took it by the door, into the fading light. Becloud? "Be cloud i' thy cups." Copse? As good read Mally's leaves. As good read *Urne Burial*, or *The Beano*, in this lightforsaken hole. Sweet hope of glory. The tinker sat snuffling and shuddering and sleeving his nose; Craobh slept interminably, a hanging silence. No one came. Ariane prickled all over. The words mocked her: sitha, Arianty, riddles. Where's thy clew?

It was darkening. They had slept late, too late. Beyond hallows. Whatever that meant, she thought: a thousand years, an afternoon. A step through an unseen door. Storm or nightfall would overtake them on the road, and then—At her back she felt the hovel changing, warping on the sly, so that when she turned and looked, the withered leaves had only just lain still. The jugs were sidling and shifting like the inventory of a dream. Arachnid shadows stared and scurried.

Quick. She turned. No witch. Wind in the door. Ashes stirring. Had the leaves been so, a moment past? Were the owl-eyes on another shelf? *He'd* not seen: he slumped, pale and guttered, with his head in his hands.

Walking back to the table, she found her notebook lying face-down in the puddled ale. It was sodden and stank, stained through, leaf after leaf, with half-moons, blood-brown like dead moorland. Cold and sick with rage, she dried it on her shirt, and shrouded it. Then frantic, she ransacked her crammed and spilling pockets, and her pack, all again and again, unable to remember if she'd brought Sylvie's tape, maddened with visions of it fallen in the leaves: a meaningless, precious, fatal loss, spoil for the ravens. There. She'd never put it—What was that she'd dropped? She scrabbled in the leaves: a button. How the rain railed!

Still the door stood open, and the witch did not come. She's done with us, thought Ariane. There would be no leavetaking, no laying on of a quest, with its consoling formality (Mother, may I?); yet she raged under the constraint of going. She could not sit; she would not cry. Resentful and afraid, she stared out at the wood he had created: dark, unhallowed and malign. No fire nor candlelight, no leaves, but wind and rain. And worse: he'd thronged it with his witch tales, like an evil puzzle, hidden wolves and ravens in his trees.

The child slept on: they could not go, could not stay, and it grew darker. Dressed for going, hulking in her backpack, Ariane writhed and paced with knotted hands and gnawed tongue, worn out by her daemon fury. As she bent to scratch behind her knee, a sudden horrid revelation thwacked and drowned her: O bloody hell, his fleas. Turning on the tinker, in a blind grinding rage, she stumbled—clang!—into the greasy cauldron.

"Wilta hush! Tha bloody great cow."

With a lungful of cold ashes, blind and black, she flew at him, kicking the iron pot to clangor, so that the jugs grinned and rattled on the beams. Wanting to bite him, she could not speak.

There was a thump and a wail. Craobh had tumbled onto the floor. She cowered lamenting, black with cobwebs. "I cannot get back. I was in the sleep, and I can never get back."

"Vixen! Now tha'st wakened bairn. Hush, lass, I's here." He bent and picked her up.

Seeing the child cling to him, Ariane felt a firedamp of rage, a choking evil. She snatched at the child. "Don't you touch her."

In her frenzy, the child was riving blindly at both, pushing at the hollow of his throat, clawing at Ariane's eyes. Wrathful, hoarse, he shouted, "I's done no harm to her. Tha has. Tha has."

She looked at him in a cold stupid shock. Stone. She sat on the floor and hid her face. Cold absolute mass of self, and dark and nothing. No soul: her light was dead, annihilating light. She did not weep.

He made no move toward her, but pried the child away, gently enough, and set her on the bed, and went out.

Craobh wailed, cold, starved, terrified: newborn yet again, too soon, and in a world of demons. It was bleak as Bedlam. A long time after, Ariane lamented, a hideous harsh barking cry.

The tinker came back wet and silent. Standing grimly in the door, he beckoned. He had his broad hat and his budget; with his staff, he looked like Charon, and the taste of bronze was on her tongue, the weight of cold and common trade was on her eyes. Ariane raised her blotchy face; past dignity or drama, moving in the tin semblance of a nurse, she thrust Craobh's body into clothes, spat and rubbed at her grimy face, jerked the comb through her cottered hair. She left the bed unmade. The tinker pulled the door to behind them.

In the mist and mire of the dismal yard, the geese waded, gabbling, grey and motiveless as spirits. Slithering and falling in the sleety mud, the travellers picked their way; the tinker carried Craobh. Ariane, bent beneath her load, saw his filthy trampled coat-skirts flap at every step. They came to the wicket-gate. He set the child down beyond the hedge, holding fast to her sleeve. But nothing waited at the door.

Ariane turned back, athwart the wind, and over the gargoyle's hump of her burden, and saw no gate, no garth, no hovel, only mist and dripping thorns. She thrust her raw hands into her pockets. There she found the witch's comb. No way now to give it back. What she desired had caught her up. She had to carry what she had wanted, light or love or vengeance: the burden of that knowing being the last, unasked, of Mally's gifts.

Sharp wind and sleet assailed them. They walked into the leafless wood, in silence, each a little way from the others, drawing near and nearer in the net of dark.

There was no beyond, only deeper in the wood: no doorway into waking light. Not caring what way they went, walking because to fall asleep was dreams and death of cold, to move was numbed forgetfulness, blank souls in harrowed bodies, they stumbled on and on. They went blindly, blundering through cat-iced puddles, whipped by branches, slithering to the verge of scars. They came to no water they dared cross: the becks ran fiercely swift and stony, fanged with ice. No one led. Nothing, as yet, followed.

The moon was hunchbacked, sunk in cloud. The night was bitter, bleak with fog and sleet that scudded thinly past, or loured, skulking sullen in the hanging woods. No owl cried out. The wind had sharpened.

Craobh kept falling. So they carried her, turn and turn about, sharing the burden with a grim unspeaking justness. Wind on tears had cracked her cheeks. She stared into the joggling darkness, wailing thinly and clinging when her weight was shifted, hung in the cold air between bodies. If they were walking in her sleep, the dream was evil.

Once Ariane, unburdened, blind and heedless with misery, came up sharp against his staff held cross her way. She saw the broad crack in the stone before her feet, heard the fierce far tumult of water. She jerked her head, acknowledging, and turned aside, and slouched on in silence.

In a stony narrow place, the tinker halted. Still and wary, with the child slumped in his arms, he nosed the air. Ravens? Ariane scarcely saw the glimmer of his face, but the hunch of his body was anxious. He plucked her sleeve. Then he thrust Craobh down in a crevice of a rock, between naked roots and stone; and crouched warily before her with his staff. He was gone, but for rustling: a drift of leaves, a copse.

Ariane crouched hiding in a dank and thorny hollow, cowering with her face in her hands. Beyond the wind's keening and the icy rain, and their own ragged scuffling of feet, she had heard nothing, thought nothing but of going on. Now, and louder than the thump and stutter of her blood, she heard it come: the thrash of a running creature, high in the woods. It was coming nearer, unstealthy, purposeful. Abjectly squatting, awkward as a toad, she waited.

I want it over with, she thought, I'm sick of this. She could crouch and be eaten; or could run. And be pulled down. She had Craobh's soul, and so was prey, the cynosure of death. Wildly, she thought of flinging the stone away from her, into the thicket. Let them take it.

The running gashed and gashed the air. What was it? What was it like? She could not endure to go blindly into dark, to have no image for her enemy. Her death. Warily, she peered through her hands.

It was running high and athwart them through the hanging woods, now on four legs, now on two, heedless as if the trees were shadows, headlong and indifferent as a fall of rock; then it sprang in a crouching leap from stone to stone down the rough stairway of a ghyll, through and through the cold shattering spray. For a moment, Ariane saw it black against the pale water of the falling beck: a naked shaggy manlike figure, with a beast's head and great backward-curving, coiling horns. The thing had scented them. She cowered in her earth.

But when it came to her, she saw a man, unhorned, with strangely wideset eyes, so pale as to be blank; broad cheekbones and an archaic changeless smile. Not tall, but square and sinewy, tough as roots of yew, that thrive on bones; naked and hard.

"Come with me," he said.

His voice was deep, passionless and harsh. It sounded in the great lightless hollow of his chest: a voice from the Delphic cave, discarnate, all-possessing, barren. The hair of his chest and body was blood-brown, glittering with wet, though on his head it was pallid dark as rotten wood. He stood smiling with unirised cloud-pale eyes, numinous, evil, ambiguous.

"Come with me. Come underhill. I have always loved you."

"No," she said, despairingly.

He came closer, not touching yet; but she felt his aura, stone cold, a fastening cold, grim and ravenous: not wood for all his semblance, but naked rock, rough and hoar as sarsen, an undecaying mockery of life. It had no eyes.

Blindly willing unbelief, she backed away. He stood behind her.

She twisted away, and he was there.

She ran, but he was before her, ever at the turning, like a minotaur: dark marrow, in a maze of bone. She stood.

"You have called me," he said. Cold, insinuating, dry: he would have her, devouring her self as carrion, undying.

Dark.

A hand touched her face, gently. Her body shuddered in wild loathing, but her mind denied. "Tha'rt none of his," said a softer, shaken voice. "Cannot see thee, what tha'rt." She opened her eyes. The tinker stood with her, between her and the dark with cold iron, his knife, and spoke a word she could not understand, unsteadily, hoarsely. Again. "Duergar." It stood unmoved. The thing cannot touch us, it hasn't touched us, she thought, unwilling it: cannot take hold, unconsented.

The duergar turned and fixed the tinker in his wide, empty gaze. The tinker's face warped in agony. He gasped. The knife fell.

"You are on my earth, beyond hallows; you are forfeit," said the duergar. "Stone under all." Ariane thought: stone breaks knife. The game had a terrible, brutal stupidity, endless denial on denial.

"No," said the tinker doggedly. "We's i't wood: cannot have us." Wood wraps stone.

"Night over wood," said the duergar.

"Comes light, soon or syne."

"Dark is elder."

There was a heart-thud's silence. No answer. Then the white gaze fell on Craobh. No! cried Ariane, but had no voice, struck mute, as the tinker started wildly and was stunned, unmoving: they were caught like stones, enduring, seeing pain. Of kind, their blood and bones obeyed the duergar. They would not consent to follow him, nor could he take them in the wood, in hallows; but he could torment, compelling frenzy or paralysis, fathering his evil on their unwilling silence.

Coming to the child, the daemon crouched, and kissed her mouth and licked her cheek, rasping and whispering in her ear. An accolade: a formal bestowing of the flesh. Moveless, helpless, Ariane looked inward, seeing with the soulstone's eye: annihilation. No scythe of iron, but the naked edge of her mortality. Unlight. Unharvest. The thing with horns.

Knife cuts wood.

The child spoke in a small wretched voice. "Ariane."

"Ariane," said the daemonic voice. "By your name, you are bidden. Eyes to ravens, soul to Annis: but the flesh is mine." He glanced from her, all greedily assured, at the child, at the man. "And all." For the barest breath, he hesitated, fleering at the tinker: so they knew he had no power to call the nameless soul. Ariane was his, and the soulless, carnal child: he could possess her as he liked.

In the flickering of the duergar's will, the tinker sprang to seize him by the throat. The dark shrugged. The tinker was hurled down against the rocks. He lay dazed and blinking for a moment; the innocent blood slid sidling down his temple. Ariane knelt by Craobh, not holding her, not now; but there, unseen in darkness. Shaken, silent, the tinker crouched the other side of her. A knot of souls, and each alone. The daemon twitched the child upright. She hung there, soulless; a branch broken down with ice, benumbed and naked fear. "She walks."

Endgame. They walked, huddled together. He was driving them to the wood's edge, beyond the witch's realm. Beyond hallows. They were his there, flesh and fell; and one called Annis waited for their unregarded

souls, stone, cup and all. Ariane felt his blank ravenous
eyes, ever at her back, unendurable. The goat's lust, and
the grave's: unglutted hell. Wormblind and cold as earth,
he would be in her, would engulf her in his greed,
devouring what was toadflesh, defiling; and would spit
away the cold and insular crystal of her soul. What he
could not crack, she thought, he would encyst. It would
not end. The fossil would endure in suffering. Already
she knew his fell weight, immense and dry as death.

"He didn't ask you," she hissed at the tinker.

"Not leaving," he said morosely. "Tha'rt my friend."

The wood was growing thin, a scattering of thickets.
They could walk side by side now; the way was broad.
They saw the blank pale sky, in which ravens fell and
balanced, fell and turned. For all the tinker's endeavor-
ing, his wood was barely a night's walk to the edge, a
little hall of candlelight in endless shadow.

Ariane sickened. The child had called out for her, for
the first time by her name; her friend had touched her
face, a hand in darkness—ah, but she was lightboned
with remembered shock, with a poignance of regret—
and the thing had twisted and defiled their goodness to
his ends, perverting trust into betrayal, and reassurance
into violation. He had robbed her of the moment of
accepting grace.

She thrust her hands into her pockets, clenching them
in grim-lipped desperate fury. One closed on something
sharp and alien: the comb. It gnawed her hand. She
clenched it harder, bitterly exulting in a pain she could
command, the last. With the sharpness, she remembered
light, the bright unwanting moon. The comb was Malykorne's, it was of the wood; she would tear the daemon's
eyes with it.

Turning on him, she felt all her forebodings of witchi-
ness, all her furies, annealed and fused in her, in one
flawed but darkly burning glass. He flinched from her,
dismayed. A hedge of thorn sprang up all round her, and
round the man and child. Unhallows. It was rootless, and
sank like a wave into the earth.

The duergar pounced.

But swifter, shaken almost to exultant madness, cawing, Ariane called forth another thicket, higher and

enwoven, earthfast; but the daemon shifted shape, assailing the wood as a storm of scything malice, a black unlightning withering the roots.

They withered, and she raised another thicket, sharper, further onward, woven of her fury, out of rage and joy and ranting terror; and he followed, gaping as the grave, insatiable. They ran before him, hedged round with quickset thorns: the child, the tinker, and the witch.

Swift as she raised her owl-wood, the stone devoured it, isle after isle of sanctuary. She saw the moorland rising like a wave of dark before her; felt dark behind them, gaping. The comb wrenched at her soul, tearing and warping like a storm of owls, lurching her sideways in staggered curves, as if her veins ran mercury, and lead ran in the marrow of her bones; as if her soul unbalanced, eccentric with desire and fear. It was too great for her, the old moon's comb of horn. Mally's brushwood. Unfast in light, and fickle: like her skein and shears, entangling who wielded it, two-edged. Each thorn Ariane set in dark's way was dragged from her, up through her gasping lungs; thorns snarled and matted in her wits, botched and black-thumbed and malicious. But if she paused, drew breath, the witchwood faded, ravelling. Stone gaped; and still the sky was dark, the ravens followed.

Stone balked before his prey, a labyrinth of walls; night harked on; and at their backs, the duergar hunted, relentless, driving them toward the naked fells and his possession. A few steps, and Ariane would fail, and all would fall to him, caught in a blind turning, and devoured on the stony hillside.

From behind the stone came a light, clear and holy as the morning star, but low and tremulous: it walked on the earth. Its shadow was tremendous wood, enhallowing; it came, and took them into light.

"Gerroff!" it cried.

The daemon vanished. They stood astounded, unbelieving, as a shape came sploshing up to them, with a lantern in its hand. Somewhere beyond, a cock crowed.

Sylvie sat up and looked about her. No trees anywhere—hey, where'd they go? No witch. A sea of huge unbreaking hills, bare as waves, and paler than the louring sky with snow. How black she would show against that white, that alien clarity of field, naked to the spying birds. Naked as stars. Orion, she thought briefly, not naming him, but seeing: a negative, striding across the simplest landscape of night, unencumbered, splendid.

She shivered absently, shaking the snow from her hair, huddling the rough cloak about her. What strange cloth, she thought, snagged on it; then fingering curiously: ill-woven and uncombed, with patches of it rough as beech-nut husks, or scant as cirrus, prickly with twigs and burs, and snarled and botched with darning. It was fastened with an iron brooch, clumsy as a thorn. She hefted the staff, hand-worn already, long and dark, ringed with a black silver band. That was incised, or scratched, but neither eye nor fingertip could make it out. She looked in the grey skin bag, and found an oatcake, a pale round cheese—oh rats—and a withered apple, all jumbled in a rag of linen; a leathern bottle—water—and, oddly, a mirror of polished bronze. Travelling light, she thought, and bit into the dull, soft, sour apple, turning it about and about, standing jigging with the cold.

Now what, Sylvie thought, and looked to the squat impassive stone. What way's the story go? The one about the ravens and the witch?

The stone was silent. It cast no shadow, had no face; though she felt with the unshaken intuition of a dream

that she had slept in its lap. It gave no sign; but she
knew its answer: tale's thysen. She had to be going, so
must choose her way. There was no wind to get back of
beyond; no fox nor hare had trodden out a way; in the
cloudy brownish dusk, no sun nor moon gave east or
west. No bird spoke in runes to her, no silvery thread
was knotted, by long ways and winding, between her
hand and her fate. She tucked the apple-core in the
pouch. Twirling the staff between her palms, she let it
fall.

That way then, toward the sheepnosed hill, the way
the stone looked out. Good: for a squinny of the sun
revealed a drab wasteland east and south, behind her.
North and west lay dazzled, cloud beyond cloud of earth,
a clearness that was sky not stone: her way.

But wait. Some glance of upright dark, the stone perhaps, reminded her of Nan's hallway, cold and narrow,
with eluding mirrors: the way of coffins. She remembered Nan stalking out through that hallway to look at
an eclipse of the sun, as one queen to another. Turning,
Sylvie touched the standing stone in farewell, brusquely,
not unfondly. She half felt a twitch, as of shy stand-offish
dignity. "Thanks for the ale. And the cloak and things.
I'll do what I can. See you."

It was strange, walking out on the hills. The world was
all of light and mass, uncolored and profoundly bare,
as though creation were in draught. Stone and cloud
and water, fell and crag. At first the way was moorland, bleak and curlewed, set with cairns in sullen
heaps. The morning had fallen out as snow, and left no
brightness to the huddled air. The sky was dark, though
bellied with a bitter light, cast upward by the fading
snow. The wind was getting up behind her. Huge and
brown, it buffeted, rebuffed her, luffing the unwieldy
cloak, fretting the icy ground to fume. Wraiths from the
stoneheaps. She sang as she went, in a daunted murmur,
coming and going underbreath, almost wordless; the
wind was smallpipes and a hollow bass, a bourdon, droning and wheedling in a narrow round: a souling wind.
Sometimes she ran, not for joy or terror, but to catch
herself gone on before.

Then moorland turned to moss, scored with groughs

of dead and brittle icy water, splintering and squelching
underfoot. The wind still urged, but the way was treach-
erous. The discord made her prickly with unease, like a
cat in a thunderstorm, uneasy and fascinated. Her eyes
went dark, looking out over murk and mire and hugger-
mugger. She fell silent. Heedless and wary all at once,
she chose her way.

Crossing the hag took all her wits. She went swiftly,
leaping from tuft to tuft of wiry grass, until an island
sank beneath her, irresolute; and turning back, she saw
no way. She went slowly, gilgamesh, gilgamesh, prodding
with her staff, picking her way over what looked like a
vile primeval chocolate pudding, all cracked-skinned and
oozy, bearded like a crone. At last she misfooted, and
sank in mud unequally, and fell and fell, devoured.
Squirming and spurning in panic, she flailed out for the
fallen staff, not quite in reach, twiddling beneath her
fingertips . . . She had it. Closed on it. She braced herself
with the staff held crossways, and wallowed out of the
morass.

With a filthy hand, she smudged back her hair. She
was shaking. The earth was bones here: cold and saturnine, a chaos of the assimilated dead. She stood unsteadily, on legs sucked marrowless. She unpinned the cloak,
to try and wrench it out; but as it left her shoulders, she
was assailed with a sense of bitter cold and nakedness,
as if she had flayed herself to the bones, as if her body
were the naked soul and the cloak her body.

Hastily, she flung it on again, and was lapped in reassuring sodden misery. A tutelary cloak, with draggled
wings. Sylvie wrung as best she could, slewed round.
There were long dark threads in the warp of it, no
beast's, but like a woman's hair. How strange. Wearing
that cloak, she thought, she would not die of cold,
though would suffer it; perhaps it had other virtues, of
walking unseen or warding malice. If any, they'd be
shrewd and scant.

But wind on that sodden wool made her bones ache
and shiver. With her teeth chattering, she rubbed her
stiff hands. No tissues. Hey, but when had she last snif-
fled? Last night? Weird cure for a cold, drowning. Or
was it getting drunk on black ale? Could use a cup now.

Wassail the mud. She longed to have a fire, to leap about a raging brightness, call down what it might. But how? Ariane, she remembered, had the matches, in another world. Wish Air were here: she always liked it winter in the game. She'd see things, patterns, threads. She'd talk. Sylvie looked around. The heath was soggy, and even if she'd had a burning glass, the sun was pale and northern, clouded over. Could she do anything with the bronze mirror? The knife—it had a flint and steel.

Sylvie leapt recklessly over the last cracked hags and tussocks of the bog onto the high moor, and pulled fiercely at the heather, dead gnarled with dead in stubborn implication, heaping it up on a rocky outcrop. The roots were sinewy and slimy. No tinder. She ravelled out a fuzz of wool from her sweater—it was torn anyway—and knelt over it with her flint and steel, and struck and struck until it caught, withering. It sailed away on the wind. Snuffed. The next she weighted with a stone. The fire took. She witched it on the heather. It burned, frazzling, then unfurling, quick and pale.

She crouched before it, warding and warming; then stood, and jigged and stamped, to stir her cold blood. The wind swaled the fire at her, and she jumped it, laughing: hey! and again. She leapt over it and over it, dancing above its greed and beauty, and rejoicing in its souling danger—O ravens, do you spy it?—bright for the journey's sake in dark, and fleeting on the stony changeless hills. She danced with the souls of earth set free as wind and fire. Its windblown, sidelong forays scathed the sparse bents, flowering and fading, taking no root in the drowned earth. When her brief fire died, she stamped the cinders, no blacker than the peat but crisp, the ashes whiter than the filthy snow, sharp as hoarfrost on the slushy mire.

Stiff-clad and ashy, breathless, but fire-heartened, Sylvie trudged on. The moor was dark and shaggy, set with rocks like wolves' paws. For some hours, she climbed, and thought of woods and riddles, and of how the witch could need her, enough to call her from another world. She had to be, somehow, at once outlandish and essential. Deea, she thought, I hope I don't wreck the whole ecology; I could be an alien lifeform. Like a grey squir-

rel. No trees, though: no acorns. I'd die out. The bare-
ness of the landscape began to intrigue her: like doing a
puzzle from the back.

The moor was bounded by a drystone wall. She ran
up to it, and halted. Hey, look, O look at that. Beyond
lay white stoneland. Chaos had become crystalline, falling out into air and earth, of purest curving, and bright
water. Bare clarity. Stone glinted, and the grassland fell
away, a thousand feet. A hawk towered below her. She
wanted to fling herself down on the wind's back and fly;
or roll, but the stones were sharp.

She walked aslant the hill. Her song came from under-
ground of her, like a keld from a hillside, clear and
ancient, running on:

> Will you go to the rolling of the stones,
> The tossing of the ball?
> And will you go and see pretty Susy
> Dance among them all?

Water veined the fells with silver; the stone laid bare was
cracked and puzzled with the agelong gnawing of the
rain. The earth was hollow here.

Coming over a high shoulder of the fell, she saw a
scrawl of darkness. Trees. Her heart leapt up. She
stared; her body bent, unconsciously echoing the line of
them, the lift and poising. Years after, she could have
danced that line; and certain turns of counterpoint, or
graces, movements made in turning from a window,
would remind her. Ten or eleven little trees, in a clump
beside a ruined wall, a sheepfold or a shepherd's cot; a
flicker, as of falling leaves, though all the trees were
bare. And something else. She clambered over the walls
between, stalking lightly, warily, among the rocks, and
crouched behind a stone.

Among the windbent trees and tumbled stones, a child
of nine or so, all in brown rags, sat beside a little spring
that filled and flowed. He tossed a handful of ash-keys
in the air, and they came whirling and flickering and
shearing down around him, dry and light. He glanced at
the patterns they made on the earth, and then swept
them up and tossed again; and once again, watching their

shoalings and their shadows as they fell. Sylvie had been still as if he were a bird, fearing to flight him; but as her shadow fell on him, he looked up and laughed.

"Have you come thrae't Clouds?"

"No, I'm real, I think. I'm not too sure about you."

He looked bewildered for a moment, then amused; but he spoke with grave courtesy. He pointed back toward the witch-stone with a hand rather large for a child's, brown and sinewy and narrow. "There's twa gates: ower yon Clouds and by Soulsgrave, and ower t'Law. Not aloft." He glanced wryly at the cloak. "Back o't moon's not so mucky."

Huh? Oh, Clouds are what those hills are called, thought Sylvie.

Then he smiled. "You've been a lang night coming. Well met." He was beech-brown and hazel-eyed, with hair of that leaf-brown that lights to gold; he had a nut-round pointed face, bemused eyebrows, and a gentle nose. He wore a brown cap, with dangling lappets. "Come in, if you can."

The wall was down. Ducking and twisting under the gnarled branches, she came toward him. It was a spare and lovely place: a maze of fallen stones, some breast-high, some brailled, with moonfaced lichens; a windbent knot of trees, thorn and ash and rowan, oak, alder and sloe, and a few stunted apple trees and hazel bushes. Each spoke through its branches a rune of the wind's: hold fast; hail morning; O lord of winter, northwind, I defy. The air was—not misty, though she thought of rainbows—elusive, full of the glint and twirl of imagined falling leaves. One flat stone was fire-blackened, and she found a shard of delft. On the clear brown water of the spring moved light inlaid, in leaves and sky, his fleet: holy at the center, stirring and spilling away down the stony hillside.

"I like this place. Is it yours?"

"Been laiking here."

"Can I have a drink? My bottle's empty. You can have some of my stuff; there's bread and cheese, if you want." He nodded. Sylvie took off the cloak and hung it out to dry on the hazel wands. No harm was here. She knelt and dipped her hands through the slow-stirring riddles of

the leaves—O how cold, her hands were silver—and she
drank. Bending over the leafy water, she saw a face
reflected, faceless as the moon and rimmed with brightness, shadowy with hair. She saw the leaves and branches
of a wood in autumn, leaves rising through the water;
saw a hand in darkness, the mirror of her reaching hand,
but other. Numbed with cold, she could not feel if they
had touched. She sat back on her heels; the child was
watching. "That's good water."

"Aye," he said.

They sat in companionable silence by the water, in
the fitful sunlight, cracking nuts with a stone. When she
reached into the grey skin bag, the apple was round
again, and withered: ah, she thought, and shared it out
with the cheese and oatcake, all but the rind and crust
and the seeds, taking care to leave the crescents to
renew. She had a feeling that she ought not cut them
with her iron knife. She was ravenous enough to eat the
cheese, grimacing and bolting, though she wondered if
she could catch the apple green. The boy picked and
crumbled courteously, looking at her, scowling at the
cheese as she did, as if for manners' sake.

After their meal, Sylvie turned the cloak in a hail of
mud and ashes, beating and brushing at the crusted peat,
leaving the burs. They seemed intrinsic. Then she sat and
looked at the child among the trees, so still, so wavering
with light and shadow, ghostly leaves.

"You're one of them, the old ones," she said at last.

He sat with his chin on his knees. "I were."

She stirred, excited: it was coming real, like the
moment before the shaken air was fire. "Are the woods
her—the witch, I mean?"

"Soft now, she hears." He bent toward her, tensed
and trembling with recollection, like a drop of rain upon
a thorn: bright enclosing dark, and heavy with his winter's tale. His voice was soft and broad, but underlaid
with the rhythms of an old formality. "She's eldest. Came
afore. Cloud's wood wi her." He glanced at the bare
hills, and drew breath.

"Time were and elsewhere, Cloud were wood, and
bough and branch were lightfast, turning leaves; as they
were earth, and flowering wi stars. I were Cloudwood

then, bare light. I were—not bone and blood like I is now, but root and leaf. I see'd them, and they were; I waked them frae't dark, and warded them frae baneful stars, walking i' my hills, back o years. Others o my kindred, lightborn, kept each wood and water, keld and beck, fell and crag and law. I ever loved t'fall o leaf, but some danced wind i't green boughs, or rime and roke; some ran afore't spring, and starred grass.

"Come wakesun i' winter, and midsummer moon's night, we kept lightfast: met as stones to dance. Turned sky."

White things moving on a hill, thought Sylvie. "But I thought the witch was wood."

"Keeps hallows."

"Oh. So she's eternity, and you're like time? Or vice versa."

"She is, and she is."

Sylvie paused. "But aren't there any people in this world? All gods?" She touched the fallen stones. "Someone built this. No one said, like, hey, no sun this year?"

He looked puzzled. "Hearthfolk, tha means? They came aftertimes. They taken and they cut our branches, teemed their milk and blood upon our stones; they browt hallowfires ont fells, ash and salt. Burnt our wood to drive dark away. Feared shadows. Some fort wintersake hanged wrens i't thornraws, waking sun, thowt they; some wanting harvest slayed their bairns fort ravens i' their corn. Felled Cloudwood wi cawd iron. Some danced at witches, ranting moonwise back o Law. Called on darkness, craving light of it, unfast and bound. Cast bones, craved rings. But they were few, and flayed of us, and fleeting."

"Witches?" said Sylvie. "Like what's-her-name, the owl? Like Annis?"

"Some has called on her."

"And not on you, you lightborn?"

"They's awdest, moon and dark."

"But you're the ones who dance."

"Danced lightfast and t'stars. They cast earth's weird atween them twa. Bare sun, bent moon. And ay and every year afore't sun's rising, lightspring at unhallows, Annis came, and cast aside her staff on Law, and turned til stone. Light rade on high then, summer lang. And nightfall, ay on hallowsnight, in turn, moon waked Annis, to devour sun, call down t'snaws. Rade out aloft and hunted souls, beyont hallows. Moon kept hallows, bound as tree. Then wakesun came, and lightfast, turning light. And so it went. But Annis craved dark o moon, dead o winter, unturning: so she bided.

"It fell out langest night and dark o't moon. She came frae't back o Law, unmoonwise and uncalled, and broke our dance; she struck about her wi her staff, and caught us stonefast, all but half; and scattered all. And sithen Annis hunt has soughten us, by dark and light. Has ta'en us, stone by stone. She's broke hallows, bound Law. Calls t'ring o stones her crown; plucks out our souls to give her sight. Come stonering is closed—"

"Ah!" cried Sylvie, fiercely apprehending. "It all gets stuck at the nadir. All dark."

"Aye. Annis would be soul of all, see all inwith her stones, and give creation ower as carrion to dark. Sall all be dark. Stars'll not wheel; moon sall not change. Hills o dead, same as yon Soulsgrave Hag."

"I see." Sylvie was hunched, crowded up with a barely restrained alacrity, intent and eager as a rache-hound. "She cares for nothing in itself, only for knowing it. Having it all to herself. But why destroy it, the dance? Could keep it turning, like a sort of little wheel, if it causes light. That's what she wants."

"Hates it. Cannot thole what she craves, for that it's eaten. Craws feed on eyes; she gizzens on souls, crams light in her unfadomed dark, and still there's light, and she mun gnaw. Sun turns, dance turns, frae dark intil dark, and all's fleeting, all's giddy. All's reborn. Nobbut dark's lasting. Nowt's endless."

Sylvie looked at him, brown as a winter leaf, real as earth. "She hasn't gnawed you. Am I supposed to keep you from her hunt? The witch was sort of sketchy."

He spoke more sadly now, and gently, not as seer. "Annis'll not send for me: I's owerlooked. Thowt I, an I had no soul, she'd none to take, would never have all on us: so I given it intil another's keeping. I see'd no other way. I'd no fastness but unbeing what she sought." He looked down, at his sort of ash-keys. "So I fade, wi't wood: cannot see it waking now, and cannot dream, as mortals do: I were not made i' that wise."

"That's rough," she said feelingly. "No woods, and staying on and on alone. Not knowing." Then a wicked irrepressible thought struck her. "Deea. And did she—you know, the owly witch—did she come to the *summer* dancing?"

"Malykorne? Eh, well. Can tha see her dance?"

Sylvie laughed: the thought of the witch frolicking crossly with a garland quite undid her. Then she asked seriously, "But why doesn't Annis hunt down the one who's got your soul? Or both of you, and put it back? She must know one's missing."

"Hush. Cannot tally. Knaws all and nowt." He looked triumphant, terrified. "'His body clouds it frae her sight: she's nowt to do wi bone and blood. Doubt she'd devour both our souls, an she knawed, and give him flesh and fell to her ravens: he'd not turn stone, being earthborn."

"Did you *ask* him?" she said severely.

"No. Not thowt on."

"Well, that's nasty!" Indignant. "Here, hold this. Back in a few millennia. Oh yeah, and watch out for ravens."

Unchildlike, unremorseful, he spoke with grave compassion, owning what he had taken from one mortality, what he had given, his burden of light. "I see now what he's tholed for me, lang years. Telled him nowt, nor asked his will. And he is good. I chosen."

"Oh!" she said, "Then he's the—I think I heard him, in a dream. I saw—" She stopped, remembering the heap of rags lying, gaunt and still, beneath the tree. Asleep. Or dead. Was that to come? Or only shadow, what might be? Long past? The witch gave nothing but was true. He'd sung with her: they'd crossed. "So anyway, he's out there. He goes on." Getting cold out. Dark. "But how do you live?"

"Laiking. Has nuts to crack, and get us sloes and crabs and rowans here. Water i' keld."

"It's cold; there won't be nuts much longer."

"Clap craws, round about t'farmsteads. Pick stones. Fold sheep. Folk leaves out meal for us, by dark. Odd eggs i' corners, sadcakes. Bowls o milk. Cannot die o want, nor cawd; but cannot thole getting witless. Sleep now frae time to time: forgetten what I knawed. Not dreamed." Small and hard, looking down at his heap of nutshells, at a fan of yellow leaves.

Then he turned to her, quick as rushlight, with his throng of shadows. "There's hearthtales telled by fires, rimes and ballads sung o't lightborn, though they call us out of our names, hobs and hallybairns. They warp and dwindle us." He spoke low. "Eh, but sooth is, we has fell away. Turn nowt. Sun wakes i' their hearths now, dark's turned by their rimes and running. Wren's t'win-tersake i' truth."

"Oh," said Sylvie. "Oh, like in the Golden Bough? They do that in my world, they hunt the wren. For luck, poor thing. A sacrifice. Round about the winter sol-stice—lightfast—and they carry it from house to house, all decked with ribbons, like a sort of totem: please to see the king. There's songs. Like that?"

"Stone dead. Have see'd them bear it, all i' garlands, wi their sad small pipe. Dancing til it wake. Sint ring were brok, all's langways, handed on. All's earth til earth. Unfast. They's wick as rushlights are, here and gone: but keep hallows. They bear light."

"It's done," said Sylvie. "It gets done. And you go on."

A silence. "Shadow's what I is. I's tale. And they has borne me, year to year. I's etten bread and salt wi them, I's touched cawd iron, sained their barley and their apples, stoned craws: all fort sake o listening i't shadows, remembering what I were." He was twisting about Syl-vie's staff, thumbing the graven ring, over and over. "Have yer come thrae Awd Mally, then?"

"You mean the witch? Deea, bet she'd huff if I called her that to her face. She likes playing old witch. It diverts her." Sylvie smiled, remembering. "Yes, I saw her last night, whenever that was; it was in the woods. They're still there, wherever she is. She gave me quite a lot of her ale, and drank with me. And I did see her this morn-ing, if she counts as a rock. She sent me to take back your souls from Annis, but I don't know how. I'll have to think about it, as I go."

"Did she say how many on us were left? I cannot see."

"She said, 'One and t'other one.' " Could be the boy

and his soulbearer, she thought, or another of the light-born, unsouled or in hiding, still free. Well, if the witch weren't gnomic, it wouldn't be a fairy tale.

"And given you no word?"

"Said I was her sword."

"I'll set you on your way, i't morning. I knaw t'gate."

It was darkening, creaking with frost. Chill and aching, she wrapped herself in the potsherd cloak. She could barely see his face by now; but shadow made of nine trees an illusory wood. Nine and one. "You sleep while morning; Annis won't come here," he said from darkness. Softly, "Will you tell me your dreams?"

The cock crowed, and Ariane let go the comb of horn. The morning star drew near. It was a woman with a lantern, walking on her earth in heavy boots. Dark and small, she came sploshing up to the travellers, and looked from face to face.

"Heard summat. Thowt it were a fox," she said. Her voice was small and harsh; her face, white-brown as winter earth, and shy, expressionless beneath a straggly fringe. She wore a man's jacket and brown sweater over striped flannel pajamas and the heavy farm boots. Standing at Ariane's shoulder, barely higher, excluding dark, she said softly, "You've done that well. If he comes back, you bear light, mind: show him."

Wordless, Ariane held up her empty hands.

"Tek my lantern," said the woman, and handed it to Ariane; then unexpectedly, she smiled, a tiny shy new moon of grave amusement. "You've brokken his heart."

Soberly, she took Craobh in her arms, and beckoned. "Come int' kitchen by fire; I'll put kettle on."

The travellers went with her through gates in stone walls, lifting and latching twine and wire loops and rusty snecks: by her lantern-fire, the labyrinth was the intakes of a farm. They plodded through slathery muck and straw, past a rope-straining, ranting, black-and-white dog—"Hush! yer daft bugger," in that hoarse gentle whisper—and into a stone-flagged, low-ceilinged room, spread with sacking and newsprint. A fire burned low.

Craobh stood trembling until the woman bent and briefly spoke to her, too softly for the others to hear; then she sank by the hearthstone in a daze. The tinker bobbed and mumbled a sort of thanks before huddling in the ashes. Ariane collapsed. When she closed her eyes, she saw thorns. Bone-white, tenacious, bodiless, they closed her in, they tore at sight. The comb lurked and loured in her pocket. When the wind blew the door ajar, she flinched. The woman made up the dozy fire, unhooked the black kettle, going out to the yard again to fill it. Ariane stirred feebly, half struggling up in earnest; but her legs were stone. "I'll . . ."

"Don't trouble. Time I were up fort milking anyroad. Phoebe's up."

So they sat by the hearth as she came and went; they huddled with the child between them, stunned and torn and icy wet. The tinker looked his age. He shuddered, though the kindling blazed, his shadows cowering with mortal cold. Ariane was aware of fire, and the muted gleam of glaze and brass; of earthy sacks and muck-truffled boots; of Craobh's caught breathing; of the sober tick of a clock; of rue drying; of a hunch and aching she had forgotten was her pack; of dim and drifting pales of whiteness all about, a ghostly fleet. She felt the woman's reassuring presence, not hovering but true as earth, tough and shy and kind.

The woman brought a huge brown teapot, and swilled and filled and steeped. She poured out tea black as bog-water into milk, and spooned in lashings of sugar. Ariane held her cracked white mug, round and lovely as if it were painted by Vermeer, as plain as morning; and she drank in silence, drank light and silence and holy commonplace.

Craobh was nodding, slumping; she could not hold her cup. "Eh, poor lass," said the woman, and took her on her lap, and pulled off her boots and rubbed her feet. She held the cup for her; she stripped away the cold wet clothes, and towelled her and wrapped her in a shirt and a heavy sheepskin coat, stained but warm. "It's t'ane our shepherd keeps fort lambing." The child slept on her lap. She rose and laid her, fast asleep, on the settle.

Ariane watched drowsily: how simply the woman moved, for one so small, as if she took her measure from the hills. She was tough-framed but saddening with age, sad and stony-faced, with something else that came and went, like a star behind clouds.

The tinker looked bewildered, slipping back into his dream, grimacing at the strange sweet cloudy stuff in his mug, yet clinging to its warmth; ill at ease with kindliness. He's lost, thought Ariane. She looked at him, all leaves, and leaves of shadow, wood by the strangers' hearth, and thought, he's none of theirs. Not now. And he's wanting them: not light, but hearth and kindred. Bread and ale, unclouded sleep. Ah, but how had he lived, these long years of winter? He'd not sprung from earth. Had no one mourned him? Cradled him? Who'd sung to him? Had others stoned the scarecrow from their doors? Or kind, incurious, thrown bread to him, odd Tom, awd Flaycraw, even as they would to birds? He must have been routed from many such a farm, when cold had driven him toward fire. Toward voices. Yet he bore their songs, made light of them in darkness, hearth in travelling; he made them wood.

He stirred, turning toward the woman with a rueful, wincing smile. "You're not to slay yon cock at crawed. He's not for seething."

The woman was filling a couple of stone bottles with hot water from the kettle. "Sad night," she said, and tucked a worn-out quilt, once blue and starry, round the child. "We've no beds to spare. Forby you're reet mucky fort house. Sleep i't laithe whiles you can get weshed."

"Thank you, ah, Mrs. . . ." said Ariane.

"Mrs. Woodfall." Gathering up the stone bottles and

a pile of wraps, she took them across the yard again, now sheepy grey with dawn, and up a steep outside stair, all of stone and unrailed, into a shadowy loft full of hay. She turned and hung something small on the lintel. "There's been travellers slept here afore. Nowt comes in unbidden, nobbut wind and our cat," she said, laying out sacks and ragged quilts, tucking in the stony jugs. Swayed and staggering with sleep, Ariane trod off her sodden boots; the tinker shirked his coat. Somewhere beneath, a cow stamped and lowed, geese squabbled, "Ta-ra," she said, and snuffed the candle. They fell at once into the deep soft scratchy beds, and slept: Ariane, at least, undreaming.

Ariane woke alone. She lay on rough sweet summers past, grey-golden; and without, the air was bleak and dark, with sleet and wind scything. She lay under the great roof-beams: ribs of wood, a sanctuary. Hallows-trees, she thought, looking up at their leaning out and reconciling, their rough shouldering grace. She marked the sagging slates, bone-pegged, and overlaid like feathers, not for flight but downward-bearing, brooding on the shape of air, the falling of the grass turned sun within, the hidden soul. A, said the roof-beams, A; and O, the cup, the scything moon turned full and full, the eye of thornwood and the haloed floor. There is hallows; there is going on, that A begins: the old hard way, beyond all hallows, toward the scything and the endless light. The journeying becomes the light, and O is flowering of A.

She took out her notebook, its pages curling, brown as oak-leaves, and wrote A and O. She looked at the comb, and thought nothing; she combed her hair. Being so long starved of solitude, she found she could not rest in it. She got up. What was it Mrs. Woodfall had left, as if to ward them from dark? She found a crooked twig, hung rune-like on a nail above the doorway. Thorn.

She came halting down the stone stairway, glassy in the hissing sleet, and edged through broad plain pelting daylight, and muck and chiding geese. House and barn and outbuildings were all of stone, slate-roofed: sway-backed and plainfaced, broad, enduring. She found the kitchen, and wiped her feet hard on the mat. The tinker sat by the dresser, devouring a hunk of brown bread, as if someone might take it from him. He pointed toward the fire. "Washing her," he said, his face moving with concern and awe, and amused foreboding. Ariane went to look.

The low dark room was hung with airing sheets and shirts and towels, on clotheshorses; four or five small solemn children crawled in and out of caves of linen, playing some game by unspoken consent, wriggling and peering and hiding. By the coal fire, behind a screen of washing, stood a tin bath. Mrs. Woodfall and an ancient woman, bent and broad and grizzled, like a mandrake Mrs. Woodfall, were bundling up Craobh in a towel.

"In tha gets," said the old woman, jerking her chin. Ariane stood mute and mortified. "Eeh, not first arse I's see'd, coming and going. Get thee doffed," said the old woman, inexorably, like a priestess in the steam; so willy-nilly, stiffly fumbling with her buttons, Ariane began to strip.

O heavens, what should she do with the soul? Between water and their watchful eyes it might come to harm; or call forth shrewd questions she had neither heart nor wit to answer. Stooping clumsily, as if to worry at a stubborn bootlace, she undid the cord and shirked it off, bundled in her shirt; she got her clothes off and crumpled round it in a furtive bunch, and poked them under a chair. She sat cowering and blushing, knees to chin in the bath (made for Woodfalls), and the old woman poured a can of water over her head. A child stared round the screen, dark-eyed and curious. Ariane emerged shivering, sanded down with yellow soap. Her clothes were gone.

"Daft to put yersel back int' such mucky rags," said Mrs. Woodfall, looking in with a bundled armload. "Forby they's wick wi lops; yer all etten up. Here's clean." She dug in her apron pocket. "And yer bead, like." Ariane stared, dripping. "Yon's me grandmother, Mrs. Owlund."

"How do you do?" said Ariane, absurdly, ducking her head. She took the stone. An odd bead to be wearing, nothing more. Naked as a needle, red-eyed, and smarting in all her scoured bites and scratches, with a strained

and sopping plait, she struggled into what had to be the
grandmother's clothes: crow-black, wide and short, crack-
ling with starch and camphor, haphazardly straight-
pinned. Sucking a pricked thumb, she tucked the stone
in the shift. Mrs. Woodfall fetched another can of water.
Small wonder, thought Ariane, the tinker looked dismayed: old Mrs. Owlund was like to scrape him down
with the side of her rusty pan, with donkey-stone and
sand and brush, before dousing him like a scabby sheep.

"What can . . . ?"

"We've no apples down. You could run up to't loft;
our Rach'll show you. Happen twenty on 'em."

Rach was not the attendant spirit of the bath, but an
older child, mole-dark and greyer eyed, with a knotted
dangling red ribbon clenched in a very skimpy lock of
hair. Ariane followed, through doors into whitewashed
northern spaces, sparely furnished, and upstairs into a
dim sweet loft full of nuts and apples. As she went, she
saw the tinker going to his bath, with a look of curiously
resigned martyrdom, or as if unsure what he should
recant, being innocent; halfway up the stairs, she heard
a wallowing splash, and a cry of "T'watter's swammed
ower!"

They turned the apples in the loft, Rach squatting
intently behind her falling lock of hair, leaping nimbly
along the joists. The rain rattled on the slates. She
looked out of the round window in the gable-end. "Can't
see Cloudlaw," said Rach. "So it's hallows yet. Our mam
can see."

"Hallows. Do you mean now? Or here, this place?"
The child looked quickly at her, wondering, and away.
"I really don't know."

Rach thought, biting her knuckle. "It's hallows while
lightfast, you knaw. Langest night. And it's hallows
where fire is, and thorn: some i't house." Light and
quick, she leapt the apples, and turned a bright grave
face, moon-round, toward Ariane's bewilderment. "And
back o't clouds is all wood there, and hallows ever; said
owls danced there, did our gran."

Ariane came down with a lapful of streaky russet
apples, coarse and sound, but small as crabs, and tum-

bled them down on the long bare table, grey with years, and rough as a cat's tongue with scrubbing.

Straightening up to shake her apron out, she caught a stranger's eye, and looked away in some confusion. He was with Craobh on the settle, a slight sharpnosed fairish man in a collarless pale shirt and baggy trousers, oddly with no shoes on such a day. Craobh touched his hand—O dear me, the tinker, and in Mr. Woodfall's shepherd's clothes. Without his swathes of rags and crony earth, he seemed dwindled, paled, like a bit of lost soap, or the moon at the bottom of the sky when the night's all run away. There was a tawny light in his hair, an autumnal flicker; he looked forlornly thin and childlike, no age at all. He nodded to Ariane, ruefully: this is none of I.

"Hullo," she said. Me neither. Craobh came to her, and briefly pressed her face against the skirts. She stroked the child's dark head, but Craobh was elsewhere.

Mrs. Woodfall was jumbling away his tattered clothes into a basket with Craobh's and Ariane's. "Yon awd haggard coat's fit for nowt nobbut flaycraw," she said.

"Aye," he said. "Gans wi me: coat's what I is."

She turned it over seriously, fingering the holes and patches and the dangling buttons, learning it; no color, any color, fall and wind and winter, leaf on leaf. "Cawd way o keeping yersel."

"Keeps others," he said obstinately, gently, with his eyebrows crouching at hare and harrier, leaping away. With his quirks and his creases coming back into play, direful or dazzled, he looked more himself.

"Eh, my souls," she said, relenting. "Can gerrit airing out, but as well darn arainwebs."

She went with Ariane to lay the cloth. "Just ten. T'mester's to Caldbeck and beyont, seeing to't sheep. Ta'en Hawk." She got the knives from the dresser. "What do yer call t'lass?"

"Craobh."

"Crieve. Eh, that's odd. Traveller's name, like."

"She's not mine."

"Aye. See'd that." So she had shaken out the dirty rags, unjudging and clear-sighted: comes with wearing. No word of the child's unearthliness, but: "Yer uneasy wi them." Ariane looked away, rubbing at the spoon she was to set.

"He's not . . ."

"Aye. Come eat yer porridge." It came in great brown bowls with a hazy blue line: good plain solid oatmeal, afloat in milk. The tinker surpassed himself. The smallest child came and stared, and knelt on the bench, gravely feeding him with a huge spoon; she put the oatmeal on it with precise, grubby fingers. He coaxed Craobh. Ariane helped herself to coarse brown sugar, and strong tea. Mrs. Woodfall went on cutting great doorsteps of bread to mop up the porridge with until even he had sat back; then wiping her hands on her sacking apron, she turned to kneading dough.

"Can I do owt?" he asked drowsily. "Milk t'ducks?"

Mrs. Woodfall hid her new-moon smile behind an immense clean white handkerchief. By now, five children, from nine perhaps down to two or so—it was hard to tell, they were so small and so grave—were standing in a solemn knot before Craobh, poking their heads forward, bluntly curious, then covering their faces shyly with their hands. Four girls in washed-out cotton frocks, long and limp and wan, a boy in shorts and a jersey: all in drab cardigans with much-rolled unravelling sleeves and scuts of hankies poking out; all thin and tough as moorland ponies, with long black eyes and straight straggly brown hair hanging over them. Hey, thought Ariane, budget Brontës. Craobh looked shyly at the red hair-ribbons. "Asta come frae't Clouds?" said Rach, speaking for the chorus, grave as to a sibyl.

Craobh looked to the tinker, uncertainly. "Aye, snawed," he said, as straight-faced, teasing and parrying.

The boy spoke. "There's holes ont moor: sheep has falled down. Forever."

"Would 'a like to hear us gramophone?" said a girl, and wound it up, a squat black horned one. She dropped the needle on a crackly, leaf-shuffling noise, then on came a chuff and a hooting. The merry-go-round broke down, over and over.

"Gi's a turn, our Beck."

Craobh stared. Ariane hugged her knees. The tinker sat between his splayed heels, as a child does, listening;

as the music took him, he sat back on his bottom, leaning
way back and gently patting and dancing his feet, so
lightly that they made no sound. Wheezing, the music
ran down. Beck said, "Sitha, Crieve," and poured a
handful of pebbles and fircones on the table turning
round. They spilled away.

Craobh said cloudily, not to any child, "Could I turn?
I knew that, I did once. Let me turn."

"Eh, lass," said Mrs. Woodfall softly. Ariane looked
up. "Could yer gi's a hand wi sheets folding? Tea's been
stood ont hob."

"I'll do," said Rach.

"No, tha mind lalluns."

The rain railed. The fire burned. The bread rose. Mrs.
Owlund knitted. Mrs. Woodfall got on with the ironing,
laying out the blanket on the table, spitting and dabbing
at the irons with a knowing finger. There was a good
faint homely smell of scorch and of bread, and apples
baking. The children played jackstones with the tinker,
and cuffed and tumbled on the floor, or sailed in the
wicker basket, with the broom as mast. The women sang
at their work, old songs, rough-hewn and worn as smooth
as any wood they handled, stone they trod; and ranting
hymns, thump and glide, thump and turn, soldiering on
to heaven: glory, down the wind-white sheets. They had
good rough voices, rising like the roof-beams of the barn:
they were where they needed to be, they met and upheld.
Ariane folded laundry, fetched irons; she peeled potatoes
badly with a sharp stubby knife.

Mrs. Woodfall thumped her iron down. "It's a thin
time o year for walking."

"Yes," said Ariane.

"Your lass wants summat more nor a candle and a cup
o milk. Have you thowt on where you're bound wi her?"

"No," said Ariane.

"Ah well, tek this." She was fumbling in her apron
pocket, and took out the rune-twig from the lintel of the
hayloft. "Lad left it, as slept in our barn. Cried and
clapped craws frae't green corn."

"Middling harvest 'at year," said Mrs. Owlund, clacking needles. "T'earth wants summat. Greener yet when
it had blood."

"Lad?" said Ariane.

"Lang gone," said Mrs. Woodfall.

"Unhallows, it were," said Mrs. Owlund.

"Were Lightfast eve," said Mrs. Woodfall. "We'd not hunted wren. Our Phoebe given him awd cap." She turned to a child, softly, seriously. "Eh, tha lal howlet, come out o yon winterhedge! Come by, tha's muckying t'sheets."

"It's my castle, I's a witch." But she came, calling to her brother, "I'll get yer back later."

"I need thy ribbon, doy." Mrs. Woodfall was knotting it firmly to the bit of twig. "Tek that to Crieve. And laik i't barn, t'lot on yer: I's fair mazed wi yer mollocking."

Beck trotted back, tugging at the rest. There was a criss-crossing of scarves and pairing of great ill-assorted hollow boots that dropped and pluffed at every step, and a fierce brief skirmish over the tinker's hat. "Bat bearaway!" he cried, and caught it from the air. He set it on Craobh's head. "Turns." He looked down at the youngest born, beating at him with her wooden doll, a spoon in a nightgown, and laughed. "Wha's this? Lang Jenny wi't ladle?"

"Wha's laiking at Babylon?" called the boy.

"Tigged last, tha's Tom alone."

"I's not. Had me fingers crossed."

They all went out.

Mrs. Woodfall held her iron to her cheek, and bent to her work. The coals fell and hissed. She said to Ariane, "You've not done too badly, what you've made of her— not touched her soul."

Ariane began to cry, terribly, with her hands in the bowl of potatoes, earth and blood and grimy water. Mrs. Woodfall gave her a hot clean handkerchief that smelled of air and iron, and she let her cry. She cried for a long time, in wrenching gasps, twisting the cloth.

"No light," said Ariane at last. "I have no grace."

"No, you haven't. But you've not gi'en ower."

"I'm tired," she cried, with battering despair. "I work and work at seeing, and she—oh, I'm hopeless. Like one of those bicycle lamps that goes by pedalling. And not even then."

"Happen you're dazzled, trying. Let be. Moon's there

to gan by. And way, i't dark." She bent over a child's shirt.

"Only to see by her, not her. I wanted—I've ruined her."

"Aye, she's bad hurt, but think on: she still walks t'earth. She and yon lad wi't cap, our flaycraw: thowt he were't last. They've not flitted wi their folk. There mun be cause. Happen you've done her good by chance, though ill by trying." She took the soulstone from Ariane's clothes, where it lay hidden, and turned it on her hard brown palm. "Clouds here, but nowt evil."

"Storm," said Mrs. Owlund, clacking her needles in the harsh grey wool.

Ariane said suddenly, fiercely, "Well, I didn't call . . . him. The one that followed. He lied."

"Aye, that he did, but he's knawed some at listened." She tucked the stone away. "Sitha, don't use comb again, it's ower sharp for you. You called lass by your lone: there's summat in you. Light, or other. You mun use yersel, afore't end."

"What *is* the end?" cried Ariane wretchedly. "No one tells me."

"You mun be bound to Black Annis. There's nowt else up here, nobbut sheep."

"What's she?" Souls to Annis, the duergar had said.

"Stone," said Mrs. Woodfall.

"Witch," said Mrs. Owlund. "She walks o nights."

"Among a ring o stones, more and less: for them at sees. They move."

"Witch," said Ariane. "Not like Malykorne?"

"Aye," said Mrs. Owlund. "Dark and light o one moon. Sisters."

"No," said Mrs. Woodfall. "They's one thing."

"Is she evil?"

"Nowt to do wi folk: some has called on her. She's eldest, same as like awd Malykorne. They is, nowt else. Unlightfast. Back o things. But you're halfway cloudwise, if you've see'd her i't wood. You can see yon soul."

"But you can see it."

"Aye," said Mrs. Woodfall.

"Can see an owl's egg," said Mrs. Owlund, rudely. "Gan by day and tek no heed o voices. She's aback o beyont, by whinnymoor. And a foul gate it is, ower't riddlestones. T'mester won't go that road, not wi'out it's a sheep strayed, and not when her hunt rides, not i' hallows."

She brushed back her fringe with one hand. "Eh! look at time, and no dinner getten. I mun see to't pudden." She turned her rare smile on Ariane, who was fidgeting with desperate visions: death or glory. "Where's thy drum? Ista marching away in yon awd petticoat? And yer smalls not dry."

Ariane smiled back, unsteadily. "No. No sword. No cap and feathers. I'll ramp away on the porridge spoon."

She washed her face in cold water, and combed her storm of hair. She peered morbidly into the inch of glass: all right, a *cheerful* death's head. She felt the lightest touch, dry leaflike, at her back, and turned to see Craobh, holding up the twig of thorn on its red ribbon. "Look what she gave me. Can you spell it?"

"A," said Ariane. "It says A."

What was that? thought Sylvie: oh, the wind in the door. Get up and latch it, or the leaves will blow away. You've left Cloud scattered on the bed. Fumbling with the strange torn quilt, leaves on leaves, yet full of bright and rusty pins, she woke and saw the boy sitting quiet as a tree beside the water. He turned to look at her. The earth was still as sleep, asleep and cold: its breath had touched his seeming-glass with mist. It was cloudy dawn.

"Oh, rats," she said sleepily. "I wanted to check out the stars, if they were the ones I know." She lay curled in Malykorne's unidyllic cloak, which was cloud and morning, as it was night and wind. She spoke softly. "I was thinking of Orion, he got into my dream. Not as stars, but like a traveller, all in rags—I never saw his face—walking through a slanting forest. Like a card I'd never turned before, but it was always there, the odd one out, the Traveller. I knew the tale." She thought a moment. "It was Cloud, in the dream. Old woods. No underbrush, just huge, spaced trees, oaks and beeches, and the light—you know, as if there was water just beyond—and fallen leaves. Leaves still falling. Like a tale within the tale, all going on the same. Unending. He was walking to a shape of music—not aloud, but like the cadence of it, fuguing—and he came to the end of the trees, out onto the scarp of a high, bare, green hill. There was another world below, green fields and woods, just coming into leaf. He had wings—not birds' wings, but like handmade, out of leaves and silk and wicker—and he flew."

"Morning," said the child. "Orion?"

"Stars." Sylvie sat up, broad awake in the closing pale mist; and gathering scattered nuts and stones, she picked out on the rimy earth the belt and sword and sprawling man. "He's in winter."

"Aye, t'Flaycraw."

Sylvie hugged her knees, caught up in wild ideas. "Hmmm. If he's—they could all be the same constellations as I was born under, with other names and myths: or does that change them? Is a Bear a Ladle? Could be like and unlike: I didn't make him very accurately. And stars drift, you know, over thousands of years. What am I saying? You really do know."

"Stars, aye, but none o yer names." He looked at her pattern musingly, as if she had brought him his hand's print, or its leafsake as a fossil, in a stone from the stars.

She touched the rune. Leaves, stones. The Traveller, if I call it so. Is Cloud another name for earth? Are all the myths one fall of stars? Same patterns, could be, but the reading's changed. Another tale. "So here could be earth, but long before or after me (when I was), or now and sideways, like a mirror world. Earth and elsewhere." She mimed with her quick hands, circles athwart. "See, the worlds, the orbits, would cross like the hoops of a gyroscope—"

He nodded. "Same as garland."

"—but obliquely. So one of us is through the other's looking-glass, that way. Backwards fortunes. Same stars, but slanted, and the drawing's changed, the lines. Same laws: gravity, light. But no cross-gravity, no warping pull: the other's always unreal. Except for shadows. Like I'm dreaming Cloud, dreaming me." What Cloud? The one I made with Air? Of leaves, stones, stars, as real as earth? Found elsewhere then. Another world. Are dreams all someplace really? "Time's sort of skewed here. And there's witches. What else is strange, I wonder?

"O the moon, yes." The other moon had risen sideways on its keel and out of phase, north above Nan's woods; she had run after it. "I hope it's clear tonight, I've got to see this. Wake me if I fall asleep."

"T'world's boxes," he said. "Inmost greatest."

"Are they? So I'm further in," she said as soberly, laying aside her pretty toy for now. "Boxes." She twiddled her hair, remembering, ah what? Wood within wood, and a fire burning, doors of dark: oh, the witch's place, her moonfast hallows. There was something, like a rime, a ring—leaves, thorns, the windy cloudy sky, not sky, but—O the stars. They'd danced in the witch's cup. "But the stars were strange when I drank the ale: not earth's at all, they *reeled*; and I knew them, I knew their names. The Ship: that's one in Cloud. From a ballad. Deea, it'd be weird if they were mine and Ariane's."

"Ballad? Frae your earth beyond?"

With her hands in her pockets, softly, in a voice sleep-rough but true, she sang:

> I'll take down that mast of gold
> And set up a mast of tree,
> For it does not suit a forsaken maid
> To sail so royally.

"Thowt on," he said as softly. "You'll not see t'Ship waking, cloud or clear: lies back o dark, nigh farthest in of all, afore all dances were. Tree's rooted i't light, and branching wi a starry crown. Fast and fleet. Came sailing wi us lightborn, out o winternight. Sails still.''

She looked at him thoughtfully: round wistful face, unchildlike long and knotty hands, brown rags. She was forgetting what he had been: ah, but so was his enemy. Briefly, from her morning dream, she saw the windblown starry figures, the words and the orb of heaven, scrawled on withered leaves. "Well, scratch the forsaken maid,'' she said. "That's beside the point. But Ariane saw the Ship, we both did: we made it up.''

"Ariane?''

"My friend, she's—well, it's funny, she's like Nan. They sort things. Keep them. They see patterns.'' She rubbed out the rune. "The tree in the song's just wood. For the rhyme. But it's real here, maybe all the stars, the songs are true, they're farther in; and nothing else is like what we imagined. Well, woods: but they're archetype.''

"See'd what I's lost,'' he said sadly. "T'wood's in your sleep, and I cannot get in. Way's shut against.''

They were sharing breakfast, crumbling the oatcake, crunched and come again, and the relentlessly recurring cheese, biting the apple turn and turn about. "What can I call you? They must've come up with something at the farms. 'Hey you' could get awkward.''

"Cobber: they see'd me i't hazelwood, laiting nuts.''

"I like that. Cobber. I'm Sylvie.'' Stiff as a heron with sleeping cold, she rose and stretched; with her eyes and with her body, she thought over the clump of trees once more. "Where now?''

"Ower t'Law.'' He pointed with his long brown hand. She peered through the drifting mist at darker cloud. Beyond the grassland rose another moor, bleak and bare and rumpled, shaggy as a starveling wolf.

"How far?'' She filled the water bottle. The rings woke and spread and died before he answered.

"Two, three days, til where I end: my bounds. All beyont's unhallows, Annis realm.'' He had a handful of the ash-keys, light and frail. He tossed them up, and let them fall unread. "You'd come by langest night.''

"Good, don't want to meet her yet, before I've had

time to think." She slung on the grizzled bag. "Sort of dropped in on this."

"Off-comed, all on us lightborn: you're nobbut last."

Ducking and twisting under the branches, they came to the last outlying tumbled stones of the ruin, and walked on, northward and away. Knife-bright and clamorous, the water of the keld fell swift beside, and lost and found itself in fissured rock. Sylvie strode, lithe and tough, in her knight's slantwise path, for the hill was steep; Cobber ran, in long curves, leaping on the stones; or lingered. In the mist, they saw a hare, crouched, then curving round the child in a swift spiral and away: a rapt and fleeting starfall dance that seemed to linger in the air, caught in stone. Like a grey-veined marble, thought Sylvie. A day-moon. A kestrel cried.

Crossing the beck, they waded, looking for stones tumbled round. Waystones, said Cobber, for a teind to Law. "Hill's hungry, it sleeps ill. Would dream on Cloud." Underwater, the stones seemed stained ale-brown, or onion-skinned, streaked as delicately as pace-eggs; but when she fished them up, they were moon-pale and celadon and claire-de-lune: they would dry to cold grey. She clacked them with cold stiff hands, to break in flint-knapped clarity, dusk-blue and autumn-veined within the chalky rock. Tales. Dreams of earth. She found one with a hole in it, another with greylag geese and clouds, and put them in her pocket.

Cobber looked at the stone he held, rime-white and almost round, with chasing shadows; then he tossed it away, clack clonk. "Moon's hagging," he said. "A' but dark."

Above the falls, they turned uphill, and the way grew steep. They rested on a broad blunt outcrop. Sylvie laid the staff across her knees, and looked at it. "It's strange," she said. "There's not much *made*, this world. Sticks and stones. No artefacts. And then this ring." She touched it. "Are these scratches? Or like runes?"

He said nothing. Then, "Is stars? All is, or nowt."

Sylvie found a stub of umber pencil and a napkin in the lining of her jacket. She tried to do a rubbing of the silver ring; but the pencil was hard and the paper fuzzy, the tracing faint and obscure. "Need tape."

The child watched closely. "Clouded ower," he said. "Is't stars?"

She held out the pencil. All in one line obliquely he drew a tree with leaves that was a bird with human hands and an immortal ageless face. It had no right way up. But the blunt lead tore through the flimsy dampened paper; it rucked unevenly. Seeing his uncertain face, she took the pencil, and drew an owl-witch, huff-shouldered, sharp and lunate. He laughed, and she crumpled them up together, and stuck the napkin in her pocket. Could blow her nose, anyway.

They walked on. The way changed slowly, the cropped grass roughening to heather and wizened clumps of bilberries, among dead rusted bracken, wet and heavy with roke. The light embrowned. Sometimes, walking close enough, she heard him sing: a wordless melody, strange sliding intervals. He had a small true woodwind voice, made harsh with crying birds.

After some hours, when the low white sun had turned, they came to the boundary wall and went over, onto the wolf-backed, stone-fanged moors. The wind blew cold from the east. They left their lightly hoarded stones on cairns, weighing down their troubled sleep with gifts of earth. There were many of these stone-heaps, solitary, or clustered like the shards of constellations, half-familiar, broken on the wheel of time.

Not speaking for the wind, Sylvie turned her thought to her coming, and her play in the pattern: like chess, with its adversary dance; and not so, for there was no array, no map, no marshalling, for all there seemed to be a dark witch-queen and her moonish rival. For example, in chess there is no sudden starfall of new pieces, unless by Thos-rules: neeeow, puzzle piece crashes on QKt-5, and takes your queen. She laughed to herself.

What did she have? Ritual and anarchy, wild conjecture, gnomic riddles, dreams. A fugue of tales. A sense of harmony, with discords and inversions, running on. A witch's cloak and staff. A chance-met child. A journey. The songs went on in her head like water underhill, riddling and running on: "*. . . for it's deep in the sea I must find my downfall . . .*" Strange, with the bare fathomless rock underfoot.

There were no stars that night. It rained ice. They
crouched in a crannied ghyll, among gnawed tumbled
rocks. A few thrawn trees stood windbreak, bare-rooted
in the stony bed, dead thorn and living tangled stubbornly, naked alike. The branches rattled in the storm.
Sylvie and the child sat close within their crack, like twigs
in a drystone wall, a child's imagined travellers abandoned to the dark. Stone tables, monstrous chairs of
stone: she half thought to find grass in an acorn-lid for
supper.

"Sad night," he said. His hands were on the earth, as
patient as roots, enduring; but his face was to the wind.

Huddled in the cloak, as wet as any maid betrayed,
Sylvie watched the sky. It was wild and grim and splendid. The sleet hissed and rattled; the lightning flicked
disdainfully, an adders' nest of tongues. "Doesn't coddle
her messengers, does she? If those are the witch's
clouds."

"Clouds and other," he said. "Cludder aloft's reet
Malykorne, but cry and cawd is Annis rade. Hunt's up."
They heard, colder than the sleet, the ring of bridles;
cold above the wind, the cry of ravens, far and deadly.

The traveller, she thought: he's out in this with Cobber's soul. He's prey. She shivered, thinking of a wild
and tatter-coated man, running, cowering from the storm
of malice. Not much cover.

"What about you . . . ?"

He sounded unhappy. "Astray. Not ta'en, hallows wi
us." He made a gesture with his hand: avert. "Cannot
knaw while t'end." She saw his pale cheek, there and
not, by wincing light. "Does cloak ward you frae unseely
eyes?"

"Don't know." Would it? Mally never—well, she
wouldn't. "Thought they weren't after me, only lightborn. I'm unCloudish. Tinfoil." Not all unglinty, Malykorne had said. Hell.

"Beyond hallows, they's leave to hunt all souls astray:
blood for their ravens' fee, and stones for their brows.
They's iron-crowned. Only lightborn mun they give til
Annis."

In their uneasy silence, they heard the cry and clamor

on the wind veer northward and return, light-lashed and
yelling in its fury, riding headlong on the fells of dark.
Pale and vast, in rough grim henges, the stones hewn of
thunder thronged the clouds. Bright as pain, the lightning
flared, it flared, like cloaks of burning silver on the
storm. The hunt rode. Far off and terrible, it spurred
over them, ice-shod with knives of sleet; and faded, muttering and lurking, into cloud. Rain and dark.

The child drew breath. "Gone back. He bears it still."

Her hands, it seemed, were stone with clenching Mally's staff. She shook the icy cloak. "Have you ever seen
him again, your other?"

"No."

"But you have the same bounds?"

"Aye, but other times; he's i't Wood, now and then.
Sky's not turned wi him. It's hallows ever, frost and fall."

"Bet he's cold, poor guy."

"Were a wanderer. He's getten his ways."

"Could've used a down vest," she said, and yawned.
"Hwah. O dear." The water trickled down her neck.
"Don't you want to come under the cloak? Drier, sort
of." It was in fact rather dank, like a stone kitchen on
washing day. He shook his head. "What'll you do when
we get closer? Turn back?"

"Not thowt. Turn and wither; cross ower and come
int' circle o my kindred, bound or light o stone. Face
witch. Fast her ring, mowt be. Or dance. Your coming's
a sign, good or ill."

She was too sleepy to debate his choices. "Oh. Hey,
sorry, I'm conking out. Take you with me in my sleep,
if I could: probably dream about missing trains. You be
all right?"

"Wake. Walk. Think on awd rhymes."

Bones to make me bread, thought Sylvie, nodding.
"Came to the dark tower, I'd rap and cry, come down,
come down. Say Mally sent me for a cup of ale."

"Hush," he said. "Yon's what you spoke on." The old
moon, bent and waning with its burden of the dark, tot-
tered wanly down the sky; but even now, ah now, its
dark devoured it, and hung alone, undying and unborn,
the dead of moon: a citadel, burred round with frost,
nine-walled, redoubted. Stone. She rubbed her crazy

eyes. No moon. All cloudy dark. Beside her, he was
still. "Yon's it seeming. When her stone is full, sall be.
Darkfastness. Annis' tower."

"Looks like we're bound there." She pulled her hood
down over her eyes. "Night, Cobber."

Waking in the kitchen, the travellers found their old
clothes beside them, folded, washed or shaken out, and
roughly mended. They looked out from the deep-set window. The morning was dark and cold, but the sleet had
ended, and the wind had stilled; the ground was white
with frost. The hills looked pale against the slate-dark
air, pale as bone. "Yon's Cloud," said the tinker. "And
ower yon is Law. Unhallows toward."

They went out into the windless, whitened yard.
Craobh caught in passing at his greatcoat, fiercely aired,
and shrewdly bitter in its scent. "Aye, wormwood," he
said wryly. "We's been flitted," and he stirred the glazy
water in the trough. No leaves. He filled his cup. Drinking, he glanced ruefully at Ariane. "Nobbut water."

Rach and Beck came out and shook the cloth between
them on the icy stones. The small birds came, the wrens
and dunnocks, whirring, light as leaves: as if the naked
air had branched. Craobh roused, softly crying out and
clapping air. They lighted. "Knap at crumbs," said Rach.
"Yer family's great, and cupboard's bare." Oboeing and
ogling, the geese thronged after.

"Serpents!" said Ariane, half afraid of the sinuous and
strutting, hissing flock; but the children fended them off
with affectionate contempt.

"Shoo," said Rach. "S'll have thee plucking for a quilt." She switched at the gander's back. "Eh, tha bezzler, knap at worms. Crumbs is fort jennywrens."

"Getten five eggs," said Beck. "We's have them to us tea."

"Were-eggs," said the tinker, teasing Ariane.

"There you are," said Mrs. Woodfall from the dairy, fleeting milk. She wore the shepherd's stiff old jacket, and a knitted scarf round her head; her breath clouded. "Gi's hand wi kirn, lass, wilta?"

They gave what help they could about the farm, fetching and tailing as the children did; only Craobh lagged and dreamed, astray. The others brought her things to see: stones and feathers, reels of cotton, a marble with a cloud of stars, the cat, the buttonbox; the babby's wooden doll, a faceless fondling. She played for a long while with the nutmegs in their silvery house, like children in a tower of the moon, thought Ariane, barbed and latched against witches.

Later, as she sat cutting strips of rags for a sacking rug, Ariane looked up and saw a strange thing, hanging in the shadows from the kitchen ceiling, with the flitch and the drying herbs, the oatcakes and the iron pans: a sort of cage of twisted thorn, an orb of twigs, all leafless, with a sad knot of tattered ribbons, white and black. And one, quite narrow, of the heartsblood red. She touched the tinker's sleeve as he went by, but he said only, "Aye, not burnt while t'sun is come."

After noon, they went with the Woodfall children to cut green branches for their winter garlands. There were no trees in sight. The fields, rimy that morning, had thawed and darkened, and the scant shrubs were hung with cold bright water; only northward of walls and in hollows did the sharp frost cling. A mist rose from the becks. Far and clear on the nearhand, browner fell, they saw the sheep like a scrape of snow, and Mr. Woodfall, stooping like a windbent tree, dry-walling. But beyond the icy mud, beyond the fallows and the walls, outby, the great cold bulk of Cloudlaw rose winter-pale: a sky of flint.

Turning from the rutted lane, they went up onto the

bare rigg behind the farm, scrunching and backsliding on
the sheep-gnawed brittle grass. The Woodfalls went
before and among and behind, bright-cheeked and raw-
handed, goose-greased for chilblains, sleeving their noses.
They spoke their brief blunt allusive language among
themselves, part grimace and part rough-and-tumble,
cuffing like hares on the moonlit common fields of their
imagining. With the strangers they were rough and shy
and kind. They looked an odd lot, bundled stiffly in their
cut-down clothes, their shawls and scarves and knitted
caps, like a nest of Mrs. Noahs; and the strangers odder
still, thought Ariane. They met nothing but a crazy ewe,
pale-eyed and querulous: a dingy sibyl. "Art strayed,
awd lass?" The tinker tugged his hat to her, and listening, nodded. "Baabylon? Up Law," he said, and left her
glaring in the mud. Their way was faint but trodden, and
steep as the sky; at last they came struggling to the top,
and over on the fell.

Below them lay a little spinney, long and narrow, slanting down: oak and alder, hazel, thorn and holly. Craobh
looked about in wonder, touching the branches.

"What do you call this place?" asked Ariane.

"T'wood," said Thomas.

"Cobber's Wood," said Rach. "Get us boughs for our
door, and garland fort wren; t'awd one's burnt til ashes
soon. Snaw's ont wind: we'll not have another chance to
come afore lightfast."

Beck said, "Our dad comed last year: snawed."

"Were ower his knees," said Thomas.

Solemn, with her knife and sack, Rach went among
the trees, and stood before a thrawn and ancient holly,
asking leave to cut of it:

> Hallybranch and hallybright,
> Out o darkfast, bear us light:
> Crown for wren and wren for stone,
> Moon for waking, leaf and bone,
> Thorn for hallows, branch and blood;
> And tha'll have mine, when I is wood.

She cut the greenest branch. Craobh bowed her head
as if assenting to the sword, and not in ritual. Her hand

was bright with blood. Perhaps she had scratched herself, coming through the thicket; perhaps not. The tinker lapped it in the skirt of his greatcoat. "Dosta want to gan back?"

Her eyes were far and fierce. "Given leave to them," she said.

They filled their sacks with green, and the tinker cut a great bundle of thorn for their bonfire, with their knives and bill-hook. They had brought ropes to bind it. "You'll want this dragging," he said. Leaving his coat all of a heap, chameleon amid the tattered oak-leaves, he clambered after a bough of mistletoe; and being lithe and light and rather scatty, and longer than a child besides, he got it. "By yer leave," he said, and cut.

Grave admiration from below. Glancing ruefully at himself, old tatters and new holes in Mrs. Woodfall's rough, patient mending, he said, "Strange acorns i' this wood," and dropped to earth. The little ones crouched in the bushes, whirring and hiding and calling out, as quick as birds to find the berried holly, picking none.

Craobh would cut no branch, but walked in the damp and durmast, longways through the narrow wood, to make it last. She woke birds like brown leaves. So Ariane would have turned the pages of a book lost in childhood, now torn and faded, its words strangely dulled: the thing a shadow and a puzzle, loved and rued, while the memory was inward brightness, a longing beyond recovery or grief.

Ariane gave Rach her bunch of holly. "Burnt?"

"Aye, they runs wi't on crook, by nightfall, ower fields: far as t'ashes falls and t'fire lights, fields are sained, they's hallows." Her face was alight with the hallowfire, the sharp frail comet fleeting eerily away, over the dark fields of her sleep; but she spoke gravely as always. It was hard to shape for the stranger what she had always known and was not spoken. "T'dark ones— hallyans, you knaw"—she turned her hand—"are caught i't thorns."

"So these"—Ariane touched the boughs—"are for another garland?"

Rach nodded. "Green crown's made aforehand, for to bear t'wren til it wake, come lightfast. And it's dark o moon. So then we's up and hunting it thrae't wood, and bring it back. Stone dead. And it's hanged i't crown. We gan a-souling for it arval. Cakes and siller for it crown, folk give us. And you munnot shut yer door, mun bid us in. Then at new moon's hallyfire: that's wakesun. And there's guising, and there's cake. And songs." She made a garland of her hands. "Then's hanged i't kitchen." Softly, so that the youngest might not hear, she bent toward Ariane, and said, "So as t'witch won't get in at door."

"Is she so near?"

"Not like in a castle, she's nowhere; but her time is."

The fells were pale beyond them, but the wood was dusk, and rising, filling like a cup of woven branches with the dark. They had crammed their sacks, and wrapped away the one rare bit of mistletoe, like a nursery of moons, hard-won. Pinched and bright, blowing on their hands, the children came together: all but Craobh.

Witches, thought Ariane. "Craobh?" No answer. Dark and trees. She caught the tinker's wary glance. An owl cried. Though the wood was small, they scattered, calling out: the elders, sharp; the children, wild and shrill, as in a game of witch by owl-light. Moon's hid and all after. Thorn's hallows. Quick and shadowy as birds, whirring and eluding sight; then gone. The rotting leaves damped their voices, and the wood was mirk, unchancy, close. Dark, thought Ariane; and touched Craobh's stone.

Cold heavens and a starry thorn, a ship of tree: and root and branch were nightfast, flowering in light. The wood was all of sky, and all; yet was smaller than a hazelnut. That O was lightself, eye, yet other: what I held, beheld. They were one and the other. One.

She let it go. As in a seeming-glass, mooncold and cloudy with her gaze, she saw the child. She was standing in a waking dream beneath a blackthorn, still as wood, of wood, enwoven in its boughs; one branch was all in cold white flower. Ariane saw it still with other eyes: still lightfast, though of earth. The wren would die.

Craobh turned and broke the wintry branch, as black as ash, all starry in her hand. The flowers fell, and were ice. It was snowing. Her face was bright and fearful. "For the crown," she said.

The homeward way was dark. They had their lantern, and the snow fell, bright within the circle of the candle-light, and nowhere else: a walking storm. Beyond was nowhere. "I's no feet," said Phib, so Ariane took her up, and chafed them, and stamped her own until they swarmed. Beck danced. "See at, I's shoon o velvet." Rach and Tom clapped hands. "Shak, shak, featherbed! Wedding's coming on." Craobh bore the lantern, and the tinker carried thorn. The children ran, dragging their cobbish sacks like shadows, imps and urchins of the dark; their old, wild, joyful terror flying out behind, like fire from a shaken brand. They called and whistled for the dogs, who came, circling like shaggy moons, black and white, shepherding their flock in quiet down the cloudy hill, toward firelight and tea.

After nightfall, and shepherd's pie, and the washing-up, Ariane wrote by lamplight, bending close to her book. The ink had come from the Woodfalls' kitchen-dresser, forgotten among candles, dishcloths, old valen-tines, and the fat bristling pincushion, shabby as a hedge-hog. Craobh lay sleeping on the settle, with an old quilt tucked around her. The children had gone off to bed with their candles, having begged for tales of giants, and burrowed when they heard them. Mrs. Owlund and Mrs. Woodfall were darning stockings, thick as leaves in Val-lombrosa, with the basket set between them. The tinker had gone out on the fells with the master, driving sheep to the high folds, for it was snowing fast.

In the quiet and uncertain light, she thought and wrote, in her small sharp hedgerow hand, little of all she had seen, but filling all the little space, and crowding in the margins. Not a tale, but a runestave: A and O.

She thought about the prophecies, about the word as branching tree: a knot of thorn, cold-crystalled; or an arainweb, rayed and ringed with half-seen patterns, stones of water; or a skein of stars. Craobh's other name. The naming stars has called them, though their spell is endless dance. The world is word, and must be spoken, rooted, danced. Cloud and clod are one root, so that a sky of stone, a fell of heaven, are the deepest magic of necessity. So flying is to walk on law. Waking sun will bid it rise. The light is borne by travelling, A springs from O. The way is earth, here and now, though it lie through cloud or commonplace; and elsewhere is the coming home.

She thought about the journey and the light, which are one: though Malykorne was not of time, unlightfast, yet her end was in her going on, O was A. She had turned the travellers out to make their way, to make her wood, dying or enduring as they must, against great dark; but journeying to come again within the thorny hallows of her realm. Their travelling became the wood. There was no turning back: no thread spun out would be unravelled, nor was death annulled; neither had they left her cot. The ship is rooted, though it sails before the wind.

For a moment, Ariane lost her graceless angst, and was herself, was tough, obsessive, insular: a crabbed and rooted thorniness, unbodied, crowned with light. Then the candles dipped in the draught, and shivering, she thought of witches.

The candles crouched again. Mrs. Woodfall got up and went out to her husband in the back-kitchen with a drench for an ailing sheep. The tinker came in, all powdered with snow, shaking himself and stamping, like a wassailer at the door. He stooped over the fire, and his shadows loomed, etenish and homely, a hearthtale of giants. There was mulled ale waiting, and he filled his cup. Ariane looked at the sleeping child; the bright, bemused and tousled wanderer; the ancient woman, nodding, with her silver thimble on her gnarled brown hand; at the fire, the row of plates, the sharp bright holly: and she saw all this with longing, as a stranger already pressed against the glass, a sharp and hungry frost excluded. She thought with cold dread of the moorland night. "What now?" she asked the tinker.

"Walking on," he said regretfully.

"Now?"

"I't morning."

She spoke softly. "Souls to Annis, he said: she's what Craobh's been running from. Gave me her soul to keep, and I've led her straight to the witch."

"T'gate's led; tha's nobbut mazed."

"Well, she's waiting, and we can't elude her; I'll bet

her castle's whichever way we set out. Now and nowhere. And there's no wood, not now. That's what's maddening: Mally won't let us in. It's all her house." Ariane looked down at her hands, scratched with holly. "Couldn't we just stay here, until it's past the longest night, past Annis's time? They'd let us."

"Sun 'ud not turn, I doubt: when we come til Annis hand is sun, and dark until. Same as like t'wren: it's hunted fort wintersake, bears light sall never see. Crown's it bier." He glanced up at the cage of thorns and shadows, swaying in the little wind. "Eh, poor awd wren, poor Jenny." Then dolefully he said, "Doubt Mally's not given thee windegg for nowt. Will hatch out storm."

"I had a feeling about this: no way beyond but through it."

His face, as he looked at child and hearth, was wistful; yet for all its creased and weathered innocence, he spoke with grim compassion. "T'lass is wren. We's nowt, nobbut daws wi dimants: can sit darkfast, or gan and be etten, for Annis cares. Not seeking bone and blood, not thowt on. So tha's hawden thy stone, whiles, and I's wood, I's beared cup. T'hunt's flet us ower, chanced. Could fall on us t'morn, or never: we could walk, and no end on it, no grave, no dance. No tale.

"But nowt's healed. Wood's here and not, but ever i't fall o leaf, ay hallows and unturned. Unfast. I's not found winter's end, nor see'd t'spring o't year and green: not come to't gate beyond. Lies thruff Annis, I doubt."

"But if she takes us . . ."

"Aye, Cloud, clogs and all," he said grimly. "That end or another: dreamed o't lad, that I given him an awd bad hazelnut that were his cup. I'd kept it ower lang for him. Were dust."

His face gentled, as he turned to her, touching Sylvie's brown-leafed twig, among the pages of her notebook. "Tha'll not find yon odd tree on Law. Other woods, elsewhere. And stars."

Sword i't leaves. O Sylvie, Sylvie's star, she thought, lightstruck with sudden hope. Craobh had come, through years and light-years and the dark, star-fallen to the earth, not as thrall but messenger, summoning her bright

uncloudish champion: a sword that Annis in her baleful
dark could not foresee.

"Yes. Yes. She comes into this before the end—Sylvie—but I don't know how. She's the Sword, the travelling, she's running on before. What Mally told. See,
there has to be an end. She led me here." She thought
of the moveless running figure, of the moon caught out
of time, in her mantle of the flying cloud, burning silver
on the wind; of the brown girl in the nightwoods, stalking
witches. "You'd like her, Sylvie: she knows a lot of
songs."

"Would that. Not heard another for a while."

But that starry crossing hung, bright and fortunate,
elusive, in a ruined web, and all their ways were blind;
their thread might lead them, not to Sylvie, but the spider, dry and brooding on her thirst. Ariane sighed.
"We'd better go early, what light there is. Get me out
the back door before I wake up."

He smiled at her, condoling; but there were shadows
in his rushlight face. Half solemnly, he poked out his
feet, heavy-shod in the shepherd's cast-offs. "Aye, cannot stay: Hob's getten new boots."

She smiled back crookedly, pierced with a sudden poignant regret for the hallowfire she'd never see alight and
fleeting, for the hearthtales and the carols, and the tinker
casting shadows for the bairns. "What about our bowl of
cream?"

"Whey and sadcakes," he said.

She bent closer, and asked unhopefully, "I wonder . . .
could Craobh, could we leave her here? Until—I don't
know what it is we're meant to do. They'd keep her from
harm. They're good. She has nothing left, and she can
still be hurt. I can't use the comb again, Mally didn't
give it to me; I don't know what the egg is for, not yet,
and I've no power, that I've learned: the witch may not
fear the light as much as hate it. And the stone's—well,
dangerous."

"Tha'rt witch, whatever, as thy lass is sword; and I is
wood: awd tattered coat's my fastness. Seeing's thine.
Nowt to bring but what we is alone. And lass is lightborn.
She mun come." He set down his empty cup. "Tha'd not
come thy ways back here, tha'd not find way: never turns

on itsel. I's tried," he said sadly. "And she'd not stay, sitha, she'd follow after yon stone, an it lay in Annis claw. Mowt die, if tha went far."

"I could, well, not give it back, not heal her, but leave it with her . . ." she began, small and stubborn, forlorn.

But Craobh spoke. "I'll lead you. The morn is lightfast eve: will be the dancing in the stones." She spoke in a small voice, far and clear as a star, as frail and cold, compelling; and their hearts' blood thumped tabor to her piping. She sat fingering her rune-twig, staring dark-eyed in the firelight. How long since she had waked? They saw her: not Craobh, but the immortal, light from elsewhere, flawed, refracted in the child's frail body. "Lightborn, if any walk in Cloud, will come, and I must dance with them in turn: the ring must not be broken."

"But the witch . . ."

"Have danced with Annis long before, have called her from the stone."

They could not answer. Mrs. Woodfall came up to them, haloed with the cold, and drowsy, heavy-booted, with her candle. A wind was in the door. She touched Craobh's cheek. "Bitter cawd i't wind: tha'd best have scarf, lass. Sleep by fire." Softer, she said to the tinker and Ariane, "Tek lantern when you go: we'll not be waking."

V

Law

"Arianty." A dry leaf brushed her face, the fall denied: a whisper. Waking, rising to the leaf from dark, she thought: then I must have slept, if this is light; there were woods in the dream, and I lay awake all night to keep the leaves from falling.

It was ashy dark. Ariane lay wrapped in the shepherd's coat, on a quilt by the hearthstone. Crouching, the tinker touched her shoulder. "Arianty? Come up, lass." The candle shivered in the dark. He held it aside, so as not to spill the burning wax; it dazzled in her eyes. He had a cup of tea for her, black and bitter, thick with leaves, for he knew no measure of the strange dry stuff. A draught for long-enduring, a kindness. No milk. She sat up, her head whingeing and wincing at the light. He set the candle down. A drop of tallow hardened on the stone beside her, and she smudged it with her thumb.

Craobh turned from the deep-set window, blind with its cataract of frost. Uncertain as marsh-light, she walked among the patient handmade things, felled and quarried, warped and pegged and fired: silent things, unrooted save in commonplace, in use and handing-down, worn smooth in joy and sorrow. She was forgetting houses. Her look changed, now far and fierce, now tremulous, bright or fearful, as the light possessed her. She knelt suddenly by Ariane, and took the stone between her cold hands, briefly. "If I fall to her, do not follow," she said.

She would not eat. She had some milk, and Ariane took the rest, to whiten, if not subdue, her black morass. Somberly, the tinker drank his cup of ale, and tossed the dregs hissing on the hearth; he raked eggs from the ashes for their way-meal. Ariane drank her tea and broke a piece of oatcake from the rack above the settle.

They were ready, with their few things tied or gathered: staff and bag and budget, cup and stone; rough blankets, food and candles of Mrs. Woodfall's providing, enough until the dark had turned, no more.

"Wait," said Ariane, and dumped out her bag, rummaging, until she found the square of chocolate from Illyria, bright in its silver paper. She left it on the kitchen-dresser, for the children. Craobh set a candle in the lantern. The tinker unbarred the iron-latched and holly-warded door; it dragged against the mat. The wind whirled in, but meeting hallows, fire and thorn, it fell: the snow took on no wraithlike shape of witch.

They left the sleeping house, walking in the iris of the light, the burr of their wavering candle, through the dim untrodden yard, from gate to narrow gate and out beyond, into the stonelaw of the frost.

It was bitter cold. The snow was dry, wind-carved in scarps and scimitars, and sweeps of ice-drift, endlessly effaced. It rose in wraiths of scythesmen, and of grass; and fell to its own blade, winnowing, unripe. In the cloud-skirts, like a sickly child, the moonrise hid: a starveling, wan and wizened. Dark of moon and the longest night would fall together.

Turning and turning to look back, Ariane saw the grey enduring farmstead huddled to the ground, old and wary, earthfast; sleeping as a great tree does, in the wind and rooted past at once. No glimmering of light shone in its windows. "Sended on wi lass, afore," said the tinker. It was lost behind the shouldering hill; it looked Cloudward, not to Annis.

Then bent against the wind and the steep of the scarry hill, as steep as cloud, they went on. Craobh bore the lantern. They followed, northward through the maze of walls, and out on the high bleak windy fellside, back of Law. Ariane saw only snow, and the tinker's grimly scrunching feet, turned herringbone for surety, his icy coat-skirts and his staff, at the wavering edge of candle-light. Craobh went lightly, slowly on before, in a curving path, erratic as a wandering star; she was walking on the wind-riggs, the spines of hardest snow. Heavier and obdurate, the others ploughed, and fell and floundered in the drifts. The wind blew sidelong from the north of east, warping them off course. Slowly, it was morning, dark with cloud. A sparse snow came snittering down, and whirled a little on the wind. The lantern made no orb. Craobh snuffed the candle.

"How far?" said Ariane.

"By night," said Craobh, "or not at all."

They went on. There was no other way, whatever end. Nor was there sanctuary, but the light returned. No den, thought Ariane. If Craobh were fey, yet she was wren and wintersake, she bore the light. They'd nothing else to go by. They would try until the last to keep her soul from dark, beclouding it with breath; as they would keep her slighted body from the cold. But at the last—Ariane looked up. White, nothing. In a tale of Cloud, she thought, she'd turn another card. The Sword. Oh, she wanted Sylvie. But no Sylvie came, striding through the drifts, astray, assured and scattering bright. Sylvie would be elsewhere, in the woods, not now, not here. She'd be her name. In all the world there was no focus anywhere, no stone round which to curve the wintry chaos, not a bird. Not even prints of animals, for the last dry drifting snow obliterated tracks. Still Craobh held to her way, and the tinker followed; Ariane trudged blindly after. No one spoke, each journeying alone.

Unforeseeing in the endless snow, they came on a spattering of red, bright as raspberries, congealed: drops of blood on the snow. Then a sheep, new-made carrion, crow-worried.

Wolves? thought Ariane, sickening at the eyeless mask, shredded to the skull.

"Starved," said the tinker grimly, and beat away the crows with his staff; but they swerved and sank again: stone-eyed, greedy, implacable.

Craobh spoke. "You have your ravens' fee. Fly now, tell your mistress that one who sought her for foretelling knows her end." Cawing and cronking derisively, they rose and scattered on the wind.

Foretelling? thought Ariane, bewildered: did she mean herself? the poor beast? Ah, but poor Woodfalls, their sheep. But the tinker bent over the carrion, and took something bright and delicate from amid the clotted wool: a ring of twisted gold, a woman's bracelet. "Don't a touch thy stone, tha'lt see her. T'hunt's wark," he said, shaken. But he spoke too late. Ariane had looked with eyes of stone, had seen the woman's bones within the bloody fell, and her long hair, stiff with jewels and blood.

Ariane stood, struck with a dark and sudden insight. Some has called on her, said Mrs. Woodfall. Witches. This was one who had been answered. Soulless she lay on the untrampled snow, in her rough cloak and bright rings. Ariane remembered the strayed sheep below the Woodfalls' wood, the pale-eyed sibyl, seeking Babylon. But where was now? The arm-ring was inlaid and wrought with an enmity of dragons, archaic, writhen gold, as from the gravemound of a queen; the ewe's blood had not yet blackened. Unseen and illusory, dragon-jewelled and maggot-ridden, witch and beast: their ancient death was bright upon the snow, and one; nor could it be unspilled. A morning's walk behind, the Woodfalls wound their gramophone. But why illusory? Did Annis mock their folly? "She doesn't know we're . . . She's not . . . ?"

"Laiking wi us? Wha can tell?" said the tinker, turning the ring in his hands. His ragged sleeve was stained with blood. "Allt same, I doubt there's a glamour on us. We'll not see owt aright. Not—tha knaws—yon bright one, nobbut her awd shift. We's not lightborn. T'lass sees." He saw a little, having borne the cup so many hundred years: a glint of gold, a dark-quilled feather, not a crow's.

Ariane thought, what did Craobh, being lightborn, see when we saw Mally? Not the dead leaves and the dusk of the hovel: the moon's true face, perhaps. Not owlish games, or not alone. For with Malykorne, she saw, illusion went beyond her toyish malice and delight in prickly metaphor. Her comb was thornwood; souls were truly in her tattered shifts. If for the wintry sun, and suns unborn, unwaked, she made them see a heap of withered apples, there was light in them, though hidden from the eye and tongue. Yet truly the light was apple, seed and blemish, and the earthfast root bore suns. As she herself was eldest and owl-witch: ladle, ragged petticoats and all.

Storm was in her clumsy carding, and pattern in her webs. What she seemed, she was, though not wholly. She indwelled.

But with Annis, illusion could be distancing, thought Ariane, denial of the earth, transcendence; or contempt: the jewel withdrawing from the toad, which, soulless, warped and shifted in their eyes. It is all one flesh. Remembering the duergar's cold indifferent greed, she shivered. *Souls to Annis*. Wool or woman's braided hair, hoof or hand: all carrion, said dark of moon. The soul is mine.

What cause had brought the petty witch to seek her death, what prophecy besought, what quest or craving, or defiant claim, Ariane could not guess. But she knew that she herself could call forth Annis, now, by taking up Craobh's soul; could see the witch and all her realm undarkly, through a glass, and so stand naked to the dark. She would not, fearing wisely, having read so many tales. As shadows, they would meet their adversary.

The tinker stooped and left the jewel by the carcass, the unbarrowed ancient bones.

The way now was strangely guarded, set with cairns, and crouching rocks, and cloaked and hooded standing stones. On the farther slopes, the snow was shaggy, here and there, as if the wolf beneath were stirring. Dulled, chilled beyond uneasiness, unwary, Ariane saw nothing: the shadowless, the white. She had set her will to walk, no more.

"Stay," said Craobh urgently, not loud. They stumbled to a halt. At their feet lay a shallow where the snow was puzzled, like the moon's face, with a blind irregular relief of scars and shadowed seas, lacunae. Near round, the place was broad as Mally's garth. Craobh stood. "Touch the stone," she said at last, "not long, or she will see that one unblind has come." Ariane did, hesitant and formal: it lay cold against her body. A flaw of clarity, a wind but lightstill, swept the snow, scattering the illusion of wholeness, laying bare the abyss.

Something here had gnawed the earth. The scars were pillars in the rock, like roots of towers, all unvaulted, or a grove of stone, unbranching; and the holes between were deep as night. Some few stones were geminate, or coalesced, like great and ancient beeches; other stacks were slender, roughly fluted, like bunches of reeds; or twisted, deeply scored and cracked, like obliterated winding stairs. Ariane drew back, half crouching, caught between paralysis and awe. She saw at once with mortal eyes and eyes of soul, the pattern and abyss; she saw the shapes of stone as leaves inlaid on water, as a scattering of wooden puzzle-pieces on the dark, ringed about with cairns and henges: Craobh's patterning on the floorboards of Sylvie's room, the way forespelled. She saw the three odd pieces, dangling on a string: the hare, the hunchback, and the moon, horn downward; and the child, now shadowing her island world, and now indwelling.

"Riddlestones," said Craobh. "The way lies over."

Not around? thought Ariane, and lost all touch of earth. The tinker stared, white-faced and wind-sharpened, stunned.

Craobh sat, and took off her clumsy boots, struggling childlike with the knotted laces, unblinding her feet. She leapt onto the first stone, and turned, all in one curving, heedless. "Where I tread: the way is spelled." She went lightly on the glazy stones, and formally, as in a dance.

Still Ariane stood paralyzed: as stone, but sliding, clenched and giddy on the brink. No earth. The void was in her head, annulling surety and sense and will. She saw dark toppling chimneystacks, and hell, and hell. "I can't."

The tinker turned to her, gingerly, not shifting his feet. He clutched his staff like a new-blind beggar. "Can tha see?" he said hoarsely. "Seen, but it's snawed ower."

He groped with his stick. They heard a brittle crust of ice break, cracked like an ancient heaven, thin and crystalline; and fall, and fall. She heard, and saw the bare abyss, that spoke to her, daunting and compelling: for *giddy* is the word for god-within; as he heard, and saw the drifting snow, and knew its frailty, and what it hid. He had seen as if by lightning. Her unblinding would grow dim; already the revelation clouded, as with mist: and she dared not touch the stone again.

"Can you see my footprints?" she said. He nodded. "Where I step." She could not. She stepped.

Swayed and stiff, she followed Craobh's way over the riddlestones, and he lurched behind her, groping with his staff on the rotten floor of heaven. They had to look down. There were long strides between, where Craobh had leapt, and the stones were broken, icy, small and slanting; and the falling was unfathomed.

Her mind fell, and fell again; her body, jerking back against imagined gravity, would twitch, aslant, unbalanced. Twice she jibbed, cold and sick and blind with fear. "Not far," he said. "Hawd on."

They staggered at last onto the cold dear stony earth; and there they lay, dazed and shaking, and the sky turned over.

Rousing after a bit, the tinker took a long pull at his skin of ale, and gave Ariane another. She drank it, coughing. They'd never have missed a corner of that chocolate, she thought regretfully. He glanced at her from beneath his ice-daggled brows, with his nut-hook face all innocence, and laughed. "Riddles, were it? Ah. What's light on wind, t'way to blind?"

"Snaw," said Ariane, solemnly; and giggled, crazy with sprung terror. "What has it got in its 'pocalypse? Tell us that, precious."

But Craobh was plucking at her sleeve; her face was strange, unclouded of the child. Her stone was cold against Ariane's throat. It pierced, a fixed shivering like starlight. "Now," said Craobh. "It darkens."

They were back of beyond. Here, on the other side, the hills were bare of snow: another year, no year, winter, north. The stones were swept bare as death, and all that country, desolate and bleak and brown. The snow lay closed in Mally's kist, feathers of her geese; for back of Law, the wind blew, cold and naked, from the eye of the black witch. The grass was scant and withered, bound in a black frost. The earth was stony. Cloud beyond stony cloud, north and west, austere, the fells of winter climbed. The sun rode low and white. Yet in all that bitter clarity, a mist, a roke, still clung dishevelled to a greener knoll.

"Well, then," said the tinker, and he took Craobh's cast-off boots from his greatcoat pockets. "Here, lass, tha'lt starve thysen," he said, concerned: for her feet and fingers bled a little, cracked with cold and stonebruised. But she looked through him, bright and elsewhere; then she turned and ran.

Barefoot, west and north, upon the naked clouds of stone, the fells of air, Craobh ran, or fleeted: for she came by law, by frost and fire, air and earth, to lightfast and the carol of the stones. Unswerving as the even-star, heedless of the earth, she went, having made this journey time before times as spirit, truly, and once now as bone and blood.

The others followed, lashed on by the wind of her urgency, fearing to lose her in the greenish dusk that mocked the spring, on the hillsides that were cloud: for she far outran them. They were amid the dance before they saw.

Elusive in the mist were scattered stones, no taller than children, storm-hued, still as earth. They were a circle and a shape within; and then unpatterned, numberless: a ring and not. Craobh ran to each, and touched it swiftly with her hands. Her moving among them made a dance that mortal eyes could not unskein. Annealed as she was by grief and passion, she seemed fleetingly to burn upon the shaken air.

They will wake, thought Ariane: the stone itself seemed tremulous as fire, as cloud, through which a hand, a curve of brow or bended knee would break, dancing to an unheard music.

But the dancers did not turn, breaking from the stone. Nor was Craobh light. The sun faltered. The tinker held his crosshilt of iron to his brow. Ariane stretched out her hand, and felt nothing, cold harsh rock. Craobh caught her hands, and held them flat to the brow of a stone. And only then with unblinded hands Ariane felt the ever-breaking and unbroken light, the body of the child within, caught striving upward, as against deep water, or wind, or time. Ariane drew back. The touch of its eyelids lingered, cold as petals beaten flat with rain.

Craobh stayed. Whirling about, she strode to a stone, a little apart from them all, and struck it, crying, "Come, lief darkness, I am come!" Her wild clear clamor died, damped like a candleflame.

A flaw of wind whitened the grass. And striding down

from the high fell in storm, amid a hurly of black kids and horned deer, came a dark-clad woman, so like Craobh that Ariane caught her breath; and unlike. The earth crazed beneath her bare feet in roots of darkness, unrecallable as lightning, as if they were the talons of the frost. At her step, the grass cowered and the wind darkened, fluttering like a ravencloak around her.

She was bitter white beneath her thornblack hair; so white that her unlined face seemed old as winter, haggard in its utter baneful beauty. It was clearcut and translucent as knapped flint, a leaf-shaped spear of stone. Her eyes were grey-black as broken stone, archaic, veined with bronze. Caught up amid her writhen hair, like a rain of blood on brakes of thorn, were dark clear stones; and others, clouded like Craobh's soul, autumnal, dusky blue or green. She held a staff.

"Who calls? I tend my flock." She looked beyond the mortals, and her blindness made them nothing; her desire alone could call them into being. Only as naked souls, unclothed of carrion creation, would they exist. They were annulled.

For that moment, deeply shaken, unwilling but compelled, as iron to the adamant, Ariane thought of taking up the stone, of calling death to make her real; but her despised hand, bone and blood, would not move. Nobody cannot act.

Then seeing Craobh, Annis changed and shifted, dwindling, dusky and birdsmall, as if to coax; but her hand bit more fiercely at her staff. "Come, lagman, all are folded; come, by the star I bid you sleep . . ."

Craobh stood, mirroring the other. On her face was bitter joy. "It is not your time, lief mother," she said.

Black Annis said, "It is all my time."

Looking from one to the other, Ariane saw the shadow-play: Annis in her shift of seeming-flesh; and Craobh, caught within her shadow, the dark of moon that is its hulk. The child said, "It turns. Will you dance?"

"It is broken on the wheel of stars, that in the crown endures."

"The crown is not yet made."

"Not yet: in your folly you have come to close the ring. Let fall that cloak; you shall wear one of mine."

Turning to a stone, she plunged her hands in it, and dragged out by its hair a naked wizened child.

It could not stand, for its limbs were gnarled with long duress; it was dazed and mute; yet about it clung a crowning brightness, a luminance, the dance of light in water, light on leaves, that made Craobh seem a withered branch. Oh, thought Ariane in grief, O Craobh. She saw how far that Craobh had died, and at her hands; how cold this endless death would be. No memory could endure that vision. Annis clawed within the child's ribs, and her scything hand was full of stone, shattered crystal of a heartsblood red. "Stones for my crown," she said. "It shall be closed: the dark unturning, the undying and the unborn light." She struck the child, and it dwindled into rock.

"Now my soul." She caught Craobh by the shoulders with her bitterwhite, annihilating hands, crying out a word to call her true shape into being. The child stood unchanged.

Craobh laughed, a cracked triumphant cry. She held up her hands, blood-streaked. "Do you see my rings? I am mortal. I am not for you." Whirling about, she caught up the tinker's knife, and lightly as a dancer, bared her throat. "Would you see it flower once with red?"

Black Annis snatched her hair, bending her head back in the moon's waning curve, and held the edge to her white throat. After a long moment, she let it fall. She spoke out of her iron dismay, harsh and mocking. "Do you not know what they have done to you, carrion? What you have become? Flesh for my jackal, and a rattling cinder."

"Unbound," said Craobh, "and unnamed. You cannot conjure me. My soul is elsewhere."

The witch shook her head in a storming of rooks. The stones glinted balefully in the underbelly of light. "Fool! All hidden things are my domain. Your dark is in my glass." And she was gone, the grass combing and cowering at her passage, struck with frost.

Craobh stuck the knife deep into the earth, as if to give a merciful death, and writhed and rubbed her stained hands in the long dank grass. As she did, her hand brushed against the stone she'd struck, as tall as she and set apart, unsouled; and she flung herself on the earth beside the vain rock, and beat at it, crying softly, ceaseless as the rain, "Lief mother, let me in."

The fire made it night. It burned, bright as autumn, in the stone-clear dusk; and kindling, leaping, closed the vast obscurity in a blind keep. No stars again, high cloud. Sylvie turned over her small hoard of things. She was seeking an insight. Witches do not fall to will: she needed something, a word, a sword, to harrow Annis, as the fire fastens on the wick, or cannot blaze. A filament. She thought that Malykorne gave nothing for no end, though her gifts were shrewd and sly. But it was hard to imagine daunting her adversary, taking on a malign and shapeless dark, a shadow; she did not know what Annis feared, nor yet the hunt. She thought not swords.

She had forgotten the iron brooch until now, simply wearing it to pin her cloak, as it was given. Now she set it with the rest. What? A brooch, a mirror, a graven ring on a staff. Iron, bronze, silver, like the choices in a tale. Or a progression: eyes like saucers, millstones, towers; cloaks of sun, moon, stars. No, such chances came by witches' law, and were taken as in sleep or ritual, unquestioned; Mally's task felt more like argument. Cat's cradles, not Irene's clew. Unless the witch's castle had three gates? Well.

What of the iron brooch, clumsy as a thorn? It pinned and it pierced. It was of iron, which the ancient of earth do not love. Did they of Cloud? It was not quite annular;

perhaps it could bewitch, could catch things in its likeness: the black ring unclosed, the talons caught unseizing on their prey.

She took up the mirror next. She could gaze in it, foreseeing what was hidden, shadowed in its face. Ah, she could spy on witches. Or else transfix some gorgon enemy—she tilted the mirror in the firelight—astony and dismay; but she would need the sun to dazzle with. It was round and cold and ruddy, subtly faceted, as if beaten out: now blank and bright, now wave-hammered, stroke on stroke, glittering, like the winter sea at sunrise.

The ring with its graven runes she could not read; she thought it would enspell. It too was round, an endless ring, integrity; of moonish silver, bright and blackening, unlike the sun's untarnishing and crafty gold: uncoveted, unwedding, fickle, pure.

Earth, fire, water. What was air? All round her. Not to hand. The staff was of thorn, and tough and stout, but woods were dying; though Annis might fear and hate creation, change, yet all her will was bent on annihilating them. Perhaps this was the ur-tree, and would take root, afterward. If there was an afterward. Perhaps it was just for walking. It had served her well in the morass—might come in for thwacking wolves.

As Sylvie sat, the shape of hills they'd traversed rose wintry in her mind, grey-white with rime or fleasblood purply brown, dovetailing with the dark or pallid sky—and always, the wind and the steep and slant of gravity. The fire was pale as horn, fierce as summer: she stared through it. Beyond lay Nan's woods in August, and the windfall in the oldest cedars, where the rotten wood had gone, and the raspberries and goldenrod had taken over, having sun: tough to walk on in bare feet. Earth. She found herself singing under her breath, and caught at the words.". . . *in her bare, bare feet . . .*" Oh, Gypsies, right: " *. . . for I met with a boy, and a bonny, bonny boy, and they were strange stories he told me O . . .*" She smiled, recalling to herself, turning to the boy. "Cobber? Hey, you're quiet."

Brown and still, he sat feeding gnarled twigs of heather to the flames. "Were thinking on hearthtales." His hair was frayed with brightness as he turned. "They—tha knaws, hearthfolk—they's no stars by night: fire and shadows. Closer at they'd hug, t'huger, loom and swale: hand's a hillside. Folk would owerlook me hid i't shadows, talking low at stones and witches. Hallows-tales. Heard awd woman say til bairn, Black Annis will get thee, if tha set foot ont moor. She's getten a blue face and iron claws, and she's howked hersel out a cave i't rocks. There she waits, and she laits after bairns out astray. Flays them o skin, all wick. Drinks blood and cracks bones.' " He turned the full of his face to Sylvie, a brief, rueful, crooked glance, out of cloud. "Dark's real enough." He was playing with the iron brooch, sliding the captive tongue of thorn from knob to knob and back. He set it down, and she pinned her cloak again; she was cold.

"And what about stones?"

"Said they danced, back o Cloudlaw; said none had telled them, nor could; said they's here and not, times, and now and nowhere—when it's all else at drifts. Aye, said another—he were awd by their telling—said a stonecutter had ta'en one away for an image; and as he set his chisel in't, t'rock had cried out; and ever t'face he would set on it had flawed away, and a bairn's face had looked out." He was crouched, still as wood, eyes of wood, that flickered with an endless fall of leaves. "As if t'ring were closed, and all were stonefast, turning nowt, turned slowly slowly ont wheel o stars til dust, and she as bound them were forgetten; but t'bairn were still—not tholing, but itsel, t'stone itsel becoming—O it dwindles i't telling. She—"

He touched the ring of silver on the staff, a small thing, hard and endless, runic, cold. "Stars were bound lang sin. Lightfast."

Sylvie said nothing.

He was quiet for a while. His face was shadowy; it trembled with the fire. He was bent, toying with the mirror, tilting it this way and that. Wraiths of autumn danced and wavered, and were still.

"T'other place, beyont thornwood, back o hollins, bairns said, tell us an hob-tale. So t'granny said, a lad were sent to get eldins i't wood, and he laiked by t'water, cracking nuts while owl-light, when he met wi Awd Flaycraw, all i' brown leaves, wi his stick. In he comes, 'Breaks tha my branches?' cries—" And Cobber hunched in the firelight, and made his throng of shadows swale and scutter, as the old woman had done, miming Flaycraw: owl-beaked and oak-handed, etenish, grotesque.

It's like a mummers' play, thought Sylvie: all thwacking and fooling, but the end's the knot of swords. They've forgotten why it's done. He's seen it death; he's been the sword, the wren. And looking at the child, she saw his face was bright with awe, with silent odd hilarity. And she thought: he's seen it wake.

"So t'babby burrowed in her apron. Well, she said, t'bairn were flayed, but he stood—

" 'I'd ha' cried, Nut-hook! said lad.

" 'Hush,' said lass. 'Hears thee.'

"—t'bairn stood, and he says til Awd Flaycraw, 'Aye, it's our dad's wood. Can get sticks for our fire.'

"And Awd Flaycraw hawded out his neave, wi summat in't. 'What's this?' said he.

" 'Hazelnut,' said bairn.

" 'Eh, no, if tha had nobbut see'd: yon's Cob's cup I cannot crack, wae's me. Wood's all within, and I's yet to walk.' And t'lad see'd nowt, nobbut wind i't leaves.

" 'Gran,' said t'lass, 'what were he laiting after?'

" 'Gate thruff hallows.'

"And lass said, 'I'd ha' ta'en his nut, and set it i't earth.'

"Then t'shepherd i't corner said, nay, he'd heard tell as it were Awd Mazy at were laiking by t'water, laiting moon in it. Thowt as he'd lost her i't clouds below." Cobber laughed a little, soft and shaken; but the grieving in his voice broke through. "Yon awd one's my other. T'one on us is ever rising as t'other falls, leaf and shadow: and we never touch. I's forgetten which I is."

She sat quietly considering. "Then you think you'll never find him in your wood, to take it back from, even if Annis falls?"

"Don't knaw. Think Annis is t'gate atween now and nowhere, time and times."

For a moment, Sylvie envisioned mirrored worlds, a narrow crossing, ineluctable: the spider-bodied figure for

infinity. "You don't have to come, Cobber, he may not
be there. She is."

"I's not whole."

That night, she dreamed of a tree full of withered
leaves, pale gold, that clung and rattled; they were the
skins of children, veined with their faces and their hands,
whorled and ragged, torn across. Prophecies. No, birds.
Not hands, but clapping wings. They blew away. She had
forgotten when she waked, uneasy, but remembered that
her sleep was tawny.

In the morning, the third since they had met beneath
the trees, they went on. Close to the shortest day, she
thought: cold, dark. It was a reluctant, pallid, misty
dawn, grey with hoarfrost. It did not thaw. She thought
it was the moorland of her witch-ale vision, like and
unlike: no wind, no solitude. But it was weird: like
dreaming of the room you're in, and dreaming waking in
it, trying to make the light with ghostly hands, or find
the door. Nothing moves, or burns; you can feel nothing,
being shadow, but the fear. The room you dream is realer
than yourself. This moorland felt like that: undreamlike,
thin. It paled her to a ghost.

Step by step, the child grew wary, silent where he had
been still: unseeing and unwood. Sylvie saw no boundary, no wall, but he walked as if against the wind, against
the will of dark. "Witch-marches," he said.

She had the mirror in her pocket now, with the other
stuff: things to hand. Touchstones. The iron brooch was
at her throat, caught fast: a baleful, a two-edged gift, for
binding and annulling; but it made no thing, not even O.

The cold and starry ring was on her staff: too high for
her, she thought. Aloof. Being endless in itself, it sought
no other, no voice breaking in upon its ancient and enwoven lightfast spell. It spoke the wheel of stars. Unturned,
turning all, dispassionate, it would not scathe nor save.
She thought it wouldn't mess with witches.

But the mirror was round and whole; it gave and
accepted common light; somehow it would not be put
away. It came to hand, now and then, edged and actual
in all the pallor of the frost. Though she did not take it

out and seldom thought of it, it was present: small and
unconsoling, like a wintry sun.

Toward evening of the brief pale day, they were wandering in an abrupt and tumbled country, all thorns and
ghylls, rough as if the restless earth had shrugged in
sleep, rucking all its heaped and shaggy fells. It slept in
wolfskins. The hills were hugely cloaked in mist, bare-
headed, bleak, austere. Cobber said it was east and
northward to the place of stones, the dance; but they
had to get up the scarp. The rock was cross-grained,
deeply scored with grykes and gullies, labyrinthine, blind
with mist. The clefts lay athwart their way; they groped
and scrambled in the wreck of stone, amid the fierce
articulated thorns and knifing water, seeking ways that
led to Annis: northward, higher, out of roke. Fog lay on
Sylvie, cold as mail. Her hair was lank and her hands
were raw; Mally's cloak was heavy as a cloud. Cobber
was hunched, folded in on himself like a winter-withered
leaf, tenacious. They found a score of ways, blind crevices and broken stairs; and one, gaunt and crooked, to
the end.

They came out at last atop a high, blunt, broken rigg,
above a bleaker face of earth, slanting downward from
their feet: the back of a stony hand, whose clenching
fingers they had climbed. It was naked to the winds of
east and north, in the eye of the black witch. The earth
was barren, stony, but for sparse and wiry bents, dull as
bronze, and clumps of crouching thorn, arachnid; it was
scarred with low and random tumuli, eight or nine, like
gravemounds half effaced. A dark and holy place, a place
of bones and coins. Back of Law.

"Is this . . . ?" she began.

"No. T'Jackstones. Knucklebones. Earthborn witches
came here for rune-casting, foretelling. And other things,"
he said reluctantly: this was not the place to speak of it.
They started down the naked slope.

Amid the barrows, there were great stones lying,
squarish, pale, but darker than the hoary earth. They
were spattered with bright blood. Sylvie flinched, quick
with fear. She cast about, swiftly, warily. No witch. No
sacrifice; no carrion nor hawk: only the blood like fallen
rain. But the suddenness had waked her, as the sharp

rain wakes the sleeper from uneasy dreams of storm.
Now and foreboding met. The blood was present death.

"Oh," cried Cobber, grieving, "O my kindred."

Sylvie stood, vainly mortal, unconsoling, alien; she
could speak only to the child in him. The dry and bitter
lamentation passed. She touched his shoulder. He endured.
"We're looking for them."

"I knaw." His voice was sad. "They cannot die. Can
thole: sitha, blood o lightborn." He touched the rock;
his hand was dry. She saw the blood was stone. Shaken,
curious, she felt it. Crystals, sharp as hail, were flecked
and clotted, paler on the coarser grey, on rock rose-mot-
tled like a swimming trout, or dark as dragonsblood, its
dearest hoard, inlaid on the wyrm's ninefold, stonehard
skin. It was beautiful. "T'hunt's wark. Soul were ta'en
here."

"What we heard, the other night? Ancient?"

"Cannot tell."

The mist was tattering in the risen wind, eastnortheast
from the witch's quarter, aquiline; the thorns were rattling, eager, hailing wind. Black sky, white earth, and
at their crossing place, the stony blood: unshadowy and
unreversed. Her spirit leapt, rejoicing fiercely.

The child called out to her. He crouched behind the
stones. Against the storm, a speck of mica caught the
light, glittering, and cried out harshly, clangorous: a
raven wheeling in the air.

Bright with fear, outrunning qualms as lightning does
the quaking thunder, Sylvie thought: fire. They hate fire.
There was wood, dead roots of thorn, amid the bones of
a dry beck. With cold stiff hands, she struck and struck
her flint and steel: no hold, no hold. They heard a rumor
in the earth, a tumult in the shaken air, a cry and blowing. The hunt had spied them out.

Mirror. Cold and sallow, it lay on her hand. She stared
at it, blankly, seeing no image or counsel, but the last
quarter of her face, a startled eye. It misted over with
her breath. She blew on it, unthinking, and the O was
tawny; as it kindled with the will and wind of her spirit,
it was ruddy, fiery, a dwarfish sun, blazing bright as
Phoebus in her hand. She cried out at the cold absolute
of pain, thinking to see a charred and bone-white frame

of hand; but it was whole, and the mirror purely light, unburning: so was joy. Her sun was cold, quick, glorious.

By its light, the fire caught and smouldered, sullen in the fog; it leapt, wind-torn and wild, from root to branch, and tree to tree. She ran to set the thorns ablaze, to pale them both with fire, but the ring was broken, and the pattern made no whole, no citadel. Wrong-handed, she snatched a brand from the fire, and turned. "Cobber. Here."

"Stay." He was dark-eyed. "Stay. They hunt what flees them."

Ravens in the air, and Annis's rade upon the stony earth, they came, hurly-burly, spurring on the goat-rough horses, in their harness of the writhen gold, until the stone-fire struck beneath their hooves, and the bitter foam sprang pale and bloody from their sides. Some huntsmen rode astride of stags, pale red as dying suns, and some on black-felled brazen kids, all wild and grim and splendid, with their lean and bitter hounds beside: the darkfast, the unlightborn, three and thirty. They were white and black as flint, and flecked with dark immortal blood: a deadly cast of elf-shot, arrowy with cold insatiate desire. Their mantles flared and flackered on the wind behind them, loud as flame, but black or pale, and one of burning gold. At their sides, they bore stone knives and swords of bronze. They wore circlets of iron on their brows, at once their glory and their torment, set with stones that were undying souls. And the ravens— They were blasted angels, a denial and a mockery of flame; yet half of witchlike shape, cold moonwhite breasts and baleful talons, nightwind hair unbound: black, ruinous, unhallowed.

They halted on a rigg beyond the stones, a brief headlong ride away, the horsemen reining in, crying back their hounds by name. At their feet lay a broken wall, a half-obliterated dyke. The ravens fell and balanced, fell and turned, now fiery white, now ashen, black and ruinous against the tattered edge of storm. The wind had died, or was bodied in the hunt. The sun had not yet set. They waited.

Then Cobber caught up a stone, and flung it in their

midst. "Craws! Craws!" He ran, drawing them from Sylvie, toward the sun.

They stooped and the horsemen spurred. "Crows!" cried Sylvie, louder, fierce and shrill. "Come take my soul."

They swung to her, dazzled. With the mirror raised she turned on them, daunting in their eyes, and so they hung, between two suns. How long? The fires she had set were dying down, rose-branched and ashy, into embers. So her perilous, unvengeful joy would choke and dwindle into rage, and hopeless fear, and death. Not yet: she held the light. Sun still.

But their daemonic clamor rose, gathering in fury with the dusk. Amid the tumult of their baffled rage, she thought she heard a far and bodiless hoo-hooing, an enjoying owlish laughter. Malykorne.

In the O of the witch's cup, the eye of storm, she heard a darker voice than hers, rising from the earth to meet, to cross her falling voice. It sang. *"And wha's undone th' nine witchknots? . . . And wha has slain t' master kid?"*

Witches, she said fiercely, not aloud; and cast her sun amid the thorns and graves.

Pale in the not-yet-night, it fell and scattered, quick-gold on the earth in shivering drops. They did not fade, but glowered, spat and blazed. Out of mist and fire, bone of the dead thorn, burning on the braided wind, came wraiths of witches: nine souls astray. Taking shape of the mirror's spell, they sallowed, sullen red at heart. Rough-mantled with the fog, with combs of fire knotted in their thorny hair, thorns woven in amongst their locks of fox-fire flickering red, they stood still as candles on the earth. There was a brazen reek about them, tallowy, of forge and gallows; but they brightened in the dusk. As the sun vanished, they were wick: they turned in mimicry of mortal terror from the hunt, and fled.

Shrieking triumph, the nine ravens fell on them, and bore them to the earth, with foot and beak; they tore greedily at the ghostly flesh, scything with their talons in the hollow ribs, the knotted hair: but the eyes, the eyes were suns.

The ravens screamed at the fire in their gullets, writhing, tearing at their own throats in anguish. They rose on flurried, dying wings in vain; and fell, by one and one, stark dead upon the earth, agape, their raked wings withering away to bone and quill.

But one last, mad and crimson-eyed, in a fury of unknown, unutterable pain, stooped on a huntsman, bearing down both goat and rider with its wings, slaying the black kid, and slain by a stone knife in the undying hand. The raven lay, a botched thing, iron-beaked and woman-faced, above its feathered, rended throat. The rider briefly stood, unmoved, his cloak slashed all to quills, and dark with blood. Dismayed, whipping back their hounds that fell upon the ravens' flesh, the horsemen turned and rode away.

Sylvie swung about. Cobber was all right; he was standing. Hoarse and harsh, fierce with mockery, she called after them, exultant, seeing riddles:

> Crawing, crawing,
> For all your crowse crawing,
> You've burnt your crops
> And tint your wings,
> An hour before the dawning!

Air, she thought, exulting. See, I'm wind, I sang the wind. The child was tugging at her sleeve. The witches flickered and went out. The ravens burned. Unscathed, but scorched about the head, grey with illusory wisdom, she laughed, and staggered, and sat down abruptly, sick with terror and the reek of death: the thunderclap at last.

Ariane set down the lantern. They could not get back, not over the riddlestones where Annis waited, not by night. Craobh had come away from the henge with them, stumbling in the moonless dark as far as a dry-walled ruin, gateless, low: a sheepfold. Or a witches' castle, a hold for such ill-fated sheep as they'd seen lying dead and raven-worried on the moor, with rings and gauded hair. A den, thought Ariane; but she could not bear to lie naked to the witch's gaze, unlaired, and they could walk no further.

There they huddled, by the wavering light of the lantern. There was no wood for a fire, and the scant and icy ling caught sullenly, burned swiftly all to ash. They dared not stray for more.

Craobh sat by herself, between them, shivering in all the blankets. "She will come. It is her turn."

"She hasn't yet," said the tinker. "Not said we s'd wait supper for her." They shared out the Woodfalls' food, morosely: haver-bread and bacon, which Craobh would scarcely touch. Having eaten his roasted egg, he drove his thumb as if by habit through the vain shell, and caught Ariane's curious glance. "So as t'witches won't sail in't . . . Eh dear." He laughed softly, fearfully, at the helpless folly of it all.

She laughed with him—she would not cry—and dazzled by the candlelight, she looked at him, cloudwise and earthly innocent, nameless and astray, endeared: the other mortal in the dark world, or nearly so. He had

borne his cup too long to be unchanged. "What'll I do
with this? Crack it?" she said, holding out the windegg.

"Can all fleet away in't," he said. "Wi thy twig for a
mast."

"Here's a sail," she said: the handkerchief Mrs. Woodfall had given her, huge and coarse, a little scorched.

"I s'll blaw in't, and tha steer. What an if hunt
follows?"

"I'll cast them out cobnuts, and they'll stoop for them.
Drop our anchor right in Mally's thatch . . ." Then she
said bleakly, "I don't know. I don't know. I wish Sylvie
were here."

As they talked, Craobh had gone to the farthest corner
of the fold, and was standing, looking out at dark. "And
I," he said. "Nowt for it. Eh, but soft now, we's all
amort: will fret yon lass."

Ariane spoke low. "I'm afraid that if we sleep, she'll
go alone."

"Aye. She'll not thole losing three for one: she's that
mortal to be fond o thee. Yet she'd not willing leave
yon—" He gestured covertly at the soulstone, hidden.

"Your other—"

"He chosen." The tinker looked unhappy. "Doubt I'd
not knaw him."

Ariane said, "What if I went, as a sort of changeling?"

"Sitha, lass, don't tha forfeit thysel, nor t'stone: not
thine to lose. T'awd one would tek lass wick; would not
slay her when she hawden her. Tha munnot give witch
soul and all."

"Mally gave Craobh nothing. No sanctuary. Dreams."

"Could she ha' kept lass and her gaud and thee, all i't
cupboard?"

"No," she said, with bleak certainty. "She wouldn't.
But we're there. It's all one cot."

Looking round the walls of rough stone, the roof of
cold sky, he said, "T'other's bed were softer."

The fold was a box of shadows; yet a kingdom was
within, of stone and darkness, huger than the hills,
Cloud's Law: and it would come, if once the candle faltered. Ariane saw nothing beyond: Annis had withdrawn
into herself all seeing, and was gnawing, gnawing even
at their rushlight. It would all be dark. An end to jour-

neying; and Annis at the dying heart. A stone in carrion, an eye in desolation: absolute. Annihilating all that's made: not to a green thought, but a black one, in a blacker shade.

For a flickering moment, Ariane saw the witch's hovel, where they were, if she could find the door. Mally's shape held Annis in its arms, the old moon and the new. Grave and cot. She saw the tinker, going with his candle into dark. Thy burden's light, she thought: what Malykorne had said, a bright and heavy understanding, something that she had to give him. Wait. But he was further on.

She started awake. She turned toward him, but forgot what she would say; her eyes were heavy, and even the candle seemed still, needle-etched upon the dark. Knowing that she must not sleep, she slept; and dreamed what Annis sent.

She saw the Woodfall children, with Molly and Tavy, Cat and Sylvie and young Thos (these last a little sepia, as in Nan's album), drawing a sled along, all laden with boughs of holly, branches of thorn. The babby's wooden doll was riding: Maire's unborn child, but its face was rough as nutmeg, rasped and wizened. They were hunting wrens; the snow was thin above the abyss. She tried to call out to them, but had no voice.

She woke, as she thought, in the fold as it truly was: no illusion but a witch's castle. She was walking in a ruined hall, in a labyrinth of corridors, worm-eaten, death-riddled: she was lost. She had reluctantly to brush through great ruined webs of arras, arainwebs, that clung, importunate as death; past burned and broken chests of papers, stained, illegible; past winged or bird-faced corbels, sentient but cruelly scarred; over scattered dim and precious things: shards of Persian jars, rings and brooches, hoards of iron, silver, bronze. A coin clinked underfoot.

Ah no, no. The duergar was stalking her through the maze, which was herself long dead, lying dragon-jewelled and maggot-ridden, naked on the fell: she was possessed. She had to find her soul, her soul was lost; but all was fading, brown and dim. Her eyes were clouded, and her hands did not bleed. She came out into a great hall, raftered with her ribs; but he was there before her, and she fled, leaving her soul behind, out of her carrion body's mouth, through the broken ring of teeth.

Dark and wingless, terrible in stooping, sheer as if the sky infolded on its stars in tesseracts of night, denying light and gravity and death, Annis came. Naked and unsexed, the witch was night made stone: skyblack, crystalline and cold. Unstarry: though the moon's hook was caught in her, refracted over and over in her endless planes of night. Her hair streamed out like molten shadow.

She stooped on the body. At her touch, it broke, dry as waspnest, scabby. Her taloned hand took the soul.

The dreaming Ariane was shaken with an ecstasy of longing: that her soul was snatched from the jackal, that cold law had taken her from death.

But the paddock thing, the carrion—herself lurched up, and with its blunt hands it shattered the witch to glittering dust. It fell; but each mote grew, distilling dark, into another Annis. She was gorgon to herself, undying, and the seed of death. By necessity, insatiate, her brood of Law took shape and were bound as one, witch-crystal upon crystal coming together, face after face, body within infracted body: a spiderseye of being, flawed and terrible. The dreamer's soul was lost, subsumed in Annis.

She woke, as she thought, in the witchfold, which was not of time. She had lost, would lose her soul to Annis, it had never been her own; her self was dead, unborn, undying: all one in Law, all naught, no matter—ah, the ravens, no.

Ariane woke, truly: dry-throated, shaking, cold with sweat. She saw the candle, the trembling unchanging little light: the wax consumed, the ill night passing. Time not stilled. She heard the tinker's gasping breath; saw his drawn face twitching, and one bright earring.

Craobh. Her face was hidden. For an evil moment, Ariane thought it was not Craobh by the wall, but a puppet-thing of sticks and rags and clots of shadow. Straightforward with despair, she went to see. The child sat unmoving; the dark unearthly eyes were open, staring at beyond. Ariane crouched beside her. The cold hard stone lay on her breastbone.

"It is not for her crown," said Ariane. "I will not give it."

The tinker slept. He were i't Cloudwood, as he thought, and lying by t'water. He cast no seeming, had no face: i't keld, saw nobbut leaves, leaves rising out o dark, leaves lighting. He were wood. Grieving all alone, he sat, long dead or all unborn, unnamed: nowt's no one. T'awd one's fool. Not ruing now but ranting. With a stone, he cracked and smashed lad's owlnut he had borne, smashed all to dust. Nowt were in it, nobbut must and dark, a greater dark as night, and starless.

But aloft he saw t'awd moon, burred round wi light, a sickle, same as cheek and chin; and as it turned, it were his dark lass, A, not dead, no more than were t'lady moon, but silent. She were bended, combing flax; and he were stood without her hedge. All around her, thrawn and thrang, stood prickle-holly, brambles, thorn and awd man's beard. He stared into the dark O of her garth.

Come in, she said, not turning full to him: press through.

And so he done that, longing for a hand to meet his hand: no shadow of a leaf, but earth and kind, rising out of dark to touch, to give him back himself. An other. Her eyes would make his face; her mouth, his name, his breath, his dying.

Caught i't thorns, he rent away awd coat, awd sark, i' ribands—ah, and flesh; but that were dry as leaves. Thorns scrat out both his eyes. He brashed it, brashed it. He were through.

Come nigh, said she frae dark: I wait. Come, lief, and all alone.

Groping stumbling on icy ground—were it stone beneath? or riddles, falling?—he came to her and ta'en her in his arms.

She were hollow. She were sticks of alder, kist of ash: moon's cage o thorn and rags. Cawd rags o musty ribands made her hair, her flesh—but they were bloody, they were flayed off men. They blawed against his face, they clung. Cage shut.

He beat, beat hands against it sides; but warping he were't cage itsel, growed fast til it; and she were at him, cawd and taloned, wi her naked dugs, her beak. She tore, she tore him til his bare bones. Would cry, but mouth were stopped. Would strike, but hands had thrawed, thrawed roots i't stony fell. She were aloft him, crawing ower wi her iron cry, spurning wi her raven's wings. But he were warping, same as wood, woodsel: were bone o branches, eyes o tree, o tree—

Hearing him muttering pitifully in his sleep, Ariane touched his shoulder, shook him. "What is it?"

He started and stared wildly. "Ah. No." He saw the light in its cage of glass and iron, saw the thin fierce frightened face in its cloud of hair. Then drawing breath, recollecting. "Eh, that were . . . that were a dreadful draught o sleep. She . . ."

"Yes. I saw her."

There was silence. She looked at the child and said, "Should we watch and let her sleep, if she can? She won't be fit for—for what happens. Or is sleep—here— is sleep a windeye for the dark, the ravens?"

He got up and bent over Craobh, touched the blankets. Not asleep, but silent, waking moon. "She's not ruing. Let be." Then very quietly, looking at the stony ground, as if he had lost something amid the stones, he said, "I't dream, t'awd one—tha knaws—I thowt I wanted her."

She spoke with a sudden fierceness that made the candle jump. "That's lies! You're good." She looked at him, dishevelled, bleak: unlightborn, bearing light. Lad chosen. "I did want her. I saw—There is an absolute in her, beyond the evil. Stone itself. She's like Mally, she's her other face; they're one thing: light and darkness, Cloud and Law. They turn. I'm one of theirs. I turn and shear. I want. She called me, but I will not go to her." She drew breath. "Well. She'll have to come and fetch me."

"Her turn, whatever. T'hunt'll be aloft, keeping cludder."

"I know."

So they drew together, each alone in dark, and silent, waking sun and moon that endless night: at hallows' end. They kept lightfast through the dying candle, and far into the next. What Craobh dreamt, open-eyed, unwaking, they would never know.

*   *   *

As she set the second candle out of wind in the Wood-falls' lantern, light and glass and iron, Ariane had—not a dream, nor a sending, but an insight, small and sharp: a witch's eye. She saw Annis: not as dark herself, transcendent, but caught in symbols, as they'd seen her on the fellside, bodied, clad like any witch. Blind Annis took her seeming-glass, bright all but a sickle edge, unfull: the dead and unborn moon, undying. At the dark of moon, her glass would be fulfilled. It was rounded over and over for her earthblind eyes, waxing as the moon in heaven shrank, devoured. It was all her earthly vision; and was fickle, waning with the rounding moon, and wandering. But what she saw was true.

By the glass, it was the last of any moon, no year, time out of time. Annis hung desiring over it, but saw no lightborn soul astray. She saw the small hard circle of her crown, now all but closed, unclosed; now scattering, now bound: all stonefast, the unturning wheel of her devouring. She saw the naked hill where it would stand. She saw witches in the castle, foxes in the fold, and sent them ravendreams, forebodings. She saw truly, but in part. When the dark of moon was full, and the starry wheel was stilled and broken, then her occult glass would show all things as O: all turning past, and endless nothing yet to be.

But now, briefly, bitterly she raged: for the last souls still were hidden—one? many? she knew only all and none—within the dark edge, the rim of vision. She saw—O but when? what moon?—she saw her hunt astray and wild, unrecallable as lightning; and she saw her ravens dead, the nine: stark black, bloodred, against the blind white O of mirrored frost.

Their third candle dwindled, and still Annis did not come. Waiting, waiting for the solstice, Ariane saw phantoms, just beyond the outwalls of light, or within her aching eyes, confounded by the blink and palsy of the candle; heard the gabbling wind as huntsmen. She was worn out with imagined battles that were lost in the foreboding: now shattering the skywitch, huge as hills, to dust; now running from the yelping hunt. The moonglass was fickle. The ravens' fall it showed was sometime truth, but it could well be falsely mirrored or unfull, a delusion and a mockery of hope. She feared to trust it. O but when, beneath what moon? The fold seemed now a sanctuary, now a trap. Bone-cold and cramped, huddled out of wind, she brooded on the lightfast stone, on Mally's vain and enigmatic windegg. Her foot slept and swarmed. Overwatched, her eyes were full of bats' wings, dark and flitter; and her will was ash.

The tinker fidgeted. His look was grim. Yet it changed with an elusive innocence, with the gleam and dangle of his earrings. Dreams. And dark: he bent his haggard face, listening, listening to the earth and wind.

Craobh sat, shadowy, aloof. They saw a child's face, but flawed and sky-possessed, unearthly still. Now and then, with a sudden tremor like the candleflame's, she would brush aside her cloudy hair or smudge her face with the back of a brown-starred, blood-creased hand.

They were endeared to Ariane: odd, frail, crazy, yet enduring beyond hope; and tough. She tried to see them whole, foreboding loss, to print them on her heart; but fear had leached away all glory and all anguish. She was dull. Not her will to love, but something else within, unlabored, sent her hand across the light and dark, beyond, to touch Craobh's face. The child made no response; none was asked.

Still no morning, still no hunt. Cloud and silence, and a cat's-fur prickly apprehension: coming storm. She's brewing dark, thought Ariane. Old mother witch, are you ready yet? No, I'm looking in my seeming-glass, I'm doing off my shadow. Nothing. Like a badger in a trap, having no near enemy but iron-jawed impassive time, Ariane could only gnaw her leg away in stubborn frenzied rage. How would she run on three?

Well then, come, she said to dark. Come on. Bite.

The tinker sighed. "Nobbut mirk and cawd; think she's etten up t'sun, and we's t'afterbite."

"Hope she chokes on me," said Ariane. "I'm nettles."

"Not shrewd as that," he said, "for all thy flyting tongue, Green crabs."

Ariane would have spoken, but the shadows stirred and swaled. She looked. Craobh stood; she turned about and felt the air. Her face was unquiet, ambiguous. "Wind is changed," she said.

"Aye," said the tinker. "Not stormed."

With a wretched twisting leap of hope—her stomach being taut with dread—Ariane thought of her vision of the hunt astray and wild, the ravens dead: all far-end now, tiny and perversely clear, unreal. It turned her giddy, so that she longed to touch the stone and go unblinded, knowing the abyss. But sternly she knelt up instead, and trimmed the candle.

Things were changing now, confused, as sliding, shapeless as a thaw. Craobh was walking to herself, from corner to corner of the fold, aslant, as if she drew an endless knot; but flawed and baffled, halting with the cold: not quite a dance, but a seeking or a ritual, a rune warding them from wind and madness, though their roof-tree was the night. Her shadow rippled on the rough-laid walls, breast-high. As suddenly, she stayed.

The tinker gathered up his staff and bag; Ariane got the lantern and the Woodfalls' things, and put the naked windegg in her greatcoat pocket, with the witch's comb: at risk, to hand.

He turned to the child. "Thy way, lass."

By candlelight, they went out through the ruined gate; but once beyond the fold they saw not moorland but a ring of dark grim standing stones around them in the mist, a greater wall, whose gaping holes were all illusion; and before them was a headless doorway.

Annis waited there alone. Dwarfed between the huge rough gate-stones of the broch, she stood, darker and more ancient than the night, and starless. She held the ends of time, as yet unclosed. Still she had kept her witch's seeming, like a dark-clad woman, black and bitter white and crowned with a bright trembling hail of souls: witchlike, for she had need of hands. Within, she was shrunken like a dying star to absolutes: unlight, gravity, desire. She was the gate.

Craobh stood. Blind Annis made no move: she could not call the child, unnamed, unsouled, nor hunt her body, ravenless; but she would take. She closed the way.

Craobh turned and sprang and scrambled over the

stones of the ruined tower, and leapt where it was lowest,
yet fathomless in roke. Ariane and the tinker hurtled
after, heedless of the fall, away—but there was no
beyond.

The moor was changed. Where the somber naked
fells had lain, they saw a maze of stones, a dark
perplexity of henges rising like an unbranched forest,
like a host of the unlightborn summoned to her dark
annulling dance: shadows without substance or mass,
unrooted, shifting; but obdurate and harsh. Annis had
wrought it all in silence, of the thunder. Her storm
had fallen on the earth, but deadly still, the stones of
heaven.

Caught in the blind labyrinth, the child ran in and out,
elusive as the moon in branches, frantic as a hunted hind:
daemonic insight driven on by mortal fear. The others
lost her, lost each other, in the stones; but Annis, holding
the pattern in her silent mind, the clew of lightning, was
the end of every way. The world she had warped was
Annis, and the further out Craobh ran, the straiter, spiralled in. There was no way out: give her play for her
life. The child ran. And ring within broken ring, enmeshed,
unturning, bound and envious of light, the stones stood,
and made nothing: no dance, no wheel of time, nowhere;
not even O.

The others ran wildly, unheeded, scattering like hares
before the scythesmen in doomed grass. The lantern fell
and shattered, and the light went out. They could not
come near Craobh, for the paths unravelled them, one
from another, turning back on the witch, and in and
inward. They came ever and only to the inmost broch,
where Annis stood and wove her storm, her seine of
knotted wind. The souls burned and shivered in her hair,
cast web on web of wincing light; yet eldest, she wove
shadow.

Near and far amid the maze of stones, Craobh fled
her, racing like the moon through rack, yet seeming to
hang moveless, still amid the hurling clouds of rock, the
earthstorm. For all her hounded brilliance, seeing snatches
of the stonelaw as it warped, unriddling dark, the child
was flagging, sobbing for breath.

Ariane came yet again at last to the O, the eye of

storm. She could run no more. It did no good; but the
terror drove her on. Annis's terror. Annis's will, she
thought. Deny her. Ariane clung fiercely to a rock,
ignored, shaking with a fury of unfocused power. Now.
Do something now. She felt Craobh's soul, cold as quicksilver, running bright and grave in her every vein, a burning cold, a tree of fire—surely no blood and bone could
cloud that light—but the witch, intent on Craobh within
her closing spiral, did not seize on her. Holding the windegg, she thought death at Annis, spells of binding, blinding, breaking: all in vain.

Craobh caught and wrenched her foot. She fell hard,
with a stifled nightmare cry, sprawled winded on the
earth. Swift, silent, Annis strode forward to take her,
and the stones made way.

"Out!" cried the tinker, and he hurled himself between
the witch and Craobh. With all his strength, he brought
down his staff against the blind face.

The stick was gone, consumed as it touched the dark.
Heedless, blind as lightning, Annis struck him down,
with one terrible, black, silent bolt. A flaw of dark. Not
stooping for his soul, she walked on, bent utterly on her
desire. Craobh had staggered up, dazed, a few steps
toward the gate. They met.

With her cold and sickled black embrace, Annis seized
the child, who fought, kicking, clawing, biting, in her
silent frenzy. But she spent her fury as the clapper on
an iron bell, and did no hurt, though the air was shaken.
Annis was unmoved. "The soul will come," she said.
Inexorable, she bore the child away.

Ariane crouched, warding Craobh's soul with her
body, head on knees, unknotted hair a storm about her
face. The stone was quick. She felt it coldly shining
through her like the moon through clouds. Her body
would not veil that light. Annis would see at last, and
that would be the end.

But she stalked by. Ariane crouched still, awaiting an
afterclap. None came. The light had not betrayed her,
nor had she saved the child. She was overlooked. Her
eyes kept seeing afterimages, floating flaring shadows: a
clot like a ravencloak, a coronal of black fire. Witch and
child. No stones, but a tortured wood, and a harpy stoop-

ing with her scathing wings upon her frailer sister, Iris,
messenger. She saw the sky of stone beneath them, broken, and Orion shattered in his fall, unstarred. She saw
black lightning strike, a flaw in meaning. Then the labyrinth of stones, the witch—O Craobh, Craobh. The tinker would come, he would mourn with her. *Arianty*? No
one.

She saw, in a moment of desperate drowning clarity,
that she was half mad with fear. She bit herself awake.
Cold earth. The soul had bruised her hand. She let go.
The stones had vanished. There lay the bleak bare moorland, and the tinker. He had not moved.

She got up, and went to him. He was sprawled on the
hillside. His eyes were open, glazing over: cloudy ice on
leaves on water, broken whence the spirit fled. She knelt,
afraid to touch him, and at last fumbled for his pulse:
but his hands were stiff already as if rooted, gnarled with
cold. No thud was in his throat. She felt through leaves
on leaves of rags to find his heart: no faintest stirring in
his ribs. No breath. He was dead as earth.

I need a mirror, she thought, to see his breath—she
remembered, if it *mist or stain the stone*—and in her
bewildered grief, she nearly took Craobh's soul. No. She
stilled her own hand with her other. She could not
believe. She could not endure to look. Death had not
transfigured him. He lay, a scarecrow heap of bones and
rags, outworn, unknown. Her friend.

Not crying, she stroked his hair, once, twice, and
touched the gold ring in his ear, with absolute detached
tenderness, all utterly unlike anything she had ever
known or done: now, here, this love, this death. She
knew no name by which to call him back. She closed his
eyes. The sky was paling now, toward morning of the
shortest day. The moon was dead.

She should go. She had nothing left to do, but keep
Craobh's stone until she died of want, or turned witless,
forgetting what she bore; or else was taken. She'd not
get far alone.

No, you fool, said something within her: no, he
chose this last. He had endured, becoming what he
bore, the cloudwood's soul, his cup. He'd kept the
children. She had taken once, in calling Craobh; now

grieving, seeing, she was called: for light is in the bearing of it, and it must not lie unborne. Grimly, gently, she searched for his cup. She found his bag, turned out his pockets. Nothing. O sweet Christ, had Annis taken that as well?

Recoiling from that vast and shadowy loss, she thought of skulking tearing foxes, wolves, remorseless greedy dainty crows; of scratching out a shallow hole—ah no, no, the eyeless staring sheep.

Then she must wake with him, and drive the crows away. Dry and grim, she set her will to lay him out, the barest charity. She took him by the ribs, and they were bare already to the bone, gnarled and hollow, choked with leaves—then with witchy hands, other eyes, she knew what had become of cup and bearer.

They were wood. She saw a living tree, girthed no greater than a slight quick man, but ancient, wintry, grey. Its roots were earthfast and enduring, and its crown was light. She knew its windbent branches, knew the flickering dancing of its twigs, its curled tenacious leaves: dry and brown, then morning-struck to palest gold. They fell upon the spring of water at his roots, by one and one, enspelled: light leaves ont water. Thy burden's light. She too was waking wood.

At his roots she found a bent and blackened mourning ring, the one that had bound his cup. It lay upon her palm, small and hard and endless, not of earth, and not for Annis. She put it on her thumb: no witch, no witch at all for tears.

VI

The Wren's Crown

The ring lay on Ariane's hand, black silver, stoneless, bent. She had done with weeping now, her heart was dry; and bending by the spring to drink, she'd slipped the ring from her thumb. It was far too big for her; she'd lose it. Turning it round and round in the small bleak clarity within her grief, she fretted that she could not read the outworn runes, nor tell if they were scratched or graven, signs or random scars: her fingers were too cold and rough, the light too bleak. She held it to her eye.

She saw brown dusk and drifted leaves; not a wood, there were webs and bones, a clutter of unglazen jugs: the witch's hearth. She saw Mally stumping to and fro about her winter tasks, shrewd and sly, in her leaf-red cap and patchy dunnish skirts. About her head, and in and out the cratch of timbers, flackering, there wheeled and whirled a skein of birds: blind owls and sparrows, finches, daws and magpies, missel-thrushes. She crossly called them down. By one and one, derisive, loving, wary, they dropped what they had brought, from beaks and talons: sallow heavy knops of bronze, that scattered where they fell, on ashes, rushes, slutswool, or in her standing cup. The robin dropped one last in the witch's apron. Mally nodded. The storm of birds rose on the air, becoming wind and leaves; their wings blew all the candles out, save one, bating wildly on its wick, and stirred the reek in draggly plumes.

Unmoved, she took the swooping, fluttered candle up, and rummaged through her kists, through feathers, egg-

shells, iron keys; through clots of wool and candle-ends,
souls, clothespegs, hoarded leaves: unearthing her spectacles at last. She perched them on her nose, and keeled
the pot, abob with apples wizening in scorching ale, as
it frothed and scudded over, storm and wreck. With offhand disdain, witchful prudence, she bent, flinging the
scum onto the rushes for the hedgehog to mumble in
bemusement, weaving off in its own hey; then she stood,
licking the broad spoon appraisingly, wiping her glazy
moon-blank lenses in her skirts, which only made them
worse. She broke herself a crust to gnaw on as she
worked. It was burnt. "Tha'd better wake, next batch,"
she said, turning her baleful glittering gaze upon a spider
in her web. "Tha'st nodded again, and t'cake's kizzened
up."

Then by one and one, Mally gathered up the scattered
bits of bronze, owling amid the green and mawky
cheeses, scrabbling in the leaves, shaking out the crumpled linens, rattling and upending jugs. She counted to
herself the tale of nine. They lay on her rough brown
hand. Unruffled and askew, peering crossly at them, she
spoke. "Turn: tha'rt sun still."

They glowered, trembled, quickened, blazing like a
skein of suns, one-turning, bright and glorious: a dwarfish Phoebus, the earthsoul, winter's eye. It faded then,
unkindling, sallowing, through sullen red, lion-tawny,
dull. The star congealed. It was a cold bronze mirror, no
wider than her hand, and thumbed and bleared. Glancing
at her fierce broad face, she huffed on it, and smudged
it in her petticoats, and laid it on the shelf. "Tha'st done
well by her; tha'lt rise t'morn."

Then Mally dipped herself a cupful of the ale, sticks,
stems, seeds, drowned wasps and all. She drank it off,
in odd and seldom gulps, setting down her cup and finding it to hand, unsought, as if she danced with it, walking
from corner to cater-corner of her dusk, thrice round, in
patterns that the leaves obscured. Solemnly, she ducked
and sidled, brushed by the dangling hoary weeds, the
shawls of ticklish cobweb. Turning from the cup, she
came to it, and drank the last. She poured out the lees
on the fire, and wiped her mouth with the back of her
hand.

With sharp swift earthy fingers, she unpinned her long
dark hair, as harled and tangled as a squall of wind in a
wintry thornhedge, vexed with burs and barbs and sparrows' claws: yet strangely wild and beautiful, nightdark
about her moonish solemn face. Combless she raked it
out, and ninefold knotted it.

She twitched down a spider's web, bright with water,
spilling not a drop; she broke no thread, but stood,
unravelling and wreathing it between her gnarled and
knowing hands, weaving its stars and clouds of stars
through all the winter constellations, talking gravely to
herself. "Here's Sword, and it's rising. Here's Cup. One
lies i't foxcastle, t'other's astray. One walks and one
wakes." She dandled Orion, and wove and unmade him.
The stars were a tree. "Wood's fast i' hallows, fleet o
leaves.

"Here's Ship—" and it sailed for her, between her
hands mazed with light. "Wha's to sail in't? Unfast and
fast. Tree's rootless that sall crown it mast; bears all and
O. Sails wi lightfall, an it's tide. Dark's unturning yet."
She crossed, uncrossed the starry web, tenuous, unbroken, fatal: not a star of water fell.

"And wha sall dance? Stone's bound til, ring's bent, if
sun and moon tek hands. Light comes o turning; nowt
of O. Nine lightfast came wi cloud bairns, darkward out
o winter night, nine earthbound, fore all dances were:
cup and staff, that's twa; and stonefast three, at riddles'
roots; four lost . . . Eh, but time's lang gone sin carols
were."

She undid the last knot of the web, and shook out the
sliding stars, bright silver on her rough brown hand: nine
then one. A stone of light. She held it still, and by it set
the clot of gossamer, now stiff and dull, yet delicate,
inwoven as a cage of bone and quill; or caddised, chrysa-
lid. Soul and shroud.

Crouching, she took up a handful of dead leaves, and
blew on it, sharply. Then she opened out her hand.

There perched a wren, newborn and ancient as the
winter sun, the morning of its death; yet brown and
brisk, made quick with passionate acuity. It whirred,
drawing blood with its rose-sharp talons, beating its

brinded wings to be gone. "Eh then, Jenny," said Maly-korne, "flet away."

The wren flirted up, and quirked at her hair, as if for haws, tugging sharply and away. "Eeh, lass, gerroff; I've just had that done. Knap at hedgehog." And the witch laughed, a dark deep bottly hooing. For a glance by fire-light, her face seemed crazy and endeared, like Sylvie's as she played with fire, and yet immortally serene: her candlelight was Sylvie's elsewhere, her elusive dazzling now.

Seeing, Ariane was moved with awe and longing: for she knew the wren that was to die was no illusion, but truly soul, blood and bone, as it was leaves and web and water. It was wintersake, itself and willful, archetype and wintry sun. It was reborn. It would be hunted by the Woodfall children, would be waked in their green crown: please to see the king.

No windeye in the hovel: how would the wren fly away? Ah, but Cloud was Mally's house, all Cloud, within and in: the sky was hooped and bound with starry branches, withies twisted in her hands. The wren's crown, its cage of garlands, was her thorny hallows, rib-anded with black and white, the nightwind and the moon-light, knots of moon and dark. It bore the waking sun. Beyond was only Annis.

Look, she would have called to him, O look: forget-ting, unbelieving death; then falling terribly through cloudy ice, she knew she was beyond, unhallowed and alone. One was taken and the other dead: her friend, her other self. And Sylvie—

The ring went blank. She held it, dreading to look up. It all was gone, she thought, all gone but silence and the wreck of love, his derelict and sallowed body. Grieving, she looked up and saw the tree was rooted still. He lay as wood, earthfast, enduring, and his pale bright leaves were starry, veined with frost. Amid his naked twigs, a browner leaf, there whirred and lit a wren.

Ariane looked up at the wren, at the winter tree: quick and still, both caught in the unimpassioned glory of the light. The wren cocked its inkdrop eye at her, and bent to whet and comb its wings, preening fussily, huffed out as round and shrewd as Malykorne herself: a wicked innocence. "Go on," said Ariane. "Go on, they're waiting for you. Year won't turn." Flet away and die.

But it stayed, scolding in its brilliant wintry voice. Light-boned with chill and heavy-eyed, she staggered up, tattered and bemused as the tinker himself, in the rags of his old unturning year, clapping and calling after. The wren flirted up, jilting its twig for another; then flitted over the moor in sallies like a windblown leaf.

She chivvied it a little way, through stones and dry heath, tinselly with hoarfrost; then came on a harder glittering underfoot: flints of glass, and the lantern lying shattered, black-framed like a wren's crown of iron, with the candle flown. Winter's door lay open.

She stood. In her grief she had forgotten half her trust. Here had been the maze, that now was naked to the morning; here, the candle, dying, had recalled the sun. Craobh had fallen here.

Ariane knelt to gather up the glass—curved, useless, incorruptible, too sharp to keep—regretfully, not knowing what to do with it, not wanting to leave it naked there. It had been Mrs. Woodfall's, it had come from within hallows. No use, no use at all. And she was left with it, alone, unsheltered back of Law. The wren, the last of light, was gone. She'd hunted it away. They would stone it; they were cruel in Cloud. They'd turned the strangers from the hearth; and the witch, the twofaced owling witch had made the wren to die, had cast them, closed them out to die beyond all hallows, in winter, in Annis's dark. There was no way back. The child was taken. The tinker was dead. Damn Mally. Damn her mocking gifts.

In a fury of despair, raging against heaven, ranting, tearing at herself, she pulled out the windegg in a tangle from her coat, and with a stone, in a storm of glass, she smashed it, smashed it—

There it lay, greenblue and round. Still round as sky. O God, the soul, had she—? Slowly, cold with dread, she touched the stone at her throat. Slowly, she slipped it on its cord from round her throat, and laid it by the windegg, by the other.

Unsoul.

O I see. I see, she thought: she held it, crystal. It was gone. No. Soul. Unsoul. But one seeming. Stone of light. An O. The child was lightborn: out of dancing, the light came. Out of nothing, nowt. Unturning stone. Illusion. Death.

She held the cold impassive windegg. She saw it in the witch's hand, as now in hers: the frail-as-rime, absurdly scribbled shell, the not-quite-runes that held no wren. A trifling, enigmatic thing. The witch had kept it in her teapot. Yet it closed within its seeming frailty the inmost, hugest dark. She would give Annis nothing.

Still with seeing, Ariane took up Craobh's soul. They lay together in her hand: the soul and its shadow, that was nothing, anything, a cloud of stone or clod of heaven. It was what she willed.

Enkindled, she sat quietly. The crown of light is brief, but springs from earthfast, tough, enduring roots, tenacious for the bearing insight. The stars are knotted in a stubborn string. The glory went. It comes and goes, but the way is there forever. Having seen it, she would make her way, by lantern-light, by flint-and-steel, by moon and dark of moon, afoot: a journey-witch, soldiering on to glory.

What then? Wind and riddles. Hush. What's that little stumpy person? said Sylvie, stalking witches with her lantern. Thy burden's light, said Malykorne. A soul for hallows' sake. Who'll dig his grave? I, said the Owl. What *has* it got in its 'pocalypse then? String, or nothing.

Malykorne had made the wren of grimy cobweb, of the unheard intervals that bind the stars, all one enweaving. Fate. Out of Mally's starry skein came lightfast, came the wren. Out of nothing would come nowt. What spell in that? Illusion. Out of brooded dark, thought Ariane, came shadows; out of shadows, what she willed. The windegg was itself, unfast. All vanity. Its spell was what it seemed, what Annis took it for. A changeling soul.

But souls are to be borne, who would bear it? Herself? A fool's errand. Craobh's stone could not be hidden, face to face with dark; could not be left. Annis looked for it. What other?

Bending over the windegg, Ariane felt a tweak at her tangled hair. Wren? No one. What's wick i't shadows? Swale-and-die, said Mally's voice. Moon's there to gan by, said Mrs. Woodfall. And way, i't dark. Tek lantern when you go. And farthest, clearest of the voices, Sylvie sang, about a lump of wax: ". . . *you must shape it as a child . . . and you must make two eyes of glass. . .*" God yes, she thought, remembering how Willie in the song had shaped it, as the child his lady could not bear; and then he'd asked the witch his mother to a christening. And how she stormed and how she swore at that cheat, thinking all her spells undone, undoing them in railing: for her rant was Willie's clew.

> O wha's undone the nine witchknots
> That was amang that lady's locks?
> And wha has loosed her left-foot shoe,
> The lighter of a bairn to go?

That other witch had seen in effigy the child she feared, the child her spell had bound, unborn, undying. Doubt moves scarecrows. So might Annis see the child she craved, and so might fall.

So. Not the soul alone as lure: a seeming child, unchild, to bear it. She would make death's poppet. Not wick, but rushlight, candlegrease. Thus lightly borne, the changeling soul might pass: for Annis, blindly craving souls, and scorning all that bears and dies, could not tell the dancer from its death. It was all tallow, and devoured.

Ariane turned out her pockets: nine stumps of candle, long and short. She laid them out formally, the windegg last, and inmost of the fall: soul and tallow. Labyrinth as body, turning, dwindling, and the moon's face shadowed in the Cup, within and elsewhere, for it was not bound. The Child reversed. From within her tranced intent, the tinker's voice, bemused, said, Ah, were-egg. Convulsed with grief, with fierce visionary impatience, Ariane clenched the cold unyielding wax.

It gave slowly, slowly in her hands. Kneading the sallow mass, she thought of Craobh, held captive, where? Not as stone. For she had a body to bestow, could hunger, shake with cold. Could bleed. The body Ariane had called, unsouled, might spare her for a time; or for a meaner death. Would Annis flay the child to find where her soul was hidden? No, thought Ariane: not willingly. Not yet, without great need. Annis had dropped the knife, let go the child at first, sickening at the hands that she had worn, despising what they seized. She'd kept her hunt for such work. Unbodied, raveness, she still could call and crave, not take; she would not scathe her hardwon spoils with pawing, but would bide till nightfall and the dark of moon, to scry her seeming-glass at full.

Not hands: but there were other torments. Annis must be drawn with another soul, away from Craobh. The bird in rand. The wren. But would she stoop? Annis saw alone what she desired. Nothing else. She'd left Craobh's soul, strode past it, bent on Craobh. She'd struck him blindly—No. That's over. Craobh's with Annis. You must get her back.

The witch was flawed. Stoneblind, thought Ariane, and queasy of mortality. The roughest idol might deceive her narrow lust. She saw only what she might possess, the soul desired or desiring Annis: stones in the lightborn children; sickly mirrors of her daemon in the witches, jewelled with envious blood, who sought to shadow her, invoked her wolfish dark. Moonblind.

But she saw through me, thought Ariane. She saw the witch.

No. Even in the dreams the witch had sent her in the

foxcastle, she was piercingly insighted, blind as stone. Annis had rifled through Ariane's earthborn soul with cold distaste, seeking Annis, like an eye of stone, amid the rags and bones of alien mortality. Annis's desire was Annis, mirrored. But the house the witch had spurned—the leaves, the webs, the hoard of stars and clay within—was Ariane. Let her have what she wills, her empty glass, thought Ariane, driving her blunt nails fiercely into wax.

There was more than a scant handful of it now, she saw, unwondering: she held a loaf of wax like a newborn child, cauled, inchoate, streaked faintly from her grimy hands. It bore marks of the ring, turning round, forgotten on her thumb: criss-cross, starry, rune on rune; obliterated and affirmed, ensealed and slurred. Strange ascendants, she thought: like the scrawled foretellings at a thousand births. Annis would have fixed its stars at death. She is law.

Then: I am like her, wanting light. I took Craobh's soul, I bound her, not in stone, but in a dying body. The child, turning from me, held a candle: even the same lure. The same desire.

No. I am Annis, I am Malykorne. The stone in the rushlit house. Dark and light of one moon. Weird sisters. I child and I devour; I am grave and lap, annihilation and O reborn: light eaten by its inward fury, crown rising from its root in darkness. I am Cloud and Law. It's Sylvie who is other. She's the travelling, the sword, the falling star; she's now and elsewhere. I am where she is not. I end what she becomes. Two things. The stone and the bow of light. Tenacity and fleeting splendor: journeying, the lightfast ring. A and O. Yet two is three, and turning we are one: whorl, tangle, shear away.

In the bitter clarity of revelation, strangely triumphant, grim, Ariane looked at the unshapen wax. All is stone to the gorgon mind, all crystal to the law of death, perfection to the artist: all that is. The rest is chaos. Let the devouring crystal feed on nothing, fall in on endless dark, she thought vengefully. Yet her grief had swelled the wax.

She unpinned her hair and shook it down, unknotting it and fraying out, over and over: for she made nothing, she unbound. She put the ring in her greatcoat pocket; it had nowt to do with witches. Then she bent to her shaping, and sang: not loud, but fiercely, as Mrs. Woodfall had sung at work, to the thud of her iron on the shroudlike linen, white as souls. *Babylon is fallen.*

Roughly at first, but ever finer, Ariane shaped a child of wax, a poppet like t'babby's doll. She had thought of corbels and of poppy-heads: small kings, naive and fircone-flighted angels. But she drew a bleaker vision from the wax. Her hands informed her image; though at back were memories of Craobh, unsleeping in the attic room, as cold, as silent in her lap; and of the naked wizened child dragged out of stone, enduring light.

It was proportioned like a dwarfish child, but framed on curves and angles like green timber, not bone. A kneaded clod. So. Ariane pinched out an unchildlike beaky nose, pressed in the hollow of the throat, tilted back the shoulderblades. Between these agate subtleties of craft, she rubbed the whole, slurring it and smoothing it with her thumbs and palms. It lay in her lap, archaic, witless, blind.

Two eyes of glass. She searched in her pack, and found Sylvie's bag of stones and marbles, long-carried, scried and licked by Malykorne. *A rare light wench*, the witch had said. *Best keep these for her.* She poured them out upon her hand. Turning each world over, cloud and clarity, she considered them: Cloud, though not this Cloud, its otherworld; Unlethe, Perran Uthnoe; green Alder, Idho, Thorn, with its still clear drops of air; Ravenser Odd, a sulky stormcloud purple shot with crows' wings; bright Anthelion, Far Lune. Other worlds than this, than hers.

She chose two marbles: greenish-grey, grey-blue Unlethe, clear but flawed with bronze, like sky-in-water and the twirl of a falling, having fallen leaf; and Cloud, like a wintry dusk, but whorled with roke. Odd irises. Set in, they coldly stared. She stroked lids of wax on them: they slept.

Fleetingly, she saw another face, not Craobh's, but of her kindred, turning from her into wood, leaf-shadowy, aloof: the face that Sylvie's song had wakened in her mind. *Turn leaves*, sang echo, rising from the cloudy dark. Ariane set Sylvie's curled dishevelled red-oak twig in the changeling's hand; and a garland of dry leaves, windfall from the tree, round its head. She hung the windegg at its throat.

Cold radiance within her hands, beyond her reach; light haloing a coinstruck clarity, like cloud about the moon: a spirit rose. It hung aloft, far-seeming: small as the moon is small, incomparable with things of earth; and moving as the moon does, in her mantle of the flying cloud, by illusion and the wind. It was a naked child, unlightborn, light of earth. In her hand was a fallow branch, horngold as moonrise, and a garland of frail leaves and starred with hoarfrost, winter's crown, was on her hair: they whispered.

O, thought Ariane, O but she is . . .

Then the child opened unseeing cloudy eyes: a flawed serenity, an umbered blue-gone-green, like winter dusk, leaves burning on the water; like the windegg twice. Unnamed and soulless, mute, she waited for the dance: Craobh's shadow, Mally's sending.

". . . *catch hands and turn, turn stone* . . ." sang Sylvie, back of Cloud.

Rising, Ariane set out a ring of Sylvie's stones: the swans, the birchwood, the leaf-eye and the rest, all round her in a moonwise circle on the earth. They made the token of a keep, frail as rushlight: a toyish labyrinth, a carol in a solemn game. Yet as the child of light, invulnerable, aloof, had risen, haloed round the bairn of wax, so clouds of children rose, unmoving dancers, from the henge of pebbles, palely marked: the swans of morning flying still, the woodland green within a brow. The dance took hands, turned hedge. An O beyond the witch's law, a castle of the moon. Unhallows, and a witch without, a witch of tree within.

Here's a bird in the bush, a bonny bird, thought Ariane, and laughed. Her soul clapped wings.

Yet her body shrank. Her blood was cold and rusted, a tree of iron and a hanging soul, picked clean, carrion no longer. Above its naked boughs, her spirit whirred and cried, exulting. She would call as Craobh had called the witch, binding her within her seeming: now, before the dark. Dry-voiced, bat-shrill, Ariane summoned Annis, calling down the wind, her death. But the act itself had called its shadow. She was there.

Annis strode down from the high fells, from the stone-law, the hoar lands: a shrunk black figure, blind, shadowless. The light behind her of the lastborn sun was cold and bright as scissors, blunted on her rock. Souls winced and glinted in her hair. She came and came forever, black as the afterimage of fire, as the denial of the sun, a scar within the eye; and stood at last within handsreach of Ariane, abysmally far: the gap was death.

Her witch's seeming was stonier, harsher than it had been, exposed in the bleak clear light: a sarsen gnawed and riddled from within, uncarved at back. Her disquiet or Ariane's refusal of her mask had marred her face; it ill fit her, being faulted, lying like a cairn on sleepless dead, yet vain: a ruined broch, a barrow unpossessed, a sunless moon. There was no one in the eyes. She spoke. "The moon is dead; the sun dies. Who calls?"

"Another," said Ariane.

"There is no other; it is mine."

"No. Your crown will ever lack this stone." Cold and feathery as frost, with unseen wings against her face, she felt the child come by her. The air had darkened. Then Annis saw: the new moon where none could be, risen in the green dusk of the windchild's eyes, herself within her airy self.

The witch struck the earth with her staff, and cried out a word to crack the air, call down the moon from its shattered orbit; but the windchild made no answer, being no one. She burned coldly, unconsuming, in the witch's eyes. Thrice Annis called, in vain.

Then shrivelling to hands, stooping in a fury of contempt to crone, she made to seize her prey, clawing at the woundless cloud in a hail and wind of malice. She held nothing.

Dismayed, astonied, Annis drew back, unshrouding of the crone. At her feet a thousand thousand winters cracked the earth, in fearful silence. She was dark, withdrawing. In her breast, there hung a stone, a gravity of hatred, no bigger than a hazelnut, and heavier than worlds. Cold, absolute, devouring light, she sucked the morning dry, the hills to husks.

Then suddenly she turned with scathing fire, unlightning, black and fierce, to blast and take the spirit from

the withered ash; but grave and joyful beyond her, coldly
serene as a moonbow foreboding tempest, now and elsewhere, still the windchild stood her air.

Annis stayed. Her clawed hands stormed herself like
rooks, tearing, flickering, raking over the souls in her
writhen hair. "Who broke the ravens' glass? Their eyes
were suns, I should have torn their eyes."

Raging and railing in her madness, she broke from
her shadow-body, dispossessed of her illusion. The witch
frayed out wildly like wind made visible, like thorn-raked
fire; flaws broke away blazing and withered: tongues of
eyes, hands, hair. About her fury she had stilled the
dark, a crystal cracked and flawed with frustrate lightning; at her feet a net of chasms gaped and flickered:
riddles in the earth. Blind to Ariane, she stormed and
swore. "And my daw is lost. Who cut its tongue, so it
would sing? What brooched the dark? Who closed the
ring?"

Exalted, terrified, encastled in her O, her otherworld
of cloud, Ariane watched Annis rant and scold to stand-
still, flaring like a dying star; then she was gone.

It was broad cold day. Glowing tawny as a sinking
moon, lying back upon the air, the changeling faded,
waned and died; like rack, the cloudy children fled
before the wind. Ashes. Ashes. They left nothing but an
eggshell and a few bright pebbles on the moor: a game
of jackstones played and drawn.

Ariane stood dazed. She gathered up the stones, and
set the windegg in the lantern; as beyond the riddlestones
the Woodfall children bore the wren in its green crown,
to slender music and sad ribands. She took the ring, and
held it to her eye a moment: a blind O, blackened,
starry. Nothing was within. She put it in her greatcoat
pocket, and went her way, no way, the tinker's gate.

The fell was cracked; the fall was endless. Sylvie halted, looking down at the riddled earth, a cold dank gaping, fanged with broken shafts of rock. Witch stuff. She dropped a pebble in. No sound. She tried an icy foothold with her stick; thought of falling and drew back, shying, fascinated. "Deea, what's this, Abyssinia?" Cobber made no answer for a long while, staring at the hollow earth.

"Riddlestones," he said at last. "Beyond's Annis."

"So you're turning back? You haven't said." He hadn't spoken for the wind, the journeying, the shock of the ravens' fall, not in a long night and a day, having said his winter's tales; he spoke with reluctance now, against great dark, as a nut breaks open under earth, unshells, seeking fastness, seeking light.

"No," he said, more slowly still. "No, I mun go on. Last night, I were i't wood. Dreamed."

Dreamed? How strange, how could he? She studied his shadowy and troubled face. Hey, Cobber? Not there, not there at all. Asleep. But no wood either. Was he turning mortal, then?

Far away beside her, he touched the witch's staff. "Were i't wood and earthfast, same as waking: eyes o leaf ont wind, leaves falling. Yet I were not light, but bound, unwitting. Hands, thowt I, no hands. Would cry, but had no tongue, no breath." A silence. "I were flayed."

Ariane lay sleeping. She had come blankly in her wandering, by long ways round, as far as the wintry unleaving tree, no longer bright. It was all the haven she knew, beyond the stones. She had thought nothing, only: hallows. She had meant to go, having taken leave; but had lingered, finding no word, no close. She was so tired, and her legs shook so that she would fall, crossing the stones. Touching the rough bark gently in farewell, in benediction, she had felt bright and heavy, trembling like a drop about to fall; had fallen, lying slumped and curled about his roots, beneath the branches of the hallows tree. He sent leaves into her sleep, a charm of pale and silent drifting birds; and from the clouds, serenely, Mally shook her apron full of feathers over her, O lightfall.

"Cobber?" said Sylvie, turning, the intent of her next leap still brightly curved upon the air.

"It's nowt," he said, puzzling out his way, hesitant above the abyss. "Wings rising out o dark, same as leaves. Voices." But he lagged, and further lagged; as Sylvie leapt, and thought her move—castle on the Queen's side—and leapt again, turning backward with her staff to give him poise.

"Not far," she said. "Hold on." He seemed astonied, swayed with dreams, but steadied at the touch of wood. She turned to go on. Then she heard the riddles' voices. As deep and sibylline as wind, they spoke, with Mally's hooing voice, Nan's voice, reading to her through a childhood fever. *You must throw yourself in. There is no other way.*

No, she said. No way. Not crazy as that. I wonder where I'd fall to, she thought; and went on, formally, as if to music, step by step, and looking level to the hills beyond.

Ariane woke, blank and stiff, to an unearthly cold serenity. Craobh's soul lay closed within her curving hand. At first, she thought the peace was fallen snow, but waking there was none, only hoarfrost and a thin still brightness lying softly on her fallow mind. Had the tinker slept like this, through years, between the falling and the landfall of a wintry leaf? She had his burden now, the light and the enduring.

She sat up and ate a little of the Woodfalls' food: half

a cold bacon sandwich, and a slab of parkin. She drank some water from the spring. A little beyond, in a hollow where it had blown, she found the tinker's hat, and put it on: *with me fine cap and feathers*. Then she looked about, to see her way.

Her soul felt strangely light, unearthly still, despite scant sleep, and loss, and cold unending solitude before her. Round her at the twelve wind's quarters of the earth lay moorland, bare and desolate. All one. All Annis Law. Sunward or moonwise, north or south: whatever way she turned, the riddlestones would lie before her; at the journey's end, the crossing. They were at once unhallows' bourne, the earth's blind eye; at once the thorny hedge round Mally's realm, and Annis's demesne's black heart: a world revolving on its death. The witches' spindle, whirling cloudwool into fate. Behind her lay the maze and the ring of stones, the castle where the raven-dreams had fed on eyes: the Law. Beyond, if she could cross, lay hallows. There lay Cloudwood and the wren, green-crowned, the Woodfalls in their earthly haven. Mally's cot.

Ah, but Ariane was there, she knew she had not left, though all she saw was otherworld: the O turned inside out. The stones were wood, the witch's crown was children, turning in their winter carol; and the foxcastle, Mally's patchwork featherbed: one thing, as ever, dark and light of one moon. Cloud Law. She blessed the ancient new cosmology, that turned on hearthlight, not on void: box within box of wood, and inmost greatest. She would find her way.

Unless the ring of stones were closed: then would be no crossing into light, no light. And Mally darkfast, and the tinker dead. O Craobh.

Not with hands, but in her thought, Ariane found and held Craobh's stone. Here. I am here. For a fleeting eternity, she saw the world encrystalled, steeped in re-echoed sky, etched and flawed and angled with refracted stars: it dangled in the heavens, now blank and bright, now darkly lucid as it turned and caught the winter sun. She saw an ancient grove, outbranching, bearing stars, and rooted in the light, lightfast; it was the riddles in the stone, inturned, as deep as high. The many trees were

one, the masted Ship, onsailing. Sylvie's voice sang
nowhere, clear as starfall: ". . . *a forsaken maid, to sail
so royally* . . ." Seeing purely, undesiring, Ariane let the
image fall.

Dark and rime, a winter's day. Yet beyond the edge
of sight, she glimpsed a flaw of moving silver in the air,
a new moon falling, twirling like an ash-key in its fall; a
sudden lightning in the cloud. Lifting up her face, she
saw a cloud-grey image on the moor, stone-high, but
striding, with a long and lithe and ranting gait—O Sylvie.

As Ariane's heart broke off in joy and disbelief, the
walker paused, intently gazing, as if considering her way.
Her round dishevelled dark head turned. Another followed, all in wintry leaves of rags—No. Not the tinker.
Far smaller, look, a child. A stranger. Ah, but like to
pierce her heart. Sylvie bent to him. She wore a strange
cloak, and a staff and bag, like the image of a traveller,
a tarot-Sylvie. Ariane dared not move, lest the vision of
the brown girl fade, the windfall child turn leaves, the
web of time and chance unravel, even as the starry crossing came: so slender was the thread.

Sylvie turned and saw a tree, odd in all that desolation.
Hey, wood. And a standing stone: awd Mally?

Sylvie ran to see, with all her old wild joyful abandon,
an arrowy and curving path, as she had run away through
the night woods of another earth, haring after the fleeting
moon. A field away from Ariane, she startled, bright
with recognition.

"Air?"

Pack and all. So she's got here, what she always
wanted. Oh, we've got to talk, I've got to tell her—

Sylvie ran to her, and just beyond handsreach, stood
still, a little breathless, alighted. "Hey, your moon's gone
out," she said, pointing at the lantern.

Ariane made the last step. She snatched a handful of
the prickly cloak. Her voice was shaking. "Oh, I missed
you. You came."

Sylvie hugged her hard, briefly; she felt the quick thin
frame beneath the wool. They stood, blinking tears and
thumping backs. Ariane drew back to look and look at
Sylvie: now, here.

"Man, am I glad to see you," said Sylvie, very seriously. "Thought I was loony tunes."

Finding love for only a dime. She had not thought of Sylvie missing her. "That's two of us; it's all right. I brought your marbles. How did you . . . ?"

"I was after the moon; and then it wasn't Nan's woods, it was here."

"Cloud," said Ariane. "We blew it."

"I don't know. Got winter right. And stones."

The child had reached the tree. He stood and gazed, then touched its branches. He was silent: still as wood, not wood, for all his leaves of rags. Unturned. But he was lost, thought Ariane.

"He's shy," said Sylvie. "This is Ariane, she's from my world. Remembers lyrics."

Ariane looked up, unsteadily, and then away: too sharp to bear, not yet. Bright Sylvie, and the child like the tinker's shadow, like Craobh. The last. The child said nothing. They'd come late, past waking for the silent tree; and not too late. The wren dies, the year's reborn. Bears light shall never see. The last. The child's the last, he's lightborn, and untaken: so the ring's unclosed, the tale's not endless yet. And so the dance could be. The sun and moon, the turning. Lightfast.

Not looking at the tree, the cup that held the light, Ariane took hold of Sylvie's rough grey cloak, most strangely familiar, cloudwool out of Mally's lap. "Wassail."

Sylvie laughed; she spoke in her deepest, sibyl's voice. "Wha's ale? Did you see her? Mally? Was she dancing?"

Hey, got her to laugh. "Did you?"

"Just to get drunk with. A crony." Sylvie pulled a fierce shrewd face: Ariane could almost see the malefic glitter of spectacles. "And folded her nighties. Kind of funky. Had to catch them first."

Ariane giggled crazily. "Chaos and old nighties. It's petticoats all the way down."

"Deea. Did you look?"

"Sacked out with her. Pinched this." Fumbling, she took out the gat-toothed horn comb. "The stars will fall like dandruff."

"You stole her *comb*? Man, she'll snatch you bald."
And reflectively, "I've lost her mirror. All the little mer-
curies rolled away."

"Alien marbles. Alley-oops." She grinned at Sylvie,
crookedly. "The birds brought them back to her. It's
all come round again, the mirror's snug ont shelf. Wi
jugs and stuff. Nutmegs. Owl-eggs. For making numen-
nogs."

"She give you any ale? Like, to take out?"

"No. Nettles. He . . ."

Sylvie touched her shoulder. "Air?"

Ariane shook her head.

Oh, thought Sylvie, drawing back. What she'd seen in
the hailstone was true. Ariane was the thorny, sort of
cloudish figure, crouched in the dark. Afraid and mourning. He was dead then, not asleep. The other. Cobber's
Flaycraw, the tatter-coated, woodbrown man. The one
who sang.

"I'm all right."

"You could sit down or something." Sylvie turned to
the child. "Cobber? What's up? You're awful quiet."

Yes, thought Ariane. Of course. Cobber's Wood, the
crow-lad in the Woodfalls' fields, the wren-boy at their
door. He'd left them, lightfast eve. The child in the
Cloudwood, bearing light. The cup.

She looked at him: an odd grave child, as tangled as a
hazel wood, as brown and sweet as any nut; and wearing
Phoebe's old rough cap. Broad cheeks, long eyes, a gentle nose. He was like the tinker in no shape, but in mien
and moving, in his look of cloudwise innocence, of rushlight, fall of leaf: autumnal tawniness. Craobh had been
blackthorn, wintry dusk. And starry, not of earth. Yet
they were kindred.

The child touched the branches ruefully: a crown that
he had lost, a cage. His eyes were bright with tears.
"Tha'st done wi thy wandering. Tha'rt fast and wood.
Cloud's thy sleep, and I's waking."

Ariane touched his shoulder; he looked round, and
saw the light she bore, her grief. "Wha's here?" said
Cobber softly, looking not at Ariane, but through her,
at the wintry thorn, the moon in its branches. "One and
t'other. I's come late."

She held out the ring. "He kept this for you. All this time. He tried." The child took and set it on his thumb. Too big. A world too wide. "Take care."

He smiled at her. "Aye, it's ower great for me, as is. Time were, I borne it."

"What's with the rings?" said Sylvie. "Here's another one." She held out her staff, crossways; it was bound with silver.

Ariane touched it. The staff was thornwood, root and branch of Cloud; the ring, allusive, runic as the other. Need that, gin we meet wi witches, he'd said. Nowt for nowt, said the witch. "Was that from Mally?" Sylvie nodded. "Then it's stars, I think. Cloud's stars. The one we found in Nan's woods."

"Deea. What's it doing here?"

"It doesn't *do* anything. It's where we are."

Cobber nodded, mandarin. "Aye, lightfast, i't dance. Same as stars."

Nine lightfast, Malykorne had said: cup and staff, that's twa. Nine rings. Had Craobh borne one of them? This one, that they had graved in earth? Still there, thought Ariane, it stays: lies changeless in the stony dark, light's grave, time's lap. All else journeys, rises, following the thread from sleep to sleep. Lightself, it dances, and the heavens are its shadow. O and endless. Almost, she could read it, could unspell the light turned ring; then the moment clouded. Late.

"Sun's going. She'll be out: she said the soul would come." The name Annis stuck in Ariane's throat: not here, beyond the stones. Not now.

Sylvie looked at her. "you've *seen* her?" Ariane nodded, mute. "You're tougher than you think. I've only seen her minions, and they're no beauties."

"Turned crows," said Ariane. "Like in your song."

"Huh? Oh, *Babylon*—you found *that*? That tape I messed up? Nan remembered it; it was a game they used to play. Like someone's witch, and if she tags you, you're stone. The song's how it starts all over, in a ring. Like all fall down."

"Oh!" said Ariane. "Oh, the ravens—was it you? They were in her moonglass, dead." She looked at Sylvie. "But how?"

"Sang them lullabies. Well, sang them flaming witches. Lunch."

"Witch-ka-bobs," said Ariane.

"And—kkkkkhhhh. All done with mirrors." Sylvie grinned. "Did she see me? Is she mad?"

"She's furious." Ariane thought of Annis, unattended, raging. "No hunt. And I've put her off." It seemed a strange, fantastic thing, not hers at all. "She thought I hung the moon."

Glancing shrewdly at the lantern, Sylvie pulled another Mally-face, wickedly askew. "I did the sun; you'd think she'd catch on. No intuition." Then soberly, "Mally's sent me to see to her. What now?"

"Have you had breakfast?"

They sat on the cold bare hillside, by the tree. Ariane gave them the last of the Woodfalls' food: crumbs, really, but ceremonial. For ragnarok. She sighed, remembering the chocolate.

"Bacon! Great, I'm getting so sick of lunar cheese." Sylvie opened her bag. "Mally's lunch, see. It keeps coming round again."

"How do you get the phases to coincide?" said Ariane.

"The bread is slow," said Sylvie with her mouth full. Her voice was hoarse; she was filthy, streaked with mud and ash, snarled and tangled, but invincibly herself, drawing in the dark to make it Sylvie.

She travels light, thought Ariane; and saw the burning silver on the wind, the wintry sun in Mally's hand. Her Sword. Her instrument of fate, called forth to act her will, and nakedly, as innocent of malice as the starry Ship. Yet Sylvie still, still willful: what she was, she did, as fire burns. A rare light wench. She'd brought the ravens' burning in a fall of cards, a snatch of rhyme, all jumbled in herself. Her star was falling, and her tale was Cloud: outlandish prophecies, that mirrored here were true and lightfast stars, the turning dance. She was essential. She was air and memory: the breath that kindled fire, the songs that came true, giving shape and spirit to the naked power of the mirror.

The child had sat turning and turning his ring, that bound nothing, turned all. He was still now. His unchildlike knotted hands echoed the tree's roots, were as quiet;

like its leaves, though a paler brown, his hair stirred and strayed. He is the last, thought Ariane, remembering the numinous and wizened child caught in stone, in Annis's uncircled crown; remembering Craobh. The last. And yet, for all his weight of sorrow and of myth, he was childlike, a comely, sweetly comic, moonfaced child, odd and hale, as the tinker had been—O heavens, had she made Craobh in her likeness?

She asked, "Did Mally send you here? With Sylvie?"

"Eh no, we's met ont way. I' Cloud. All ways there, wood or no."

Sylvie thought, he's in his story, in the wood. He's forgotten which he is, leaf or shadow. She looked at Ariane, gazing at Cobber as if she saw another in his face: the old moon in the new moon's arms, the hare in the puzzled sky. Old Air looked unfamiliar, somehow, oddly suited to her rakish draggled coat; and strange and right with it, she wore a beggar's-opera slouch. "I like the hat. For questing."

"It fell," said Ariane. "He . . ."

"He sang, I heard him. Saw him. In the cup. I didn't know." Sylvie drew a shaky breath. "He was in a sort of brownish ragged coat. Under a tree." There were no other trees, this side. No grave. They'd seen the witch, and now Ariane was here alone: would she have left him lying for the crows? "Did Annis take him?"

Ariane caught her hand. A stone, a sort of crystal round her neck, swung and glinted. Sylvie blinked. As in the hailstone, Ariane was huddled, cold and grieving, stubborn as a windbent thorn; the moon was caught in her. Then Sylvie saw: within the hallows tree, the racked and sprawling man. Stark dead and staring. "Ohh. O poor Air, how terrible." Their glances nearly met, and shied away like magnets, north to north.

Cobber looked up, bright as leaves against a stormcloud. "Chosen well. Cup's cracked and sprang up green."

"Poor old guy," said Sylvie, touching the gnarled roots. "Not his kind of earth at all: scrub firs if anything. But she didn't annihilate him, why? And left Cobber's soul—that's crazy."

"I don't know," said Ariane. "She was after—O Syl-

vie, she's got Craobh. Another child. I was with her,
travelling. I—I called her." Trembling, she undid the
knot, and held out the stone.

Sylvie studied it, not quite touching. "Oh, it's a little
world." An arch-marble. It twisted, depth beyond depth
of clarity, elusive, inward; and forgetting Annis and herself, she would have taken it to gaze at, and gone in.

Cobber did. In his face there shone a bright severity
of joy, or grief. He held the stone in his two hands, as
a traveller holds water from a spring: the more he drank,
the brighter glory ran undying through his fingers.

O the ring, thought Ariane, it has a star. She wanted
him to look forever, holding Craobh as light.

He spoke, but to no one there. "Aye, coming. Seen
wood i't riddles, stars at roots." Still immensely far from
them, as ageless, clear and trembling as the shepherd's
star, he smiled. The stone was dusk, unclouded, where
his star would set. Craobh's afterlight still shone. "Moon's
way. Will be brant to follow, and i't dark. No stair. No
candle."

He looked up at Ariane, gave back the stone. Dark
now. "You hawd that yet."

"She has your twig. Mrs. Woodfall gave it to her."

"Eh, she's a canny one, for hearthfolk. It were left as
sign."

"Taken," said Sylvie, musing. "And the guy, the other
changed: I'll bet old Black Hole never thought of that,
not wood. That looks like Mally butting in. She's meddle-
some." She thought of the stumpish witch-stone, looking
out on the naked fells, as solitary as this tree; she thought
of owls: a prickly comfort. "She's formidable." Her face
clouded. "What about Craobh? Will Annis hurt her, try
to make her talk?"

"No. No, I saw them," said Ariane, reluctantly.
"She—Annis—she hated touching her; she's had her
hunt for that. She takes."

Sylvie nodded. "It's like their iron crowns: they hate
iron and they have to wear it. Craobh's the setting for
the soul, to her."

"I tricked her. She may kill her out of rage."

"Time will," said Cobber.

"And it's her time," said Ariane. "Sun's dying."

"All right, then, we'll try some witch-crunching."

"Spells won't work," said Ariane. "She undoes herself. The Witch reversed. It's something obvious. A riddle. Something gnawing at her dark. She said, 'Who broke the ravens' glass?' That's you." She shut her eyes, recalling. " 'And my daw is lost. Who cut its tongue, so it would sing? What brooched the dark? Who closed the ring?' "

"Got birds on her tiny mind," said Sylvie.

"Stark raven," said Ariane, "the two of them. 'Craws ower crown,' Mally said. Her prophecy. She sounded cross. And triumphant. Do they turn on Annis, I wonder? Do craws eat daws?" She called on inspiration, but her sky was blank of wings.

Sylvie knelt up. "Look, what do we know about her? She's Mally's dark of moon. Wants souls. She's grabby."

"Falls for illusions," said Ariane.

"Stoneblind," said Cobber.

"But her mirror's full, it's dark of moon," said Ariane. "She can see now."

"But she can't see things. They don't exist for her. Like trees." Sylvie touched his bark. "Like mortals. Us. I think that we are's essential: voices, hands. What I sang came true; what you made was real. We're the unexpected. Wild cards." Sylvie paused. "Mally said I was her sword."

"The Sword," said Ariane. "It's in the fall."

"What Mally gives is true, it all comes in."

"I took the comb. That's out. I've used up the windegg."

"What was that, your moon? What happened?"

"It made a sort of wraith, a pseudo-Craobh. Like Willie's baby. Annis stormed at it: that's when I heard her, ranting about birds."

"And the mirror's gone." Sylvie looked to Cobber's hand, to her staff. "Rings won't mess with her: they're for something else, I think. For afterward. Or forever."

"Lightfasting," said Cobber. "You'll not cage dark wi stars."

Sylvie unbrooched her cloak, and held out the dark-of-moon iron clasp: a rough, cold, malefic thing. "All's I've got left is this." Ariane took it up. She weighed it

on her palm, and turned it over. The long, curved pin
swung loose.

"Looks like a bird," she said, and so it did: the essential raptor, nothing but a beak of iron, and a blind eye,
through which its talons hung and hinged. She perched
it up, hunch-shouldered, baleful, gibbous, like a hoodie-
crow. Why is a raven like a writing-desk? What brooched
the dark? Unmoon. "It's her daw," said Ariane, and
knew a fierce dark rising joy, like the sea within a fretted
cave, inexorable. "She said she'd lost it. She was furious—she was scared. I wouldn't use it, I'd set it free. It
hates her."

"Daw?" said Sylvie.

Ariane said nothing. One by one, but in her mind, she
turned the cards; she read the daw's nativity. The Ship.
The Harp of Bone. The Tower, and the evil come of it.
The Hare. What's turned is turned. The Cup—ah, the
Cup was this fierce dark rising in her, filling, filling, and
unspilled; wood held it. She was in the ruined maze. She
brushed aside a muddle of leaves on the deep, and saw
the stars in it, the labyrinth. And looking up, she saw
the stars again. But which was shadow? What was fall
of leaves, foretelling, and what lightfast, and the end
foretold?

"The Witch," she said aloud, abstracted.

Sylvie stared. "Hates which?" She touched the brooch.
"Her daw. Hates which of them?"

"Whichever," said Ariane. "Backwards fortunes."

The fall that she laid out (she saw now) was an endless
knot: not A nor O, but either. Both. The journey and
the end. The eye of Cloud. The Witch lay at the crux: a
mirrored image. Light of darkness, leaves of shadow: in
the wren's rebirth, the ravens' darklong lightward fall.

"Keeps?" said Sylvie, riffling airy cards.

Ariane nodded.

The fall is A and O: a tree and yet an endless ring.
The Ship is at the lightspring of the fall, its root; its
flowering—O yes the Swans. Bed within the witch's cot;
cot within the thorny hedge; hedge within the endless
wood: and all the starry world in Mally's bed. Sun, dark
of moon and stars turned mirror, brooch and lightgraved
rings: the great maze in the less. No less. The dance

on Law turned heavens, Cup held Cloud; as Cloud and heavens, light and Law caught fast in Annis's crown, turned stone. O's fast. But light or dark? The fall's ambiguous: Witch ever, as the card is turned.

And A? Unfast. The travelling, the fall of stars. Ariane looked up at Sylvie, at her bright uncloudish champion: a sword that Annis in her baleful dark could not foresee, cold as Orion's, yet unlightfast, strange and sharp against her stoneblind ancient power. Light of darkness. She would turn the Sword; held back. Not fallen yet. Not yet: but soon.

The knot's undone, she thought. What's left? She saw the children in the hedgerow and the huntsmen aloft: the crowns of iron and the wren's green cage. She saw the stony ring, not endless yet. She saw, all one in the maze of stars, the Woodfalls' stone-flagged kitchen, Mally's patchwood, leaves on leaves, the sheepfold back of Law, dark with wings: the dance, the crown, the Ship and the abyss. Cloud's riddles. And they made one pattern, if she knew the key.

She held it.

Ariane laid down the iron brooch: the Wren reversed.

"Unbind it," she said. Sylvie jumped. "We unbind it. Look, the wren won't die without its shadow, so it won't be truly born. Without this other—raven, sort of. Daw. Whatever. They're one thing. Like the witches, see, they're dark and light: they turn the year." The entranced and tumbling words spilled on. "Mally's kept her turn, and set hers free—the wren, I saw it—out of leaves, but Annis—"

"Whoa. Hey, fell off the sled back there. What wren?"

"The one that Mally makes."

"And they hunt it? Got you." Sylvie thought. "And this daw's what Annis does? Her turn?"

"It should be. But Annis is afraid of change, of being turned. She's death, not dying. She's kept this bound and blind and hidden, and now it's lost. Well, all right, we'll give it back to her." Ariane glared fiercely through her long dark hair, and crouching, clawed her hands. "Eat metaphor, witch!"

Sylvie laughed at that; but Cobber looked wry. "You wake it, then," he said. "It hunts."

"You mean this thing's *alive*?" said Sylvie. "Like a sort of spare raven?" He nodded. "Dawn breaks." She took the brooch, and made it peck, peck against her palm, and strut, and cock its iron-rimmed unlidded eye: a sinister and comic mime. The cloak, unpinned, was slipping from her shoulders. At last she said, "Mally had it. Why didn't she turn it loose?"

"God knows," said Ariane.

"Well, I don't. Not my sort of thing. Witchy." It sulked in her hand. "Maybe it won't work for her. Maybe it hates them both."

"Mally," said Ariane dolefully, "likes being difficult."

"Or maybe she mislaid it."

"Did she look in the teapot?"

"What teapot? Mally—"

Cobber looked up. He was fanning out a handful of pale leaves; his face beneath the tangled, fallow hair was grimy and composed. "Mally's closed wi winter, in her way. Craw's nowt of hers. Wren's hers: not turned once forever and hid deep, but ower and ower. Same as dance."

"So is this—crow—her creature, then? Her rival?" Sylvie looked from one daft moonface to the other. *Just tell me where it goes.*

"Annis? No. Meks nowt, not even dark. Yon craw's wren's other: soul and shadow."

A spirit bound, thought Ariane. *Not elder than Annis, nothing is; but ancient. And of this earth, elemental.* "Law," she said. "Not Cloud. Unlightborn."

"Let me get this straight," said Sylvie. "Mally let hers go. Annis won't, so we do it for her. So it's spring." She slid the curving beak from claw to iron claw and back. "It threatens her somehow, so she's caught it; but not to gloat over, it bugs her. She can't or won't annihilate it. It's precious, or she wouldn't have freaked when she missed it, but she hates it enough to've lost it. What's she afraid of? Something too like herself. Or her antithesis."

"No, that's Mally's wren, that's stars," said Ariane. "The endless dance. This is iron, and denied."

"Herself. Like the giant's heart. How'd she let that out of sight?"

"The witch," said Ariane, struck cold with seeing. "On

the fell, beyond the riddlestones. Not Annis. Dead—O
God, she was horrible, like a dead sheep, with the crows
at her. She was after the brooch, I think. A rumor of
the brooch, a power. For her own." A castle. Ravens.
Prophecy for light of eyes: the ravens' fee was eyes.
"Foretelling."

"Witch?" said Sylvie, turning to the child. "Like at the
graves, like the ones the mirror called?"

"Aye," said Cobber grimly. "All fell. Tried Annis
shifts on Annis, when bone's bane til her. Cast spells.
As good drown fish."

Sylvie said, "Should've just stolen it. Like Mally said:
Annis loses track of real things, she's too narrow."

"Stoneblind," said Ariane. "Sees one thing at a time."

"So what do we do with it? Not being witches."

"O!" said Ariane. "We have to make it nothing: O."
She mimed the zero with her hands. "Annis said, 'Who
closed the ring?' It maddened her." She paused, thinking
of the grey crown of stones, the silent children, stilled in
their winter carol. *And we'll dance in a ring, love.*

Sylvie was turning round the brooch, wary of the spine.
"Looks more like a Q. Hah!" She stabbed the air. "Then
where does the sword come in? 'Cause I'm it. Mally
said."

"Bloodthirsty wench."

"Not malice. It's law. Turn and turn."

So many rings, what ring? thought Ariane. The dance.
The stars, stones, rings of silver and of ravenblack; the
sun's round and the moon's: were they to close them all?
And which had the windchild seemed to close? Crying
out against her downfall's shadow, Annis had forespelled
it, darkly: in her fury at the end, there lay the means.
A clew, but all in knots: and in it, her undoing. Turn
and turn. A ring, a tangled thread, a sword. Ariane
remembered Mally's solemn hey about the hearthstone,
out of which, somehow, the wren was made. Or was her
spell in the figures of the starry web, or in the cup, or
knotted in her unbound hair? How would they unbind
what Annis bound? Unmoon, the maze of stones.
Undarkfast.

"Maybe, somehow . . ." Ariane told off the cruxes on
her fingers. "If we knew the spell, and made the raven

sing, and danced it out, unsunwise like a mirror, like the
Witch reversed—if we danced in the stones, the circle, if
we closed it without closing, being mortal, the spell
would break, the year would turn . . ."

Sylvie still held the brooch in her two hands, turning,
puzzling at it. "No," she said. "No, it'd be what she's
overlooked. She's obsessed with those stones." She
frowned. "Not illusion, this time. We've got to get round
her blind side. Hands."

"Do we need a forge? A fire? O poor tinker—was it
meant for him? His hands? Ironwork."

"Tinker? Oh, Cobber's—No. No, simpler. Hey, like
this." Offhand as Malykorne, and then intent, she tried
to close the ring, pushing hard. No go. She wiped her
palms. Stubbornly, with all her wiry strength, she bent
the wrying ends together, warping, sliding, biting deep
into her hands.

As they met, she cried out. Her face paled and
warped, running slack and sharp like burning tallow in
cold wind, as a crooked brightness stormed through and
through her, a lightning with intent. The bird was in her
marrow, like burning metal, and she bent it shut upon
the forge of her own spirit, with her heart's quick ham-
mer: bone and blood were its only masters. Yet forging,
she was forged by it, and tempered in the zero storm.
She was a sword in Mally's hand, outlandish, bright,
essential.

Shielding her dazzled eyes, Ariane reached out through
the burning cold, and touched her friend.

"Sylvie?"

Sylvie heard the wind in the Ship's leaves; she heard
the ring of enweaving music, endless, small and clear and
ancient, the carol of the cold rejoicing stars. She heard
the darker voice than hers, the other's rising out of sleep,
and Mally's owl-voice closing up the ring. *Hold fast, and
fear it not,* they sang. It tears. The howling tears, she
cried. But still they sang, *I'll weave my love a garland.*
And of the daemonic gabble of the raven, she sought to
weave and break and bind a music, as she would make
a garland of the thorn. She would bear the raven to the
hollow stones, to Annis's blind heart.

As Ariane watched, Sylvie rose, swayed and staggered

on her feet, like one whose veins ran silver: dazed, but
dauntless still. Mally's cloak fell off, unpinned, unheeded.
The glory flared and flagged: another's shadow, a fury
winged and taloned, black as the devouring unmoon,
black as Annis, rose in storm, and rent and rent the air
above her. It would break from her, uprooting soul and
all in branching silver. But she sang, and held it fast.
*"The moon's my constant mistress, and the lovely owl my
marrow . . ."*

"Sylvie?"

*". . . She held it fast, and she feared it not, and it did
to her no harm . . ."*

"Sylvie? You all right?"

"Hey, crow's got my tongue," she said, in a hoarse harsh
gasp between notes. *"Will you drink of the blood . . . ?"*

Now the ravenshadow whelmed her light, dark-winged
and framed on darker fire; now Sylvie shone, drawing in
the dark to make it Sylvie.

Handfast, thought Ariane: the dark and light. One
star.

*". . . we exchanged rings, love, and aye the best was
mine. Yours was the purest gold, and mine but false tin
. . ."* Sylvie took and forced and twisted the brooch down
her narrow hand onto her wrist. Ariane felt a weird
shudder at the imagined touch. *". . . to call my true love
to the dance . . ."*

As she had gone from Nan's woods, ah, but slowly,
Sylvie ran, cloaked with burning silver, bright on the
wind of its burning, flaring out; and crowned with
shadow. She fleeted toward the riddlestones: no slight
moon now, but full, bright and heavy with her burden,
quick with mingled fires, light and dark; complex, like a
star and its occulting moon.

Ariane stared after. Her eyes were scarred with light,
with claws and beaks of fire. She turned round to the
child. He had gone.

The cloak was heavy as a cloud. As Sylvie let it fall, the boy, the lightborn, took it up, for it was Malykorne's, of her winds and weaving, and she gave nothing for no rhyme or reason. No one saw. They were elsewhere and otherwise by now, in Cloud, all three: his other dreaming in the earth, and through his bones of wood, and into leaves; the stranger, green and leafless still, but crowned with light, the soul caught in her like a star in winter branches; and the walker, overshadowed with the dark-winged malefic spirit she had loosed, eclipsed by it and waning, and then bright, a coronal of silver fire flaring out. She held the ravenshadow. O but it knew the child of old; it turned its blind devouring seeking gaze toward him. So swiftly then, to be overlooked, he happed himself in Mally's cloak, and went into the song that she had woven.

He was alone on the moorland, in the mist and thorns. Beyond him stood a little clump of windbent trees: nut, thorn, and oak; and in the branches of the last there perched a raven, with a ring in its beak. It took the iron bauble in its claw, and cocked its knowing pebble eye at him. "Riddle-me," it cried and cawed. "Ashes, ashes, we all fall down."

Cobber clapped his hands and yelled. The raven flew.

The child was shivering. He wore no cloak; but cloud and hills of Cloud were all around him, cold and heavy, rough with thorn, with heather prickling through the rags of snow. It was his landscape, woven out of dreams and myth, witch-gathered, combed and carded as the other

291

sang, by dwindling rushlight; spun by dark of moon, the spindle filling with its bright and heavy skein: time was and elsewhere. It was warp of winter's tales and hearthlight, as the tinker's coat was rags of autumn, years of dreams. Wood for the sleeper in his drift of leaves, and Law for the lightborn, stolen child; but cloud for the child unseen, the last and soulless.

He had crossed into his other's tale. He was the traveller, unnamed and changeless, though his rushlight burned away, elsewhere. The lass was in the witch's castle, under fell and over water, bound in riddles in the utter darkness of the light inturned. He would go after, were the gate beyond the moon: for that he came.

He began to walk back over the fell, toward the riddles whence the voices came. No other way, they said, no stair nor candle: you must throw yourself in. He went, not over Cloud, nor by Stonelaw, but the other gate, aloft. The way was brant and narrow.

By his lone in all that wilderness of rock and cloud, he thought on hearthtales, lilting softly in his small true woodwind voice, made harsh with crying crows. He told old thrums of cradlesongs, hush ba and lilly ba; told rimes and ballads heard in shadows, got from knitters by an ashy hearth, from shepherds and crow-lads and nightfall travellers, from waits at a windy door, in sleet and mud: all songs his other knew, had borne; or ballads of that ancient root, its leaves. He wove them into one tale, his journey, as the black and pale and rudded wool, death, dreams and bloodred birth, cross-warped with nightwind hair, were made the web in Mally's hands, between her iron combs. He made a coat of hallows. So his other had; and so had made his endless way, his wood: the leaves on leaves, the rushlight burning.

A rent, and Annis's nothing would fly in, and tear and take; for the mortal guise is thin, their hallows frail. Beyond waits Law.

He went on, to the measure of their slender piping, dub of drum. Their dance is brief, from dark to dark. They go longways, yet rehearse with awe, with mirth, with grave unease, the carols of the sun and moon. Their journeying is endless: turning in their starry chains, they bear the crown, the staves, the cup and swords; they turn and hand them on. Another and another takes the Fool, the King, the Witch's part. And yet for each in time the ring is closed, makes nothing; the knot of swords takes all.

Cloud beyond cloud, he came amid the ring of stones, his kindred, stilled in their winter carol. They were no taller than the child, but stonefast, shrunk and shrouded in their cloaks of earth, spellbound upon the farthest of all journeys. Slowly he walked among them, as through the dance. For the mist, they could not be told, they made no rune. But two among them were merely stones. Any face could be set upon them. They turned nothing. He stood, twisting and twisting the loose ring on his thumb: cold and endless, starry, it would not let him in. He turned and went on.

The sky was very dark, and the fells were white as bone against, or fleasblood brown. He saw a black and ragged shadow hanging, shaken like a man on the gallows tree, a scarecrow in the wind: strange on these barren hills where no green swath is cut, and blood, not corn, is raven's fee. It seemed his other going on before him; but he did not follow, and he saw it shook and sidled over no rock, but bleak and depthless hag.

A pack of silent hounds, black and pale and sullen red, came hunting him, thronging fiercely at his throat. He hid his face in the crook of his arm; but he walked on, and did not run from his body's death, and they were thorns and burs, and withered bracken.

Softly, warily, he crept past the cave where shadow-Annis, hearthwitch Annis crouched, with her blue face and iron claws, and gnawed and cracked and cast her bloody bones. The tree at her door was hung with skins of children, flayed and ragged, flackering in the wind; but as he looked on them, they were withered leaves that blew away. The leaves half falling to the earth, and whirled and whelmed, they rose a charm of birds.

He crossed a black water, that rose and vanished in narrow cracks of stone. Leaves were drowned in it, though they fell from no wood. When he knelt by the spring, and filled his hands, they were dry and full of shadow. How dosta like Cloud ale? said no one. Not well, said he: cannot drink bout a cup. He walked on.

High, high on a rigg, there was a brown bent owlish woman plucking wool from the thorns, her apron full; but as he came to her, the crone was a crouching bush, all hung with mist. The witch was beyond. She could not come where she was not.

What's aloft? said he.

Hanged souls out to dry; they'll not, this dearth o sun, they'll not bleak fair for dark o moon.

Wren's flet away fort sun, said he.

Aye, but not come back.

Will I fetch moon frae't dark? said he.

Aye, frae Annis cupboard.

What gate, awd mother?

Back o't wind. Tha mun fall.

And she was nowhere. He went on, remembering an old voice by a fire, a spindle falling, shadows: ". . . *it were Child Rowland to't dark tower came . . .*" Almost, he set his foot on nothing, and flinched back. The stones gaped at his feet. He looked round, and all was other-world, all cloud, save the riddles' hunger. The other child was deep within, the star at the riddles' roots, at the wellspring of the dark. There was no stair, nor candle. So he fell.

Cobber was gone, and the cloak was gone, and Sylvie reeling into dark. Ariane looked wildly round for him: there was nowhere on the moorland he could hide, nearer than the stones. The tree. She touched the branches, and he spoke through her, as he had sent leaves falling through her sleep. His spell was leaves of shadow, waking light.

Lad walks, said branches. See tha wake.

It's closed, she said, I'm going. Sylvie's gone.

Hawd fast, said leaves to roots. Bear light.

She felt herself as tree, her witchroot fast in stony earth and sibyl's leaves adrift, the fleeting crown of flower and the stonehard, fragrant, bitter fruit. For a moment, thorn and nut tree stood enlaced. One's t'other, an tha sees. Not else.

Dream well, said Ariane. Then drawing breath, she turned and ran helter-skelter after Sylvie.

She was far away already, wavering on the rim of sight,

nearly blotted out beneath the raven's shadow. As Sylvie was eclipsed, her fiery coronal flared out, brief, annular. They set as one beyond the brow of the hill.

Ariane ran breakneck, heedless of the rocks and wiry tussocks, crashing through the cat-iced becks. A cloud beyond, she saw Sylvie, lurching, swayed under her burden. She bent upon her staff; above, the mingled lightnings, black and white, fled back in storm.

Then in her, through her, Ariane saw a dark-clad, heavy-booted figure, brown as earth, running wildly over steep hoar fields in dusk. She bore a sheepcrook with a cage of burning thorn blown out behind in knots of ember, whirling flakes of snow and fire. Mrs. Woodfall. Between cloud and stony earth, the sharp frail fleeting comet hung: the old year's crown.

One's t'other, an tha sees. The wren's crowned with green and burning branches, so the raven's bound; they're borne from hallows to the Law, to wake the sun. Please to see the king.

Blinking, Ariane saw no visionary star and shadow, but Sylvie wildly staggering, as if drunk or heavy-laden. ". . . *we have powder and shot, for to conquer the lot* . . ." she sang, defiantly. As Ariane came close, she saw that there was blood on Sylvie's tangled hair. The dark had talons.

Crows tearing at the clotted fleece. Blood on the tinker's hand, his ragged sleeve. He knelt beside the witch, and took the jewel from her naked shankbone. Carrion. The brooch on Sylvie's hand was like that armring: though black not firegold, and rough not intricate, as strange on her brown wrist as writhen dragons were on bone and hoof, and far more baneful in its clumsy shape. The ring was made in the raven's image, the unclosing O: adorning thralling dark. The dead witch had known it; she had worshipped it, and feared and coveted its power.

"Sylvie," said Ariane. "It's her shadow."

Chanting hoarsely in a harsh wild voice not quite her own, like a beggar on a bridge, like a child with a rattle-bag, Sylvie glanced at Ariane. ". . . *by your leave we will sing, concerning our king* . . ." Her face was shaken with an intensity of terror and of reckless joy: a burning glass. "Oh, he's pulling . . ." she gasped, between breaths, between catches.

Hold fast. Bear light.

She could hardly see Ariane's face, exalted, anxious, torn in ribands, black and white; could hear nothing, for the weaving music out of chaos. It was hard to focus. Still she sang, ". . . *in ribands so rare . . .*"

Ariane saw Sylvie like a cage of bone, pale within the ravenshadow, and the heart, the wren beating madly; saw the wildly fluttering ribands: frost and thornwood, moon and Law; and one, quite narrow, of the heartsblood red. Sylvie's blood. Outlandish, real. It made it real. The wren on the bloody snow, the stones. The ravens tearing—No. Mally's thornhedge hung with souls. They danced.

By long and light to Babylon—Hey, where'd they go? Sylvie thought of Mally's cold wide lap, her nightblack hair and comb of wind, that had combed away all the old stars from the heavens, Nan's stars: chair, crown, huntsman, bear, unconstellating as they fell.

The Sword's herself, thought Ariane. A star, a tale, foretelling. Something else. Hands and will. Her blood, against a shadow.

Tha's my sword, Mally said. No hands. If I let go—

Nightfall, thought Ariane: by dark, or not at all.

". . . *bonny lasses to carry my pall, give them broadswords, gloves, and ribands all . . .*"

They hastened through the wintry dusk. Light waned, and Annis Law lay waiting. Time would be done. The moon and sun would die. There was a black frost on the naked hills, and the sky was dark, yet strangely clear, with cloud beyond cloud turned stone, and turning. Now I know the shape of wind, thought Ariane: the sky is flawed with it. The sun was caught in the stony heavens, dying where it hung.

Sylvie fell on the ice, her body queerly angled, as if she could not use her hands to save herself; and sliding headlong, all but fell into a deep ghyll in the rock. As Ariane ran up to her, she sat, dazed and cut, sharply laughing—an unwilling vixen's bark, torn from her—but holding what it was, the darkness, still. "Whoopsy. Almost lost him." Her face was deathly pale. ". . . *his*

spirits white as lightning would on my travels guide me
. . . Lightning in the ground."

"Hold on," said Ariane. She bent to raise her up, and
felt no shadow of the scything wings—ah, strange—no
fury, but a shock of cold. They touched.

". . . *catch hands and turn* . . ."

Again. She heard the clamor, saw the glory rising out
of dark. Again. Catch hands and turn. As clear as that.
She'd had it wrong, the fretting after words on tape, the
riddling with the cards: the dance is in the taking hands,
the light is in the fall. Hold fast. Let fall, as fall it may.
The dance is turning.

Ariane hauled Sylvie to her feet, heavy with the
shadow. "Can you make it?"

"Running out of lyrics . . . *The moon would shake,
and the stars—*" Her face changed. "Oh, it's turning
now!" cried Sylvie, and she ran.

Reeling, stumbling, she came to the brink of the riddlestones. They gaped and howled at her feet; they broke
her music with their clamor, and the raven beat its wings
in fury: a scrawl of inverse lightning.

For an endless moment she held back, assailed and
daunted.

Sylvie, said Ariane, and turned her card, the last. The
Sword. A leap in dark. A journey and rebirth. Of the
stones, she made the green dark wood that hid within its
maze the thornhedge and the witch's cot; of the raven,
the new moon. A star hung falling in the dusk; a traveller, lithe and light and ragged, drew a naked sword. Ariane held all inturned, not Law but Cloudwise, leaves not
stone, rightways for Malykorne; then she laid it down,
in its pattern, inmost of the fall.

Sylvie leapt. She flashed, brightly curved upon the air,
perseid: a recklessness resolved, a sword long-forged.
Starfall. At the earth's blind heart, she turned and struck
her staff against the rock.

"Come on out," she cried, and the raven beat its wings
of shadow. "Annis! Come and take me."

The fall had not broken him, the child thought. A wind that was the witch's hair, woven in her cloak, had whorled and borne him up, so that he fell as lightly, wildly, as a leaf. He lay in utter dark and cold, unfathomed, at the riddles' roots, the tower of the dark of moon. And yet he was no windborne shadow: for he ached. He was bruised and dazed and shuddering. Behind his eyes he fell and fell, still whirling on the northwind blast. Still dimly in his ears it hooed and raved. The dark caught in his throat, a sharp and bitter air that pierced his ribs in breathing, and the weight of downfall crushed him.

As he lay, he felt about him, numbly, nearly stark with cold: the earth was bare rock, gnarled and twisted like great roots of trees, but rising to no leaf, no seed, no light. Ah, but he was turning stone, he was for Annis's dark crown. Against great dread, he stirred himself, and sat huddled and shivering. Slowly he saw shadows. A cold grey dimness fell from high, high above, through unbranching trunks of stone. Looking up, he saw no sun, no heavens, only darkness and a scattering of stars: one, bright and tawny, might have been the Lantern, at the masthead of the rising Ship.

No other child was to be seen, and he dared not break the silence, calling. He stood and fell, and stood again, clinging to the rock. His blood was brittle as a branch, and there was ice in his hair. He took up the broken thread of his song, and wove silently: *he spied his sister wandering, as pale as any ghost* . . . She could not be far, he thought. The stones, though fathomless, were strait, a narrow cell no greater round than a broch.

Step by step, feeling before him with his hand for the blind rockface, stooping, clambering, he went on; but found no circling wall, only great silent trees of stone, and serpentine roots, and deathly stillness. Not a leaf, not a bird, no sound of water, though all was black with ice. Could he be wandering in a maze of circles? No: no wall was there. The stones were inmost of the Law, of Annis's domain, and therefore endless: the otherworld to Cloud, a labyrinth without heart or compass. He looked up. Though the stonewood was huge, oppressive, still he saw the sky: an O no greater than a wren's eye, as dark. He went on. The song would lead him to the child.

No sun, nor moon, but mirk o night . . . He thought he saw a glimmering shadow going on before him, pale and fitful, wandering like the spirit of a fallen star. *No star, but black as hell. Awa' and fled her leet, leet wraith . . .* The rushlight flickered, and was gone. He held to his tangled clew of thread. Deeper and deeper he went into the wood of stone; and now the trees had branches, interlacing far above his head. A mortal terror seized him: I am lost.

O he rade on, and farther on. No way, but what he sang.

Then blindly he touched a face, like his own but cold as death, cold stone. Beneath its childlike brow it had a raven's beak. It was cracked through its eye and gaping, and wept ice. Ice had gnawed it. Sick at heart, he recoiled, and felt another stone, a child with a bat's shrivelled face.

The stones had faces here, and captive bodies, thronged, solitary. They were huntsmen and witches, blind, but wary in their rock: some beaked, but with long dank hair, and batwinged; some with goats' rough haunches, but with manlike trunks, and eyeless branching skulls; or wolfish, but with witches' naked dugs, and hawkish talons, riving at their stony flesh; or stark, starve-winged like ravens, manfaced, spined like scaly wyrms. They were caught in the riddles, writhing, crawling on their bellies, wrenching upward on vain wings. Not Annis's

creation: bound by her, or bred like crystals, blindly out
of stone, the seed of Law. Winter had effaced them,
cracked them; rain had warped. They hated and knew
nothing. Wary of their sleep, he passed; they made no
stir, but bided, darkfast, in the dwindling, breeding rock.

At last, deep within the labyrinth, he saw a silvery
glance of light. Softly, he crept closer. It was a spring of
still water with a dark shape huddled over it, unmoving,
haloed in reflected light, and black against. Not Annis.
He felt no bitter cold at bone, yet something strange.
Unblind, unlike the witch, the gazing figure bent, and
scried the water. No leaves. He saw no fall of leaves;
but coming out of shadow, he was dazzled. He came
near. The keld was blank: not water, but a seeming-glass.
The child bent over it was of his kind, and like him,
nameless and unsouled. He had not seen another since
the dance was broken; he had forgotten their own
tongue.

He knelt, and touched her face, blindly for his tears,
and he kissed her cheek and chin.

She embraced him in her turn, as in the dance; but
for a heartbeat lingering, the mirror of his grief; not as
lightborn, but a child. She spoke. "He is dead, your
other. For my sake. For nothing."

"Nay, sitha, he is wood." He sounded soft and rustic,
dwindled, in the face of her harsher ruin. He felt among
his rags and brought out a handful of the withered leaves
that had fallen on the earth above, the burden of his
other's sleep: the light and dark. A sibyl's hornbook.
One by one he let them fall to the seeming-glass, grey
and silent in that windless dark, by chance in a pattern:
the Ship.

She looked long and silently, and then held out her
hand. In it were seven rings of bent and blackened silver,
of the nine. Not earthly silver, nor of time, but lightfast,
light indwelling, out of winternight beyond: made O,
made endless, by the carol of the stars, lightfasting in
their turn the sun and earth, unturned and turning all.
They were the dance. Yet in themselves the nine were
shadows. They were borne as emblems of the starry
dance lightgraved in them, as runes and tokens of an
ancient vow: the handfast of the light and Cloud. They

worked no spell, nor gave hallows. The children who had
borne them long were stone, set in Annis's darker crown,
the O as yet unclosed. She had cast the rings away.
"They are nothing to her."

He said nothing, but mutely showed the eighth ring,
that had bound his cup, a world too wide on his gnarled
brown earthy thumb. He had lost the music of it, cold
and starry, but the cradle-rhymes ran on. *One is one,
and all alone . . . What is your nine-O?*

She touched it. In her face was still a shadow of the
lightborn. "The eldest holds the ninth and last; was in
the green hill where they slept. He gave it, your other,
for foretelling."

"See'd. Mally given it to her outlandish champion,
against Annis fall; for that sake, my other's wood, and
yours walks moonwise. They's wakened craw. Were it
not i't glass?"

"I looked not for prophecies, but sought a door." Her
eyes were dark and elsewhere, on the leaves on the keld
of stone.

"I were sent to fetch you back. Moon said." So a shepherd lad might say: the star bade me fold. "Tale's what
I is."

Still gazing in the glass, she changed, lightening as if
the moon shone slowly through her cloud. "O the wood,
O see, the new witch holds the dark inturned, unriddles:
only now the way, the light, the journey. Stars beyond,
and the Ship sailing." She lifted her face. "Will you go,
will you go with me?"

He stared at her, astounded, struggling toward the
half-forgotten light. Had he so changed, forsaking wood,
that he was earthblind? For he saw no wood, no stars:
he saw her face, blank and shining with a pinched,
exalted fear. The rings lay scattered in her lap.

She spoke more simply, as one wakes a child by dark,
gently, that the rushlight might not dazzle sleeping eyes.
Come, look, the stars are falling. But the hand that held
the candle shook; the child she waked, still dreaming,
was herself. "The door stands open. Will you leave this
earth?"

"How?" he said, and touched the rock beneath them.
"Stone is stone." But he was shaken with a bitter long-

ing, a grief reborn: to leave behind this husk of body, and the dread of stone; to dance again the wheel of stars, not on Cloudlaw at the sunreturn, but endlessly in spirit, as they had done, the lightborn, long before this dream of turning earth, before the Ship had sailed. He looked to her. "But how?"

"Through the seeming-glass." Her hand was hovering, enrapt; it brooded on the face of light. O but quickly, said her eyes; her eyes were fearful. "As the leaves have fallen, so we rise. Light's fast through it, beyond time's lights and all the changes, the dying and rebirth." And truly her hand was in the water in the stone, all silvered, ring beyond bright ring spreading outward. The leaves rocked and drifted. As he looked, he saw their faces shadowed in an ancient wood, far branching, fast in light; he saw the starry crown, its leaves: he knew their tale. The Ship was sailing on. A hand was reaching out to draw them, hand in hand, into the dance.

But as the seer bent, the rune-twig dangled from her knotted ribbon. It was one that he had set upon the Woodfalls' door, a country charm for wayfaring, as rings for hallows and for handfast. It travelled with the unborn child, the shepherd on the hills, as O kept fold and hearth; it waked with the dead on their long journey. A, it said, whose crown and flowering and root is O; but A is travelling, endures: that green would arise from fallows, and the wren from its bier of thorns.

"No," he said, unwilling, and drew back. "No, we munnot leave our kindred stonefast, or t'earthborn bound forever to our souls. Cloud or none, they chosen for our sake to thole and dare. They mowt die, or worse, at Annis hands. And think on: if her crown is brok by us fleeing, nowther is t'carol danced. Will be no sun." He touched the ribbon. "Pledges ha' been changed: cup borne for hallows' sake, as twig hawds way til end. Ta'en is ta'en, runefast same as rings. Annis brok faith. We munnot."

Grey as stone, as silent, she knelt at the water's edge.

"The wren dies," she said, drawing back from the glass gone hard as crystal; and the silver fell like dust from her dry hand. The stone was dark. Then very softly, "I am cold."

"Tek this." He fumbled at his throat to find a brooch, a fastening to the cloak, though nothing could be seen there, nothing felt.

"No," she said sharply. "You would leave the tale, and see what this place is; and it would go near to kill."

So he held her. She was cold as stone. And so was he, as if they had died in a ballad. *Hand in hand they lay ungraved, Thorn blaws so bonny O. T'robin and t'wren browt leaves* . . . But he could not take her in: the song was his alone. *And crown's o' th' holly O.*

Still kneeling, all astray in thought, he gathered up the leaves from the witch's glass, and each was a word, a note, of his other's endless dream, his tale of hallows: still the traveller slept in Mally's lap, the earth, and the burden of his sleep was light. The child spelt from them, and they were woven in his hands: "*. . . he wrapped her up in a cloak of gold . . .*" It hung from her shoulders, wanleaf, scant and ragged, shining pale as the new moon rising.

"We mun go," he said.

She rose, and took the seeming-glass from where it lay. "She will be blind without. The moon turns."

The glass was not quite round, he saw: the barest edge was dark. It was the old moon hid away, unborn and dead, all one to Annis. So this was her cupboard: he remembered Mally, and was comforted. He thought of souls in her wicker basket, that were truly there and elsewhere, where their bodies waked or slept. But he and the lightborn lass were soulless, fell and bone; in dark and nowhere else. He had fallen, borne on the witch's wind. The lass was brought. How had Annis climbed when she was witch? Not all her hunt had wings.

"Has servants," he said. "Happen there's backstairs."

All by the glimmer of her cloak they walked, seeking a way upward, like children harrying birds' nests. They tried, where the stone was most ruinous, to climb the cracked and glazy winding stairs: the work of winter's gnawing. The ways led nowhere, or they broke beneath the searching hand. The children fell and fell again; they backed and slithered down a rockface scaled by anxious inches, leading only to sheer rock slick with ice. They came no nearer to the sky. Stone-bruised and bleeding, cold and grim, they tried blind crevices, and holds that even his gnarled fingers could not clench; and fell again, half stunned.

The creatures in the rock creaked and stirred, as if waking in an evil dream: a brood of malice in that windless place, a breeding storm. They clacked their beaks, their racks of horn; they chafed their rasping wings.

The children halted. He had brought no bread with him; they had no water, and when for thirst they licked the stone, their tongues fastened to the ice. She put aside the hair from her brow with a filthy hand; looking full at him, she said, "Your brooch is strange."

"I's none," he said. But he felt a tickling stirring on his neck. It was a tiny moon-white spider, and it dropped away on a long arc of dim silver, and was gone. They followed Mally's clew, like all her gifts equivocal and tenuous, on and upward through the labyrinth of stones, out of lethe, out of dark. The thread was now a clew, and now a cable, fine as gossamer and strong as twisted will, that they could hold to, though it bit cruelly into their hands. The way was intricate and willful, and so he felt the witch's hand in it, her weaving and her thought.

So they went, till they came to a fault in the stone, a narrow crack in a great pillar like an ancient tree, marrowless and rotten; and within, they saw a broken stair. It was spiral, and so steep that they must clamber it like chimney-sweeps. Across the crack from end to end and up and down, they found the clew a web, a fitful crazy tangle with one bleak tattered leaf in it, caught up.

They did not beat it down, but hand to hand unskeined the thread, unwove the leaf, that was a small brown bird, its breast stained red as blood. It lay stark in his two hands, until she breathed on it; then wick as wind it flew away, straight for the O of sky, while they must wind the stair.

As they crept in, a clangorous inhuman voice cried out, "The wren's away, mother, and the redbreast flies."

"Annis! Come on, come and take me!" Standing at the earth's blind heart, uncloaked and mortal, naked to the witch's eye, Sylvie called again. No answer. In the tumult of the raven's wings, she could hear nothing. She stared hard, hard at the Law. Nothing came. No witch. But what was it she waited for? A stone, a shadow? The raven shuddered in her veins, uprooting. She could not— she held it still. Then suddenly she felt within her, cold and heavier than the cinder of a galaxy, but clear, a malice and an utter silence.

It was Annis, shrunken like a star to absolutes: an atom of intense desire, unlight and hatred. She dwelt in Sylvie's mind. Yet the air and stone and water of the fells were Annis, and the lightning Annis, stilled in vaunting, vaulting heaven: she was form and grave of all. Her stony clenching hand had cast the Bones; her nails had riddled earth. The dying sun was pinched in her, a flaw, a fleck of mica in the stonestruck sky. Flint-white and black her fells stood up, sharp-knapped and glittering, against the clouds of rock. All were Annis, and denied: her domin-ion now was naked mind, a maze, a crown of souls. Long since, she had cast off the earth her bones. It lay as carrion, yet uncorrupting in her bitter cold: stone dead, denied and untranscended.

Sylvie stood. She saw it clearly. She was Annis now, a small domain: Cloud's eye, the bones of Law. Assailing her, the witch withdrew her seeing from her ancient realm. Her crown lay derelict, a scattering of stones; her lair and seeming-glass unwatched. There was a gate through her, a way beyond. Her will was bent on the outlandish rival who had slain her ravens, put to flight her hunt. Who closed the ring? Who calls? Riddles not her own: nerves, labyrinths of cells. In cold perplexity, but closing, in the maze of the unlightborn mind, Annis sought her rival's soul.

Forever, for another breath, Sylvie held the raven back: it was a flaw in the terrible crystal, a shake in the silence. Then crying out, she loosed the storm. The ravenshadow flew. Shrieking to crack the sky, it towered, stooping on the sun that was bound in stone, to bear it down with beak and claw.

Ariane, at the riddles' edge, saw it rise, wild and black in its fury. O the shadow's Annis, she thought. She's torn it from herself. She'd fear no other thing, no rival: her shadow in herself was bane and being. So she's torn it

out, denied and bound it in cold iron, for its torment—
O as Mally's made the wren her shadow, light of leaves,
and set it free; but that is given and returns: the ring is
closed, the dance is danced. This thing is hoarded, hated:
she'd not slay herself. What is the raven? Anarchy,
devouring hatred, darklust—ah, she's greater now, without her fury: not as evil, but as stony law and death.
Unflawed and absolute. She *is*.

There was a broken measure, a heartbeat mislaid
before the bolt of thunder. Annis fled her prey, striking
after the shadow. Sylvie stood. She numbly felt the dead
cold ring of iron on her hand, its cruel disjointed beak:
the husk, the moulted offcast of the raven's new instar.

Ariane saw the witch flare out, overtaking her shadow.
She was fiery crystal, a burning tesseract of stars: the eye
of nightmare from the witchfold dream, but inverse now,
cold radiance to harrow sight. She cracked through at
the raven's cry, in the bitter cold of revelation, splintering and falling, falling from the air, from cloud into a
colder edge.

The raven stooped.

But falling she was knives to rend the shadow; so the
bird was wind, still-closing, to elude the swords.

So Annis was stone, to withstand the tempest. Huge
as a hillside, cold as a ruined angel ribbed with ice, she
stood, with her hair like molten shadow, long as wind,
silver-black. It whipped about her face; it roiled and
lifted. In the rending wind, she streamed away into her
hair, sublimed, like grey-black lustrous iodine, from
stone into a heavy brumal mist, crawling and writhing,
fraying out in sickly turmoil. The wind was choked.

She was dark and doubt, to blind and smother it; so
it was lightning without thunder, wincing, vivid, riving.
They had counter-changed: glare falling into formless
dark, and shadow twisted into light.

From the darkness, Annis spoke: she called out to the
raven, iron words, to warp and bind. In her dissolution,
it took shape, and burned on her abyss of cold. Fiery, it
towered in the air, unshadow: a creature neither bird nor
woman, iron-beaked and naked, quilled and taloned, in
a storm of swirling hair.

The dark shrank into Annis, standing cold and clear

in the bleak twilight. The raven ringing upward in its widening spiral stooped. She spoke again. Her spell caught it stark in midair. It fell to earth, and falling, shrank and dulled and hooped. It clanged on the naked rock. It was a brooch, new-bent upon the forge of Annis's will, unclosed and bound, still glowing sullen red.

O hell, no end to it, no end, thought Ariane.

Annis stood and coldly raged, dark-clad and bitter-white and blind.

Only knows the one trick, thought Sylvie. Is that all? No sword? Could grab, and—All again? That's wrong. Gets nowhere. Watch. She wants it and she doesn't. If she moves—

She's won, thought Ariane. So why's she furious? Seen that before. She's driven to her witch's body. Hands. Why? Ah, to take it up. So she's not won yet: the raven's downfall was its last and mocking shift. Her triumph is embittered, galled, by this earthly need. The old brooch, the old thorn in her psyche, was unbound and turned against her. As unwilling hands—O Sylvie, do you see? It's hands—she needs must cast this new brooch deep in her abyss, beyond all spells, beyond all thieving or mischance. This time—No, thought Ariane, she *is*. She knows neither past nor to come, nor grudge nor cunning, only *I want, I have*: the children, one by one, until the ring is closed; the raven bound and bound again, now, forever, under Law.

The witch's eyes were clouded. In the coil of malice, serpentine turned thorn, that was her hair, there hung a trembling hail of stones, blindwhite as were her eyes, souls touched with frost; or bloodred drops. She strode to where the brooch had fallen, on the riddlestones; for that, she had no need of eyes.

But Sylvie had sprung first, and snatched the ring: a great leap on the stones, and a sudden balance, twisting.

"Look behind!" cried Ariane, and Sylvie wheeled about as Annis tried to catch her staff, and cast her down among the stones of the abyss. She would have her brooch—ah no, and broken flesh to slake her jackal's lust, eyes to lure her scattered crows, a soul—The witch, behind you!

Wheeling, Sylvie swung the staff at her, to drive her back.

The witch leapt over it, light as fire. Blind as Annis was, the stones were self; she could not fall.

But flailing vainly, Sylvie overbalanced, toppling, and went over sideways with the staff beneath her, caught between two stones. It held. She tumbled up, cat-quick; she had the brooch. As Sylvie sprang away with her unchancy prize, the witch pounced. She snatched at air.

Stone to stone, the brown girl dodged, and Annis hunted; now as creatures do, to take; and now obliquely, spelling out some darker fate than capture. She struck, random as the lightning, now and nowhere, everywhere, intent. Bright, elusive, quick as mercury, Sylvie jumped for her life, for the marchland beyond the witch's realm.

In vain. There was no farther shore. All was center. In her fury, swift and silent, Annis broke the stone of earth, ranting it to riddles at her feet. A net of chasms gaped and flickered, widening. She would have her prey.

Yet she flinched from the ravenbrooch, even as she struck, recoiling. She'd torn it from herself. "Don't run! Turn and pin her!" cried Ariane. But Sylvie was too far away, unheeding, desperate.

Calling, Ariane ran round the edge; but there was none, it fell away, devoured in a sudden wave of void. The stones had overtaken her, she was on them. Reckless, Ariane leapt after Sylvie, skidding wildly on the stones and shouting, in and out of Annis's blind web. "Sylvie!" She can't hear, she's got to hear. "The brooch. Stab her."

Sylvie turned suddenly on Annis, and caught and held her by the waist, burning cold and biting, strong in fury, changing shape as swift as storm. An ambiguous embrace: they swayed at death's edge on the rock. But Sylvie held her fast, through all changes, struggling to raise her hand that held the brooch, spine outward. The witch's sark, her seeming-body, was sinewy as wind, as death; but Sylvie broke her grasp. The thorn of glowing iron pierced Annis at the throat.

A great dark jewel of blood came slowly, a stone inset in stone. With numbed and trembling hands, intently, Sylvie pinned the circle shut. The brooch was fastened,

binding Annis within the body she had taken, in the turning of the dark of moon, and wheel of stars: within the
dance. The witch was still, though brimmed with malevolence as with envenomed blood, silent, unresisting, under
Law.

They stood unmoving on the riddles: one and the
other, close as if they wound one skein; the third, aloof
and gazing.

It is sealed, thought Ariane: but what is bound within?
Annis gives nothing for nothing asked; her soul is blank,
unless it take the impress of another's will. She must
swear, and by nothing mortal: I am ashes on the wind
to her. But I have what she must acknowledge, envying;
if I can hold it. So she saw, with cold detachment.
Grimly, daring all as Sylvie had, in swordsedge act, she
touched Craobh's soul.

"Annis."

By the shock of cold, she knew that Annis saw her,
saw the child within her like the dead and unborn moon,
undying; and the windchild round them like an icy halo:
threefold, presaging storm.

"By this stone," said Ariane. "The sun."

"Is turned," said Annis.

"And the moon."

"It waxes."

"The souls."

Cold silence. Sylvie thought, well, it's my turn. Tha's
my sword, said Mally, and Annis won't give them.

With her blunt, half-bladed jack-knife, Sylvie cut the
stones from Annis's black hair, as they were knotted in
beyond unravelling: the bloodred crystals falling like a
thaw, like sleet from shaken thorns, in rose-splashes on
the earth. They stained her hands. She cut the soul-
stones, one by one: the children of the northlands, fell
and cloudwood, keld and law. Haily, fiery, or green in
leaf; fall dusk and glory, storm and iris, star and sun and
moon. O but they were beautiful and perilous, the souls
of lightborn beings, other worlds: a handful of bright
stones.

She held each few stones most anxiously in her cold-
numbed other hand, fumbling, trying to bestow them
safely in her pockets, never taking her eyes from the

witch's face or body, lest she spring. Again and again she
cut, bluntly hacking, tearing, like a scythesman through
weeds, like a hedger at thorns.

At last Annis stood shorn, maleficent, as small and
cold as death uncrowned. She made no stir, unmoving
even to touch her ruined head. Maybe, thought Sylvie
uneasily, she's stranded on her rock. Can't see. She
thought of Mally's moonish spectacles, her fierce and
knowing glance. Yet they were sisters, dark and light of
one moon. Turning back, she stared at the blind eyes,
cloudy, veined like quartz, like pebbles dulled with keeping. Out of awe and fascination and a terrible unwilling
pity, she gazed; impulsively, compelled, she touched the
cold eyes with her living hand, her tongue. Grey eyes for
eyes of stone. They saw.

Unblinking, Annis looked on the mortal face, as on
the sun her death. "You have taken and have given:
ask."

In that stony gaze, she could think of nothing. "Oh.
Oh, the stars here. I'd like to see the stars."

Annis said, cold-voiced, "They turn. Long silence for
your star, and long its falling into darkness, I foresee:
your death is in the heavens." Then quick as silver in a
crack, she cast herself down the riddlestones, by dark
ways, and was gone.

Beyond the stair the lightborn climbed, the Lantern
rose in heaven, bright and tawny, and the Ship sailed on
toward winternight. Then a darkness not of cloud obscured
the heavens, hurtling down: it rent the sky. They heard
it wailing in its cold dismay, dry-winged, iron-taloned in
the rock. The winding stair was shaken, and the stones
of the way were cracked.

"Air? I can't . . ." Sylvie's voice was shaking, small
with shock. She stood hunched and trembling on her eyot
of stone: like Nan going out to the eclipse, tall and
dishevelled, in the autumn of her wits, to talk with death.
"I'm stuck. She—oh man, I'm dizzy."

Ariane was no steadier. "All right, hold on. I'm coming for you." The earthwounds of the witch's rage had
closed at Annis's fall, leaving Ariane dry on moorland,

Sylvie stranded on the riddlestones, the ancient and heal-
ing heart of death. The moor lay seemingly unbroken
around them. Step by step, gingerly, Ariane came to the
farther edge of the riddles, not five yards from Sylvie's
hand.

Greenly, grimly comic, Sylvie turned to her. Like
clagged and rusted clockwork overwound, tin heron and
tin stork, they crossed toward each other on the stepping-
stones, and met between earth and elsewhere. Steadying
each other, with voices, presence, touch, they staggered
to unbroken ground.

There they huddled, crying with relief, with cold, vexation, fear; and Ariane with the unnerving strangeness of
consoling Sylvie. Awkwardly, she touched her hair, but
Sylvie shrugged away. No use. They drew apart, each
into her own despair, crouched or restless. They were
silent, hearing in their minds the witch's prophecy, her
curse: the shadow of their deed, ambiguous. *Long silence
for your star, and long its falling.* They had turned the
sun and stars, that dark would come in turn. Their death
hung in the sky, a baleful star.

"Cobber?" Nowhere. Sylvie turned. "Air, did . . . ?"
Silence. Sylvie's heart lurched within her. Gone. She
saw it in that ashen face. And the other child that was
taken—hell, and Ariane's poor tree. Her tinker. She
hadn't thought to ask for their lives. She'd had the
chance. All wasted, for a curse. She felt sick.

Beside her, Ariane grieved bitterly. O Craobh, O my
poor tinker. And his other now was lost, she'd lost him.
Sylvie's boy, Craobh's kin. He'd gone to look for her.
They were down there, in the stones, in dark, where
Annis went. *No stair.* She touched the stone: cold
silence. Dark. She wept, raging at her blindness, at her
witch's cold and heartless insight. She'd played her fall
of cards, for what? A handful of stones. *For light*, said
her stiller voice: what they themselves had willed. The
dance. But she had lost them, lost their faces, voices,
hands. They were captives, bound in wood or rock,
astray and dying, dead. Their hostage souls had been
their only surety. Annis now could slay, hack wood, hurt
flesh. Binding the raven in her, Ariane and Sylvie had
diminished her, had made her vengeful, turning law to

wanton cruelty, and being into evil will. They had driven her to hands.

She looked to Sylvie, bleak-faced. There was blood on her own lip. "I—when I made her swear, I should've—"

"No, you asked what you had to. The three things. It's a tale." Sylvie's face was wan and beaky; her hair, lank with sweat. "I had the chance. Free will. And they—I'm sorry."

"You didn't know. You didn't know them." Ariane drew breath. "I think whatever you had asked, she would have twisted it."

Sylvie turned the iron ring. "We have to have faith," she said at last, somberly. She was streaked and grimy with her tears, but not so ashen. "Mally sent us. You don't get sent from other worlds for nothing: it's unbalanced. Wasteful." She sat tugging fiercely at the cold black ring of iron on her wrist, the raven's dead instar: its beak lay curved upward in her palm, or lolled and pecked unmeaningly at her sleeve, awry and broken-necked. "Damn. It's stuck. I'll have to soap it."

"Goose grease," said Ariane. A pale joke, revenant. "Knock at Mally's and ask. She'll love that." She thought of the witch, cross and busy, with the wicker basket on her hip, and the grey northwind hissing rancor on her ash-heap. She grinned wryly. "Poor awd Annis. Lost her marbles."

"Hey, well, there's that." Sylvie smiled, recalling. "Deea, she looked pretty punked out. Spiky. And her safety pin."

"Mally does her own hair, when she can find her comb. Or whatever, hedgehog." Then soberly. "Can I see them?"

Sylvie fumbled in her pockets, and brought out the stones, by twos and ones and little handfuls, from the torn linings: all the souls but one and the other, stone and tree. In that bleak and wintry light, they were subdued, clouded. There was winter even in the greenest stone, a frost; and some were cold as hail. She wiped them very gently on her threadbare knees, and laid them out beside her on the earth, on her old grey and brown scarf.

Turning each stone round, she looked and looked at

them, curious, rapt, a little awed: caught up in them, as
light is gathered in a lens. She held them to the light.
"See, there's patterns. They're related."

Ariane said nothing; but she saw.

Taking up and setting down, Sylvie changed them:
pairs and odd ones out, and taken in, in country dances;
starry wheels and pleiades, and a lone clear shepherd's
star. In a knot of stones, one inscape, ghyll and oak-
wood, shaded from frost through leaf to fire of the turning year; but as Ariane looked, she saw another knot
within: a timeless dusk, one green diversely flawed, blue-
green, as hill and water, cloud and wood.

She made a henge of them, a ring and not, unnumbered and elusive.

Then Sylvie changed her changes, turn and turn, as in
their old game of labyrinths on Sylvie's quilt, all else
forgotten for a moment. But the fall was endless. It
would not come out.

Ariane took out Craobh's soul, that she had borne so
long. It was no cloudier than many, colder than some,
flawed: a wintry dusk, a slanting woodland hoar with
mist, a clear and trembling star. Surely, it would darken,
if . . .

Sylvie looked up. "They're strange—not stories. They're
like music." She gathered up the souls, regretfully. Ariane gave her the shabby velvet bag to put them in, and
knotted up the spilled-out marbles, common glass, in
Mrs. Woodfall's handkerchief. "What now? We can't
stay here."

"Give back the souls. The children—where they dance—
are stones. A ring of stones. Not far," said Ariane. "I
don't know the way. I think it finds you, if it's meant.
Or not. They take you in."

"Oh, the dance. Forgot that. Mally said."

"And it's lightfast, it's their turn," said Ariane. She
thought of the nameless naked child, dragged in ruin
from the stone; thought of it as Craobh, as Sylvie's odd
sweet tattered crow-lad. How would she and Sylvie go
to heal such children, even with their souls? And if they
danced, if stones—Could he not wake, the tinker, racked
within his wood? "We could go by the—the tree. He
might be changed, if—disenchanted, when she fell," she

said uncertainly, remembering his staring face, stark limbs. Unspelling might be naked death, carrion for crows; or sleep; or nothing. As if he had never been.

Sylvie nodded. "Cobber'd go there first: it's his wood, it's the only place there is, this side." she said. "Hope it's back to your old guy now." She peered at the sky. "We better hurry. I think they've got to dance by night-fall, or it's curtains."

Ariane looked to the hills, to the dark yet clearing sky, the cloudbanks lifted in the rising wind. The white sun, like a watermark, rode low. On the fells, the snow blew thinly, desolate. A dreary day, what was left. From northward came a flight of birds, storming black as leaves against—"O look, look, O Sylvie!"

Rising out of dark and in the northlands, haloed round with a cold radiance, a glory, were the sun and the new-bent moon. They hung just at earth-rim, at rise, and coalesced. Within the great brough of light, the O, the winter's iris, they were children. Hand in hand they rose, one happed in a cloak of burning gold, the other in a mantle of bright cloud, and crowned and garlanded with winter stars.

They were what Annis in her ranting fury had fore-seen: rebirth, enacted in the windchild's tawdry mum-mery, and shadowed darkly in her glass; but now seen face to face, beyond death's stony hand. They were light, the sun of winter and the turning moon. The earthborn gazed.

A dark wind rose, full of rack and scurry, like the shadows of a wood in storm. The cloak of light was borne away in tatters, leaves of fire, leaves of fall. The glory fleeted, and the daylight stood. Two figures, all in wintry rags, and small as birds, stood hand in hand: the robin and the jenny wren. They were the lightborn children, coming slowly from the stones. Craobh held a silver mir-ror, scarred and tarnished like the moon's face, not quite round; and withered leaves were in her hair. From Cob-ber's shoulders hung Mally's cloud-grey cloak, unclasped and draggling behind. The old, the dying sun combed out their shadows on the fellside, long as wind.

Sylvie laughed for joy, and ran to Cobber, and whirled

him round, so that the cloak flared out and fell away, and still they danced, giddy as two stars.

"Oh, you came, you came back!" cried Ariane. Craobh stood. "You're shivering. Look." Clumsy with joy, she unknotted the soulstone, dangling on its thread, now this way, and now that. A star in her hand. She held it out. "And all the others: Sylvie took them."

"Not yet. Bear it yet a while."

Sylvie left off whirling suddenly, bright-cheeked and breathless. "Hey, another one," she said.

Craobh looked at her with dark strange eyes. She took Sylvie's hand between her hands. "The Sword: thy star is not of Cloud, unfast. A bright ascendant, crossing dark: a brighter passing still." Sylvie gazed at her in silence, wondering.

Craobh turned to Ariane, and kissed her cheek and chin. "Well done, though not yet done: she is not dark and light, but turning. After, if the ring is danced, she will be sun and moon. Thou hast seen rarely."

Ariane shook back her tangled hair. She knew the words; she saw the pattern, leaves amid a fall of leaves: and seeing, let them fall. "By owl-light," she said. "Still journeying: the way is hallows. The wren is born, and dies. Dark's fast, the wood bears light: the tale's not endless yet."

"Bright lass," said Cobber. "Sees thruff stones."

"Are we going to spring the tinker?" asked Sylvie.

"Aye," he said. "Crack nuts." His round face for a moment was so dazzled and bemused, that Ariane laughed. Wassail.

Sylvie turned to Craobh. "Is that her seeming-glass? It's like Mally's little sun." But Craobh held nothing.

"Gave it back."

In the west hung the setting moon, new-bent, a ring of palest gold unclosed. It pinned and pierced the shadowcloak of night; it brooched the dark.

VII

Lightfast

He walked in the Cloudwood in the endless fall of leaves,
rising from the dark to touch their falling shadows, bright
upon the water. O, they said, alighting, waking rings
of silver: O, and flet away. He was the tale the leaves
told, falling. They were scattered on the wind. Ah,
the leaves were birds, yet had no voices, only fleeting
shadows, flawed and freckled in their charm; and the
water ran swift through him, veining with delight the
darklong endless turning of the wood. His coat was
ragged, leaf on leaf of dreams falling light away. *Thy
burden's light*, said wren. *Tha'rt waking wood*, said owl.
But he was light himself, naked to the bone, but for his
belt of stars.

Turning over, turning deeper into stony dream, he
knew he slept. He walked in his body's sleep, self in
woodself, rooted fast in Mally's stony lap; she bent,
combing out his leaf-fall hair by rushlight in the shadowed cot. The candle faltered. *Hush, ba. Sleep.* He was
her song, her waking wood. The leaves fell on her
windlong hair, unbound, and spelling sleep.

But there was something clouded, tangled at the roots,
still hands, and scarred and bleeding: they clenched and
scrabbled at a sharpness, fire-wrought and alien. A ring
of twisted gold. It pinned him through the heart to earth.

Did he sleep, or did the owl-witch wake his body, this
ae night? He walked in the wood's heart, beyond the
doors of sleep, and doors beyond of horn and bone, the
further in the huger. All was I, all known and undiscov-
ered. O but it was strange, being wood and wanderer,

bound and boundless, lyke-wake and childbed, moving still; but fleeting strange, forgotten as the wind stirred. He walked amazed. The wood was endless, bone of branches, eyes of tree, of tree.

And yet he knew, had dreamed, that now and nowhere, again and yet again in wandering he would come within a thorny hallows, bright with haws: an orchard where a dark lass, low as blackthorn and as wild, sat combing flax amid her goats. The lass would love him, running barefoot after; she had loved, betrayed him, or had dying borne their child; nor had she ever glanced, but scorned. He knew her changing face, its dark and bright. He had seen a thousand times anew its curve amid a cloud of hair; had seen its fierce aloofness and desire, drawing on; and strangest, furthest and most loving, its serenity, brooding on his sleep. Her face eluded, even as he held her body, sweet and brown as any nut, as deep as Cloud-wood, and her tale as endless. He knew her green enduring and her frailty, her crown of light; was known, held, loved. And now and yet again, he'd come to her, and lie in hallows: two, and turning one.

Yet even as they loved, their graves were green, the sloe-thorn and the nut embraced: coat of ragged leaves and smock of thorn cast by, pale flower from the naked boughs, the thorn the bright blood follows. Death was no end in the witch's cot, he saw, but root and crown: the wood was ballads. Green, the wood was silent that felled and strung with hair would speak: *I died for love.* He was all things: the fool, the hanged man, and the harp of bone. He had gazed, would gaze at her, all-having and unholding, trammeled and unbodied as a sort of stars: his own ascendant.

Stooping, sidling, through the bright and dark of leaves, the slanting forest, he went on. All ways were one. He had crossed with his other, becoming Cloud-wood: bone of tree that bore the nut, as yet unfallen and unsprung, unfelled, that held the cup unturned. Yet long ago the cup was earth, and earth a leaf had fallen in the endless tale. The turning was his dance, the leaves his voice; he dreamed of waking wood. Oak-handed, green at heart, he shook the birds from his nightfall hair. He wore his ragged coat, his mantle of the withered gold:

the traveller, great-rooted and far-branching, bearing stars.

He saw a shadow coming, crowned with horn: an other, like a scarecrow in the heart. Unfast in earth. He stood. *Breaks tha my branches?* cried. Wood's what I is, and death is trespass, an iron share.

But the other was no shadow, but a child astray, all in brown rags, bent under a great burden of thorn. Those sticks were never broken in his wood: no leaf had fallen that he had not felt. No thorn in hallows grew so pale. He came and stood before the child, and barred the way.

The child said nothing; but he gazed.

Stands so bold, and will not fly? By these stars, Cock Wren s'd die. The traveller clapped hand to his belt. No sword was there. Stars? He saw how brown and gnarled his hands were, same as oak-roots; how his coat of tatters swaled, like rushlight shadows. Hob i't hearthtale, he thought, bemused, remembering fire, a spindle falling. Wind i't door, and stamping. Voices. *In comes I, wi sword and stars.* Guisers. Laiking at wren and sarsens, come winter, come to dance. Awd Moon sweeped in afore them, wi her broom. Tha weared t'fool's awd coat, and got thee slain wi swords, and rose: so winter died. After, tha did off thy coat, and drank. T'bairns were flayed, and lasses peeped and smiled, aback o doors. Thinking on, he laughed. Wha's sword? Awd flaycraw's what I is. Then: poor lad, lies heavy on him.

"Will I carry sticks for thee?"

The child stood, pale as a morning candle. "An you give me leave to set it by."

"Wi all my heart. Will light us both."

"Think on: cannot be given over, an you take it up."

His hand were on it: it were cold as hail, and sharp, and heavier than all the world. It were like uprooting earthfast bones, a barrow's weight. He saw. It were not sticks, but a fardel o bones, wi fell and hair and iron rings. A death. His own. No. Shaken, cold at heart, he let it fall.

The child looked at him, unhopeful, unregretful, owning love.

"I met tha once," the traveller said. "Wood's thine."

It hung fire about them, gold and shadowy: not his,

no more than was his breath, though he had borne it long and light. No more than was the cup. Though what's been drunk is drunk, he thought: seeing's mine. He looked at the hale and holy trees, earthrooted, crowned with light; beyond all ravens' malice, though founded on the naked stone: their commonplace, his and lad's. O how the leaves became him. No, he thought: coat's not what I is, but bones.

Uneasy, he remembered journeying, all the long way to this wood's end; remembered stones and hunger, hail and wind and lice, cold and love; remembered strangers, chance and featherbeds: the world beyond the wood. The birds sang there, shrill, bereft. He would not know their tongue. Gone was gone: the wood was felled, the wren lay cold in its green crown, the lass was dead a thousand years, and dust.

He thought on hallows, where no winter was, nor grave. Nor spring—Had he not seen? The thorn was starry, cold as any snow. It bore no earthly flowering, nor seed, nor song of birds. The wood was silent, falling. All ways in Cloud beyond were endless, one: no dance, as stars hung still; no journey, nor to grave nor birth. The children she had borne were wraiths of air. And the lass—ah, but she were true as Cloud, he thought. What's loved. Not held, but turning, same as moon. Not leaves, but deep as roots. What's crown, wi'out it's branched of earth? Unfast.

But i't journey, hand took hand; i't dance, t'sun were turned. Fool died, and rose and drank; or died, and were laid i't grave, and another weared t'coat: so dance went on. I's been wood, awhile, and lad sall be, i' turn. Cup's wood, not I, he thought. Cawd comfort. Law. As coat's fool, as dance is turn o't sun: so candle after candle wastes, and all one fire. He was made wick for bearing light, long or short; had legs for journeying. Longways yet through winter, and beyond, sweet hope of spring. Green's there: would lie on grass. Or under it.

He smiled at the rueful lad. "Ah. Goose walked ower my grave. Come thy ways, then: it's a sad night toward." He took the burden up. Were not that heavy, as he bent his back to it. So that were settled. They walked on.

"How did tha get on, lad?"

"Drank water," he said. "Clapped craws."

"Drank ale, times. Cup and all."

The child took his sleeve. "Did well. It's bitter, at t'last."

"Were sweet as apples, times. It kept."

In the quiet between them, he heard the cold dark river. Beyond it lay no wood, and he must cross. The silent one, the stone-eyed boatman, kept the ford, would claim his toll. Panicked, the traveller cast down his load of thorns, and could not: they were self. He hung upon them like a scarecrow. None had put a coin by him, for crossing, nor on tongue nor eyes; no gold hanged in his ears. No salt nor earth nor candlelight. No name. So beggars died, and crows mourned them. He scrabbled through his rags, and found nothing: a handful of withered leaves, of ash-keys, husks, haws, brambles; last, an owlnut, worm-eaten, yet heavy in his hand, as if it held the dark and all unmaking.

"He'll tek nowt," said the child, "but what's saddest borne. Give him as he asks: here's nowt." He touched the owlnut. "Gate were Annis: you crossed then. Coin were gold." Glancing at the yellow leaves, his face lightened. "Light-comed, and fleet away. None's crossed his river thwart, afore." Then shadowy and ruing, he said, "I can give you nowt."

"Asked none," the traveller said. He was shivering; a wind was in his ruined branches, and his roots groped in barren earth. "No matter. Nowt's what I comed wi." He looked at the ragged child. "But tha'rt cawd. Would tha like awd coat, then? I'd gan lighter wi'out." Forgetten what's a'neath: tattery awd sark, he thought. Hedge-got.

"No," said the child. "Let fall. Sall all be light." He looked about him at the drifted leaves. "Coat's outworn. I's whelmed in't. I mun thole winter starving, and a green coat comes wi't place."

"San't need stockins mending where I's bound."

"No," said the child. "No, you've yet to walk." They touched, a shy embrace, askew, each fearing he was shadow; and then hard, forgetting which was other: they were one. Lad's hair were rough. "Travel well."

It was darkening. "What gate?"

"Winter," said the child.

* * *

"Hey wait," said Sylvie, turning back. Ariane halted, fretting with impatience. There is nothing so frail as fortune, it is a cast of light, and she wanted to get back to the tinker's tree—touch wood—before the glory faded. She wanted not to lose Sylvie, not again. The others stood, the strange dark Craobh aloof, and Cobber elsewhere. "Mally's stick thing, I dropped it . . ." called Sylvie; so there was nothing for it but to come and look.

It was where it had fallen, but the riddles' crack had closed. Caught fast, the thorn had rooted, springing up and whorling outward, slowly, like a dancer from its roots of dance, a music stilled. It branched, windbent and black and bare; then starry, cloud-silver as it caught the moon a-sail: no staff, but a tree in flower. "O," said Ariane. "O look."

Though slight, no taller than a child, no greater round than Sylvie's wrist (her fingers closed in wonder: O), the tree was ancient. Yet unbowed with age: a dark girl's spirit, frail, enduring, fierce, lived green within. Earthfast and crowned with light, gnarled, and greyed with lichen, it was thousand-ringed, emboxing year on year, and wood in turning wood: and inmost greenest, Cloud. No green yet showed, nor fruit, nor fall: its branches would be shrill with birds. Ariane stood gazing; Sylvie touched the starry petals, cold as snow on leafless twigs. A blackthorn.

Ah, the journeying's the light, thought Ariane, rejoicing: for the pilgrim's staff of thorn was rooted, as the Ship is lightfast, crowned with a fleeting glory, sailing on before the wind. *Sails wi lightfall*, Malykorne had said. *Bears all and O*. It turns. Only in sailing, the starry haven; only in journeying, the wood's green heart, unmoved.

From elsewhere, the children looked on, all shining through their clouds of rags, like rainbows; but the tree was moonrise. "There it is," said Craobh. On a thorntwig, turning loose as on a bony hand, hung Sylvie's bent black starry ring, Craobh's ring, that she had borne as light, and graved, and found beneath the hill, and the tinker given for his death foretold; the ring that Malykorne had laid on Sylvie in her turn: the last. Stoneless, yet it bore a stone of water, bright and trembling beneath. Cold. Craobh took the ring and set it on her hand.

"Good," said Sylvie. "That's all three. I hate loose ends."

They turned away from the rune-tree, the odd thorn, outlying and foretelling spring, woodspelled: the staff in Mally's hands, the thorn at Annis's bare throat, Cloud and Law. And the moon's old riddle, ever new: the Ship forever sailing, bearing light; yet woodfast, fast in time, in hallows, and the heart of all the turning world. Now one, now another looking backward, they went up the stony fellside.

O but his tree was so close, thought Ariane. They were there already, and she could only think, how small. And desolate, so obstinately tree and out of place, standing on the huge bare hill, knee-deep in fall: huddled, sere and shabby, with its scant leaves curled and shivering against the sad bleak wind. Cobber laid his hand on the bark, with a look of fond and trusting commonplace—Late now, can we go home? He spoke a word or two, but softly: to himself, perhaps, or to his other.

No leaf fell, but a winter turned, riming veins in rising light; then slowly, wick as candleflames but still, the sharp buds swelled and broke, unpleating in thin leaves and dandled and endearing catkins, quirky as eyebrows. The leaves grew taut. The tassels fell, and the green nuts ripened, burred in their prickly husks, amid the leaves turned palest gold. Flickering, they began to fall. A cobweb glinted on the air; a rime would turn the rough hulls starry. Cobber glanced up amid the boughs; then ducking, twisting under branches in the glint and twirl of falling leaves, the flit of shadow, he reached up and plucked a nut, but only one: his soul among far other woods. As he did, a storm of small birds rose, leaf-brown, unwithering: his crown of wings.

The tinker lay there, stark and scrawny in his rags. His coat was gone, but for a few scant threads and tatters, like the skeleton of a leaf. His breath clouded, faintly— did they see? Or was it roke? An eyelid twitched. Slowly a stiff brown hand uncurled.

Ariane and Sylvie knelt plunk in the cold mud and stared. Ariane touched his sleeve. Tink?

"Cawd," he said: a cracked whisper, dazed and dry. "Were i't hand."

Ariane, in a fury of tenderness, turned out her bag— no last drop of Woodfalls' ale for him, no tea in this goddamn heterocosm. But Sylvie hauled him up, and wrapped him, scrawny as a hare, in Mally's unidyllic muddy cloak, unburdening herself of shrewd witchery. That's that. He lay across their dryish knees, drenched with hoarfrost, stiff and knobbly as a load of kindling, bearing up beneath their ticklish ministrations.

"Oh, you're back, are you really back?" cried Ariane, earnestly thumping and chafing. He shook with cold now, shuddering; had found his breath. Old rattlebag, old scarecrow, rags and bones.

"No pockets," he said somberly, pawing at the cloak, his fingers clumsy with the cold.

Sylvie eyed him, kindly, sternly. "You shouldn't run around like that. You'll catch your death."

"Not chasing it." He gazed at Ariane, resplendent in his feathered hat, at wraggle-taggle Sylvie, at the lightborn children, marvelling: Is allt stars fallen? Has I tummled ont moon? They all stared back. "Dreamed," he said at last.

"O but you were . . ." Ariane bit her lip. He raised his brows, all shrewdly innocent. ". . . wood."

"Sin I were born," he said, regretful.

"What did you dream?" asked Sylvie. Ariane grinned. Dryadopsychology. Jung Tam Lin's away, brave boys.

"Were i't witch's lap: no featherbed." His face was February, doubtful, dazzled. With his thawing hand, he stroked Craobh's tangled hair, tweaked Cobber's old brown jacket. *Wassail*. The wren-boy laughed. Kneeling, face to face, Craobh touched his earringed cheek. *Bear light*. Her ring shone briefly. Drawing back, they sat together at his feet, and watched in silence, in their maze of light. His gaze followed them, a little wistfully. "Nuts i' May. Seems I's slept thruff a verse or twa."

"Not much," said Sylvie. "Witch-crunching. The gory part." She turned to Ariane's protesting face, and asked, "So who's the guy?"

She grinned, abashed: well, it did look odd. Tom o' Bedlam? John a' Rednose? "He never . . . oh dear, well, he's the *tinker*."

"Wha's a tinker?" he said, sitting up. "Never said I were—" He sneezed.

"Bless you," said Sylvie and Ariane, together.

"I's no such craft, nor kindred." He looked sadly— coat's what I were—at the muddy cloak. "No potter nowther, for all it looks. Nobbut stray." He glanced at Ariane. "But where's tha bent? Here's craws i' cock's feathers."

What? Oh, the *hat*, thought Ariane. And welcome. Bowing low, she gave it back.

He set it on, his old way, at a rare brave slouch. Imped out, he grimaced sternly. "And wha's t'wench? Thy brown ranting lass, were it? Where's her drum?"

"Tough lass," said Ariane: reflected glory. "It's Sylvie from my world, Mally's sword. She came, I found her. She brooched Annis. Took the stones."

"Pooh," said Sylvie.

He eyed her. "Lost thy petticoat?"

"Skirt's not what I is," said Sylvie.

Ariane giggled. "Once more into the breeches. Shiftless wench. Tha'll 'a to borrow Mally's. Broadly speaking."

"Deea." Sylvie groaned. "Do they come off? I thought they were part of her. Like a cabbage."

He looked his old self now. "Ah. Tha'll not queen it far i' witch's smock. Send her awd geese to fetch it back. By't strings." They laughed. Ariane thought of Sylvie dangled, furious, aloft, arsy-varsy from the snappish beaks.

"With her apron flung over her, they took her for a swan," she sang. "O but Mally thieves from the hedgerows, she pinches from clotheslines. Burkes petticoats by dark of moon. Owls fearfully. Her swag is souls. I met her midnight in a lane, with a man's smalls on her shoulder. Said her skin was prickly ont inside: Mrs. Were-Tiggy-Winkle. Seethes nettleshirts and foxgloves. Ladysmocks. All souls. She tumps 'em out." She glanced down at her draggled clothes. "Throw in my last-year's Laurel Ash-Tree. Dryad-clean only."

"She's like this," said Sylvie.

"Aye," he said, amused. He looked about. "Law's changed." With his coat, thought Ariane: it would. The fells were rimefast, silver in the slant of light. The ling was translated—Lappish? Old Icelandic? Finno-Ugrian?— sharp, complex, unshadowy. Not songs, nor hearthtales now, but runes and spells. Grimm's Law.

"*I's* changed," he said. Shivering in Mally's cloak, an overcast, a blasted heath, the tinker—no, the traveller, her friend—looked ruefully at the ruin of his coat: nowt left but Mrs. Woodfall's darns. A spider scurried bleakly down his sleeve, no doubt despairing. No more twist. "Past praying for," he said. "S'll want my awd sark mending."

"It'll do for Mally's porridge," said Ariane. "All adds richness."

"And stockins, for a whet," he said.

She nodded. "Long time travelling."

". . . *on dirty toes* . . ." sang Sylvie, thrumming softly, watching the spider fall away. *A horse of air.* The moon's dark tower. Malykorne. "That brew of hers, that wha's-ale stuff, was *strange*. It came true." She fell silent for a moment, looking inward: the woodcut traveller climbed the stony hill, bent with her stick and bag; the tree sailed on; the ravens stooped. "You know," she said, "the song was you, I heard you. In the witch's cup. You sang how to kill the ravens." She leaned toward him, alight and serious. "Did she get you drunk, too?"

"Aye, and ranting i' me cups. Copse. Sang for her. Awd rimes. Forgetten what: I were bosky." He mowed at Ariane, a teasing glance. "Waked i' featherbed, wi yon lass."

"*Hmmm*," said Sylvie, wickedly gleeful.

Ariane looked fierce: her best malefic glitter. "Annis *soit qui* Mally *pense*."

Politely ignoring this, Sylvie turned to the tinker. "You're coming back with us? Oh, good."

He smiled. "An tha will."

Ariane, scarlet-cheeked, had stopped crowing. Sylvie whispered to her, "A very endearing fellow. Kind of puny, though."

"Well, he's not an evil cheese," she hissed, indignant.

"Now, now." Sylvie looked at him. "You wouldn't happen to know the way?"

"Gate's when it's opened," he said.

They looked at the lightborn children, Craobh and Cobber, yet unknown, unfast in earth: now brown, now shining, like gossamers on withered heath, at once unearthly and familiar. Stars through wintry leaves. The traveller said nothing. He had watched the children all this time, as if the stars shone once, were brief as hoarfrost, and would vanish at a breath.

They left one thing unspoken: that the children would not come, were there already, furthest in. They are the wood, thought Ariane, they tent the sky; and we can never come so far, but in sleeping, never see beyond the cot and counterpane and dusk.

Sylvie tumbled out her store of souls, bright and strange, in the traveller's two hands. "Hoard. But we have to give them back."

He turned them over on a lap of cloak, as if they were his dreams, and strung and knotted on his being; as if without the beads there were no thread. They made him pattern, made him garland. Eyes of Cloud, thought Ariane. She watched the play in silence, as he told the carol of the stones. It would not come out: one soul was still a knop of wood, a nut; and one bestowed elsewhere. A broken game.

Ariane touched the hailstone at her throat. Now. The children would be turning Cloud, be turning lightfast with the sky. It was their dancing day. She rose, and coming to the child, she touched Craobh's mooncold face. Not like that, she said softly: not as dust. She saw the way. But I was meant to see, thought Ariane. Unstrangely, as the clouds were stone, as the root in dark was flowering, she knew that she was witchborn, Mally's daughter. She had never left the thorny hallows of their realm, that O: her journeying would end in birth. Seeing with her eyes of wood, she knew the witchknots in the child's hair bound her to the earth, to travelling without cause or crown: dying and undead, unfast in light or dark, nor yet reborn. A fixed last crescent. When the last knot was undone, the child would turn, the lightborn would go on.

Ariane took out the comb of horn. It fit her hand. She had had to carry what she had wanted, light and love and solitude; and in bearing had become her burden. As another, for a draught of sleep, unasked-for, had become the wood; as Sylvie, bright and heedless as a falling star, was made the sword. Cup and sword and stolen comb; envied or endured, or carried lightly by a grace inborn, or anxiously and yet unbroken, like the windegg, frail and tough: Mally's gifts were sly, bestowed with tutelary malice. Sly, but true, thought Ariane. She turned the crooked comb. It was a gate of the north wind, and a wolf for gnawing; a weaver of thorn-hags, of hallows and of cages, sanctuary. It ringed the moon with storm, and barbed the virgin's tower with bright ice. It was for sleep and death, forgetfulness: the weir of lethe, and the lord of partings.

With Craobh standing at her knees, she combed the dusk long hair, Craobh falling from the child no longer Craobh, no longer child. Against that twilight, neither dying nor immortal, Ariane would hang the star, the soul. As she combed the falldark hair, she sang, riming and unspelling.

> O wha's undone the nine witchknots
> That was amang that lady's locks?
> And wha's ta'en out the combs o care
> Woven in that lady's hair?
> And wha has loosed her left-foot shoe,
> The lighter of a bairn to go?

The spell was done, undone. She slipped the soulstone from its knot; hung back a heartbeat's space, a breath. Through the dusk, she saw the traveller. He had knotted up the souls in Sylvie's scarf. He spoke to Cobber and hugged him, briefly, hard; spoke and touched his cheek: be good. As one would say to the sun: be risen. He turned to Craobh, too late. The child he saw was nameless, shadow; though she walked the earth, her soul was elsewhere, fleeting to the dance. The star had risen.

Sylvie, odd one out this set, stood with her hands in her pockets, and listened to the north wind. Hoo, it said.

They walked to the ring of stones in silence, over Cloud-law, through the greening dusk: the darkfall of the longest night, the hinge. It was windless on the Law. The fells were hoar with mist, huge tranquil storm. On the unbreaking coldest wave of earth, the stones lay light as clots of foam, as clouds of rock, no witch's sullen crown: their rune, a ring and not, obscured, elusive in the mist.

White things moving on a hill, thought Sylvie: clouds in Mally's cup.

Sad dance, the traveller thought. No dub, nor piping, nor no garlands.

Time, thought Ariane.

The children walked amid the stones, slowly, mazed it seemed. Their moving made no grammar. Ariane hugged her coat close round her, shivering. The small mist hung in drops cold as mail on the harsh wool. She stared at the circle with her witch's eyes. Was that a child's face turning, or a flaw of light? A crack and shadows, or a knarry hand, caressing air? An eye encrystalled in the rock? She turned, and it had fleeted: all were stones. Had the dance that moment fallen still? Shadow beyond shadow in the sliding dusk: how many stones? Ah, but they must not be told; that witch's knot would bind them.

O they have to wake, thought Ariane, for that we came, the turn of light, the dance—O was it now? For in the cold, still air the stone itself seemed tenuous as fire, or as cloud before the cold bright headlong moon:

a veil that stirred by a wind of spirit would fly out and flare, enhaloing, revealing form. But no stone wakened, dancing to an unheard music.

Now the wintry sun, like a struck flint, glinted fierce and sudden; it caught, hung cold between cloud and fell. At once, the light within the stones congealed. The children stood. The sun would die unturned, thought Ariane: the dance undanced forever.

Caught in the bleak bare light, the stones endured. She saw them, small and hard as milk teeth, fixed, enumerate: a broken ring. Deathpale and derelict, they cast long raking shadows, mocking portent. They were a crowd, no dance, each huddled to itself, immeasurably alone: rough still things, shrouded, stonefast.

When they dance, thought Sylvie, do they move? Or is it in another frame? Stars don't, we spin away. Not here, maybe: maybe on this earth stars dance; it's been cloudy, I don't know. No evidence. What Annis—No. No good freaking, I'll see what I see. They danced in Mally's cup, but I was drunk. They *reeled*, she thought; then graver: but they're children. They're inside, they turn the sky: a sort of little crazy clockwork. It was strange. Stars and Cobber's odd sweet moonface. Stones. Curious, she looked at them. "They're awful small."

"They're stone," said Ariane, and thought: there's nothing left that wakes, nor any close. No ring: the fossil of a stillborn dance, a cog, a crown whose realm is ashes, an unmeaning rune. She who bound them was undone; her O, her nothing would endure, turned slowly, slowly on the lathe of stars to dust.

Poor bairns, he thought ruefully, looking at the still ring and at the two who walked, forlorn amid the colder desolation of their kindred. Stone-naked's cawder yet nor rags. How will they call lightborn to't dance, sin they are earth? Cannot rap and cry, *Come out, come out wi us and soul*. He thought of the wizened bond-child in the witch's hands, its gnarled and stunted glory; and he shivered with a stranger thought. What an if i't dance they turn to stone? And if they cry, not: *Come and soul*; but, *Let us in*? Lay down their bodies that t'stane would break. They would die. Ah, no. But it were true. Light wears no body but as cloak. Wood's guise for wandering, and stone for turning death. No dance, but they mun die as bairns. Dark now: their burden's stars.

Not ghostly quite, thought Ariane, looking at the light-born children, standing, holding Sylvie's scarf, among the stones. They still have faces, still are cobwebbed in mortality; in having slept and travelled, rued and dreamed and cried. They have been loved. These knots can never be untied, though all else is spirit, all quintessence. They are meddled, neither breath nor blood, but flawed things, frail and bonefast. They cannot cross. Between spirits caught in stone and bodies, the frailty that dies and the immortal, obdurate and cold as death, there lies abyss.

Then the leaf-brown child broke the knot and spilled the souls into the other's hands. They caught the dying light and flashed: brief stars in falling, a handful of dark stones. The dark child held them close to her, and breathed on them. They kindled with her spirit, brightening as the old sun died, through owl-light, rushlight, rime under wintry moon, until she held a skein of stars between her hands; held all the labyrinth of heaven, strung on air, on darkness in an endless knot, time's thread: stars and clouds of stars and all the dance. Light-fasting earth.

All souls, said the dark child, not aloud, and scattered them. They fell, a web of stars on the cold earth, a secret frost that shone and vanished into rock.

The children woke; yet did not turn from stone, nor break their shrouds of earth: their light was inward. They walked, and the rune was changed. Old beyond all things save gravity and light, grey-hooded, they wore cloaks of stones, no longer bound by them, but as the burden of the dance, its cope; as for lilting times of summer they had worn their leaves and wood. Two stones only stood vain and dark.

Gravely as angels, the lightborn embraced. Each two were one, and coalesced, like grey-boled beeches, winter-crowned; then turning, one was two again, and hailed still others in their fleeting turn, ardently, a little stiffly, contrafuguing in their formal complex joy. Their moving was a slow and starry hey, a word unspoken. Yet a sadness shone and trembled, not of the dance, but on it, like rain upon a web. Wind-bowed, bending at the knee, they kissed the others, cheek and chin: the dark child and the lad, as brown as winter leaves. The two were threadbare and ungarlanded, estranged by blood and bone; yet as their kindred wore the stones, so they their bodies, as a guise, a garland in their solemn play: their husks were calyces of light. Embracing the immortals, they were touched by frost. Their tattered cloaks would fall to wind.

The dancers quickened. In their turning now the clouding stone blew back, so Ariane caught glances of the light within, their inessential bodies. They were sky: a lapidary blue-gone-green of clearing storm, serene, unearthly, yet trembling on the rim of dance, as on a rising star. Now one, now another would cast back his hood; their bright or dark long hair was wind, was coronal. Their faces were occulted still. Dancing they would brighten, letting fall their cloaks of stone and years, newborn and naked as the sun.

Yet the dance was at the stones: was of the earth, and elsewhere. They would dance as stone, as souls, the cloud itself becoming halo. Turning, the enskied and starry dance was stone, the ring of stones was light made carol. They were the burning glass, the heavens' eye, the O and the beginning: winter's crown.

A hand was raised, night clear, cracked through within, refracting myriads of knots of stars: it wore a ring.

Now, thought Ariane, O now. Lightfasting earth and heaven.

Sylvie blinked: was that a star? Her eyes were dazzled with long staring. She rubbed them and they chequered. Closing them, she heard a ring of enweaving musics, endless, far and clear and ancient, like a carol of the cold rejoicing stars. Bright and small and crooked, inwardly, she saw a game played with green-blue sort of misty stones on a winter grey-brown field. They were moved in complex knots and pleiades; but the rules kept changing, and the stones were lost in the wiry grass: it would not come out. It was shadowy, but somehow set to that high cold starry music. Counterpoint. They were slant-

ing, rolling down a long dark hill—but that was herself,
falling asleep where she stood.

Waking sharply, Sylvie stared: mist, and rocks, and
the two children flitting strangely in the cloudy dark, at
random, not looking for the stones they'd scattered. It
was all a puzzle, rings somehow interlocking as light, as
dance; but she was tired. She would sleep on it.

Through all the turnings of the bright strange dance,
the traveller watched his own, his other and the lass.
Wrens, he thought. Yon garland's leaves o gold, and
knots o moon and stars; but wrens is bonnier. What dies
is fairer yet nor crown. But they'd not die. They'd turn,
as leaves among bright leaves, and blow from him, mortal as he stood and earthfast. Law's turned ower now,
he thought: it's hallows flaws away, t'journey's still.
Leaves fleet away i' light, untelled; stars whirl frae us,
all folk at dies and cannot dance but langways. A, but
earthfast's what I is, at heart o dance. He stood. Took
joy in stars, but never solace. What he loved was low and
earthborn: his lass among the green leaves. Whitethorn.
Apples. Bairns. What love's i' light? Has no face. Sitha,
how she moves, as light as any leaf ont wind; and see at
lad, his bonny face.

Longingly, he gazed. Each time they turned from him
would be the last. Would be their rising.

Slowly turning in their figure, the carollers took hands.
Hand in hand, they drew the dark child into their ring,
like the shadow of the star she held; and still they held
their hands out, for the last to close the ring.

Ariane felt her soul hang shivering on her skin: it
burred her round with brightness, it haloed her; within,
her heart cracked through with longing that was greater
for the light, was joy. Ah, but seeing she was light. She
stayed. The child would dance for her, forgetting and
fulfilling, as the flower from the blackthorn root, as the
stars from the riddled dark. The lightborn waited. Yet
the leaf-brown child turned, looked backward for a
moment, unregretful, seeing and recalling all that dies;
then slipped into the endless dance.

O it was too much, too much, the wanting being light.
Blind with awe, with riving joy, Ariane turned away. For

a brief eternity, unbreathing, she bent outward, against the whorl of time, the vortex of the spindle falling. She bore something broken in her hand, toward darkfall, from the wreck of seeing: a rune, a ring as heavy as a crown of stars, bright absolute gravity. She could not endure it. It was gone. O but what was it she had longed for? A whirl of leaves in the wind. The light was ashes.

Stumbling, unblinding, Ariane was on the hill, turned round, within the ring of stones. Sylvie caught her arm, as if she had waked her from dreaming: where have you fallen from? What did you see? The traveller was there in darkness, very quiet: sleepwalking.

"We should go," said Sylvie. "Dark now." They went on.

Not far beyond the stones they came upon the bodies of two children: seemings, husks, as scant and stiff as winter birds, as light as leaves, outworn. They knelt in silence. Ariane saw that within the pale and dark of tattered ribands, within the cages of the fragile curving ribs, lay rings of blackened silver, old and thin; a cracked nut, a clouded pebble. The heads were bare, and crowned with frost. A wind rose, full of wings, a storm of the small birds blowing leaves on leaves to cover them, wrenbrown and ruddy, wan or bright or fallow gold, foretelling and fulfilling what was spelled within their veins: that winter's kings should die.

Ah, but that was myth, out of time before the dance was danced. They knelt within the eaves of an ancient wood, great-rooted and far-branching, dark and tall, unnumbered dancers. On the boughs hung yellow leaves, as few as stars against the sky. The boles and branches were half seen and shadowy, intangible; but underfoot they trod a dry sweet earthy scent, a fragrant bitterness of leaves on leaves of autumns past, and touched with frost: green slept within that earth. The traveller cast a handful of dark leaves on dark, and rose. The wood lay endless, all behind them, hallows; and beyond, perhaps, a crooked door, and dusk, and fire.

But their gate was winter; so they turned, and walked slowly over Cloudlaw. It was mirk night, below the wood, and colder. The moon had set, and the sky was huge and sad above the stony fells. A few sharp-sided flakes of snow were falling, whirled. The wind rose. The snow gathered. The three drew together, hand in hand, very quiet, close; weary beyond concern or grief or longing, keeping still an inward wonder. At long last he sighed. "Would we were by't fire, and wi ale to hand: this night were better past and hearthtale."

The snow fell thinly, ghostly, as they walked. Their death could not catch them, as in a dream, though it flurried, moth-pale, importunate; or death itself was dream, was common dusk. They were now and nowhere, in the dark between the dying old and the new-born, milk-blind year.

Sylvie shook herself. "Hey, over there, a light!"

Ariane saw a star jig on the stony clouds, saw a sharp frail comet fleeting wildly, eerily, down the drifted fields of earth, whirling out away in flaws of fire, flakes of snow. Stumbling on unwieldy legs, elated, they ran toward it. As it came, slowed against the steep and cumbering drifts, it shrank and darkened to its bones of redder fire. It trailed jauncing behind a clot of shadow.

"Oh, she's come for us, she's come," cried Ariane.

"Hush," said Sylvie. "Who's that little stumpy person?"

Mrs. Woodfall ploughed on slowly, slowly with the hallowfire, the wren's crown of burning thorn. It hung from her sheepcrook in knots of ember, flaring, sullen, dying, embers, ash. It crumbled from the staff. Flinders hissed

on the snow. Lightened, she lurched onward a few steps,
dark against the fell of dark, and stopped, raling for
breath, just shy of a ruinous drystone wall. There the
hallows ended; beyond was law.

As they came to her, she lit a lantern from the embers.
With her body, she kept it from the wind; the wick
swayed and steadied, and she shut the iron door. They
were in the burr of light.

The traveller bent, and picked up a bit of the scattered charred wood. Mrs. Woodfall bit off her mitten,
scarlet, rimed and ashy, mended on the thumb, to take
the charcoal in her hand. "Sad night," she said, and blew
her nose on a huge cold hanky. She was dwarfish,
swathed against the snow with sacking on her head and
shoulders, hoary brown: shapeless, dark-clad, heavy-
booted. She was earth and hearth and heartwood, sunwise and hallowfast, enduring and enkindling years: holy
commonplace. She looked incuriously, steadily, at Sylvie,
at the traveller in his wintry cloak, at witch-locked Ariane: bone and blood, all three. *Right then*, said her face.

Ariane, babbling out a confusion of comfort and joy
and bewildered sorrow, said, "She's gone with the others. Her others. The dance."

"Aye," said Mrs. Woodfall. "Moon come: so it's
turned."

Suddenly giddy with relief, knowing the weight of what
they had borne and done, Ariane felt the stony fellside
as a brittleness, a doubtful cat-ice thinly glazing the
abyss. "The riddles . . ."

"Ower yon. I don't come that road." Void's where I
isn't.

"Good," said Sylvie, heartfelt. "I'm getting sick of
witches." She peered into the dazing light and bobbed
her head. "Oh, hi. Are you from the farm? Cobber
talked about you; he liked the stories you told, that you
remembered them. The old ones. Even witches, even
stones. You kept them." Hard to see the woman's face.
She craned. Deea, she's short: you'd have to pick her up
to say hello. Close to the earth. Like a tough little
stunted tree, not woodsy though, windbent and by herself. Not apple: wilder, darker. What birds eat in winter.

Thorn? No flowers. Rowan? Yew? Maybe alder. "He
was by the fire. He heard."

"He were a good lad. Getten a new cap and he were
gone."

"He's wood," said Sylvie. "He and—well, *they're*
woods. Back there." The shadows and the gold, the
leaves.

"Aye, not seen." Her voice was grave and small. "I's
never walked i' Cloudwood, but me grandmother mother
did, and thowt on, and telled it us." Mrs. Woodfall
smiled at them, a tiny shy new moon of brightness in her
sad brown face. "Yer daft, clappin craws i' winter."

Crazy in the dead of winter, on the stony hills. No
green. Sylvie saw Mrs. Woodfall glance at the ring of
cold iron on her wrist, and she tugged down her sleeve.
She grinned back. "Crazy, hunting wrens."

The one's t'other, thought Ariane: the wren's crown's
ashes and the raven's cage is iron, so the sun is turned.
Mrs. Woodfall's Sylvie, earthfast, bearing light; and Mally's both of them, elsewhere. Weird sisters. O the bonny
mad lasses, the brown ranting girls: cloudwise and moon-
bent, fire-bringing.

"Stark wood," the traveller said. "Cried ravens frae't
fells: reaped nobbut stones. Felled tree to crack nut."

Mrs. Woodfall looked shrewdly at him, up and down.
Her mouth twitched. "Yer coat's changed."

"Aye, snawed ower."

"Bad bit o weaving."

"I's no other."

She hung her lantern on the iron-shod crook, and
steadying it in her bent elbow, bit and tugged her stiff
red mitten back on. Following her, they started walking
down the fell, in a thin wind that stirred the lying snow.
"Not far: she's biding for you."

Not going to the farm, thought Ariane. Not seeing
them. Green branches and dark eyes. "How are they?
The children?"

"Bairns? Eh, they's grand: hunted wren aback o't
wood. They'll be hunting me next, an I's lang. We's having us t'wren's arval. Year-ale. Killed awd goose at
flayed thee."

Goose, he thought lovingly: eat fat and lie soft. Fire

and ale. Crack nuts. He sighed, regretfully. No: we owes t'awd witch wassailing, sin she bore us. More grace and less goose. Doubt she'll bait us fair, i' season: stewed holly and ivy. Haunch o spider, well sodden. Cloud ale and cawd comfort.

Ariane thought of the fire, the row of plates, the sharp bright holly; of the dresser with its hoard of sheep-draughts, patchwork, nutmeg, a silver thimble, rushes, valentines. She thought of the wren's green crown, the garland, hanging with its knots of ribands and its shadows. And all the little children that round the table go. Hearthtales and winter carols, rushlight; and then sleep.

No. The dance had its end where it began, with Mally: in the O of thorn, the colder hallows. Winter's eye. The Woodfalls kept her door, were hearth and fold and memory. They watched her fields by night, and waked the sun; but did not meddle in the tales of witches, light or dark, without great need. They three had met with Mrs. Woodfall, not for sanctuary, but as tidings. They had borne their part. The Cloud carol would be said by her fire, this ae night of the sun's wake, and every night and all—but O the children. Ariane gazed at her bright image of them; hallowing, she closed them round, the witch excluded, sharp, illuminate and avid, staring through her cold white tangled hair: a frost at the window, a wind in the door. "I've nothing for them. Take them my love."

Mrs. Woodfall nodded. "Found chocolate. Thanks."

Ariane turned out her bag again, as always, for the Woodfalls' broken lantern; she untied the rough quilts, grey and brown as winter earth, as clouds, and there, a splash of heartsblood red. "Thank you. We did need them, we needed them very badly in the dark. They kept us."

"No, you keep them yet. They's given while you've no need on them. They'll come back."

"I don't get it," said Sylvie. "We're not going back with you?"

Mrs. Woodfall glanced at their tatters, wryly, ruefully amused. "Eh no, we's had t'guisers. Nine year back, it were." Then soberly, softly, in her harsh small voice, she

said. "Cannot. Yer bound where yer mun be. We's no
door at yer."

"Mally's," said Ariane.

"Eeyukh. How unfestive. And drunken. And damp.
And I've dropped all her presents. Wassail, though. Bet
her sister serves geodes."

"Ah. Bitter." The traveller hunched, shivering.

Mrs. Woodfall touched his sleeve. "An you find t'gate,
walking on, come ower times i't winters. Fire and ale,
and a bit o bread. No latch ont door, nobbut thorn."

"Aye, but bairns is a ranty fierce lot, as'll knap me
up." His face was rushlight. "Eh well, an you've not
etten him, t'awd cock knaws me. Forby't geese and
dogs."

"Bitch pupped," she said. "Tha knaws, Sweep's Fury's
Lass. Had Bendigo of her, and Knap. Yer've not met
Tinker."

Ariane gaped. Sylvie choked. They both cracked up in
startled glee, dismayed, hilarious. "Who's a tinker?"
cried Sylvie.

He drew his face together sternly, all knotted brows
and grimace; then he dazzled, laughing. "Tinker, were
it? Ah. S'll bite yer heels, wenches. Ha." They giggled
helplessly. "Sneck up, yer lot." He grinned at Ariane.
"Awd cur I is: meks tha dog's gossip." Then very man-
nerly to Mrs. Woodfall, who was quite stone-faced with
perplexity, "Grand name, if you've sheep wi holes. Do
you want any ducks tinkering?"

"Tales," said Mrs. Woodfall. "And ballads. Sad tales
for winter."

Sylvie said, "Don't look at me, I never said you were
a tinker. I'd like to hear you sing, wherever, Mally's. I
haven't. Not awake." She turned to Mrs. Woodfall. "Is
this the way?" No woods.

"To't back door." They went by way of earth. They
walked within her little trembling room of light, her rush-
castle, unwalled, invulnerable. A wind was driving on the
cloud, high, high above them: storm and rack, and star-
blink in the upper heavens. It blew thinly at their backs;
as they went over the wind-carved rigg, they were sheltered. They were folded.

Back of the wind, beyond Cloud, the snow lay shoaled

like dolphins. In the blue deep sky the stars blazed. Sylvie stopped, and laughed for joy, and wheeled around and round, head back, gazing, giddy: O the bonny light horseman, the scarecrow, the ship, ladle swan harp of bone unborn child gallows wren witch fool virgin tower horseman . . . O all the ballads of the heavens danced for her, in one carol. The beginning of the world. And if the patterns of the stars were strange in this sky, she did not know: the songs were all the songs she knew, and were creation. She had sung the night, and it shone for her.

Mrs. Woodfall cast a shepherd's eye on the heavens. "T'Ship, sitha. It's there and not, winters. Ship's for a passing."

Your death is in the heavens. Remembering Annis's cold prophecy, Sylvie felt fleetingly sick and dizzy, bone cold. But that blackness was a flickering eclipse, far amid the glory. She was too wild, too cold and reckless to agonize. Lightheaded. Pooh, she thought, what does Annis know? Stoneblind. If I weren't so wet already, I'd flop down and make snow-angels. Hi to the sky.

Ariane looked up. "Where? O the children," she said. "The dance. It's come for them. Sailing."

"Poor awd Wren," he said. "Not much pick on yon bones."

"Eyes to the blind," sang Sylvie, hoarse as a crow, taboring her hand. *"Legs to the lame, pluck to the poor . . ."*

"O there's Orion," said Ariane. "Look." No rags of cloud, a ceint of sparks: night-blue, naked and defiant. She sang, not aloud: *a Briton fights in seamless tights, completing unenCumbria.*

"Wha's awd Rianty? Yon's Flaycraw."

Tinker the barbarian. Ariane giggled.

". . . *bones to the dogs, says everyone,"* sang Sylvie, shrill, oblivious.

"Cawd," he said to Orion, plaintively, condolingly, and sleeved his nose. "No pockets neither."

No hanky. "Poor guy. No salt, no oatmeal . . ."

"No goosefeather bed." He sighed.

"No Sword," said Mrs. Woodfall. "Mind thorns."

By her lantern, they saw bright scratches of scarlet against the snow: alder withies, along the line of a beck.

They came to a little wood, long and narrow, slanting down by the water: the same, perhaps, where they had cut green boughs to bear the wren, where the ashes had been thorn, year behind turning year, to the sun's arising. The bare branches were snowy, harled and blurred and entangled, plumed with cold. They pushed through thorn and eider-drifted thicket, and shook them black.

"O lord," said Ariane, catching her sleeve, unsnagging her hem, then her icy braid. "This feels like Mally's hamper. Her doormat. Her hairbrush."

"She's got a *house*?" said Sylvie. "Woods. Woods. Look, is that mistletoe? I've never seen it wild."

"Ouch," said the traveller.

They stopped, rather scratched and breathless, by an ancient thrawn holly, glittering shrewdly by lanternlight, gnarled and wary, with a lap full of snow. O lilywhite smock. Mrs. Woodfall blew on her fingers, and stamped her snow-clogged boots. "Prickle-holly bush. Door's thruff here." She stood, dark and earthfast, with her star of horn. They turned, covering their eyes, and thrust in against a cold asperity: sharp leaves or will, or cross-grained time; unmoved, her light went with them.

Cold and ticklish perplexity: a throng of holly-leaves, hailsharp as a whirlwind of witches, as thick as hell's thatch, with quickset thorn, a cross-grained wicked crowd of twigs and knees and jostling elbows, firs prickly as frieze; and cold kittle feathers everywhere, or eider-drifts of snow. A star in the branches, a chink in the door.

"Bugger this for a game of soldiers!" cried Ariane, hard thrashed and lashing out, and laughing with vexation.

"Craws," the traveller muttered.

Sylvie swore.

Someone's hand in the hurly-burly struck a latch, and they tumbled out all of a heap onto Mally's earthen floor, amid the cairns of apples, and crockery and leaves.

The witch stood glaring at them, beladled, broad and fierce. She was owl-beaked and moonfaced, with a cap of the heartsblood red; her spectacles glinted malefically. Untangling himself, he touched his feathered hat to her—forlorn hope—with a demurely impudent panache. "Hallows wi yer. We's come down frae't clouds, fort wren's arval."

"One on you's dole enough," said Mally. "What shall I do wi three?"

"Supper," said Sylvie, recklessly, rubbing her elbow. "O God, not us. In us." She looked back suspiciously at the innocent cupboard-bed. Bare as a bone. Not a leaf. Ariane just sat amid the apples, all feathery, and grinned.

Mally stumped to the fire, and keeled the louring pot; it looked like sheep-dip, head and horns, fleece, hooves, fleas and all. "Boots i' me good bed! Rout o tinkers, you is," she said, and licked the spoon disdainfully. Her face wried, and she flung the scum onto the rushes. No hedgehog came. "Reyk yersels plates," she said. Grub.

They looked woefully, furtively, at one another. Sylvie sighed, and groped stealthily for the grey skin bag with its giddy green cheese and oatcake and apple. Out of the ashes, Mally howked an earthen jug, and stirred it round with her ladle, in a cloud of reek.

"Crow soup," whispered Ariane, wickedly.

"Hare," he said faintly, lovingly; and snuffed the air again, in awe and disbelief. "Wi sloes and crabs, by't tang on't. Forby a good few gills o bitter."

"Caught i't hedge," said Mally, dolloping it out into the porridgy-crusted bowls, with shards of burned oatcake, and broad horn spoons, and a generous sprinkling of ash. And it was lovely, though rather full of little occult bones, and peppery. They ate and ate, dazed with good fortune, drowsy with fire. Out of the shadows, with a slow dry roar of leaves, came stumping and girning a grim-masked, black-and-white and ash-streaked badger. He nosed and craunched the spill of apples. The witch caught Ariane staring, and said, "It brock, but I mended it."

Mally went owling about her hovel, thrang at her obscurer wintry tasks: pottering and prying with her rush-dip through her hoard of leery jugs and frails and coffers, turning over clots of wool and storms of eiderdown and leaves, webs, mirrors, skeins of birds' claws, souls and iron keys. Light hallowskeeping. "Mek it do: piece out," she muttered, smudging her glasses in her petticoats; then turned their glitter balefully on nothing. "Airs and graces!"

No answer: but Ariane watching saw a spider by the witch's nose flirt out in a flourish of gossamer, descanting on her web.

"Happen tha mazed well at riddles; but thy darning's disgraceful: allt stockins is out at heels, and tha will not keep an eye ont cakes. Tha'st let all kizzen up. Bait brock wi thee."

Silence, and the lashing of silk.

"Light wench." Mally stalked away; and rummaging, at last she found the teapot, under some washing. Ariane's heart leapt up; but the witch dumped out the hedgehog, stuck with withered holly in a dismal ball. "By yer leave," she said, and fastidiously picked and chose some fleas for the spider. Then she clapped the lid to.

Sylvie ate. Now and then, doubtful, sly and sudden, she peered back: still a bed, narrow and rumpled, with its bulgy ticking and its counterpane of patchwork, grey and brown. No woods. Or not when she was looking. All these paradoxes were exhausting. She polished her bowl with a raspy bit of oatcake, absently picked off a crust of nettle, and handed the bowl back up. "Could I have some more stew, please?"

Mally glared. "Thinks sloes and apples grows i't hedges? Tha's etten days sall come now, willy-nilly: dowce wi bitter, stone and rind and maggot, moon and keeping sun. Goose-summer, green and gale."

"Aye, and Tib's eve come Tuesday," said the traveller,

rattling a little stone in his bowl. He held it out. "Wha's forfeit, then? Or has I drawed t'fool?"

"Gi's that," said Malykorne. "And tek it wi thee."

He sighed. "Hares runs mad i't moonlight, moon turns full, and I's etten mine, neck, nippins and all. S'd like another help o March."

"*I want* gets nowt." But she filled their bowls, and Ariane's, who said nothing, but watched the badger craunching apples, the flawed years and the sweet.

"O dear," said Sylvie. "I nearly forgot." She handed up the skin bag. "Thanks for the groceries. They were very—uh—sustaining."

Mally took it with a shrewd fierce glance, and shook it out. Nothing. Dust of leaves. Her mouth twitched. "Small change." Disdainfully, she dropped it: the shrunk and grizzled budget by the cramming badger. One was grey as the other. Both had paws. "Time will mend," said the witch, and stumped back to her brewing.

Getting forward wi't thaw, thought Ariane, as Mally prodded the morass: Woodfalls'll be in ower boots, come fore-end. Mucky March. But there was a smaller cauldron back of it, seething crabs and ale. Wassail. She caught the traveller's eye and grimaced, mowing at the witch's back: owl-huffed, redoubtable. Broom? he mimed, all bustle. No: she did him Mally, stumping with a shovel. His face crimped, and he hid it; some rather curious choked noises came from behind his sleeve. The witch turned her sidelong haughty stare on him. "Bone?" He shook his head. "Tha'rt silent, sudden."

"I's saving me cough fort singing."

Mally's face bent slightly, wry, unwillingly amused. "Cawd watter's stuff for a throat." But she ladled full her cup of bitter, stems, sticks, seeds, drowned wasps and all. "It's turned," she said solemnly, and drank.

"It's turned," they echoed; and turn and turn, lovingly, curiously, gingerly, they drank wassail to the sun's waking and the wren's soul, from the witch's old great wooden cup, by the embers of her fire.

They were quiet then, dazed or dreaming, drowsy, all adrift on ale. Mally filled three cups for them, and sat, with her lap full of winter, combing clouds.

"Air?" Sylvie whispered. "What did you see? Back there?"

"The dance—O it was, it was light."

Sylvie considered. "I didn't—I saw the stones, and the kids. And you were—It was like when, you know, Irene took Curdie to see her great-grandmother's lamp, and he saw the withered apple and the heap of straw. And he didn't believe in her. But it's as true: the sun's an apple, and the stars are rocks, and the thread's faith and it's spiderweb. They're both. Like the children were. You just go on."

"Indwelling. Things are what they seem, though not wholly. Mally's a little stumpy person. Drinking light. You've spilled some."

Sylvie wiped her mouth. "You know, when she got me really drunk that time in the woods, sort of crabbed me out, I saw her. Mally's face."

"I haven't."

"Like the moon in a thunderstorm, and birds. Only it wasn't."

"Moon," said the traveller, nodding cloudily. "Gi'en light." He drank.

Ariane sipped and grimaced. The cup was a bitter solemnity; it made her head whinge. It gave her no visions, but clarity, detachment: as if sleep were a dark small thing she held, not herself, but pendant. "Next time, we'll go to one of your worlds. Lots of nice headsmen and axes and racks. And intriguing evil cheeses. Prince Heathens."

Sylvie giggled; and he began softly, hoarsely, to sing: no dark high ballad, but a childish rhyme. *"By lang and light til Babylon, catch hands and turn, turn moon . . ."* Sylvie looked at him, a slight man, bemused and tattered: beak nose, rough quirking brows, the thin gold rings in his ears waking, weaving light. She closed her eyes, and saw a cobweb in the tall wet grass, in the gold morning; there were yellow leaves in Nan's old wicker basket, where she sat, and a linen rag still hung, forgotten, stained with pear-juice, on the line. "Oh, I like that, I remember now," she said, not quite aloud. Leaves rising from the dark. The cup.

". . . turn sun," he sang: his winter carol. A minor

tune, slight subtle mordents: rushlight, true and live and innocent, intent, for all its flickering measures.

After a time she found a countermelody, and sang with him; then as he fell silent, she sang on alone, a while. Old ballads.

Lass sings true, he thought: green notes, for all she's lang and rantin. Brisk as nightengale, and brown as oak leaves, and her bonny brown specked face, like thrush's egg. He saw a green wood, a standing stone, saw nightfall and a fleeting star; saw fox cubs tumbling by a beck. He saw a fire, and a woman's face, all shadowy; he saw a bairn's hand, brown and starry. Were his awn hand, reyking up, for what? Gaud hanging by her cheek. Awd moon. And after a time, he came into the song, as into the green wood with his rushlight, following and fleeing the other, wilder candle, Lang Jenny-wi't-lantern; laiking at touchwood, by the old paths that mazed and crossed beneath the branches, ancient and new-leaved this very breath.

Ariane sat and listened, still at the heart of winter's turning. She felt a pure felicity, a not-yet sorrow, clear and recollected as a drop of rain unfallen from a thorn. They sang, now one, now the other, and as one: the dark voice rising to the other's fall, neither leaf, neither shadow; each the other's light, and crossing. Closing her eyes, she saw the starry hanged man, the wanderer, unskied and walking on the clouds of earth; she saw a green tree rooted in a hill of sky, not cloud but light-years deep and starry. The Ship. But Sylvie by the hearth was singing:

I will set foot in the bottomless boat,
And I will sail the sea.

O when will you come back again?
My love, come tell to me.

When the sun and the moon dance on yonder hill,
And that may never be.

"O but they have. They have." Ariane spoke softly, light-possessed. The children, hand in hand, had risen from the dark. "The Ship's come for us, they've danced for us—our passing, not their own. It's in the sky. Not death: sailing, sailing like king's daughters. There, and never back again."

Sylvie's face was troubled. "Where's *there*? Downfall. I don't like this."

The witch with her lap full of cloud and her iron combs looked up. "Til thy door. Same as journeying, thy end: dark and light o one moon. Thy death's nobbut rising elsewhere." She looked wickedly amused. "Tha asked what Annis see'd. Eeh, stone-blind: would call wren raven."

"You mean if she hadn't cursed us, we wouldn't get home?" asked Sylvie.

Ariane clapped her hands, and cried to Malykorne, "The leaves! *You* spelled it with the leaves, the sailing, when we came to you. They made a ship. And scattered on the wind."

"One drowned i't ale," he said, drowsily.

"Happen," said Mally. "Were't Ship i't leaves, or Wren, or Gallows, all and nowt, or summat else; then sort changed. What Annis tells i't sky, I's spelt, times; and times, what she gnaws. I's knawed forehand. Stone-blind and stark wood. We's sisters." She looked shrewdly at the three: drowsy, draggled, sleep- and ale-drunk, hectic or bemused. Snug i't ashes. "Is tha fettled? Tha mun travel light."

Out of the silence, the little knot of souls, Sylvie drew breath. "It's all gone, what you gave me. The mirror got scattered, and the ravens ate it."

"Sall rise t'morn, and year-morn, and stay: thy setting's elsewhere."

"The stick took root, and the ring's with them. The dance."

"Sall need thy mast, and shrouds o stars."

"Well." She tugged at the iron brooch.

"No," said Mally. "Tha keep it. Tha'st earned it."

"How do I get it off?"

"Need anchor, or sall never fall til earth. Forby't raven knaws way. Tha follow beak."

Ariane held out the comb of horn. "I took this. I used it, for doing and undoing knots, knowing and unknowing what it is: windfast, neither good nor ill, but what must be."

Malykorne looked long and fiercely at her, no doubt enweaving knot for knot: snarls of wind by night, to clot and tangle her long hair, to vex her sleep with ravelled dreams of owls, and thorns, and mazes. "Thy noll's none sleeker for't."

But what's been borne is bone and nerve, thought Ariane: the comb's become me, the seeing's mine. She looked unflinching with her witch's eyes at Malykorne, at her ironset and glazen wintry moons. "Shall be a wind following, if you will."

Mally took the comb. "For a reckoning. Sall tek thy first dream o birds, good or ill." With her sharp swift earthy fingers, she unbound Ariane's braid, and took a third part, and a third of that, and combed it out, long as wind, and dark: a strand of starless swift unweaving night; the dance unstrung as naked moving, longways and no turning back. Nine threads of wind of time. "Unfast and fast," said Malykorne. "No farther."

The traveller looked at the witch. "And does I sail away i' riddle, wi a spoon to row by? Or a kist, and a sark for shroud?"

"Nowther," said Mally, eyeing him. "Tha'rt earth, not cloud or law, for all thy imping out: tha can walk. Gi's ower yon cloak."

He bundled it over, not unwilling: it was unidyllic wearing, hagged and clagged and hairy, cloudwool as it was. "Hempen hampen," he said. Could walk back o beyond o't moon i' yon cloak—aye, and sneeze ilk step, see nobbut fog. Cloud's not what I is, nor wood. I's my ownsel. And scant else, he thought ruefully: nobbut hare and holes. No knife, no salt. No fire-flint. And nowt to char. Nowt ripe. Or all gone by, and where's to beg? Stone birds, but they's wary; and bed's where I lie. Awd sark. No stockins. Fell and bones. Ah well, sall gan naked to chance, green or dark, and allt wind's changes. Could starve i't ditch fort craws to mourn—touch wood— for it's bitter cawd this night. Could yet sleep full i' feather-bed, could dance ont green. But not i' Cloudwood.

Ariane looked sadly at him, all bones and tatters and faded fallow hair: as sparse and ragged as a wood in

November, wind-rattled, with its branches showing through
the stubborn leaves. And scarce a shirt to his back. Nothing left in the room but a ragged petticoat and a winsey
gown. Fumbling in a fury of tenderness, she turned out
her bulging pockets, and flung off her mole-dark and dan-
gling-silver-buttoned, fleece-heavy, filthy, parcel-of-rogues
or beggar's-opera, ranting raffish greatcoat.

"Here," she said. "It's cold out." He stared. "Pock-
etses."

He felt it, and stroked it; then put it on. It hung to
his heels. He wheeled about and laughed, heedless of the
crockery, flaunting in delight; and all his throng of shadows swaled and danced. "Ha! a cloak and a hood. Hob'll
never do mair good."

Sort of Christmas, thought Sylvie, and felt in her
jacket. Cough drops, fircones—Ah. "Could you use this?
It's not very sharp." She held out her blunt, half-bladed
jack-knife, horn and iron: the one that had cut the stones
from Annis's hair. Sword, thought Ariane: Orion. Here's
a sword for the Mole, here's a sword for the Badger.
Mince pies to feast the fairies: what the bonny mad boys
of Bedlam sang. "It's got a flint and steel," said Sylvie.
"And a corkscrew, for when they invent beer-bottles."

He touched his feathered hat to her, all crazy gal-
lantry; then turned to Ariane, hung back, a little shy of
her. He hugged her, fiercely, suddenly. She felt him in
her arms, half elsewhere: light and sinew and old jacket,
like a moon-mad fleeting hare. He turned to go.

"Not so light," said Malykorne. "Tha's forgotten what
tha owes." Music and washing, extra.

"An I's owt to give, whatever's yours."

"Not soul," she said. "I's enough needs washing. And
there's bones and to spare i't jug. No. Gi's thy name."

"I's none," he said sadly. "It were left i't cup. I't
wood."

"Then I has it somewheres. Tha tek it wi thee: cannot
be always turning out cupboard for't." She nodded at
him, sharply. "There's gate. Gan well, Tom Cloud."

He turned his bright face to her, as water to the moon,
all dazzled with the recognition: tha'rt O, in me and not,
aloft; and I is I. He kissed her, a shy dry fervent clumsy
kiss, on the corner of her eye. Pink and primmed, and

sharper-nosed than ever, with her glasses all askew, she glared at him. "Cheek!"

Then she opened her low door on the rimy morning. The sun, fox-red as shepherd's warning, round and hoary-bearded, rose above the hedge, hung fire; and the thorns glittered bright with rime. All the O of the witch's garth was blank with glory: stones, weeds, rags, her pattens of cold iron, and the crow's-foot stark abandoned rake. No geese: for they were wind and frost. The spring had spelled itself to sleep. Beyond, the wood was endless. Stooping through the witch's door, Tom Cloud set out, turning back and back again to stare; and so went on at last through winter's gate, his uncertain endlong way: through trees all naked with the newborn year, cloud beyond cloud, and turned, after so long a tale of falling, toward the green wood at winter's end.

Sylvie and Ariane were crying. The wood dazzled with tears and frost and sunrise. Mally took them in her sibyl's arms, tucked under, all a-dangle, plump and limp as geese to pluck, and tumbled them into her bed. "Mind stars," she said, and shut the door.

Sleeping even before they fell, soft and light, through clouds, they saw the great full Mally moon, all gold and cross, and not forsaking them. Round-cheeked and wintry-spectacled, owl-beaked to knap at stars, she left the sky unswept of clouds, in the wind of her nightdark hair, and went serenely owling after souls: aloof, and sailing by them, in her bright cloud, in the branches of their green and starry mast.

VIII

Shepherd's Hey

Moon, thought Ariane, asleep and laughing: hey, the moon's after me. Owl-beaked, it quirked at her, teasing, tugging out a nightdark strand of hair, as long as wind, to which it clung and clawed, kite's-tailing out behind her, burred with frost: a prickly glory. Tumbling cold through the clouds, she wound the quilt about her, to burrow from the owl in sleep, but it was full of holes, was flying leaves that—Thump! She fell through the sky's back door and out of bed.

She lay in a strange green world, all wood and leaves, and the light through leaves, in the sway and shift of light-skeined shadow, green as underwave. And there lay Sylvie, drowned in summer by a greenwood oak, out-landish as a fircone there, absurd and tousled in her wintry clothes. Far other worlds, and other seas. We're drowned, thought Ariane, or caught in Sylvie's greenest marble. Unlethe. And I am I, within the wood, and yet I hold it, flawed and starred with light, cracked through with genesis. A green thought, as green as the tinker's earthly paradise. O strange. Is this his dream? Have we fallen out of dreams of Cloud, and tumbled into Tom Cloud's sleep? Stilled in wonder and unravelment, Ariane looked up, and at last said softly, "But where's this?"

Sylvie sat and stared. Green, she thought: full leaf, but barely summer, only now, this week, this morning—O the freshness, the green and tumult, the water running loud, the birds gone crazy in the trees. Not there. Not winter. Here and now. Red oaks and swamp maples, larch and buckthorn, hickory and paper birch. That whale-

backed hill, that red oak with the windfall branch—
"Nan's woods. Back of Maire's. See, there's the castle
rock."

She sprang up, turning eagerly, wild and quick with
joy. "You can't see the house from here, not when the
leaves—" Then the green wave broke in salt, and
thwacked and dragged and drowned her; and vehemently
she cried, "But I missed it, I missed *spring*!"

The green crown lost. Poor Sylvie, after she'd done
all, chanced all, for Mally's spring; and all for nothing
for herself: no spell, no garland, but an iron ring. Not
even withered gold. And I've my witch's eyes, thought
Ariane, and said, "But we're here, we've made it back.
And there's summer still to come."

Sylvie thrashed among the leaves, and swore. Summer
when, how many springs? What star had they fallen
from? They could be old as light, that travels for a thousand years unchanged, they could—She halted. Now hold
on, don't get freaked: that oak's pretty much the same.
It's probably this summer, give or take a bit. And we're
here, we're home; we could still be falling. Toward
nowhere, or worse. She touched the rough live bark, the
leaves; crumbled the yellow fungus on the rotten branch.
The wood's the door, she thought, or is it the solstice?
She said darkly, "I just better not be my own grandmother, that's all."

But Ariane, all over leaves, said, "I just hope we're
born." She laughed for heart's ease, for giddy wonder.
She was still light-touched with sleep; though all her
dream but the memory of having dreamed, of being light,
was lost. Within, yet out. She shook herself. The leaves
of other woods, of winter and the Ship forespelled, were
scattered, fell to dust. *"O Proserpina, for the flowers now
that, frighted, thou let'st fall*—clumsy wench—*from Dis's
wagon: daffodils . . .* and what? *The winds of March* and
something . . . *pale primroses that die unmarried, ere they
can behold bright Phoebus in his* cups . . ." She still was
laughing.

"Hush, what's that?" said Sylvie, standing still. "Not
birds."

"Sheepsong." Then Ariane heard it, the music on the
summer wind, the flute, the fiddle and the drum.

Sylvie tugged off her boots half-laced, and her socks
stiff as boot-trees with dirt, and ditched them; left her
ravelled scarf and hat, her jacket and her Jacob sweater
hanging, fluttering from the branches. "That'll freak the
crows."

Rejoicing in the leaves, in the windrush and water and
the dance of sun, in the birds on each green bough, she
went, barefoot and wincing. The sharp twigs pricked and
the hard stones bruised her winter-shy unhardened feet.
Fine as a lady's, she thought in disdain. She wandered
toward the music, more or less, for she swerved joyously
to greet her paths and places: the stones of the ruined
farm where gentians grew in autumn, and apples fell, the
last of its bewildered garden, and an oak far wider than
the walls had cracked the hearthstone through; the stand
of hemlock where the owl's nest was.

"Whoa. Hey," she said, "how'd this get here?" She
caught up a stick, not rough, but shod and silvered:
Nan's. She tossed it to Ariane, and darted off through
the needles. "Tanager. There. Gone." She sauntered by
the brook, with flags and dragonflies and sedges; through
the windfall in the cedars, where the wild raspberries
were still in flower, and the fruit in hard green knots,
tough to walk on in bare feet. She saw a flying squirrel.
She found half a thrush's eggshell, and an owl-cast, and
leaves of trillium; the fox's earth was there, but deer had
killed some birches, gnawing bark. The air was full of
bugs. She came down by the shady patch—"Look, Solo-
mon's seal"—through the brushwood, witch-hazel, alder
and chokecherry. She plucked and pinched, and snuffed
and tasted—sorrel, birch twigs—looked and laughed, and
scolded back at birds.

Ariane followed, the dryad's understudy: curious and
shy of the music, which eluded her and led her on, stumbling, still unearthly light and morning-eyed, pricked
only by the branches, unregretful and awake.

At the wood's edge, beyond the wall in the deep
meadow, was a woman in a clear bright turquoise dress:
an ash-brown woman, fine-grained and strong-framed
and easy, walking, dangling a pair of bright sandals from
one hand.

"Hi," said Sylvie. "You seen Maire?"

"Dancing with our brother, last I saw." The woman grinned. "Where've you dropped in from?"

"The sky," said Sylvie.

"Oh. Thought you'd been after the goats. Old shoes." They stared at her. "The sheep were Thos's idea. He's fallen in the brook already, chasing the ram. Should cool his ardor." She laughed, a deep enjoying sound, and brushed back her hair; turquoise-and-silver bracelets fell down her brown bare arm, all in a fine glitter of sun. "You haven't seen a retiring husband, have you?" They shook their heads. "Well, get Maire to give you a drink. And some strawberries. Dangle your feet in the brook." A small white-polled boy ran by the far wall with a switch, teasing a dingy and unshorn, beribboned sheep, and the woman wandered after, lightly.

They went on to the farmhouse, still a field away. The dancing music broke and started, branched and wove; far bright figures moved. Down through the wind-silvered meadow, grass and flowers all uncut, and deep and sweet; across the stony, gnawed, bare-knuckled pasture they went. On most of the sheep's horns were knotted bunches of muddy ribbons, green and blue and red; some wore garlands round their necks, by way of salad. A few wore knots of bells. "Compulsory morris," said Ariane. The sheep glared and grazed vengefully.

Beyond the gauded flock, there was another low stone wall, and suddenly a bewildering crowd of people on the rough lawn beneath the trees, all brightly clad or softly as far hills, some dancing and some standing talking. Fall-haired Molly gravely fiddled, and a dark young man caught up the tune, and turned it, playing with a spare and hurling grace; the flautist changed to bombard, and the russet lad on bodhran snatched a drink. A long table was heaped with brown bread and wine and strawberries, cheese and sandwiches and cake. Two small children lay under the spindly lilac bush on a faded blanket, bright-red-cheeked, fast asleep.

As Ariane and Sylvie came near, the set ended, and the dancers broke, stilled or scattering and light of eye, diverted from their inward-weaving measure. A bad moment to sneak in. They two crept rather shyly round the edges, slinking for the back. Someone tittered; others turned politely, rose-pink, to the punch-bowl, or glanced and coughed; the fiddler scrawled his strings derisively.

Maire came up to them, barefoot in a long green dress, with a baby on her hip. "Good. Glad you could make it," she said, and dandling the baby in the air, she kissed its tummy, nuzzling, so it crowed and starred its hands, and pulled her garland all askew. "Ah ba!" Then to them, "There's no hot water, but if you can get to the coffee before it's made . . ."

Ariane blushed and hugged her elbows: reeking, she knew, as high as a shot crow hanged for warning. "Thank you," she said, and meant it, though she bit her lip to hold her giggling, and tried not to glance at Sylvie. You and I are sure together, as the winter to foul weather.

"No trouble," said Maire. "Or the kettle."

Sylvie plucked with cheerful disdain, fastidious, at her stiff cords. "Hmm. S'pose we're a bit funky. For company."

"Molly," called Maire. "Hey, Molly, love," and turned back to them, jigging the baby. "Whatever you can find that fits . . ." Then the dancers called her to the dance, and took the baby, and took hands.

Ariane and Sylvie followed Molly, self-possessed in muslin, through the bulging, bellied-out screen door into the cool dim house, and up the slight bent deer-legged stairs. "In here," she said.

"What's going on?" said Sylvie.

Molly looked at them in cool wonder. "The wedding," she said, and left them in Maire's room. It was low-eaved and wide-boarded, slanting, with a huge thin wavy window full of tree, panes of leaves and light. Her quilt, the one she had thought to call Drowsy Maggy, was done. All finely stitched with whorls of stars, on breaking and resolving starry wheels of blue and pale and darker cloths, it lay unrumpled on the bed. Bunches of green herbs were tied to the plain thin bedposts. All was swept. There was a basket full of clean diapers in the cold shallow grate; there was a jug and basin on the washstand, and a pine chest overspilling with faded tumbled finery, like milkweed from its rough pod, and shawls and petticoats were drifted on the backs of ladder chairs.

They stripped, piecemeal, and scrubbed in the cold

water, with rough clean towels and smooth brown soap, faintly hayfield, faintly lavender. Sylvie knelt and looked out the window. "Oh! Hey, there's Cat. Talking to some auntly ladies. And the fiddler. Must be Maire's getting married. I didn't know she had a guy. Well, I knew she'd had a *guy*, but . . ." She broke off, laughing, looking at the baby's shirts, and a string of wooden beads, for teething. Now she saw amid the light thin finery a man's check cap, and an old, gnawed toy, a wooden sheep; and a tobacco tin lying on the sill. There were two pairs of work boots under the bed, well-dubbined, side by side.

"You don't know him?"

"No. It'll be good for Maire, the company, winters; hope he's a country sort of guy. There's a lot of work, with the farm and all." Her face fell. "Work. Hell, when we get home, kitchen'll be full of mice. And spiders."

"And the mailbox stuffed with valentines."

"I wish," said Sylvie mockingly; but she sang a little at her washing, a tune and then the words: ". . . *we'll pipe and we'll sing, love; we'll dance in a ring, love* . . ." Scrubbed scarlet and glowing, she wrenched away at the barbaric iron brooch. "No soap. Guess I'm stuck with it for life."

"Bet there's a farrier in the crowd. If not, it'll come in handy at the buffet: like sort of a runcible fork. Ha!" Ariane tugged ruefully at her knotted hair. There was one long strand rimed with silver now, that she'd never seen. "Damn! I dropped all my hairpins, back there. They've taken root, thousands of years ago by now, and grown like crowns of horn. The enchanted tortoiseshell forest. Extremely deciduous."

"Plastic. You've wrecked the ecology."

Turning from the glass, Ariane sighed. "Well, I'll just go as I am. The curse at the christening."

"Oh, wear it down for once. It looks nice." Rummaging, Sylvie found a T-shirt—it said "Shepherds are honest people; let them sing"—and a long gypsy skirt to go with it. She sat cross-legged on the floor, and prodded rather gingerly at her left sole. "Splinter. Stone-bruise. I haven't had time to toughen 'em up."

Ariane found a long-sleeved cotton shirt, all white-work, and a petticoat dyed blue, rather coarse but clean, with tucks and a bit of crotchet lace, and several three-cornered tears, but secure with a pin here and there; and hanging on a peg, a broad fine straw hat with a faded wreath of rosebuds. The witch of Endor, by Julia Margaret Cameron.

Clutching their bundled winter clothes, they came down through the quiet house, feeling shy and wild and silly. Yet cloudwise still, thought Ariane, still dreaming: I will never quite awake. I am still in Mally's bed, and earth's light as elsewhere, by her moon. I know the green wood in these timbers; I know the feet that have worn them dark and thin with years, slow or dancing, the faces in the wavery glass; I know the fields where the straw was cut, and plaited, round as the sun that burned it gold.

Hope there's some strawberries left, thought Sylvie; hope there's wine. That music's *good*, I like the way the fiddle swerves, and the drone. Modal stuff. Soon as we ditch these rags—But where? She looked about. Molly and another child were on the landing, whispering, playing jacks; a long thin man, bald as a new bird, though youngish, lay stretched out on the jaded couch, reading; the cat slept under the loom, in the warped sunlight; two or three friends were in and out of the back kitchen, beating eggs and making coffee, gossiping. No cover. Furtively, they stuffed away their sordid winter rags behind the woodpile. "We could come back some dead of night, and smuggle them through the sheep-dip," said Ariane.

They paused on the front doorstep, blinking at the sun. Suddenly, there was a scrabbling and a mad barking and a flurry of tail; and Sylvie's black dog leapt joyously on her, licking and lurching on her hind legs. Then over went Dinah, writhing on her back, with one blissful ear turned inside out; and down fell Sylvie, romping and tickling, and over and over they rolled in the grass. ". . . girl!"

Cat Farrander, neat and round as a wren, but plumed kingfisherlike, came tripping up with a wineglass. "You might've said hi before you hared off upstairs. So how was Tibet? What on earth have you been up to?"

"Oh, messing around," said Sylvie vaguely, sitting up, and scratching Dinah. "So who's this guy Maire's found?"

Cat grinned. "He came to fix the stone walls, and sort of stayed. That's him, with the baby."

Sylvie stared. "Hmm. I'd've grabbed the fiddler."

Maire's new husband, small and tough, and somber in his good black suit and white shirt, prim-hued amid the bright or earthy pagan throng, was marching solemnly up and down the lawn, unfussed by the baby wailing in his arms, like a bagpipe that goes of itself. Patiently, workmanlike, he hushed it and cuddled it, and as it subsided, gasping, through hiccups into sleep, he wiped its furious quince face with his huge clean hanky. Never put work away wet. He had a grave round face, a neat dark silky head: like Ratty, thought Ariane, smiling. He was so odd and monkey-puzzled, with his long dark eyes, amid all the green-pine or willowy young men. But as he turned to Maire and nodded that the baby slept, she knew him, shrewd and steadfast; and she laughed for wonder, for the absolute and teasing fitness, the hilarity of it. Had he fallen from the clouds, cap, boots and all, to rock t'babby? Or windborne, rooted in the stony ground, until he wakened to Maire's kiss? Had she broken but a branch of him, to keep her warm? Close, thought Ariane. By moonlight, with her other eyes, she saw them growing still in one embrace, the oak and thorn: earthfast, though their bodies waked and walked. O not strange, not strange at all, she thought: earth's where he is, and hearth and fold; so they've wed. It's all else that's clouds and moonlight.

Weird, thought Sylvie, he's like—oh, what's her name?—that tough dark little woman from the farm, the one with the lantern. Mrs. Whatsit. Woodfall. Well, why not? She brought us to the door: maybe they know other doors, that family. Into other worlds. Other beds. She caught Ariane's eye, and they giggled.

Just then came a tumult of barking and bleating and baaing, and a frenzy of bells; and in through the pasture gate onto the lawn tumbled and blundered and weltered the flock of bedizened and bewildered sheep, with the evil ram hindmost, glaring and garlanded, with weeds all rakishly askew in tatters on his horns. Weeds dangled in one topaz eye. Round about and at their heels skirmished a rag-tag of heathen dogs, crazy with joy. "Dinah!" yelled Sylvie, as her heedless bitch tore after, madly barking. They were driven by a rout of guisers, some with horns and some with sticks, and one with a pipe and tabor, good as silent in the pandemonium; and all in light fantastic garb, impromptu: leaves and tatters, and an old top hat with peacock feathers, pink flamingo hightops. And here and elsewhere, in and out, quicksilvery, ran Thos, tawny-haired and thievish, with a sheepcrook wreathed in ivy.

Their reeling and unruly morris came onward, to wild laughter. Maire yelled, "My seedlings!" and bolted off to shut the back gate. The bridegroom stood, all alight with mischief, and the joy of battle; then tenderly thrusting the baby into the nearest arms, he whistled up the dogs, and ran to recapture the riot.

Unnoticed in the receding uproar, Ariane and Sylvie ventured out and surveyed the table. The Wreck of the *Hesperus*, but plenty of it. O glory, half the tiered cake at least, a beauty: dark within, and dense and sturdy, with handmade swirls of frosting, and bunches of sweet imperfect flowers, rosebuds and violets. "Chocolate," said Ariane, faintly, lovingly. "It's chocolate." She grinned triumphantly. "*Bitter* chocolate."

"After all that greasy bacon, you need vitamins," said Sylvie sternly, handing her the carrot sticks and broccoli.

Ariane broke out singing, high and cracked and breathless. "*Crudités, crudités, puer est natus, ex Maire-ia virgine, crudités . . .*"

"Deea," said Sylvie, giggling.

"Cream cheese with your strawberries," said Ariane, and stuck one on the raven's beak. "Hah! I don't hold with wearing ironmongery, whether it wears well or no." She cut herself the first injudicious hunk of cake. "Chocolate," she said, "is a sacrament."

Sylvie kept eating the smallest ripest strawberries, lovingly and slowly, another and another from the blue-and-white bowl. The grass was full of hulls. "It's almost worth having been gone; it's like getting them in January." She stirred the wine-punch. "No wasps." She tasted, and

ladled out a cup. "Fizzy. Maire's extravagant." With her
glassful, she got herself a formal dish of strawberries,
with a spoon and lots of cream. "Hey, it's not goat."

"Ewe?" said Ariane, and lavished some on her cake.
Fishing out a fruit slice from her second cup, Sylvie
looked wickedly at her. "Have some wine. Go on, it's
full of fruit and stuff, it's sweet: you wouldn't even know
it's in there. Not like bitter." She raked the orange rind
with her teeth. Ariane shook her head, happy to be
teased, untempted. "Oh, go on. I've never seen you
drunk. It's your turn."

Thos came haring up, breathless and wet and wicked,
and snatched a devilled egg on the fly. "Did you see?
Did you like it? The attack of the baa-barians. Hi, Syl,
what's with the Captain Hook act?" And he was off.

"Bedlam baas," said Ariane. "Well, half a glass. For
ceremony."

The woman in turquoise strolled over, dandling the
baby on her shoulder. "The hat! Wonderful. Celebrate
the summer," she cried to Ariane. "I'm Tib. The other
sister," and she took a strawberry. She bit it, laughing.
"Lewd, O wonderfully lewd, those horns!" she said,
dancing the baby. "He's cornered them down by the
soggy end, rolling in a sensual sty, poor things, in all that
wool. Maire's had to put off shearing till it thawed. And
now the wedding."

"Been cold," said Sylvie cautiously, casually, damping
her leap of guilty joy. Poor things: sleet and hail and
frost, and now no buttons on their fleeces. And I missed
it.

"Two foot of snow, Easter Thursday, and damn poor
sledding still, up north." She hitched the drooping baby.
It was nodding, fierce and dreamy, with a berry mangled
in its fist. "Must just rinse the crotch." And she ambled
off.

Now the dark young fiddler was sidling up, picking
with sweet disdain at the violets on the cake, and toying
with the rosebuds, licking warily, wickedly, at their
almond-sugared prickles; and eyeing Sylvie. She looked
down at the bowl, near empty. "O dear, it's down to the
green ones," she said, unblushing for her greed.

"I like raspberries still better," he said. But Ariane

missed what Sylvie said in turn, for the two auntly ladies bore down on her, and she turned from the dalliance, and refilled their glasses.

The taller of the aunts, black-browed, and brown and grizzled, gnarled of hand, and badgerly of arm and shoulder, with a deep harsh sibyl's voice like an old traveller's, looked straight at Ariane, and said, *"And we fairies that do run by the triple Hecate's team from the presence of the sun, following darkness like a dream, now are frolic."* Ariane, half-hidden in her witch's hair, gazed back: so you know me. Which face of three is which of us? Oh, but of course, we take it turn and turn.

The old lady glanced at her, and sipped. "I was Puck, and a spottier and more sullen sprite you never saw. On this very lawn. In the Paleolithic."

The other, stout and wrinkled, with brief ragweed, hawkbit, gone-to-seed white hair, and mad innocent blue eyes, said, "O my dear, not nearly so glum as poor Bottom, with the wires on her teeth, she married that young fool Greylag, most improvident, and prophetic, come to think of it, only backward. There was never such a year for strawberries! Not Hermia, the other one, Cobweb's sister, was sick."

"Well, I like Maire's rude mechanical. Snug. At least he's not a cousin. Or a clavichordist," said the taller. Then to Ariane, "This is Kate Thompson, and I am Caroline Hughes. Maire's aunt. We were always the incest-and-folk-dancing set. Though I must say we never thought of sheep. They looked unremarkably like Aunt Sibylla's ladies' morris class. The rolling eyes. The bottoms."

Ariane laughed, delighted. "O but Cotswold: the goats are northern . . ." she began; but summoned by lesser aunts, the ladies turned and sailed away. What we do is manners.

Cut short, she looked about, and found Tavy, grimy and intently grubbing with a bent spoon and a silver caster, squatting under the table at her feet. She crouched. "I dreamed about you. You were in the snow with some children, riding on a sled a long long way. You were picking holly."

"I don't remember being there," he said, puzzled. "Was it fun?"

"It was cold. Is that your castle?"

"No, it's the king's." He went on digging, and took no more heed of Ariane, but beat against the hillock with his spoon. "Open up your city gates! Come open at my call!"

Sylvie was still talking to the fiddler, though they'd drifted to the grass beneath the trees. Caught herself a blackbird, thought Ariane. He was a wild and windblown young man, lithe, with long dark curls, and a three-cornered face, all slyly innocent. Reynardine, she thought: but a coal-fox, not a tawny. He'll be off in his green castle. With a goose on her back. But as Ariane came nearer, they were arguing about cosmology, and Sylvie'd cornered him. ". . . I don't like Aristotle's, all that stuff about the Unmoved Mover: it's stand-offish. All that glass and cold pure nothing. No. Creation's going on, it's like a river. The going on's the end. It's messy and complex, and God's involved in everything there is, grubs and wasps and mold. Except free will. We have sort of crystals of will."

"Is that where you'd risen from, so brown and beggarly? The river of creation? Primaeval mud," he said, mocking; yet he looked at her. "You're the farther from grace by a washing. Wilfully combed."

With a face half pleased, half puzzled, as at an unexpected card, a fool's hand or a hidden cunning, Sylvie looked up, and seeing Ariane, she called her in. The Queen of Spades. "Hey, what's the universe like, then? He thinks it's a Christmas-tree ball."

"Oh, infinitely recurring disorder," Ariane said lightly, lofty as Miss Hughes. "It's like a dance."

So to turn the two and one again his way: "Astonishing," he said, in his soft quick lilting voice, turning round the raven's brooch on Sylvie's thin brown wrist. "About sixth century B.C., and its queen'll be after waking, she'll be wanting it back. Is it that scared of fairies you are?" And sly, "Does it prick you in bed?"

Sylvie laughed, frankly delighted, daring him. She loved a reckless game, though she'd not lose lightly, nor lay down her heart, but for his. But he'd played his jack at last. Ariane, still playing witch, said, "Her troth is plighted to a troll beyond the hills. We've scrubbed her up for the wedding. It's his ring; it was his mother's thumbnail."

He'd not let go her hand. It lay in his, like a crazy tableau of Van Eyck's marriage portrait, with Ariane as mirror. "Will it come off?"

Maire, going by in her long green dress, saw him slide the iron ring and thorn, and turned to Sylvie. "Take mine, it's not so sharp," she said, and lovingly, lightly, she held out her golden ring.

"Does it lie so heavy on you?" said Ariane to Maire. "Or do you hold it light?"

Maire smiled, unruffled. "Light as breath."

"It won't bite," said Sylvie, teasing him. "It's mine that has the beak."

Glancing at the fiddler's quick dismay and fallen face, Ariane laughed. Great virtue in that handfast O, as good as salt or candlelight, and better far than iron for the laying of spirits. Thowt it were a fox. She grinned wickedly at him. "Do you vanish at cockcrow?"

Then the bridegroom, all bright and jaunty like a terrier with a mouthful of trouser leg, came back, wearing the tup's great muddy garland as a breastknot on his good black suit. He gave Maire a dripping bunch of it. "Don't say I never done battle for you, my love," he said. "Where's that young Thos gone?"

Maire took the weedy garland. "The fiend! That's my flax." But the fury in her voice was absent-minded; she was smiling fondly at her husband. "Was for your shirt, love."

"Who needs a shirt?" he said, and laughed at his boldness. "I'll get him back later. We'll have a dance while it's light." He took her hand.

Maire turned back to Sylvie, bright, impulsive. "You'll sing for us? As a wedding present."

"Oh. I hadn't—Like *this*?" Maire nodded, coaxing; Sylvie melted. "Well, all right. If you want me to. I haven't brought you a ladle or anything." Then ruing a little her consent, reluctant, "When it's dark."

"Is it better then?" said the fiddler. The bridegroom looked wryly at him, amused—get back to your other fiddling, lad, as you're paid for—and he got up, green-stained and lithe, springing up as light from his dismay as a branch bowed down with heavy dew, to the sun of his inward conceit.

"Could you start with *Tib's Maggot*?" called Maire, and he nodded.

"I like that swervy sort of fuguing part," said Sylvie. "The way it doesn't quite cadence, then does." As he glanced back at her, she smiled. "See you."

Ariane, delighted, gazed at Maire and her bridegroom as they went, hand in hand to the dance: the wedding of Cock Robin and his Jenny Wren. Maire went knowing what she did, serenely shining, like the great full moon, in her dress green as wheat; and her bridegroom, flown with ale and wonder, bright Phoebus in his reeling glory. After them, each lad and lass took hands.

Unwary as she looked at them, Ariane found herself drawn in, as the sets were made, longways on the sweet bruised grass, for as many as will; and the musicians plucked and pegged away, or hooted mournfully, at tuning. The long shy fellow, the *eminence chauve* who'd been reading on the couch, came up and said abruptly, "Do you dance? Or just mudwrestle?"

"The nine men's morris is filled up with mud," she said, inconsequently. "You should see what they give the women." Then as his eyes flickered, and his mouth quirked, covertly amused, she added meekly, "I can try."

He talked her through the measures, brief and lucid, and she tried vainly to remember them: a sort of celestial fox and geese. But she was distracted: a voice behind her was saying ruefully, ". . . so we thought of calling ourselves Gabbleratchet, but then our brass broke up with our smallpiper . . ." And another, bluntly, ". . . and March hares, you know, when they dance, they aren't mad for love, it's the females rebuffing the males— Pow! in the kisser . . ." And a White-Knightish guest aslant of her, in an old linen suit and odd socks, was talking socratically with Molly on the mathematics of the hey, odd and even. Sylvie was walking through the dance with a fairish and faded-jeaned partner; Ariane saw her, far beneath the trees, obliquely as a falling star: intent on now, and elsewhere.

As the music started, a lilting eluding air, Ariane turned and tried to recall the crossings and recrossings, the stars and heys that would weave her in the dance. For a while, her partner's sardonic gaze compelled and dared her, kept her straight; then somewhere in the maze she dropped his clew. As she blundered away in an access of lyricism, he murmured, "Left." So lyrically she turned, and he said dryly, "Your other left." Miss Hughes caught her arm in passing, as she ducked. "No, that's right. Left. I am a gentleman, this set."

O heavens, thought Ariane, it's like the rules of Irish prosody. So much for ramping Pegasus. She sided with a rhinocerine old fellow, with a romping white bunny, and a duck and a dodo, a precisian cock sparrow in gloves. So deliver I up my apes, and away to Saint Peter. From hand to hand, and in and out, she went, bear-led and basilisked, bandersnatched and flirted at and whirled and whelmed, dropping stitches and laddering all down the line. O must I ravel out my weaved-up follies? Breathless, she ended where she had begun and a bit, and made her confused courtesy. To the same partner, for a wonder. "Thank you," he said. "It's been random; therefore you were sometimes right."

Ariane stood, laughing quietly: well then, the dance was not what she did, but what she saw. She was the witch, the other. *One is one, and all alone.* Another slower dance began, and she withdrew, from pleasure less, into her green world. It was late now, there were shadows, and the birds were still. The light and weaving music plucked at her skirts, sent burred and wind-borne notes to follow. She went on. The woods along the sheep-field wall were darkening, their proper and peculiar inscape and complexity of leaves becoming all one shadow: wood. Only here and there were blots or paler streaks, firs and birches, drowned in a still greener air. There were alders by the brook, where light hung, wavering. The field was stony, sloping, odd. When she came to the far-end wall, she climbed over, and walked on through the rising dusk, beyond in the long meadow.

The grass, wind-silvered, tarnishing, grew deep above her knees, adrift with flowers. The dark rose and floated them on its slow tide, cloud-pale, nebular, unfast. The sky still was cloudless, still was light. The unearthly flowers when she caught at them were tough, wiry-stemmed and starry, with a dark speck at the heart. The grass grew scant and coarser toward the hillside's stony crown.

Black against the sky she saw a rock and a thorn tree whisper together. The stone was wide-lapped, crouching, and the windbent thorn stooped shrewdly over it, gnarled and gaunt and green. So close did they crony that the stone had bent the tree, the tree embraced the stone. A bird on the wind had brought the seed; slow ice had borne and left the stone that fire had shaped, time worn: they two were earthfast. Ariane—air, water, fire and earth—had walked. Yet all three met now and elsewhere, in their element. As one. She touched the stone and tree, in silent greeting. Then she turned, looking back on their domain, the way she'd come. She stood, and swung her round straw-plaited hat, and gazed.

In the sky gone green hung a great unwavering star and a slight moon, and in the tall grass, the little stars came out, the fireflies; below in the green-leaved dusk, the dancers turned. It was all one skein, one weaving: stars and clouds of stars and all the dance. It was midsummer, at the turning of the dark and light.

She saw the dancers had become the suns and crescent moons of the Dancing Master's book, not black and white as on the page, but bright and living alchemy, the souls of stars. They moved, fiery in the dusk, and turning with their slow and starry heys the air to music. Their bodies were exalted by their act, their mooncurved cheeks and chins turned silver, their faces and their flying hair to gold; each Phebe and her Silvius to sun and moon. Dancing, they became the dance. Not as the starry crown, the O, but longways: yet they turned within their endlong set, in chains of starry whorls and rings and wreaths of hands, journeying as time does, that is always and never the same: for now and ever now a bright new sun and moon led off the endless dance, on the green earth as they did aloft.

Above the dancers, at her feet in the dark grass of the

hill, there wove the low and fleeting stars, the fireflies, all shining in a maze of light, now and nowhere, here and gone. Their web was star-hung prophecy, a mute and airy babel of foretelling: riddles, runes, light-falling chance. They spelled in passing all the stars of summer, and of winters past and yet to come, of earth and elsewhere and of cloudlands long ago; told fates of dancers yet unborn or dust, and dreams of the undying. In their scrawl of fire she read of the wren's death and its wedding, and the grass's fall. She saw the Ship turned Wren turned Ladle, scattering like sibyl's leaves, like sparks of fire on the wind. She saw Orion dandled on the grass, cat's-cradled swiftly through the Fool, the Harp of Bone; she saw the Pleiades kite's-tailing Perseus, and in his upraised hand Medusa's head, which is an eclipsing binary, light and occult spiralling, each about her other— or else saw something else. And then the sort was changed.

Being starry in the deeps of grass, the hillside mirrored heaven: darkly, as in moving water, still bright creation swirled. She saw the moon below her, in the sky-in-river of the hill. She saw the thorn tree's shadow, drowned in cloudy windy dark, branching downward with its roots in heaven, lightfast. With her witch's eyes, she saw them, fast in the fell of heaven, in the lightyears deep and night-black starry, the uncrystal, drinking of the springs of light. So time is rooted in the dance; so light indwells in cloud and moving. Overturning in her thought, she saw the tree itself, not shadow, in the grass and flowers of the fields of night, where no star fell before the scything moon, nor withered, yet they danced: the windless sea of grass wherein the Ship sails lightfast, branching in the stars of heaven.

Turning slowly, she looked up. The heavens were—O green and starry, of that same unearthly blue-gone-green, but flawless, as the soulstone she had borne; serene as were the lightborn bodies of the dancers, then seen fleetingly, unclouded of their stone, but now laid bare, pure element: as if they had uncrystalled to become the night. The sky was all one soul. She stood, a mote in that abyss of sky, yet at its heart, which is everywhere, and all else nothing. For a brief eternity, she was herself that rounded clarity of air, that O, cracked through with skeins of stars; yet held it, small and infinitely complex and clear, a green-blue marble in her hand.

It was still. The dance had ended. Ariane stood, a little dazed, and touched the stone, the tree: still there. And still there her simple gift, her seeing, though her hand was empty: still her eyes were green.

Then slight as cobweb, elusive, ineluctable, she heard a small frail piping and a heartsthud dub of drum, not from the lawn below, but from the wood, higher up and farther in; and with the music, small and sharp and sad, hopping light as bird on briar, there came a faint dry clack of clashing horns, and thrash of leaves, a clear cold seldom *ting*. Out of the dusk woods, gravely now, there came a sort of guisers, crowned with horn, and shadowy, their faces moon-blank in the darkfall, and their coats as tattery as leaves; and in and out, and elsewhere in the maze, there wove a moonpale mothy fool. They were huntsmen now and prey, not shepherds: a darker hallowing. The blood beat to their tabor. Softly, formally, they set to, and clashed their racks of horns, and lightly paced. They came within handsreach of her, soft as owls and wary; yet they gave no sign of heeding, as if she or they were shadow, elsewhere to the other. Last of all, the Fool with his broom of thorn whorled slow about her and awry, light as a falling leaf. To their slender haunting music they moved serpentine, away toward the wedding; they would circle nine times sunwise round the house, wherein the bride-bed lay, and on the bed, a bunch of flowers.

She watched them till they were shadowy amid the shadows; then, not aloud, she spoke: O sisters, hallow with me. Thrice as childing moon, and thrice devouring, and thrice again, the old bright bow of heaven. Slowly, moonwise, by herself and one of three, she turned and turned about the stone and thorn tree, nine times in wise and clumsy patterns that the wind obscured: her own dance, her benediction.

It was near dark now. The moon was lying back, all gold, above the roof-tree. Lanterns flowered on the lawn, were hung in the branches of the trees. The fireflies wove nonsense. Time to be going in, she thought, all grave and giddy, reeling. With the sky on my head. *Like Antipodes in Shoes*—O heavens, Andrew green-blue Marvell—*How Tortoise like, but not so slow, these rational Amphibii go* . . . She tied on her haloed prickly straw, with its garland of weeds. She heard a murmur of voices and laughter from below; then quiet and a low voice speaking, Maire's. Then Sylvie sang.

Ariane smiled: a strange song for a wedding, a true-love forsaken. Her fiddler would tease her for that. Ariane imagined Sylvie by lantern-light under the leaves, brown and thin; she heard her clear dusk-blue voice and the fiery star within it rising to the end:

> But she said that she'd led
> Such a contrary life,
> She said she would never be
> A young shepherd's wife.
>
> Here's my sheepcrook and my black dog,
> I give them to you.
> Here's my bag and my budget,
> I bid them adieu . . .

The music began again; the dancers and their shadows moved. Ariane walked slowly down through the long midsummer grass, carrying stone and soul and thorn within her, the green wood and the starry heavens, toward the dance.

FUN AND FANTASY

Buy them at your local

bookstore or use coupon

on next page for ordering.

WORLDS OF WONDER

BEYOND THE IMAGINATION

Buy them at your local

bookstore or use coupon

on next page for ordering.

If you and/or a friend would like to receive the *ROC Advance*, a bimonthly newsletter featuring all the newest and hottest ROC books and authors, on a complimentary basis, please fill out this form and return it to:

ROC Books/Penguin USA
375 Hudson Street
New York, NY 10014

Your Address
Name _____
Street _____ Apt. # _____
City _____ State _____ Zip _____

Friend's Address
Name _____
Street _____ Apt. # _____
City _____ State _____ Zip _____